THE LOST FLEET

BEYOND THE FRONTIER

LEVIATHAN

JACK CAMPBELL

TITAN BOOKS

The Lost Fleet: Beyond the Frontier: Leviathan
Print edition ISBN: 9781781164686
E-book edition ISBN: 9781781164693

Published by Titan Books
A division of Titan Publishing Group Ltd
144 Southwark Street, London SE1 0UP

First edition: May 2015
10 9 8 7 6 5 4 3 2 1

The right of John G. Hemry to be identified as the author of this work has been asserted by him in accordance with the Copyright, Designs and Patents Act of 1988.

What did you think of this book? We love to hear from our readers.
Please email us at: readerfeedback@titanemail.com,
or write to us at the above address.

To receive advance information, news, competitions, and exclusive offers online, please sign up for the Titan newsletter on our website:
www.titanbooks.com

A CIP catalogue record for this title is available from the British Library.

Printed and bound by CPI Group (UK) Ltd, Croydon, CR0 4YY

To Glenn L. Sparks, an old friend who lived a very good life and left this a better world for his having been here. There is never time enough.

For S., as always.

THE FIRST FLEET OF THE ALLIANCE

ADMIRAL JOHN GEARY, COMMANDING

Second Battleship Division

Gallant

Indomitable

Glorious

Magnificent

Third Battleship Division

Dreadnaught

Orion (lost at Sobek)

Dependable

Conqueror

Fourth Battleship Division

Warspite

Vengeance

Revenge

Guardian

Fifth Battleship Division

Fearless

Resolution

Redoubtable

Seventh Battleship Division

Colossus

Encroach

Amazon

Spartan

Eighth Battleship Division

Relentless

Reprisal (returned to Callas Republic)

Superb

Splendid

First Battle Cruiser Division

Inspire

Formidable

Brilliant (lost at Honor)

Implacable

Second Battle Cruiser Division

Leviathan

Dragon

Steadfast

Valiant

Fourth Battle Cruiser Division

Dauntless (Flagship)

Daring

Victorious

Intemperate

Fifth Battle Cruiser Division

Adroit (lost at Atalia)

Sixth Battle Cruiser Division

Illustrious

Incredible

Invincible (lost at Pandora)

Fifth Assault Transport Division

Tsunami

Typhoon

Mistral

Haboob

First Auxiliaries Division

Titan

Tanuki

Kupua

Domovoi

Second Auxiliaries Division

Witch

Jinn

Alchemist

Cyclops

Thirty-one heavy cruisers in six divisions

First Heavy Cruiser Division

Third Heavy Cruiser Division

Fourth Heavy Cruiser Division

Fifth Heavy Cruiser Division

Eighth Heavy Cruiser Division

Tenth Heavy Cruiser Division

Emerald and **Hoplon** lost at Honor

Fifty-five light cruisers in ten squadrons

First Light Cruiser Squadron

Second Light Cruiser Squadron

Third Light Cruiser Squadron

Fifth Light Cruiser Squadron

Sixth Light Cruiser Squadron

Eighth Light Cruiser Squadron

Ninth Light Cruiser Squadron

Tenth Light Cruiser Squadron

Eleventh Light Cruiser Squadron

Fourteenth Light Cruiser Squadron

Balestra lost at Honor

Lancer lost at Atalia

One hundred sixty destroyers in eighteen squadrons

First Destroyer Squadron

Second Destroyer Squadron

Third Destroyer Squadron

Fourth Destroyer Squadron

Sixth Destroyer Squadron

Seventh Destroyer Squadron

Ninth Destroyer Squadron

Tenth Destroyer Squadron

Twelfth Destroyer Squadron

Fourteenth Destroyer Squadron

Sixteenth Destroyer Squadron

Seventeenth Destroyer Squadron

Twentieth Destroyer Squadron

Twenty-first Destroyer Squadron

Twenty-third Destroyer Squadron

Twenty-seventh Destroyer Squadron

Twenty-eighth Destroyer Squadron

Thirty-second Destroyer Squadron

Zaghnal lost at Pandora

Plumbatae, Bolo, Bangalore, and **Morningstar** lost at Honor

Musket lost at Midway

Kururi and **Sabar** lost at Atalia

FIRST FLEET MARINE FORCE
MAJOR GENERAL CARABALI, COMMANDING

3,000 Marines on assault transports and divided into detachments on battle cruisers and battleships

1

"Five minutes to exit from jump space," Captain Tanya Desjani said from her seat next to Admiral John "Black Jack" Geary on the bridge of the Alliance battle cruiser *Dauntless*. "All systems at maximum combat readiness."

The warships commanded by Geary had left the blood and fire of Atalia Star System in pursuit of the dark ships that had carried out the destruction there. Geary and the others called them "dark ships" because their hulls were a duskier shade than most warships', perhaps because of special stealth materials. It hadn't been the crews of the dark ships that had committed the atrocities at Atalia and at Indras Star System but the dark ships themselves. The dark ships lacked human crews who could have overridden automated systems that had developed deadly glitches or perhaps been deliberately sabotaged by any of a variety of malware. Having finally won the century-long war against the Syndicate Worlds, the Alliance government had decided not to place its faith in the men and women who had paid the price for that victory, instead placing its trust in robotic systems that had already set ablaze two star systems.

Geary's Task Force Dancer had left Varandal with twelve battle cruisers, eight heavy cruisers, thirteen light cruisers, and twenty-five destroyers. The battle cruiser *Adroit* had been lost in the fighting at Atalia, along with the light cruiser *Lancer* and the destroyers *Kururi* and *Sabar*. Four battle cruisers, *Leviathan*, *Dragon*, *Steadfast*, and *Valiant*, along with some heavy cruisers and destroyers, had remained at Atalia to assist damaged ships and recover wreckage from destroyed dark ships.

Only seven battle cruisers were left in the pursuit force.

That would be enough. If they could catch the surviving dark ships, which had fled from the destruction they had wrought at Atalia.

"Are automatic software updates disabled for *Dauntless*'s systems?" Geary asked.

"Yes, sir." Tanya could be informal at other times, but now she was sharp, precise, and dangerous, a human weapon honed by the last decades of the brutal war with the Syndics. "My people are actively monitoring all systems, and if something tries overriding the block on updates, they have orders to shut down those systems and do a cold reboot from last-day backups."

"Good," Geary said. "It's a hell of a thing not to be able to trust our own software."

Desjani shook her head. "We could never completely trust our software. It wasn't just flaws and glitches, it was also all the malware that enemy hackers could come up with to cause our software to misbehave. Humans separate from the machines are the only firewalls proven to be reliable enough. That's why we always kept humans in the loop, for those times when the software got its artificial little brains twisted."

"'Always' until those dark ships were built," Geary said, his tones tight with anger.

"Yes." She leaned closer and spoke more quietly. "If the dark ships went berserk after they arrived at Varandal, like they did at Atalia, stopping them from doing a lot of damage might be impossible for us. They were nearly two hours ahead of us when they jumped for Varandal, and if they accelerated after they left jump space, they will have opened that lead. And none of the defenses at Varandal will be able to see the dark ships at all to counter them."

"I know," Geary said, trying not to let his frustration sound too clearly. "Thanks to official software updates designed to keep us blind to the dark ships. Are the software patches that fix the damage caused by those updates ready to send as soon as we arrive at Varandal?"

"Yes, sir. The First Fleet ships still at Varandal will install the patches on your say-so because you're the fleet commander, but other Alliance forces not directly reporting to you may not," she reminded him. "They'll argue that these are unauthorized modifications to official software, so they need approval from their own chain of command to install them."

"If they're already getting shot up by warships that are invisible to their sensors, they may be motivated to ignore regulations concerning unauthorized software modifications."

"One minute to exit from jump space," Lieutenant Castries called from her watch station at the back of the bridge.

Geary fixed his eyes on his display. A marker to one side confirmed that *Dauntless*'s weapons systems, like those of the other warships in this pursuit force, were set to open fire immediately if any dark ships were within range when the Alliance warships left jump space. He didn't think they would be, though. The artificial-intelligence routines governing the dark ships' tactical decisions were apparently closely based on Geary's own methods, and under these circumstances, if he had been the commander of the dark ships, he would not have attempted an ambush against a force with as much an advantage in firepower as Task Force Dancer still possessed.

The jolt of transition from the gray nothingness of jump space back to the real universe hit Geary. He was barely aware of the sudden reappearance of the stars in the endless blackness of space, his mind dazed by the transition, but even while fighting off the effects of the exit from jump, Geary noticed that none of *Dauntless*'s weapons were firing.

His display swam back into focus as Geary concentrated on it.

Desjani was a second faster than he was in getting her mind working right again. "They're heading for the hypernet gate."

"To attack it, or to use it to get away?" he wondered aloud. "At least they're not moving into the star system to attack the ships and facilities."

Space had no up or down, no east or west to determine directions, so humans had made up their own. Every star system had a plane in which planets orbited. One side of that plane was labeled up, the other down. Any direction toward the star was starboard or starward, while any direction away from the star was port. The conventions were simple, but they worked to give common references for ships that might be pointed in any direction, upside down or at right angles to each other.

The dark ships that had escaped from Atalia, two battle cruisers, one heavy cruiser, and five destroyers, were to port of Geary's ships and diving down slightly as they moved at a steady point two light speed for the hypernet gate orbiting six light-hours from the jump point where Geary's ships had just arrived. "They're three hours' travel time ahead of us. We won't have any chance of catching them before they reach the gate," Desjani said. "We'd better hope they're running and that their warped artificial brains haven't decided the gate is also an enemy target."

"Status signals from the gate indicate that the safe-collapse mechanism is operational," reported Lieutenant Yuon, the weapons systems watch-stander on *Dauntless*'s bridge.

"Thank you, Lieutenant. At least if the dark ships do attack it, we don't have to worry about the gate's setting off a nova-scale explosion when it collapses. They'll reach the gate in another twenty-seven hours." She ran some quick calculations. "There are two destroyers at the gate. Maybe . . . damn. The only other units already at Varandal that are positioned to be able to intercept the dark ships are several more destroyers and light cruisers."

"Those wouldn't stand a chance even if they could see the dark ships," Geary said. "We may not be able to catch the dark ships, but we can stay on their tails." He tapped a comm control. "All units in Task Force Dancer, immediate execute accelerate to point two five light speed, come port two five degrees, down zero three degrees."

"Are we going to chase them through the hypernet gate?" Desjani asked.

"If we have to," Geary said. "We have to find their base, wherever it is." He checked the fuel cell status on his ships and let out an angry breath. "I'll have to leave our destroyers here if we do that. Their fuel supplies are getting too low. Now, let's get the word out to everyone here," Geary added, his mood and his voice grim. He could see the many defenses at Varandal, the numerous warships and installations, all at standby readiness because the war with the Syndics had at last ended. "Why aren't they reporting peacetime readiness instead of standby?" Geary grumbled.

"Because nobody but you remembers what peacetime readiness is," Desjani reminded him. "And if the attack on Indras by those dark ships causes the Syndics to retaliate, this peace business may already be over with before the rest of us can figure out what it means."

"I hope you're wrong about that. At least if the Syndics attack our defenses, we will be able to see *them*." Even after experiencing on these ships how secret software modifications had left Alliance sensors unable to see the dark ships, it was still hard to grasp that everything else in this star system would be totally unaware of the dark ships that were passing through. Many of those defenses were too far off to have seen the dark ships yet regardless, of course, let alone the more recent arrival of Geary's ships. Light only moved at about eighteen million kilometers a minute, so with distances inside a star system measured in hundreds of millions or billions of kilometers, even light took a while to get places.

But other defenses, other ships closer to this edge of the star system, should have seen the dark ships by now. If their own software were not blinding them to the presence of the hostile forces.

"What you are about to do will raise hell," Desjani commented.

"I know that," he replied. "Are you advising me not to do it?"

"No." Her grin was fierce. "I'm looking forward to it."

Geary couldn't help a tense, humorless smile in return, then composed himself, touched the transmit command, and began sending the message he had been rehearsing during the long days in jump space since leaving Atalia. "All units in the First Fleet, there are hostile forces in this star system that your software is blocking all sight of. These are not, repeat not, enigma warships. Our best estimate is that these are fully automated combatants that have slipped whatever controls were supposed to limit their actions."

He paused a moment to let that sink in before continuing. "We have engaged in combat with those forces at Atalia, where they, without provocation or warning, attacked Alliance as well as civilian shipping and caused extensive destruction and loss of life. These hostile warships have already attacked Alliance warships and killed Alliance personnel. My task force is in pursuit of these ships, which are currently en route to Varandal's hypernet gate. Based on their actions at Indras and Atalia, it must be assumed that any Alliance or civilian ships they encounter will be attacked and destroyed.

"Attached is a set of software patches you are to install on your ships. Disable automatic updates and permit no other updates until I personally authorize it. Your combat, maneuvering, sensor, database, and other systems contain hidden subroutines that mask the presence of the hostile warships. Once you have implemented the software patches we are sending, we will forward identifying information on the hostile warships. If we sent that information now, your own communications systems would strip out all traces of anything related to the hostile warships. These software patches are personally authorized by me as commander of the First Fleet. Geary, out."

He tapped in another command, this one aimed at the two destroyers on picket duty at the hypernet gate. "*Mortar, Serpentine*, this is Admiral Geary. There are hostile warships in overwhelming force approaching your orbit. You cannot detect those warships until the attached software patches are fully applied to all of your systems. Immediate execute, accelerate to point two light speed and proceed on a vector toward Ambaru Station while applying the patches. Geary, out."

"That should have them nowhere nearby when the dark ships reach the gate," Geary told Desjani.

"If they follow that order," she said. "And if they don't head back to the gate as soon as they apply the patches. If they do. Those two destroyers are not part of the First Fleet. They belong to the Varandal local self-defense forces."

"I know that."

"You told them that enemy forces were approaching," Desjani added implacably. "They're not going to run."

"I didn't tell them to run," Geary insisted. "I told them to head for another orbital location while fixing their system software."

"Same difference, Admiral," she said. "You'd better get Admiral Timbale to send them those orders if you want any chance of their being obeyed. Ambaru Station is currently three and a half light-hours from us, and the destroyers are about five light-hours from Ambaru, so if Timbale sends maneuvering orders to the two destroyers within a few hours after we warn him, there is enough time"

"I'm calling Timbale now," Geary replied. Another command entered, then he spoke with quiet intensity. "Admiral Timbale, this is Admiral Geary. Be advised that there are hostile forces operating within Alliance space, and that hidden subroutines in our own software are preventing us from seeing those forces. A mixed force of hostile battle cruisers, heavy cruisers, and destroyers inflicted catastrophic damage at Indras Star System, damage which the Syndicate Worlds' authorities at Indras blame on the Alliance. Courier ships must be sent as soon as possible to alert fleet headquarters and border star systems that the attack at Indras may trigger direct retaliatory attacks on Alliance star systems by the Syndicate Worlds. The same hostile warships caused extensive loss of life and property at Atalia and conducted a deliberate and unprovoked attack on the Alliance picket ship watching Atalia, destroying it without warning. They also attacked my ships, destroying one battle cruiser, a light cruiser, and two destroyers, and inflicting serious damage on other Alliance warships. I have reason to believe that these hostile warships are completely automated, with no human crews. They are very heavily armed, very maneuverable, and a force of them is currently traversing Varandal en route to the hypernet gate. I am in pursuit of them and will engage them again if possible. I have ordered the two destroyers on duty near the gate to reposition, but do not know if they will comply with orders from me. Attached is a set of software patches that will allow you to see the hostile warships and retain information about them in your databases. Geary, out."

He sat back, feeling *Dauntless* accelerate as her main propulsion drove her in pursuit of the dark ships, the other warships of the task force arrayed around *Dauntless* and matching her movements. There was nothing else to do now. Space was too big for anything else to be done. All he could do was wait, and react when he finally received replies to his messages, which would take hours to reach the ships and places to which they had been sent, and hours more for replies to cross the same immense distances.

"At least there aren't any surprises among our fleet," Desjani remarked as she frowned at her display. "No ships missing since we left."

He grimaced at the data being displayed. "But they're still sending out false readiness status reports. I'll need to find out what shape they are really in, and how much progress Captain Smythe's boys and girls have made in repairing broken systems and battle damage."

"We broke some more at Atalia," Desjani pointed out. "Or, rather, the dark ships did."

Geary nodded, keeping his eyes on his display. "Smythe was worried about how well *Adroit* would hold together when so many systems on her were built on the cheap. He was right. Why would people bother to build a warship and cut so many corners while doing it?"

"The Alliance was close to broke after a century of war," Desjani said. "Remember?"

"They still are," he said. "But they found enough money to build those damned dark ships, which might have already caused another war to start."

She gave him that look, the one he hated to see, the one that believed Black Jack could do what others could not. "You can save it."

He knew what "it" meant. The Alliance. "Tanya, how can I, how can anyone, save the Alliance? It is so much bigger than any one man or woman."

"It's not bigger than Black Jack," Desjani reminded him. "He is the Alliance as far as most of the people are concerned. He came back from the dead when we needed him the most—"

"I wasn't dead!"

"Technically, no. I'm talking legends and belief here, Admiral. Black Jack is also the one who reminded us of how far we had strayed from the things our ancestors believed in. He's the one who finally beat the Syndics. Are you going to argue either of those points?"

He gave her a cross look. "Since when have I been able to win any arguments with you?"

"You give me an order, and it will be done," Tanya told him. "But if you ask my opinion, you'll get what I really think. And I really think that Black Jack can save the Alliance. Because most of us believe in him. Maybe during that century you spent frozen in survival sleep, when everyone thought you were dead and the government built Black Jack up to be the greatest hero ever, maybe the living stars and the ancestors really were talking to you. And maybe they still are."

"Let's hope so," he said. "But, if they are, what they are telling me is that Black Jack alone can't do the job. Just like beating the Syndics took a lot of brave men and women, saving the Alliance isn't a one-person show. Even the Black Jack a lot of people believe in is going to need a lot of help."

"He's got it."

"I know." Despite his worries, Geary managed to smile at her. "Black Jack may be what gives others hope, but what gives me hope is knowing people like Tanya Desjani have my back."

* * *

Messages moving at the speed of light tore across the vast distances separating objects in space, moving much faster than the ships humanity had built but still feeling slow given how long it took them to reach their targets. It took six hours for the first replies to start coming in from the nearest of Geary's First Fleet warships that had remained at Varandal. Startled and bewildered, all ships indicated that they were applying the patches but all were wondering what was going on.

Given the distance to where the battleship *Dreadnaught* orbited, it required almost seven hours before they heard from Captain Jane Geary, who had been left in command of the majority of the First Fleet that had not accompanied Admiral Geary. "I'm glad you're back though I don't understand what happened," she said. "We're applying the software patches now, but some units have reported to me that they have received orders supposedly from Admiral Timbale instructing them not to apply the patches."

Jane Geary shook her head. "I haven't heard from Admiral Timbale, though, which is odd since he has contacted me whenever a matter concerned First Fleet ships. I've asked Admiral Timbale for clarification, but also told every First Fleet unit to comply with your orders, Admiral.

"You should know that I was interviewed by some government inspectors regarding the fleet repair work. I told them what I knew, which was that all repair work was necessary and funded through appropriate channels, then referred them to Captain Smythe. Geary, out."

"Smythe is going to be glad that Lieutenant Jamenson is back," Desjani commented, as Jane Geary's image vanished.

"He had Jamenson prepare plenty of reports before she left," Geary said. "That woman really is amazing. She could make the simplest thing impossibly confusing, and yet do it all by the book. I'd want her on my staff myself, if I had anything I wanted to hide. But what Jane said was true. All of the repair work is needed, and it's all been done by the book. Maybe the book didn't intend that we do things the way we did, but no one broke any rules."

Tanya twisted her mouth in a half smile. "If there were a rule against confusing things, fleet headquarters would find itself up on charges in no time."

He didn't smile in return as he gazed at the display before his command seat. The three hours of travel time, or about thirty light-minutes, that had separated Geary's ships from the dark ships was closing very slowly as the long stern chase offered no chance of actually catching the enemy before they were able to escape. If they turned to fight, he could finish them off, but as of a bit more than a half hour ago, the dark ships had kept forging steadily for the hypernet gate. "Tanya, I need a gut check from you."

"That's one of the reasons I'm here." She nodded toward where the dark ships were indicated on her display. "You're wondering if we should follow them through that gate if they take it?"

"Yes." He didn't bother asking how she had once again read his mind. In this case, the worry was the sort of thing anyone should have had. "We know the government was building twenty battle cruisers and twenty battleships in their secret fleet. We destroyed four of the battle cruisers at Atalia though only because we had a two-to-one superiority in numbers. If those fleeing dark ships are going back to their base and we follow them there, we might run head-on into the rest of the dark battle cruisers and battleships."

"That thought had occurred to me," Desjani said. "As did the thought that the resulting battle might be very short and very unpleasant for us. Can we afford to run that risk?"

He gave her a startled look. "You're saying that?"

"Yes, I'm saying that. Somebody we both know helped me realize that charging into a fight regardless of the odds might be brave, or just stupid. It depends. I agree that we have to find their base. Since as far as we know all sensor software has been rigged to not see those things, and the odds of anyone's making an actual direct visual observation of anything in space are as close to zero as doesn't matter, the base could be anywhere. Maybe even at Unity, where the government would think it would provide maximum security for them."

"I don't think so," Geary said. "Yes, nobody would see them in space, but at the base itself, when the dark ships dock for maintenance, repair, and resupply of weapons and fuel cells, people would see them. And sooner or later, some of those people would talk to other people in whatever star system it was."

"But you said no new facilities have been built."

"Not as far as Captain Smythe could find out," Geary said. "Following the money is the best form of intelligence we have on this mess, and the money says no new base facilities were constructed along with that new fleet. They must have a base where they can't be seen, but where could that be?"

Desjani grimaced. "If we chase them there, we'll get the answer. But how many ships should go? Should we send what we've got knowing that the odds against us are likely to be bad wherever those dark ships are going? Or should we just send a single ship with orders to take a quick look, then immediately head back here? Admiral, my best recommendation is that we wait to see where those things take the gate to. If it's somewhere that might be their base, we won't need to chase them immediately. But if it's a big system, something like Unity, we'll have to follow because the dark ships might be glitched enough to target things there, and we'll have to stop them."

"That would be the only thing we could do," Geary agreed. "You're right. If their destination is someplace a lot less populated, some border star system that was part of the defenses against the Syndics, that would point to that place as their base. Maybe a star system like Yokai, which was turned into a Special Defensive Zone, with no citizens allowed in to see things that they shouldn't. It's possible, though, that we'll see some destination that's ambiguous and leaves no clear guidance for what to do."

"It's a good thing we have Black Jack in command," Desjani said. "He'll know what to do."

"Very funny." He scowled at his display again, where the situation nearest the hypernet gate was unchanged. "*Serpentine* and *Mortar* should have begun moving by now."

Desjani shook her head. "I told you they wouldn't move. They have orders to guard that gate, and, by their ancestors, they'll guard it and not run from some invisible enemy. And based on what Captain Jane Geary told us, I will lay you odds that those two destroyers have received orders, supposedly from Admiral Timbale, that tell them not to download those software patches."

His gaze focused on her. "You and Jane have both used that term. 'Supposedly from Admiral Timbale.' Why?"

She paused, frowning. "I'm not criticizing the actions of a superior officer—"

"Which is something you'd never do."

"Who's being funny, now?" Desjani asked. "I don't believe that Admiral Timbale sent those messages to some of your ships because from all that you've told me and all that I've seen, he has been a pretty reliable supporter of yours. He's backed Black Jack a few times when it was obviously hazardous to his career. He's also kept arm's length from anything he did not have to be involved in, so that you would have freedom to operate. Why would that man send orders to some of the ships under your command telling them not to do what you told them to do?"

"He wouldn't." Geary looked down at the controls on one arm of his command seat. "But the biometrics built into the comm systems are supposed to ensure that anything sent under someone's name actually did come from that person."

"And the sensors on our ships are supposed to ensure that we see everything," Desjani pointed out. "But they weren't. Why wouldn't whoever is behind this dark ship stuff work to protect their lies by also messing with the comm systems? We already *know* that they've been messing with the comm systems in other ways."

"That's a good point," Geary said. He studied his display, thinking through possible options, many of which would burn bridges behind him if he took those paths. "They think they're right. Just like the people who wanted to build those dark ships. So anything they decide to do must be right. Once you've already done a criminal amount of deliberate sabotage to comm systems on your own ships, why not take it another step to try to keep anyone from learning about the sabotage?"

She nodded, her eyes angry as they met his. "What are you going to do?"

"I'm going to do what I think is right," he replied, reaching to tap his comm controls. "*Mortar*, *Serpentine*, this is Admiral Geary. I am invoking my rank and an ongoing emergency situation in Varandal Star System to issue orders directly to you. Immediate execute, accelerate to point two light speed and proceed on a vector toward Ambaru Station. I repeat, this is an order given by me personally under emergency authority in the face of an imminent threat. Acknowledge this order and carry it out without any delay. Geary, out."

There was a good chance that he had directly and openly overridden orders issued in the name of another admiral. It wasn't just bad form, it was the sort of thing that impaired discipline and the entire chain of command. "This could tear everything apart," he muttered.

"Admiral," Desjani added, leaning close to ensure they were both inside the privacy field that kept their conversation from being heard by others on the bridge. She only did something like that when she considered it absolutely necessary. Since she and Geary had married during a brief interval while both were captains, they had both followed policies of acting strictly professional while aboard *Dauntless* or any other warship. Anything that might show they were personally close, something other than admiral and captain, was avoided, as was any form of personal contact.

"We didn't set this mess into motion," Desjani said. "You've been keeping your superiors aware of what you're doing, you've been following orders, and I know better than anyone that you have constantly questioned whether or not you are doing the right thing. The people we're dealing with have been lying to a lot of people and keeping what they're doing secret, so no one could question it and whether it's actually all that smart. They've lied to us, they've lied to the people of the Alliance, and odds are they've lied to a lot of people in the government itself."

Geary gave her a surprised look. "You think some of the senators don't know what's going on?"

"Yes. Which is weird coming from me, I know. A year ago I would have been certain they were all rotten and plotting against the fleet." She made a face. "But talking to you, and having a chance to actually get to know some senators, have made me realize that it's like evaluating good tactics and strategy for a situation. You have to learn as much as you can about whom you're facing, and not depend on preconceptions or prejudiced judgments or stereotypes, when deciding the best courses of action. You've told me you think Navarro is all right, and I saw enough of Senator Sakai to form my own judgment."

"And Senator Unruh," Geary said, recalling how she had impressed him. "But then there are people like Senator Wilkes, who struck me as a total opportunist. I think that Senator Costa is sincere in her beliefs, but she's also willing to let anyone else pay the price necessary for what she believes has to be done. I admit that I haven't entirely figured out why Senator Suva would have gone along with this stuff."

"She's scared," Desjani said, her tone making it clear what Tanya thought about people who made decisions based on fear. "Scared of people like you and me, who don't fit into the way she thinks the universe ought to be. Scared of a universe that isn't working the way it ought to, whatever way that is. People do dumb things when they're scared. But I actually like her better than Senator Costa, who tries to come across like she's the number one supporter of the fleet but just wants to use us for her own games no matter how much that might cost the men and women she claims to support with all her heart."

Geary sat back, thinking, not really looking at his display for the moment. "Victoria Rione told me more than once that the government is like a clumsy giant, with one big hand and lots of little minds trying to make the hand do what they want. If enough of the minds are in agreement, the hand can get things done, for better or for worse, but if the minds are focused on fighting each other, then the hand just flails about."

Tanya never liked it when he brought up Rione.

"That woman has been involved enough in such things to know all about them! Admiral, in this case it seems to me that some of the minds managed to get the hand doing things without a lot of the other minds knowing what was really going on. Suva thought the dark ships would keep her safe, but Costa probably just wanted a new, dangerous toy that would follow orders and not ask questions."

He looked at her. "That attack on Indras, which could cause the Syndics to retaliate against us. We've talked about that, but we haven't been able to figure out why someone ordered something so stupid."

Desjani inhaled deeply, then met his eyes. "Looking at this situation now, and what else may have been done to our comm systems, I think our problem was we assumed that everyone else would realize how stupid it was. The Syndics have been violating the peace agreements in lots of ways, including covert actions coming out of Indras. Someone figured the appropriate response to that was retaliation."

"That's an appropriate response when you're at war," Geary said.

"So? People today don't know peace. They know war. A lot of people don't know how to handle peace, so they're responding as if the war is still on. A war that justifies them and what they want to do, a war that keeps things just like they'd been for a century." Desjani looked away, then back at him. "Even people in this fleet. Roberto Duellos is facing a tough decision that never would have come up if the war hadn't ended. He doesn't know what to do. He's not the only one."

Geary shook his head. "No. That doesn't make sense—"

"It doesn't make sense to *you*," Tanya said forcefully. "To you, war is still an aberration, a temporary, unusual state of affairs. To us, war was how things always were. You, the legendary hero, threw out the certainties of our lives and replaced them with uncertainty."

"Tanya, the Alliance was on the verge of collapsing from the costs of the war," Geary said. "The Syndicate Worlds has collapsed in many areas, and—" He paused as he remembered something.

Desjani nodded firmly to him. "And the Syndic leaders have been trying to get the Alliance to attack again because the war justified them, too. The Syndic government wants everyone in Syndicate Worlds space to see us as the threat and themselves as the protectors. Whoever ordered the attack on Indras might have given the Syndic leaders what they wanted, and maybe the people on the Alliance side who gave those orders wanted the same thing as the Syndic leaders, an active enemy to validate what they want to do."

Geary looked away, fighting off an impulse to reject her words. "You're right. I can't put myself in the same mental and emotional state as people today. I can't imagine wanting to perpetuate war because of feeling that's the way things should be. But I have seen the disruption that peace has caused, the people like Duellos who feel unmoored, and Duellos is lucky because he hasn't been downsized and kicked out into star system economies reeling from the costs of the war and the sudden cutbacks in Alliance spending as defense expenditures were slashed. But I can't imagine anyone seeking war as part of some cynical plan—"

"No." Desjani shook her head, wearily this time. "You still don't get it. They're not being cynical. They've convinced themselves that they are doing the right thing. You and I met those former Syndics at Midway, people who have spent their lives serving the Syndic despots and an ugly, dictatorial system. Only a few of them struck me as evil, the sorts of people who did what they did because they wanted power and money and didn't care who suffered and died. Most of them seemed like average people, who somehow rationalized serving the Syndics. I don't know all of their reasons, but I suspect they were doing what they thought was the best thing. You met Captain Falco. How do you think he saw himself?"

"I know how he saw himself," Geary said. "As the savior of the Alliance. As someone who knew the right things to do and would do them. He was wrong on all counts, but he was sincere. You think that's what we're dealing with?"

"You already said it," Desjani replied. "Back at Atalia. They thought the dark ships were the perfect solution to all of their problems. And now that perfect solution has come home to roost."

His eyes went back to his display. It would be hours before he knew whether or not the two destroyers had followed his orders. Or whether they would hold their ground, determined to do what they saw as their duty.

Usually, waiting was the worst part. This time, the worst part was knowing what was going to happen.

2

"Admiral Geary, what's going on?"

Admiral Timbale sounded as if he was torn between confusion and rage. His expression reflected the same tangle of emotions. "I received a fragmentary message from you, which then disappeared from the comm system. My comm techs were trying to find it and discovered that several messages had gone out under my name countermanding something you had sent even though I had no record of whatever that was. I don't know why you're heading for the hypernet gate so fast, or why comms between me and most of the ships in this star system are as messed up as if we had a corps of Syndic meegees at work here. I am requesting that you detach one of your destroyers to physically courier your latest messages to me, so I can be sure I have them and know what they say. Timbale, out."

"He hasn't even picked up on the threat, yet," Geary said, appalled. "He thinks it might be the Syndics." The term "meegee" was an ancient one, derived from an old acronym for electronic warfare techniques like intrusion, jamming, and interference. The equipment employed had changed considerably since the term was first introduced, but the basic concepts for sabotaging and confusing enemy comms and sensors still applied.

"How could he understand the threat if the software is deleting anything that might clue him in?" Desjani asked.

"Could there be Syndic meegees at work here? Or is this all the work of our own meegees?"

She laughed. "The lines blurred on that so long ago that no one knows. Our people weaponize some code, their people find it and mess with it a little and shoot it back at us, then we rework what they did and fire it at them, and who the hell knows where most of it came from anymore? There are more viruses on our systems than there are viruses in our bodies, and the ones in our computer systems keep evolving a lot faster."

"All right," Geary said. "But Timbale had the right idea. I'll detach *Hammer* to carry my information to him."

Her eyes were on her display. "She won't get there in time."

The dark ships were only ten hours' travel time away from the hypernet gate as they held their velocity at point two light speed. Two light-hours' distance. Roughly two billion kilometers. It was a very, very large distance. But in this case, it wasn't nearly large enough. From where Geary's ships were, the destroyer *Hammer* would take nearly seven hours to reach Admiral Timbale at the vast orbiting complex named Ambaru Station. A message sent from Ambaru to the two destroyers guarding the hypernet gate would take four hours to reach them. Even if Timbale sent that order immediately, it would get there an hour too late.

Geary sat morosely on the bridge of *Dauntless* as he watched the inevitable taking place, the dark ships getting closer and closer to the oblivious destroyers at the hypernet gate. The only good thing was the number of his own ships here, battleships, heavy cruisers, light cruisers, and destroyers, who were calling in to acknowledge having downloaded the software fix, usually accompanied by startled questions as to what the dark ships were and what were they doing at Varandal.

But with the dark ships only five hours' travel time from the hypernet gate, Geary frowned as a sudden thought came to him. "Tanya."

She was still on the bridge as well, of course, looking totally unruffled by the hours spent up here. "Yes, Admiral?"

"Suppose I were commanding those dark ships—"

"As best we know, the artificial-intelligence routines running them are based on what you've done," she pointed out.

"Exactly." Geary pointed at his display. "I know I'm being pursued. I know that if I flee through the hypernet gate, I will reveal the place where my base is located, allowing the enemy to attack it and cut off my entire fleet at the knees. What do I do?"

Desjani frowned as well. "You? You sure as hell don't use the gate. Not you."

"No." Geary sat up straighter, glaring at his display. "I realize that I can't get away without betraying the rest of my fleet, so I have to stay here, and since that means being destroyed, I have to do whatever damage I can here before all of my ships are lost."

She stared at him, then focused on her display, hands flying as she tested courses and actions. "Ancestors preserve us. They're going to go for Ambaru, aren't they?"

"Yes. If we keep charging after them, and they turn aside from the hypernet gate at the last moment and head for Ambaru, we won't even see the maneuver for nearly three hours. My battle cruisers won't be positioned to be able to intercept them before they reach the station and blow apart the central command-and-control node for this star system."

"Why not just throw some rocks at it?" Desjani demanded, using the fleet nickname for kinetic bombardment projectiles, which really were little more than smoothed hunks of metal. "No one could—They've run out, haven't they?"

"Yeah," Geary said. "I think so. They used up their rocks beating the hell out of every possible target at Indras and Atalia. So they get us out of position chasing them, then charge at Ambaru and take it out at short range with their hell lances. They'll know exactly what to target on the station."

Her expression hardened into anger. "Because they'll have blueprints for every ship and station. Because the Alliance government was so worried about internal threats, it assumed its own military installations might have to be potential targets."

"That's what I think," Geary agreed, studying his display. "But if I'm right, we've still got time to mess up their plans. It won't be easy, though. I can move battleships to blocking orbits, but against something as maneuverable as the dark ships, that may not be enough."

"Focus on countering what you would do," she reminded him.

That required thinking a bit backwards. First, using the simulator on his display to figure out how to best position the battleships that could reach blocking orbits in time. Then, shifting perspective to look at those battleships and try to figure out the best way past them to reach Ambaru. It was as difficult, and as unsatisfying, as playing chess against himself. "Tanya, there's something wrong with this."

"What?" She leaned over, eyeing his display.

"Those dark ships are programmed to do what the programmers thought I would do, not what I would actually do," Geary explained.

"Not entirely. They based a lot of it on the battles you've actually fought. But I get your point," Desjani admitted. "You have to think like Black Jack the hero of legend as they think he is, because that's also who the dark ships will be thinking like. So what does the great hero do here?"

He took another look at the dark ships. Two battle cruisers, one heavy cruiser, and five destroyers. Then at his plans to defend Ambaru. There were twenty-one battleships left in his First Fleet. Several of those were laid up undergoing major repairs. Several more were not in orbits that would allow them to move to block the dark ships in time. That left seven battleships he could get into blocking orbits in time to meet the dark ships if they headed for Ambaru—*Warspite*, *Vengeance*, *Resolution*, *Redoubtable*, *Colossus*, *Amazon*, and *Spartan*. There would also be several divisions of light cruisers and destroyers, but the battleships would form the armored shield for the defense.

"Admiral Geary," he said slowly to Desjani, "me, that is, would swing wide and either up or down, outmaneuvering the blocking force and getting to Ambaru before the battleships could have any hope of lumbering into new positions."

"What would Black Jack do?" Desjani asked.

"Imagine that you knew what I'd done in past engagements, but still saw me as you once saw Black Jack."

She thought, eyes hooded, then looked at him. "That guy, Black Jack, would have gone out in a blaze of glory. Again. Seven battleships form the core of the defensive screen. And Black Jack would have five destroyers that were already running low on fuel cells."

"Yeah. Five destroyers without crews."

"The programming running the dark ships has to care about losses," Desjani pointed out, "or those ships would have fought to the end at Atalia rather than taking off. They'll try to save their battle cruisers even if they're willing to sacrifice the destroyers."

He ran one finger through his display, tracing a possible path. "They could do it. A firing run on Ambaru, then bend their vector toward this jump point. All right. I think I know what they think I would do. Let's get this done."

Just looking at it from the godlike perspective of the display before his seat, the necessary maneuvers appeared simple. Move this ship here, move that one there, and so on. In practice, changing orbits was pretty complex. Fortunately, it was a complex math problem, and computers were very good at math. All Geary had to do was designate a ship, tell *Dauntless*'s maneuvering systems where he wanted that ship to go, and the necessary commands and vectors appeared so quickly that it seemed instantaneous.

He sent the commands to the individual battleships affected, as well as to the commanders of the light cruiser and destroyer divisions that would back up the battleships. Space was huge, so even the many ships he was sending out would form a very sparse screen indeed, but the point wasn't to build a wall. It was to position mobile units so that they could move to intercept anything trying to get past them.

"What are we going to do?" Desjani asked.

"Hold course for now until we see the dark ships head for Ambaru," Geary said.

"If we do that, we won't be in a position to intercept them before they reach Ambaru!"

"I know. Even if we turned now, we couldn't catch them in time. Every minute they spend heading toward the hypernet gate draws them farther away from a straight shot at Ambaru and allows us to try for an earlier intercept. We'll wait until less than three hours before the dark ships would likely maneuver. That way they won't see us changing our vector before their own planned maneuver. If they saw that, the dark ships would probably turn sooner and accelerate faster, and make our intercept impossible. Even if everything works right, it will be close. If the worst happens, I've got sixteen heavy cruisers that I can move to stop them after the dark ships clear the battleship screen."

"Sixteen heavy cruisers?" Desjani shook her head. "Against two battle cruisers like that?" She paused in thought. "Maybe. If they at least make the battle cruisers divert their courses and mess up their firing runs—"

"It will be insurance that we'll have time to catch those dark ships," Geary finished.

At two and a half hours before the dark ships should reach the hypernet gate, Geary sent more orders, secure in the knowledge that the dark ships would not see his maneuver before they had very probably planned to change their vectors. "All ships in Task

Force Dancer, immediate execute, turn starboard zero six four degrees, down zero five degrees." *Dauntless* swung in response to the command, her maneuvering thrusters pitching her bow toward the star and slightly below it, the other battle cruisers, heavy cruisers, light cruisers, and destroyers with her matching *Dauntless*'s vector change.

Task Force Dancer. So named because it had hastily escorted back toward their home space ships carrying representatives of the alien species that humans had nicknamed Dancers. "What would the Dancers think of all of this?"

"They said they'd be back soon," Desjani said. "How much do you think the Dancers knew about the dark ships, and how did they discover things we didn't know?"

"I think the Dancers may have pulled a few strings," Geary said. "I'd like to know why, but I can't shake my belief that ugly as they are to our eyes, the Dancers are allies to humanity."

"I hope you're right. The living stars know that humanity already has enough enemies, most of them homegrown."

Geary kept hoping his display would show new information, but *Mortar* and *Serpentine* stayed near the hypernet gate. He could easily put himself in the place of the crews of those two ships, imagine them watching the odd movements of Geary's ships and listening to whatever fragmentary and contradictory messages had reached them. They had brought their shields to maximum strength, had their weapons powered up, and were doubtless scanning space, watching for any threat, unaware that the software in their own communications, sensor, and weapons systems had been secretly directed in hidden subprograms to hide or delete anything related to the dark ships. But even if they had seen the oncoming dark ships, Geary did not know if the two warships of the Alliance would have fled. As he had learned after being awakened, in a century of war with the Syndicate Worlds the Alliance fleet had forgotten how to win but had become uncompromising in its willingness to die trying. The two destroyers did not maneuver in the last minutes before the dark ships reached firing range, and they did not fire as the dark ships closed on them.

The dark ships tore past *Mortar* and *Serpentine*, hurling out a barrage of fire at the Alliance destroyers. To the destroyers, the attacks would have seemed to have come out of nowhere, not that they had any time to be shocked by that. Shields collapsed under hammerblows of hell-lance particle beams, after which the weak armor of the destroyers offered little obstacle to the enemy fire. *Mortar* exploded, vanishing into a ball of dust as her power core overloaded. *Serpentine* shattered, breaking into several pieces that spun away helplessly, a pitiful few escape pods breaking free from the wreckage to seek safety for the small number of surviving crew.

It had happened nearly three hours ago, only now the light revealing the deaths of the two destroyers reaching *Dauntless*. Few humans could watch such images and not feel as if they were seeing something as it happened.

"At least everyone will have to believe us now," Desjani said, her voice low and furious. "Everyone saw that."

"I wish we hadn't lost two ships providing that evidence," Geary said, feeling the same emotions. "Look. We guessed right."

"You guessed right," she corrected him.

The dark ships had suddenly changed their vectors, whipping through turns that, while immense by the standards of distances on a planet, were comparatively tight when measured in terms of spacecraft traveling at twenty percent of the speed of light, or about sixty thousand kilometers a second. Without human crews, the dark ships could manage more intense maneuvers than Geary's ships, but even the dark ships were limited by the amount of stress their hulls could endure.

"Enemy formation is steadying out on a vector toward Ambaru Station," Lieutenant Castries announced. "Estimated time to intercept of Ambaru's orbit is twenty hours, ten minutes. Maneuvering system recommends we adjust our vector to bring about an earliest-possible intercept with the dark ships in twenty-one hours, six minutes."

"Do it," Geary said. His display showed the dark ships diving toward the star, and toward the thin screen of warships that was slowly assembling in their path. Behind that screen of battleships, light cruisers, and destroyers, sixteen additional heavy cruisers were converging into two box formations on orbits that would bring them close to the path of the oncoming dark ships.

"If I were in command of the dark ships," Geary commented, "I'd see all of this, realize that my plan had been compromised, and come up with another plan."

"Never turn aside," Desjani said. "That's another Black Jack quote. Did you ever actually say that?"

"No. Why the hell would I have said something that stupid?"

"Well, Black Jack supposedly did," she reminded him. "Your battles show you maneuvering, but also staying focused on hitting the enemy. It will be interesting to see how the artificial intelligence guiding the dark ships interprets that."

"Interesting?" he asked.

Her answer was cut short by an incoming message.

"What kind of supernova did you set off?" Admiral Timbale's image asked. "I've read the material you sent aboard *Hammer*, but when I tried to copy it to my own comm system it kept disappearing. So I downloaded that software patch you sent and ordered my systems people to run it. Before it could complete installing, I got calls from security people I didn't even know were on Ambaru Station who informed me I was in possession of illegal software and was in violation of Alliance rules and regulations that I also didn't know existed."

Timbale had a stubborn look in his eyes and a firm set to his mouth as he spoke. "You say there's an active threat in this star system, and based on the vid you provided of what happened at Indras and Atalia, it's an extremely dangerous threat. I've sent orders to the destroyers on guard at the hypernet gate to reposition, but—" He paused as if having trouble speaking. "But those orders may not arrive in time based on what information you've given me. If the worst happens, it will be the direct result of whatever and whoever messed up our comms and other systems. There's been a lot of talk in recent years about the enemy inside, and I never cared much for it. But here we are, deliberately blinded as we deal with a threat to life and property."

He took a deep breath. "I am insisting on confirmation of the authority of those security personnel even though everything they have checks out. I've told them I won't follow any instructions from them unless and until higher authority directs me to comply. And I have informed them that if anything happens to any ship in this star system, I will be sending military police to arrest them on charges of conspiracy and sabotage. Timbale, out."

A momentary silence after the Admiral's image vanished was broken by Desjani's comment. "Somebody pushed him too far."

"I noticed," Geary said, thinking of how Timbale would react when the light from the destruction of *Mortar* and *Serpentine* reached him.

"Could this push the Alliance too far as well?"

"Not if I can help it."

She nodded, then stretched with slightly exaggerated motions. "It will be fifteen hours before the dark ships reach weapons range of the first screen. I'm going to get some rest while I can," she added pointedly.

Geary sighed, rubbing his eyes. "You're right. I will, too. I need to be at the top of my game when we encounter those dark ships again."

"They're on a clean track inbound," she pointed out, gesturing toward the curving trajectory of the dark ships. "Unless they alter vectors, the next thing they encounter will be our defensive screen."

"A defensive screen that I'll start converging on their tracks when they're a lot closer." Any move he made now would be too easily countered by the dark ships.

He had always hated this part of space combat, just like every other fleet sailor. The enemy was in sight for days, with attack runs sometimes lasting for several hours or more before contact occurred. Human instincts formed on the surface of a single planet could never be comfortable with the idea that an enemy you could see charging you was not an immediate threat. It would never feel right to set up your own attack run, then go to the mess decks to eat before catching several hours of sleep, knowing the enemy would not be in range until long after that. Half the trick of handling space combat was learning how to deal with the many ways in which humans had trouble handling space.

This time was particularly bad because physics made it unlikely that he could intercept the dark ships until just slightly too late. He could accelerate his ships to cover the distance faster, but then would have to decelerate them to ensure he could actually hit the dark ships when he caught them. The time saved just wasn't enough, the distances just too large. But he would have to watch, hour by hour, as his ships could not quite get where they needed to be in time.

We'll never really be at home in space, Geary thought as he lay down on the bunk in his stateroom, gazing up at the slight imperfections in the overhead that had grown comfortingly familiar in the months since he had been awakened from survival sleep to discover that a century had passed in what for him was the blink of an eye. He had spent a career in the Alliance fleet at peace, only to reawaken to a fleet and an Alliance staggering from a century of war. Since then, he had fought battle after battle, some against alien species unknown to humanity a short time before, but it seemed like most of his battles had been against his fellow humans. Not always combat, but battles over who was in charge and what to do and whom to trust and what to believe.

But now the fight was against something that didn't care

about any of that. Artificial intelligences who just did what their programming told them to do even if that programming was compromised or glitched or riddled with bugs.

No, that wasn't right. The fight wasn't just against the AIs running the dark ships. It was against the people who were more willing to trust artificial-intelligence routines than they were their fellow humans, who thought the right solutions could only be found through keeping secrets and making decisions that no one else was told about. The Alliance could survive the dark ships. But the Alliance could not survive if people stopped believing in the ideas that made the Alliance what it was.

He had beaten the dark ships once. Could he also beat the mindsets of the people who had ordered those ships built?

"They're still coming in on a direct trajectory," Desjani told him as Geary took his seat again on the bridge of *Dauntless*. "Very Black Jack in their tactics."

"Should I be flattered?" He studied the flat curve of the projected track for the dark ships, running through the center of his loose defensive screen and on toward an intercept with Ambaru. With the dark ships diving in toward the star that Ambaru Station orbited at a distance of about eight light-minutes, Geary's battle cruisers coming in on an intercept from the side had managed to close the distance a great deal. Relative to Geary, the dark ship formation was to port and slightly behind, almost exactly thirty light-minutes distant. The defensive screen ahead of them was formed into a flattened oval facing the dark ships and orbiting to maintain a steady position relative to them. That screen was only twenty-two light-minutes away. If none of the ships changed their trajectories, the dark ships would go through the screen at nearly right angles, while Geary's battle cruisers would meet the screen at an angle as they continued to close the distance on the dark ships. Five light-minutes closer to the star and Ambaru Station than the defensive screen was the secondary blocking force, sixteen of Geary's heavy cruisers formed into two blocks of eight each. "I've punched through enemy formations before, so that's consistent if they're programmed to follow my examples."

"You can't tighten the screen down much," Desjani commented. "The dark ships are so much more maneuverable that they could just swing around an edge if you do." She gestured at her display. "They're going to try for *Warspite*, *Vengeance*, and *Resolution*."

"You think they're just going to target three of the battleships?" Geary asked. "*Warspite*, *Vengeance*, and *Resolution* are closest to the center of the defensive screen, where the dark ships are aiming for. But the dark ships have enough maneuverability to aim for other battleships as well."

"They do," she agreed. "Now, think like a computer. Calculate probabilities. The dark ships could have run a hundred thousand simulations of their upcoming encounter with that screen by now without overheating a single circuit. The dark destroyers have to be low on fuel. The heavy cruiser will be better off, so they'll save it for their encounter with our heavy cruisers. But they'll burn off all five of their destroyers. A single destroyer targeting a single battleship will have a certain chance of getting through to its objective, especially if it accelerates to a velocity fast enough to produce a serious problem for our fire control. But it won't be a hundred percent chance of a kill. Even if all of our shots miss, if the destroyers are going fast enough to mess up our fire control, they'll also be going fast enough to complicate attempts to ram. Even a battleship is pretty tiny compared to the space around it."

He nodded, understanding where she was going with this. "If I had to make a wild guess based on my experience, I'd say maybe a fifty percent chance of a big enough piece of the destroyer getting through the defensive fire and striking the battleship."

"And if it's two destroyers targeting each battleship?"

"Pretty near certain, I'd guess." He hunched forward, studying the situation again. "We need to start hitting them as far from the battleships as possible, but the farther ahead of the battleships our destroyers are, the more likely that they'll get chopped up by the dark battle cruisers."

"What would Admiral Geary do?" she asked.

He moved one hand to trace the movements of ships. "Send out several formations of destroyers and light cruisers to hit the flanks of the dark ships as they approach the defensive screen. I'd try to take out as many of the dark destroyers as possible before they reached the screen, and maybe cripple or destroy the heavy cruiser. So the dark ships will expect me to do that." An idea came to him, causing his lips to form a cold smile. "But if those dark destroyers are going to accelerate to hit our battleships . . ."

Desjani smiled back. "Yeah."

"Let's set this up, Captain."

There was an undeniable sense of satisfaction in using the computer systems aboard *Dauntless* to swiftly come up with plans that would hopefully trip up the plans developed by the computer systems on the dark ships. Looking over the plan carefully, Geary nodded. "Captain Desjani, I need to talk to the battleship captains in the screen as well as the commanders of the destroyer and light-cruiser divisions."

Desjani gestured to the comm watch-stander, who hastily put together the conference message. "Ready, Captain. Circuit three."

"Thank you," Geary said, touching the necessary comm control. A real-time conference was out of the question with the ships separated by at least twenty light-minutes. Any message sent to them on wings of light would still take twenty minutes to get there, and the replies would require another twenty minutes to cross back. There were few things more annoying than a conversation in which at least forty minutes separated everything said and each reply.

"All units in the screening task force," he began, "this is Admiral Geary. Your status updates indicate all of you have installed the software patch on all of your systems. It is critical that you keep those patches intact because otherwise all of your combat systems, sensor systems, and comm systems will be blinded to the dark ships and open to false messages.

"You will have all seen the reports from Atalia. These ships are not as maneuverable as those of the enigmas, but they are better than our ships. They are also individually much more heavily armed than our ships. Do not underestimate them.

"Captain Armus," he addressed the commanding officer of the battleship *Colossus*, "it is likely that the dark ships will attempt to employ their five destroyers in suicide attacks on our battleships." Was suicide attack the right term when it was an artificial intelligence that would "die"? "If the dark ships hold their current trajectory, I expect *Warspite*, *Vengeance*, and *Resolution* to be targeted, with two destroyers each going after two of the battleships and the remaining destroyer going after the third. We will attempt to hit those destroyers before they reach your screen.

"I am transmitting maneuvering orders to you now. The screen will contract toward the contact point with the dark ships, but not by much because of the ability of the dark ships to outmaneuver us. Captain Armus, if we succeed in taking out the destroyers prior to contact, do what you can to cripple or damage the dark battle cruisers and the last heavy cruiser remaining with them."

He paused, his thoughts somber, then spoke again. "Even though the AIs controlling the dark ships appear to have been programmed using my tactics, these opponents are otherwise more alien than anything else we have encountered. They will fight without mercy or reason. They must be destroyed before they can inflict on Alliance star systems the kind of damage they did at Atalia. To the honor of our ancestors, Geary, out."

Desjani, her chin resting on one hand, glanced over at him. "I used to think that about the Syndics."

"What?"

"That they fought without mercy or reason. But you're right. Compared to the dark ships, the Syndics are models of compassion and rationality. Even Syndics were capable of questioning their orders."

He sighed and sat back, knowing that it would be three-quarters of an hour before he would see any reaction to his message. "Too many of them never did. The dark ships are still holding at point two light speed."

"Conserving their fuel cells," Desjani said. "If their destroyers are going to sprint the last distance, they'll need everything they've probably got left. So, we've got about an hour and a half before the fireworks start, assuming we guessed right."

"Have we heard anything more from Admiral Timbale?" Geary asked.

"Not a word. Nothing at all from Ambaru Station even though we sent them a warning as you directed. There's a good chance those secret squirrel security goons who tried to muscle Admiral Timbale messed with the software patch."

"Them or friends of theirs," Geary agreed. "Following their orders. There was a word for that in a language on Old Earth. What was it . . . kadavergehorsam."

"Ka-what?" Desjani demanded.

"It means 'corpselike obedience,'" Geary explained. "The idea that subordinates should do exactly what they are told, unthinkingly, and only what they are told. One of the greatest strengths of humans is our ability to think, to adapt, but how many organizations have done their best to mold their people into unthinking drones?"

"Like the dark ships?" Desjani said. "The ultimate example of trying to create something that will only do what it's told. But the software is so complicated, and so prone to glitches, and vulnerable to malware, that they've ended up acting on their own anyway. Hey, if those people on Ambaru have blocked the software patch because they are unthinkingly following their orders, it could mean they'll die at the hands of something that is also supposed to be unthinkingly following orders."

Geary nodded, his lips twisting at the ugly irony. "I'm sure if we could somehow question the dark ship AIs, they'd tell us they were only following orders."

At forty-four minutes after his instructions had been sent, Geary finally saw movement among the screening forces. Some of the battleships swung about ponderously and began adjusting their positions in the screen to be closer to the place where the dark ships would penetrate. Most of the Alliance destroyers and light cruisers did the same.

But four squadrons of destroyers and two squadrons of light cruisers leaped out of the screen, accelerating toward the dark ships.

"Just what they'd expect," Desjani murmured with satisfaction.

The two dark battle cruisers were running side by side. Trailing them was their sole heavy cruiser. Two dark destroyers ranged out slightly to one side, two were on the other side, and the fifth was slightly above. A far lesser tactician than Geary would have sent in escorts to try to shave off the dark ship escorts before contact with the screen. It was a predictable maneuver, and also in accordance with the doctrine Geary had learned a century ago. Doctrine he had reason to believe had also been programmed into the dark ship AIs.

He had set up this engagement, but could only watch it, still several light-minutes away and thus unable to communicate in time to control events. Everything he was seeing had already happened several minutes ago.

The Alliance light cruisers and destroyers charging toward the dark ships had drastically increased their rate of closure on the enemy. As they reached the right positions ahead of the dark ships, ranged above the track the dark ships were following, the

Alliance warships pivoted and began both braking their velocity and swinging their trajectories downward to where the dark ships would pass.

Geary realized that the bridge of *Dauntless* had fallen silent as everyone waited to see who had outguessed whom.

"Yes!" Lieutenant Yuon whooped as the dark destroyers suddenly began accelerating at a rate no human-crewed warship could match, their main propulsion shoving them ahead of the dark battle cruisers and toward where the screen of battleships waited. "Sorry, Captain," Yuon muttered as Desjani turned a withering glance his way for a second.

But Geary had felt the same exultation.

If his intercepting light cruisers and destroyers had been coming down to meet the advance of the battle cruisers, they would have completely missed the dark destroyers charging ahead, and instead found themselves tangling with the massively greater firepower of the dark battle cruisers.

But Geary's orders had told his ships to bend their intercepts well short of the battle cruisers, to assume the dark destroyers would be out ahead and accelerating.

"Estimated relative velocity at contact will be two point three light speed," Lieutenant Yuon reported in a painfully professional tone of voice as he tried to make up for his earlier outburst.

"Too fast," Desjani grumbled. As objects accelerated to fractions of the speed of light, their visions of the universe outside them became increasingly warped by the effects of relativity. They no longer saw things where they were. Human ingenuity, always at its best when it came to working on ways to war with other humans, had managed to counter those effects somewhat. At velocities up to point two light speed, human-designed fire-control systems, sensor systems, and maneuvering systems could compensate enough for the distortion to allow hits on other ships as they flashed past at incredible velocities. Beyond that, accuracy fell off dramatically with every increase in velocity.

"That's why I sent out twenty-seven destroyers and eleven light cruisers," Geary said. "Even if most of their shots miss, there should be enough shots being fired to score some hits."

Several minutes ago, the Alliance destroyers and light cruisers had raced downward past the dark ships at a high angle, their automated fire-control systems hurling out hell lances, ball bearings (still known as grapeshot) if the range was close enough, and specter missiles from the light cruisers. Automated systems had to be used because humans could not possibly aim and fire in the tiny fraction of a second during which the forces were within weapons range of each other.

The dark destroyers fired back with implacable and emotionless precision, but their fire-control systems were just as hindered by the velocity of the engagement as those of the human-crewed ships. Even though each dark destroyer carried as much armament as a human-crewed light cruiser, there were still only five of them against thirty-eight of Geary's ships.

The Alliance squadrons plummeted away from the encounter, turning back upward but unable to alter course quickly enough to engage the dark battle cruisers and heavy cruiser that rocketed past above them. Geary watched red markers appear on some of the Alliance warships, indicating hits from the dark destroyers. But aside from two blows that had knocked out some of the weapons on the light cruiser *Croise*, Geary's ships had taken only minor damage.

But only two of the dark destroyers had emerged from the encounter still on their trajectories toward the screening force. Two others had been knocked off course and were tumbling helplessly, maneuvering systems too badly damaged to control the ships. The fifth had tried to stagger onward after the first two, but several specter missiles fired by the Alliance light cruisers had swung through tight turns to slam into the stern of the dark ship. It vanished in a flare of light and heat, leaving an endlessly expanding ball of dust where it had been.

"Still accelerating," Desjani commented, displaying no elation at the damage done to the hostile forces. The two surviving dark destroyers were pushing their velocity higher, which would make targeting them even harder for the Alliance warships in the screen. "What's Armus doing?" she grumbled in a voice too low for anyone but Geary to hear.

"He's setting them up," Geary said. "*Warspite*, *Vengeance*, and *Resolution* are holding fixed orbits, so anything aiming to intercept them will have to come down a predictable path."

"Oh." Desjani grinned. "Sorry, sir. Battle cruiser captain here. I tend to think in terms of maneuvering."

"Whereas Captain Armus knows battleships and thinks in term of forts and firepower," Geary said.

If the dark ships had attempted to dodge, to simply tear through the thin screen of widely spread Alliance ships, they would almost certainly have succeeded in making it through intact. If the Alliance ships had not guessed that the dark ships intended to ram, they would have faced a difficult fire-control solution for their weapons. But the two survivors bore down on their targets, one aiming for *Warspite* and the second for *Resolution*, and the Alliance fire-control systems only needed to solve for one, simple solution. The two battleships and the remaining Alliance light cruisers and destroyers near them hurled a wall of fire down the bearings along which the dark ship destroyers had to come, and the two destroyers hit those walls and disintegrated under the blows.

Coming on behind, though, were the remaining dark ships, and those were just trying to run through the screen. The two battle cruisers and the trailing heavy cruiser tore past the still-thinly-spread Alliance ships and onward, without any hits being scored on them.

Geary's jaw tightened as he checked the maneuvering data again. His battle cruisers were still angling in toward the dark ships, but the intercept point was far ahead, past the place where the dark ships would be able to fire upon Ambaru Station.

None of the fixed defenses near Ambaru were showing any signs of alert or alarm. They were all apparently still blind to the presence of the dark ships.

All that lay between the surviving dark ships and Ambaru Station were the sixteen heavy cruisers forming the last defensive barrier.

3

"How do we stop two battle cruisers like that with sixteen heavy cruisers?" Desjani asked. "If they were typical battle cruisers, we could do it, but the dark ships are not typical."

Geary indicated the intercept point on his display. "We don't have to stop them. We just have to push back their time to reach Ambaru and push up the time when we get within range of the dark ships."

"Make them maneuver off a straight shot at Ambaru?" She nodded, then tapped a symbol. "The heavy cruiser formations are under Commander Rosen. What do you know about her?"

"That she's commander of the First Heavy Cruiser Division," Geary said, "as well as commanding officer of the *Tanko*. And that in previous engagements she has shown a tendency to hit hard."

"Then you need to realize that when you send Rosen after those dark ships, she's not going to just dance around," Desjani said. "She's going to go after them and try to land some hard blows."

"Rosen has seen the data on how heavily armed those dark battle cruisers are."

"And she's going to try to hit them hard," Desjani repeated.

"I know," Geary said. "That's the idea." He saw her surprise, then the dawning realization. "Because," he went on, "I wouldn't do that, throwing heavy cruisers against battle cruisers in a head-on fight. I'd order a feint, and a diversion. Something to fool my opponent into doing what I want, which in this case would obviously be to throw those dark ships off a direct vector toward Ambaru."

"Even if you fool the dark ships," Desjani cautioned, "that won't fool their fire-control systems or prevent them targeting any heavy cruisers that close to firing range."

"Hopefully, I've got a solution to that as well. You know how our fire-control systems are programmed. They prioritize targets based on threat and on the highest hit probability." He touched his comm controls. "Commander Rosen, this is Admiral Geary. Your orders are to try to stop those dark ships. Get in close enough to hammer them. Try to knock out their main propulsion or maneuvering systems. My estimate is that they will not attempt to evade a firing run by you but will hold their vectors, assuming that you are conducting a feint. Set up your formations and attacks so that two leading heavy cruisers in each of your formations will clearly represent the highest hit probabilities for the fire-control systems on the dark ships and have those two heavy cruisers do last-second evasive maneuvers to throw off enemy targeting on them. I'm trusting your skill in this, Commander, as well as the skill of each cruiser commander. Geary, out."

"You're trusting in the finesse and subtlety of Sel Rosen," Desjani grumbled. "Good luck with that."

"She's not going to do exactly what I would do," Geary replied. "That may be our best hope of stopping those dark ships before they can hit Ambaru."

Five light-minutes separated the battleship screen from the heavy cruisers. The dark battle cruisers had maintained point two light speed, so it would take twenty-five minutes for them to reach the heavy cruisers. If the heavy cruisers accelerated to contact, that time would shrink, but Geary knew that Commander Rosen would be smart enough to instead bring her warships in at the battle cruisers from high angles in order to keep down the relative speed of the engagement.

The sixteen Alliance heavy cruisers were formed into two boxes, each composed of eight warships arranged in two columns, with each ship a little higher than the one ahead of it so that the formations stepped upward from front to back. One heavy cruiser formation was above and to one side of the projected track of the dark ships, while the second formation was below and to the other side. It was a classic positioning, which would allow the heavy cruisers to react effectively even if the dark ships made some major course changes to try to evade the Alliance defenders.

"She's taking into account the maneuverability of the dark ships," Geary noted approvingly.

"Let's hope she's taking into account their firepower," Desjani said. "We're still closing, but too slowly. We'll be within two light-minutes of the dark ships when Rosen's heavy cruisers hit them."

"Still nothing from Ambaru or any of the fixed defenses?"

"Nothing, sir," Lieutenant Yuon replied.

"If the dark ships continue down their current vectors,"

Lieutenant Castries added, "we will still be thirty light-seconds distant from them and twenty minutes' travel time from intercept when they reach Ambaru Station."

Thirty light-seconds didn't sound like much, unless you knew that a single light-second was the equal of three hundred thousand kilometers of distance. Nine million kilometers, the equivalent of thirty light-seconds, was hopelessly distant in terms of trying to defend Ambaru.

"Once they've hit Ambaru," Castries continued, her voice professionally unemotional, "the dark ships might choose to alter vector toward the nearest jump point."

"In which case, we will have zero chance of catching them before they reach that jump point," Desjani said. "Rosen better slow them down, or we'll have no chance of saving Ambaru or hitting those dark ships again."

"Fifteen minutes until the dark ships are in weapons range of Commander Rosen's force," Lieutenant Yuon said.

They were so close by the time the forces rushed toward contact, only a couple of light-minutes to one side, that the images were almost real-time. As the dark ships neared them, Rosen's heavy cruisers accelerated out of their orbits. Both formations pivoted around one of the leading heavy cruisers, as if the formations were rolling up to stand one corner, and headed toward the paths of the dark ships, the upper heavy cruiser formation diving toward contact while the lower formation climbed toward the enemy.

This time the dark ships reacted in the minutes before contact by abruptly jerking upward and to one side, toward the higher heavy cruiser formation. The dark ships plainly intended concentrating their fire on one set of Alliance heavy cruisers while avoiding the second formation.

The moment of contact was so quick that there was no hope of seeing the events happen, but Geary was also focused on what the lower formation of heavy cruisers was doing, bending their climb up and over to compensate for the change in the vectors of the dark ships. Instead of missing them completely, the lower formation hurtled past the sterns of the dark ships a few moments after the enemy battle cruisers had encountered the upper formation.

"Damn," Desjani muttered as the results of the engagement were reported by *Dauntless*'s sensors and data feeds from the heavy cruisers.

As Geary had instructed, Rosen had ordered her leading heavy cruisers in each formation to evade at the last moment, shifting from targeting the dark battle cruisers to instead aim for the dark heavy cruiser trailing them. The change in vectors had been enough to throw off a lot of the dark ship fire. And the dark heavy cruiser, hit by four Alliance heavy cruisers, was staggering along and sliding off to one side, trying to regain maneuvering control.

But the two enemy battle cruisers had also aimed some shots at the second row of heavy cruisers in each formation. *Diamond*, *Bastille*, *Hori*, and *Presidio* had all taken significant damage, losing weapons, shields, and in some cases parts of their propulsion and maneuvering thrusters. Personnel casualties were only estimates, but all four heavy cruisers had taken losses.

The twelve heavy cruisers hitting the dark battle cruisers had done their job, though. One of the dark battle cruisers had lost half of its propulsion and been slowed by hits. The other had been battered along one quarter but did not seem to have suffered serious damage to its propulsion or maneuverability.

"Not enough." Geary sighed, trying to accept the fact that there was nothing more he could do, that catching a force of warships which did not want to fight was nearly impossible when all of space existed to offer escape, that the distances in space meant sometimes there was no way to get somewhere in time to make a critical difference.

"The dark battle cruiser with the damaged propulsion is having trouble regaining its velocity," Lieutenant Yuon reported. "We can catch it before it reaches firing range of Ambaru."

"Which leaves one battle cruiser to shoot up the station." Geary tapped his comm controls. "Commander Rosen, use your heavy cruisers to finish off that dark heavy cruiser. Be aware that it will likely carry out a power core overload once helpless, so stay clear of the damage radius. There are light cruisers and destroyers coming your way from the screen which you are to assume control of to coordinate their attacks with your own."

He looked at Tanya. "Let's get that damaged dark battle cruiser. Too bad we can't—"

"Captain?" Lieutenant Castries called, sounding baffled. "The second enemy battle cruiser is pivoting. He's . . . braking his velocity."

"Why the hell . . . ?" Desjani demanded.

Geary was staring, trying to understand, when Desjani laughed.

"They programmed them to do what you would do!" she said.

"And I would throw away my chance to hit Ambaru?" Geary said.

"You would if it meant not abandoning one of your ships to the enemy!" Desjani laughed again. "Don't you get it? You come back for injured ships, you don't abandon comrades, that's how you've fought, and those dark ships are programmed to fight like you did."

Geary realized that he was smiling. "Nice. The dark ships aren't thinking about it, they're not responding to any moral imperative, they're just doing what their programming tells them to do in a situation like this." He hit his comm controls again. "All units in Task Force Dancer, immediate execute, come port one four degrees, up zero two degrees. Engage assigned targets when in range. Geary, out."

His warships angling in faster to hit the slowed dark battle cruisers, Geary made sure that enough of his warships were targeted on each to ensure they would be knocked out. *What would I do if I was on one of those battle cruisers? Dive down. And port or starboard? Starboard, to get back on a direct vector for Ambaru.*

He ordered a slight, last-moment change of vectors on his warships as his formation slammed into the dark battle cruisers from one side. The seven Alliance battle cruisers and the remaining heavy cruisers, light cruisers, and destroyers in Task Force Dancer threw everything they had at the dark ships, three of the Alliance battle cruisers passing close enough to the dark ships to unleash their null field weapons that ate chunks out of the enemy warships. One of the dark ships deployed a null field as well, taking a fortunately small piece out of *Intemperate*.

Geary called out orders sending his formation curving up and over for a second firing pass in case one of the dark ships was still a threat to Ambaru. But as the results of the engagement were evaluated by the sensors of the Alliance ships, it became clear that wouldn't be necessary.

One dark battle cruiser was gone, replaced by a spreading cloud of debris. The second consisted only of its forward portion, tumbling off at an angle, which self-destructed while Geary watched.

The dark heavy cruiser still survived, but Rosen was leading her heavy cruisers at it. When her firing run was complete, nothing was left of the dark heavy cruiser but pieces of wreckage.

Desjani let out a cross between a whistle and sigh, pointing to her display.

Ambaru Station was only two light-seconds away, everyone on it apparently still oblivious to how close they had come to destruction.

"All units in Task Force Dancer," Geary sent. "Well done. We're going to brake our way around the star, so that when we're back in the vicinity of Ambaru we'll be able to match the station's orbit easily. All destroyers are priority for fuel cell replenishment."

"What are you going to do about Ambaru?" Desjani asked.

"It looks like we may have to invade it."

The Marines came off the shuttle ramp in full combat mode, their battle armor sealed, their weapons active. They took up positions around the landing dock, scanning for threats. Behind them, the shuttle pulled away, making room for another shuttle also loaded with Marines.

Ambaru had a lot of docking stations. Right now, a dozen of those stations were receiving Marines who were equipped for battle and moving as if conducting an invasion of an enemy-held facility. General Carabali was aboard *Dauntless*, which had moved in close to Ambaru to oversee the assault.

"Admiral," the Marine captain in charge of the force with Geary reported, "all we have in sight are two civilians, no weapons visible, broadcasting identification as station officials, dock supervision department."

Geary studied the view from the captain's battle armor. The two station officials, the sort who normally met incoming traffic, were staring at the Marines in shock. But despite their astonishment at being on the receiving end of an Alliance assault, both were smart enough to avoid doing anything rash. The two stood absolutely still, their arms extended to show empty hands.

The captain had waved forward two scouts, who scanned the surroundings outside the dock. "My scouts report all clear, Admiral. Just civilian pedestrians."

"I'm on my way." Geary, wearing only his working uniform, came down the ramp and nodded to the officials. "I'm sorry for this, but we don't know what the situation is aboard this station. My ships have been unable to communicate with you."

"Unable?" the senior official of the two asked, surprised. "There isn't anything wrong with our comm systems."

"Then you might explain why my ships kept getting an 'incompatible message protocol' response when we tried to talk to anyone on Ambaru," Geary said.

The officials exchanged baffled glances. "We tried calling you on your inbound, Admiral," the senior explained. "But our comm system said it couldn't shake hands with yours. Are we . . . are we prisoners?"

"I hope not," Geary said. "Where—"

His words were cut off as General Carabali called, her voice calm but authoritative. "Admiral, we have troop movements detected near shuttle docks seven, nine, and twelve. No specific data yet, just indications of troop presence in those areas."

"What kind of troops?" Geary asked.

"Alliance ground forces."

"Make sure your Marines hold fire until given authorization to shoot," Geary said.

"Admiral?" The captain commanding this force of Marines sounded urgent enough to shift Geary's attention instantly.

"What is it?"

"Our armor systems are fending off attempts at software upgrades," the captain reported. "None of the updates are asking permission, just moving in and trying to apply themselves. If not for the firewalls we had added to our armor's systems before boarding the shuttle, the new software would already be installing."

"It's all coming through official channels?" Geary asked.

"Yes, Admiral. All codes clear."

"What are your suits replying?"

"Admiral, we've got the Potemkin-software routines running as a quarantined outer shell. Whoever sent the updates thinks they've successfully installed."

Desjani had been listening in as well via Geary's comm link. "Somebody tried to take out your Marines."

"We have similar software upgrades being attempted on all Marine battle armor aboard Ambaru," General Carabali reported. "All intrusions have been repelled but have mimicked successful intrusions to fool whoever sent in those upgrades."

"Sir, our Potemkin routines are trying to disable our weapons and targeting systems," the Marine captain with Geary reported.

"All ground forces detections on Marine battle armor have vanished from the Potemkin-sensor picture," Carabali said.

"Same old game," Desjani commented.

"But what are the ground forces seeing?" Geary wondered. "How is their armor reporting the Marines?" He looked outside the dock, seeing the area beyond now apparently deserted. "Someone has cut off this area from normal foot traffic."

Geary checked his data pad, trying once again to access Ambaru's internal comm net and once again finding all channels blocked to him.

He looked back at the two officials, who were still standing nervously, awaiting instructions. "I need your help."

Both of the officials reacted with a mix of surprise and elation. "You need our help? Black Jack needs our help?"

"Yes." Now wasn't the time to express how much he disliked that nickname. "There are ground forces soldiers nearby. We don't know what their armor's sensors are telling them about our Marines. I need to talk to a ground forces officer. Not by comm link. Face-to-face. Will you go out there, locate someone, and tell them I need to talk to them? There may be some danger, but you two are the least likely to provoke any overreaction, and so are the most likely to succeed without any adverse events taking place. I give my word of honor for the personal safe conduct of whoever agrees to talk to me."

Both officials nodded, their eagerness shadowed by obvious concern over the prospect of being caught in the middle of a firefight. "We'll do our best, sir."

Geary watched them walk slowly out into the now-deserted areas outside the docks, knowing that ground forces soldiers must have those areas targeted and hoping that the software messing with comms and armor sensors did not provide a misleadingly threatening image of the two officials that might lead someone to fire. "How does everything look?" he asked Carabali.

"They're waiting," she said. "I don't know what for."

"Orders?"

"If I were them, Admiral, and receiving commands to move against what looked in every way like fellow Alliance personnel, I would be asking for confirmation. Especially since my Marines are just holding position and not trying to advance."

"Good. Keep your people in place and keep their fingers off their triggers."

A single shot could trigger a major fight.

Between men and women who were on the same side.

After five very long minutes, a single figure in ground forces battle armor stepped into view of Geary. "Everyone hold," Geary ordered the Marines. "Do not target that soldier, do not aim any weapons in the direction of that soldier."

He nerved himself, then took a couple of steps forward.

The soldier began walking as soon as Geary stopped, moving with a steady stride until coming to a halt directly before him. One hand raised and the soldier's faceplate popped open. She saluted. "Major Problem, Admiral."

He returned the salute. "What problem do you—"

"Excuse me, sir, that's my name," the soldier interrupted in long-suffering tones. "Major Jan Problem."

"I see. I'm sorry," Geary added, not able to think of anything else appropriate.

"I've gotten used to it, Admiral. Mostly. What's going on, sir?"

"You tell me," Geary said. "What is your armor telling you?"

She gestured toward the Marines. "Hostile forces. Contain. Disarm."

"As you can see, they're Alliance Marines."

"Yes, sir. I did see that, which is why I know they should not be hostile, but if I try to disarm them, they are likely to become very hostile. My colonel has told us to hold position until further notice."

"Did he give a reason?" Geary asked.

"Yes, sir. The orders to contain and disarm allegedly came from the ground forces commander in Varandal Star System within two minutes of your forces arriving on this station, but that officer is known by us to be on the primary inhabited world, five light-minutes from here. It would have taken at least ten minutes for our general to see what was happening and send those orders back to us. My colonel is trying to confirm where those orders actually came from."

"There have been false orders issued in the name of Admiral Timbale as well," Geary said. "I assure you, we are not here to act against the Alliance or in any unlawful manner. We are here because the software in Ambaru, all of it, including that in your battle armor, has been infected by malware which is selectively altering your sensor picture, blocking and changing communications, and possibly causing other harm. We have patches you can use to reboot your systems and give you full control over them again."

"That's why the Marines aren't answering us?" Major Problem asked, her eyes widening in surprise. "Their comms are messed up?"

"Actually, the Marine comms are fine. It's your comms that are blocking transmissions from the Marines, and from me, and who knows what else."

"Excuse me, sir." The major began speaking into her comm system, paused, spoke again, paused, then muttered a few words under her breath. "I tried telling my colonel, and my own comms cut off."

"You'll have to do a face-to-face," Geary said. "Like we are doing here."

"This is the Syndics, right, Admiral? Playing their damned games again."

Geary took a deep breath before replying. "We don't know for certain who is responsible. We only know that the malware involved is coming in through official updates and has all of the latest code approvals and accesses." He offered some data coins. "These contain the software patches you'll need."

The major took them, eyeing the coins dubiously. "These are going to impact official updates? Who authorized the patches, sir? I know my colonel will want to know."

"I've authorized them," Geary said.

"You're not in our chain of command, sir, but I'll leave that up to my colonel to decide." She frowned, listening as a message came in over her armor's comm circuit. "Sir, we just received orders directly from Admiral Timbale. Not just the colonel. All of us."

"Those orders didn't come from Admiral Timbale," Geary said. "I haven't been able to contact him myself for some time. Until I talk to him face-to-face, I won't believe any messages I receive, even if they have all of the proper authentication codes."

"I need to pass that on as well. With your permission, Admiral, I will rejoin my forces and personally brief my colonel on what you have told me."

"The sooner, the better," Geary said, returning the major's salute.

He briefed General Carabali and Desjani on what he had learned as he watched the major walk briskly back to her lines. "Make sure the Marines know the ground forces don't intend moving in, and they should not target or fire on the ground forces under any circumstances. I don't want anyone accidentally letting off a round at Major Problem."

"If I were Major Problem," Carabali commented, "I'd get myself busted to captain as fast as I could. It looks like the ground forces are handling this professionally, but I think I see something else in their reactions."

"What's that?" Geary asked.

"It feels as if the ground forces didn't entirely trust their sensors or comms before now. They're double-checking orders, and they're doing visual confirmations of what their sensors tell them. Things must have been happening that have caused the ground forces to adopt such measures."

"Problems with the official software that created problems for even routine operations by the ground forces?"

"That's entirely possible, Admiral. The software we use is so complex and interrelated that if you pull one string of code, it creates knots in all kinds of places. Those secret subroutines might have been causing problems all across the board, problems that were having a growing impact on the effectiveness of our combat systems."

"It's a good thing we beat the Syndics when we did," Desjani commented. "From the look of things, we were well on our way to defeating ourselves."

That might still happen, Geary thought, hoping that he hadn't accidentally said it out loud. "Once we get this situation stabilized and find Admiral Timbale, I'll meet with all of the senior military and civilian officials on Ambaru. Then we'll have to brief the senior ground forces and aerospace forces commanders as well."

"A lot of other people could have gone to Ambaru to set up that meeting," she said. "You shouldn't be risking yourself."

"Everyone needs to know that I am giving the orders they are seeing," he said. "My being here in person is the only way to make sure that happens. Would those station officials have risked walking to the ground forces if anyone but I had asked?"

Desjani changed the subject quickly enough to make it clear she knew she would not win the argument. "We're not spotting any unusual activity in space. No shuttle launches, no alerting of station defenses. It's all quiet out here."

"That's good." He looked around, seeing what still appeared to be a perfectly normal view from a shuttle dock on Ambaru if you didn't count the total lack of passing traffic. "But from here it all seems quiet inside the station as well, and we know it isn't. Hold on. More company is coming."

Instead of another ground forces officer as Geary had expected, two civilians were walking into the dock, one man and one woman. Neither were the officials he had sent off earlier to speak to the ground forces. Both looked official even though neither wore an obvious uniform. Somehow, though, their generic suits gave the impression of still being a kind of uniform.

They stopped before Geary, and the elder of the two smiled politely at him. "Admiral, we have to speak with you urgently. It is a matter of Alliance security."

"Is it?" Geary asked. "I'm sort of busy at the moment with matters of Alliance security."

"We're going to defuse all of that, Admiral," the younger of the two said in tones of utter confidence that grated on Geary's nerves.

"Are you?" he asked. "And just who do you work for?"

"The Alliance, Admiral."

"That's nice. Exactly what part of the Alliance?" Geary pressed.

"Sir," the younger of the two said, "we can tell you that when we are in a secure location, you are briefed into several very important programs, and the necessary security oaths are given—"

"No," Geary said, holding up one hand, palm out, to emphasize the word. "I'm waiting here. Anything you have to tell me you can say here and now."

"I'm sorry, Admiral, but we're not allowed to," the elder explained. "Please. We don't want to have to insist."

"I don't want you to have to insist, either," Geary said. "What's wrong with the comm systems on Ambaru?"

"Once you are read into the appropriate programs and swear to the nondisclosure requirements—"

"No," Geary repeated.

"Admiral," the oldest official said with what seemed to be feigned reluctance, "now I must insist. If we have to arrest you, we will. We have that authority from the government."

Geary gestured toward some of the nearest Marines in their battle armor. "These Marines are loyal to the Alliance, but I think you'll find that they aren't inclined to trust you."

The younger official smiled. "What they think doesn't matter. They can't even see us or hear us."

"You think so?" Geary activated a comm circuit. "Captain, have two of your Marines target these two, one on each."

"Yes, sir."

Two rifles came up and around, each centering on one of the officials, whose expressions had gone from smug to worried. "You can get away with a lot when you control the software," Geary said to them. "But when other people figure out that there's another source of malware, one coming through official channels, they can figure out ways to block it. Now, you two are under arrest for threatening an officer of the fleet. You will stand to one side of the dock under the close personal attention of some of my Marines. I assume you know that there are very few people who actively seek out close personal attention from Marines? You will wait there until I have had a chance to find out exactly what is going on here and have been able to get security reestablished on Ambaru."

"Admiral," the eldest official said, "you are risking the compromise of the most important secret programs—"

"You mean the programs that may have just restarted the war with the Syndicate Worlds?" Geary asked, surprised that his voice didn't tremble with anger. "Did you bother looking at the vids that were sent here of what happened at Indras and Atalia?"

"We were not authorized—"

"You weren't authorized to pay attention to what was happening, but you were authorized to risk the lives of everyone on this station?" From their expressions, Geary realized that his voice had gotten a lot louder. He scaled it back. "You idiots. We barely managed to stop an attack on this station, an attack the station was blind to because of your actions. Literally *blind* obedience is not a virtue. Don't say another word to me until I ask you to, and don't do anything until I tell you to, or you will both regret it."

After only a couple of minutes, another ground forces soldier appeared. The soldier advanced with open hands held out, then popped his face shield when close to Geary. "Colonel Kochte, commander of the ground forces with primary responsibility for defense of Ambaru," he introduced himself.

"Are we good, Colonel?" Geary asked.

"I'm not moving my people until we get things cleared up, Admiral. Our systems are a mess," Kochte complained. "The problems seem to be spreading throughout Ambaru and the star system."

"You've got official software fighting official software," Geary said. "I provided Major Problem with software patches that will fix the problems."

"Yes, sir, but with all due respect, since you're not in my chain of command, and as far as we can determine the patches are not officially approved or authorized, that creates some other problems for me."

"Colonel, I want to ensure that no Alliance troops end up shooting at each other because of the problems with the software on this station and their battle armor."

"We are in agreement with that, sir." Kochte hesitated. "Admiral, if this was some Syndic sabotage, I could act immediately."

Geary considered that. "I cannot rule out Syndic involvement in one way or another. I don't know with absolute certainty who has been creating this problem."

Kochte smiled. "Then I can have those patches installed, based on your assurances that they are necessary to the defense of this station."

"They definitely are necessary, Colonel. I understand in their current configurations, your battle-armor systems are designating Alliance Marines as hostile forces."

"And the Marines are not. Or they shouldn't be." Colonel Kochte looked at Geary. "Admiral, since you got back, it has looked like you and your ships were doing some sort of fleet mime game, pretending you were fighting something that wasn't there. But our systems spotted damage occurring to some of your ships even though there was no indication of anything firing at them. Does this have anything to do with any of the aliens?"

"I don't think so, Colonel." He couldn't rule it out, of course. Maybe the enigmas had figured out a different way to mess with humanity. But he had no evidence for that, and substantial evidence in the other direction. "I suspect this is purely human mischief, but by whom I do not yet have sufficient information."

The colonel's eyes went to the two officials standing stiffly with Marine rifles held in ways that covered any movement they might make. "Who are they, sir, if I may ask?"

"I don't know. They thought they could give me orders."

Kochte looked uncertain again. "Is it happening, Admiral? They said you wouldn't."

"Happening?" The meaning of the question hit Geary. "Do you mean am I moving against the government? No. I am acting lawfully, dealing with threats to my forces and to the Alliance. I am still trying to sort out who is behind this. Even if these two are legitimate, which I think is far from a settled question, I do not think the government really understands what has happened, that layers and layers of secrecy have kept too many people in the dark about what I suspect was actually going on, and that too many other people have used secrecy as a way of avoiding having their actions questioned. I am not moving against the government. I am still trying my best to defend the Alliance."

"But if those two really are from the government—"

"I know what they claim. I don't know who they are, and I don't know where they are from," Geary said. "Do you recognize them?"

"No, sir." The colonel took a deep breath. "I do know I still haven't been able to get comms with my general. Therefore, I am placing my forces under your command as senior officer present. What exactly are we doing?"

"Making sure no Alliance soldiers trade fire with Alliance Marines. I'll stand down my Marines. You do the same with your soldiers as fast as you can get those software patches loaded. After that, our priorities are to get Ambaru Station working again, find Admiral Timbale, make sure Varandal Star System is ready to defend against any Syndic retaliatory raids—"

"Syndic—?" Colonel Kochte again looked at the two officials standing stiffly to one side. "Retaliation for what? Something they did?"

"Something they're involved with," Geary said. "They may not even know about it even though they've been helping to make it occur."

"Ancestors. What the hell happened?"

"A century of war. I keep discovering more people who seem to have learned all of the wrong lessons from it."

"He's in there," the Marine sergeant declared confidently as he worked on a panel next to the hatch for Admiral Timbale's private quarters. "There's some kind of override on the security software that is locking him inside and blocking comms in or out."

"How long until you can get it open?" Geary asked. He was acutely aware of the fully armored Marines still escorting him around, but for once he did not object to the presence of such bodyguards. The discovery of the two apparently innocuous agents hidden among the population of Ambaru had rattled him enough to submerge his usual concerns about seeming too obsessed with his personal security.

"Another minute or so," the sergeant declared confidently. Something went *snick*, and a row of lights inside the panel changed from red and orange to green. "Or less."

The hatch opened slowly, as if still reluctant to free the occupant of the quarters. Admiral Timbale was indeed inside, looking furious enough to eat his way through the armored bulkhead. "Admiral Geary. Thank you."

Timbale's voice sounded slightly strangled from both his anger and the humiliation of having to be freed from his own quarters. "I should have guessed you'd be the one to get things under control. If the Syndics think they can—"

"I don't think it's the Syndics," Geary said. He turned to the Marines and gestured for them to withdraw down the passageway, so he could talk to Timbale with a small measure of privacy.

"Have you seen them?" Timbale asked. "Two people in civilian suits. They claimed to have authority from our government."

"I've seen them. I've got them," Geary said, displaying a picture upon his comm pad. "These two?"

"They said they had authority to override fleet command structures!" Timbale seethed. "I had never even seen them before. Why wouldn't I have been told if someone like that was on a station under my command? When I insisted on verification, they left to allegedly get it, and I found myself locked into my own quarters with all forms of comms cut off. I don't care what authority they claim to have. I don't even care whether or not they are Syndics! I won't tolerate being treated like one of the enemy!"

"How long have you been trapped in there?" Geary asked.

"A couple of days, I think. With all systems available to me frozen or off-line, I can't be certain. What happened while I was in there? Did *Mortar* and *Serpentine* get clear?"

Geary took a moment to reply as he realized that he would have to deliver some very bad news. "No. They held their orbits."

"You said there was a threat. Was there a threat?" Timbale demanded with worry growing in his voice.

"Yes," Geary said, his own tone flat. "A serious threat. Due to malware in official software updates, both *Mortar* and *Serpentine* were destroyed without ever being able to see that threat."

"Damn." Timbale couldn't say anything else for a moment, then began again, his voice now trembling with anger. "Any survivors?"

"Seventeen off *Serpentine*."

"Seventeen," Timbale repeated. "From the crews of two destroyers. Those two . . . agents. They're the ones who kept me from sending new orders to *Mortar* and *Serpentine*. Is that right?"

"I believe so," Geary said.

"Then I don't care whatever they are or whoever they work for. I want them shot! Right now."

"I understand why you want that," Geary said. "But—"

"Dammit, Admiral, I have asked nothing of you for the support I have offered! This is clearly a war zone once more, and that means I have the authority to order those two to be shot without trial!"

Geary waited, looking back at Timbale's face, which was distorted with rage. "Is that really what you want, Admiral? Those two might be able to tell us who gave them their orders."

The light of reason and calculation reappeared in Timbale's eyes. "Who gave them their orders? I do want to know that. Especially if it was someone supposedly from our side."

"So do I," Geary said. "I request permission to take them to a fleet warship for interrogation."

"You—?" Timbale gazed back at him with suspicion. "Why a fleet warship? Why not here? We've got excellent interrogation facilities."

"You told me that you didn't even know those two agents were on this station," Geary explained. "What if they have friends here as well? Friends who would keep them from talking by any means necessary?"

The rage was gone. Timbale wasn't a screamer, the sort of commander who ruled by fear and intimidation, and now his native caution and control had reasserted itself. "Very good point, Admiral, though I'm surprised that you thought of it."

Geary made an apologetic gesture. "I've been talking to Syndics.

Former Syndics, that is, at Midway Star System."

"They'd be good instructors for this sort of mess."

"And I've spent a while around Victoria Rione," Geary added.

Timbale actually mustered a cold smile. "She could probably teach the Syndics a few things." The smile vanished. "Do you think Rione could be involved in this?"

"No." Geary shook his head for emphasis. "I am certain that she is trying, in her own ways, to find out the same answers that we want, and for the same reasons."

This time, Timbale nodded somberly. "Her husband. The people who messed up his head to block his ability to talk about that classified research program he was involved with might well be the same bastards behind this. The end justifies the means, and at some point they forget what the end was supposed to be, and the means justify themselves. And then you and your enemies have turned into two sides of the same coin." He inhaled deeply and met Geary's eyes. "You reminded me of that. You reminded a lot of us of that. Too bad some people didn't listen. All right, Admiral. You have my permission to take those two prisoners to one of your ships for interrogation, on two conditions. One, I want to know what they tell you. And, two, I am not relinquishing my right as commander of fleet forces in this star system to order them shot at some future time."

"Understood," Geary said. "Many of your subordinates didn't know you had been malware-exiled. They're working now to get the station fully operational again using software patches my code monkeys are supplying. The ground forces assigned to Ambaru have placed themselves under fleet command until they manage to reestablish reliable comm links to the star system ground forces commander."

"Good. People are thinking. I never assume that's going to happen, so it's always a pleasant surprise when it does." Timbale took another long breath, composing himself. "It's time for the boss to walk around so he can find out what's going on, and so he can look like he knows what he's doing. Damn. *Mortar* and *Serpentine*. This isn't supposed to happen. We're at peace."

"Some people didn't get the memo," Geary said.

4

Lieutenant Iger did not look happy. "Admiral, I am very uncomfortable with the idea of interrogating Alliance personnel whose identification materials appear completely authentic and who indicate security grounds for their actions."

"I understand your concerns," Geary said. He could just order Iger to do it anyway, but he had long ago learned that dramatically different results could come from someone's pursuing a task willingly and enthusiastically as opposed to someone ordered to "do as you're told or else." "But no matter what their identification says, and no matter what they say, they were directly involved in actions that caused the destruction of Alliance warships, the death of fleet personnel, and attempts to corrupt the systems in the battle armor of our Marines."

Iger nodded. "Yes, sir. There doesn't seem any doubt of that."

"So what we need to know, Lieutenant, is who those two are really working for. Isn't there a term for someone who seems to be one of ours but is actually working for someone else?"

"A mole, Admiral." Iger's eyes narrowed in thought. "They could be moles. The identification could be completely legitimate, they could be part of a covert Alliance agency, and they could still be plants working for the Syndics."

"Exactly," Geary said. "I need to know whose orders those two are really responding to, and I am certain that we are more than justified in wanting to know that answer given events in this star system as well as at Indras and Atalia."

"Yes, sir." But Iger hesitated once more. "Admiral, it is likely that they will refuse to cooperate with interrogation and refuse to reply to any questions. We can still learn some things by monitoring the reactions of their bodies and their brain patterns to specific questions, but we would not be able to identify their true superiors using something that vague."

Geary considered the statement, wondering what Iger was driving at, then abruptly understood. "Do not take any actions contrary to good interrogation procedures, the laws of the Alliance, or fleet rules and regulations. I want accurate, actionable intelligence. And when the time comes, I want to be able to greet my ancestors knowing that I did not shame them."

Iger nodded, a smile flitting across his face, then saluted. "Yes, sir. Me, too, Admiral. I will do my very best to get the answers you seek, sir."

"I never doubted that," Geary said.

As Iger left, Geary leaned back in his seat, grateful to be in his stateroom aboard *Dauntless* once more. His ships were gradually assuming assigned parking orbits and taking on new supplies. A message from Captain Smythe had provided a real picture of the readiness of his fleet, one which wasn't nearly as good as could be hoped but wasn't nearly as bad as it could have been. Varandal's defenses were now on alert, and the software patches were gradually being introduced throughout the star system to clean out at least some of the dangerous subroutines hidden in the mass of official software.

All of which left him in the unenviable position of trying to decide what to do next.

He called Desjani. "Tanya, who can we trust as a high-level courier and afford to spare?"

She was in her own stateroom, absorbed in the many and unending responsibilities of a ship's commanding officer. Desjani looked back at him, rubbing her forehead with a resigned expression that implied she was also trying to deal with a few headaches. "Jane Geary," she replied after several seconds.

"My grand-niece?" Geary grimaced as he considered the idea. "All of the battleships in her division are laid up in dock. *Dreadnaught* won't be underway again for . . . five weeks."

"Right. Long enough to use the hypernet to get to Unity and back." Desjani shrugged. "Unless you're planning to head off with part of the fleet—"

"I hope not."

"Then Jane Geary won't be needed to help hold things together here."

"Will she be able to get to the right people?" Geary asked.

Tanya gave him one of those looks that told him he had said something that betrayed his lack of familiarity with how the universe worked a century after his supposed death. "She's a Geary. Descended from Black Jack."

"Descended from my brother," Geary said.

"Close enough, since you didn't have any children before the battle at Grendel. The point is, if Captain Jane Geary shows up and says, I need to talk to so-and-so, she'll get to talk to so-and-so."

"All right." He looked away, thinking. "How much should I send?"

"Who are you sending it to?"

"Senator Navarro and Senator Sakai."

"Navarro and Sakai?" Desjani gave him a doubtful look. "How much experience do we really have with Navarro?"

"I have seen him enough to have formed an impression," Geary explained. "And Victoria Rione said he could be trusted."

"Oh, well," Desjani said archly, "if that woman vouched for Navarro, I guess that settles the issue."

"Tanya——"

"Do you have any idea where she is?"

"She——? You mean Rione?" Geary asked. "No. Why?"

"Because you should send it to her, too." Desjani smiled thinly at his expression. "Hey, I may not like her . . . actually, I definitely don't like her . . . but I know she would get that information to places where it would do some good."

"True," Geary agreed. "But since I have no idea where she is, all I can do is authorize Jane Geary to pass Rione a copy if she runs into her."

"That's the best you can do," Desjani said. "Now, as to how much to send? Send everything. Make it clear that absolutely nothing has been held back, that you are not keeping anything from them."

"That's good advice," Geary said.

"Why, thank you, Admiral." She lowered her forehead onto her palm, resting it there. "We've done the easy part. You know how hard the rest might be."

"The rest of the dark ships?"

"Yeah." Desjani raised her gaze to look into his eyes. "They've still got fourteen battle cruisers and twenty battleships, all superior in combat capability to ours. That's not even taking into account the accumulated damage and wear and tear on our ships, whereas the dark ships are all shiny and new. I have no idea how to beat a force like that."

"We have to hope that the rest of the dark ships haven't slipped their leashes," Geary said. "That they are still under control of humans who can shut them down."

"If it's a virus or other malware, not just glitches, the other dark ships could be just as badly infected." Desjani rolled her eyes. "Crazy artificial intelligences. Driven mad by malware or just problems in programming that was too complex for anyone to really understand. How many horror movies have used that plot?"

Geary shook his head. "Apparently not enough. The government got convinced that this time the AIs couldn't be corrupted or develop serious failures."

"I used to think fleet headquarters had first call on idiots," Desjani said, "but I have come to realize that the government must be requisitioning some of them. Aside from the ones that the citizens elect, that is."

"Tanya, I know some of the men and women we've encountered in the government appear to have been born without any common sense and lost ground every year of their lives since, but if we start believing that as a rule the citizens can't be trusted to elect their representatives, then we've stopped believing in the Alliance. We might as well change the name to the Syndicate Worlds and pass control to an unelected elite."

She sighed heavily. "Doesn't all that idealism ever make your hair hurt?"

"What?"

"Look, I understand. We all do. But it's kind of hard to believe the way the Alliance is run reflects the best of all possible ways of doing things!"

"It doesn't," Geary admitted. "Somebody once said that allowing the citizens to vote on their government was the worst way of doing things, with the exception of every other way that humans have tried."

"It's the least-worst option?" Desjani asked. "That I can believe. Now, I'm going to use my dictatorial powers aboard *Dauntless* to get that package of material assembled for your courier. You need to put together an executive summary for it, though. Something with bright colors, explosions, and short words so our leaders don't let their attention wander."

After ending the call, Geary glumly turned to the task of trying to very quickly and very clearly explain what the mass of data he was sending meant. *First, a secret Alliance program is out of control, threatening the Alliance itself. It has already launched unprovoked attacks on Alliance citizens and property. Second, the Syndics have threatened to start the war again because of the attack on Indras by elements of that secret Alliance program. Third, Atalia, a neutral star system, was savaged by the same elements of that secret Alliance program, which then launched an unprovoked attack on fleet units. Fourth, Atalia urgently requires humanitarian assistance.*

Fifth, software for critical, official systems is riddled with "features" that aid and allow intrusion and misuse, and place those critical systems in jeopardy of being unable to fulfill their functions. Sixth . . .

Sixth . . .

Dammit, why didn't you place your trust in the citizens of the Alliance rather than in secrecy and technology?

The courier ship carrying Captain Jane Geary and multiple copies of Geary's report on multiple backup systems departed through the hypernet gate three days later. "There have been a lot of civilian ships leaving since we got back," Desjani commented, "but this should be the first official reporting of what has happened that gets to the government at Unity and fleet headquarters."

"What have I done, Tanya?" Geary asked. "I've knocked over the first domino. How far and how wide will the reaction be?"

"You didn't knock over the first domino," she replied, giving him a crooked smile. "Whoever sent out those dark ships to hit Indras . . . no, whoever authorized the whole dark ship program . . . the war . . . there was a century of dominos falling in that war." Her gaze on him shifted, becoming appraising. "Or maybe the first domino fell when you were the last person off *Merlon* a century ago, and your damaged escape pod put you into survival sleep, to be lost until the fleet found you on our way to Prime to try to beat the Syndics once and for all. Maybe that's when this whole thing got put into motion."

He made a scoffing sound. "You make it sound like a plan."

"Maybe it was. Maybe the living stars knew that we'd need you, and for some reason that I admit I don't understand, maybe they thought that we deserved being saved from our own follies." Desjani smiled again. "And if that's true, then you'll figure out a way to stop the dark ships."

Geary shook his head at her. "No pressure, huh? Tanya, right now I have no idea how to stop them."

He looked back at the depiction of the hypernet gate, knowing that at any moment a fleet of dark ships might erupt from it, and wondering what he could do to lessen the disaster if that did happen.

Captain Tulev's battle cruisers arrived at the jump point from Atalia a few days later. His own ships battered in the fight with the dark ships at Atalia, Tulev had been left behind to assist damaged ships, pick up survivors of destroyed ships, and provide what pitifully small aid he could to the ravaged human cities in Atalia.

He had come aboard *Dauntless* to provide additional details because recent experience had only emphasized for them all that even the supposedly most secure forms of conferencing and communication were not truly safe from eavesdroppers. Geary had invited Desjani to attend the meeting in his stateroom as well, they sitting on the short couch together while Tulev occupied the chair opposite them. Tulev rarely displayed much emotion, but even he could not avoid occasional flashes of anger and distress as he reported in detail on the damage done to Atalia by the rogue dark ships. "The only good thing, and this only from the perspective of the Alliance, is that the people of Atalia are convinced that the dark ships must be Syndic in origin because they attacked us and we destroyed many of the dark ships in the subsequent fighting."

"At least we finished off the dark ships that escaped from Atalia," Geary told him.

"Yes. I regret missing that action." Tulev paused, thoughts moving behind his eyes. "Can it be called vengeance when what was destroyed were only machines?"

"I derived some satisfaction from it," Desjani said.

"But of course, Tanya. I would expect nothing else from you." Tulev bent the corners of his mouth in the briefest of smiles at her.

"I'll be even happier if I get to blow away the fools who thought building those dark ships was a good idea," she added.

"This, too, I would expect of you," Tulev said, then looked at Geary. "Do we have plans, Admiral?"

"I'm trying to get the fleet in the best possible state of readiness," Geary replied. "I've sent a very detailed report on what happened at Indras, at Atalia, and here at Varandal, to the government and to fleet headquarters. They will realize that we have to do something. Hopefully, they can deactivate the surviving dark ships. If not . . ."

"It will be difficult," Tulev observed with typical understatement. "My ships will be ready, Admiral."

Desjani had been watching Tulev closely. "Is everything all right, Kostya?" she asked.

Tulev glanced at her. "Has everything ever been all right, Tanya?"

"Not in my memory." She leaned forward a bit toward him. "We've been through a lot, you and me. Fought in a lot of battles, lost a lot of friends, seen a lot of things we'd rather forget having seen. I'm a little worried about what I think I'm seeing now. Is anything in particular wrong?"

This time Tulev took a few seconds to answer, his gaze distant, then he looked back at her, then at Geary. "I'm waiting for the war to end."

Geary nodded. "I know that this peace feels a lot like a war at times."

"That is not what I meant, Admiral." Tulev frowned slightly, his eyes on the table before him. "I'm waiting for the war with the Syndicate Worlds to end. The war that destroyed my home, and so much else. A peace agreement was signed. Officially, the war is no more. But that happened outside of me. Inside . . . the war remains. It still goes on. It doesn't end. I don't think it will ever end, in here." He tapped his chest with one forefinger.

Geary looked away, trying to find words. "I'm sorry."

"I know how you feel," Desjani said. "If not for——" She broke off, looking away, uncharacteristically embarrassed-looking.

Tulev showed that shadow of a smile again. "It's not something that should not be said, Tanya. You found someone." He nodded very fractionally toward Geary. "It must help a great deal."

"It does," she whispered, still not looking at him, and sounding guilty now. "There's something in my soul besides the war."

"And that is a good thing, what I would want a friend to have, just as you would be pleased if it were me who had found someone."

"Is there anything I can do?" Geary asked.

"Thank you, Admiral, but you are not my type."

Desjani snorted a brief laugh and shook her head at Tulev. "That's the guy I used to know."

"He is still inside there. But . . . so is something else. It is war." Tulev shrugged. "In the histories, they give dates. A war begins on this day, at this hour, and then it ends at some precise date and time. All very neat and clean. But you and I, all of us who have fought, we know that wars don't end at some moment dictated by a peace treaty. There's nothing neat about the endings, if they truly end at all. I remember too many things, Admiral. I remember too many people. Many of them I don't want to forget. But I cannot forget any of them. I have no home left to me. And so the war goes on, inside."

Geary nodded. Tulev did not often talk about the destruction of his home world during the war. It was something everyone knew about him, so it did not need to be discussed. "The price of war goes on, too. Histories tend to calculate that in terms of money and casualties during the war, not in terms of what it does to those who fight and experience the wars. We've been . . . talking to . . . some official representatives who were involved with supporting the dark ship program on Ambaru Station. They haven't told us much, but one thing we did get out of them was one of the concepts behind the dark ships, that by turning fighting over to artificial intelligences we would eliminate the impact of the killing on humans. They said it would make war less horrible."

Tulev fixed his eyes on Geary. "They said that? Tell me, Admiral, what would you call a person, a man or a woman, who killed without concern, without thought or regret, simply because they had orders to do so? What would you call someone who felt nothing at all when they killed, never questioned an order to kill, and never hesitated, but simply killed, then moved on to the next target?"

"I'd call a person like that a monster," Geary said.

"A monster. Yes. Because those who we send to kill must know what they are doing, must realize what life means, must feel the pain. If killing becomes too easy, those who issue the orders become too fond of it. We know this from history. There have been too many times and places where it became easier to kill than to think, easier to kill than to debate, easier to kill than accept differences." Tulev frowned, revealing great anger for the first time since Geary had met him. "And they would make war 'better' by turning it over to monsters who don't care? Who feel nothing when they kill?'"

"An ancient military leader supposedly once said that it is well that war is so terrible, because otherwise people would grow too fond of it," Geary said.

"He or she knew much more than the fools who sought to give war to the uncaring minds of machines," Tulev said, still frowning. "To the dark ships, what they did was not terrible. It was simply a task, an order to be fulfilled. We will stop them, Admiral? We will not accept official assurances that next time there will be no malfunctions?"

"I will not," Geary said. "I will use every bit of my authority and influence to stop them. I don't care how many peaceful tasks are supervised by artificial intelligences. They're good at a lot of things, as long as someone is watching for times when something goes wrong by accident or malware. But not war. Not if we're going to stay human."

"Welcome back." Admiral Timbale led Geary out of the shuttle dock and toward one of the main commercial areas of Ambaru Station. "Things are still a bit unsettled here. Everyone will be immensely comforted by the sight of Black Jack."

"It's that bad?" Geary asked.

"Enough word of what happened, and what nearly happened to this station at the hands of those dark ships, that both the civilian and military populations of the station are jumpy." Timbale smiled and waved at a passing group in civilian work clothes. "I've been going through recent shipping reports and finding some very disturbing things," he continued, Timbale's relaxed tone of voice and outward demeanor clashing with his words.

"Disturbing things?" Geary asked, nodding and smiling at passersby who brightened at the sight of him.

"Yes." Timbale glanced sideways at Geary. "Shipping losses. You understand, we're used to a certain level of those. Syndic raiders slipping into border star systems. Sabotage. Accidents due to rushed manufacture of the ships or hazardous materials being transported. Stuff happens. Once the war officially ended and word of that filtered through the Syndic border star systems, we had a big change for the better. Shipping losses declined by over seventy percent."

"That's good."

"Yes. But less good is the fact that, according to the reports that have come in, we saw a resurgence of losses in recent months." Timbale looked down, his mouth working. "Freighters and other shipping that never reached their destinations. Sometimes wreckage was identified, but with all of the wreckage in most star systems within a score of light-years of Syndic space, that hasn't been possible too often."

As he returned salutes from several passing ground forces soldiers, Geary somehow managed to keep his smile fixed despite an urge to snarl. "Mysterious, unexplained losses."

"And no survivors from the crews." Timbale reached one hand up and back to rub his neck. "We had thought, well, that's the Syndics. They've been messing with us, like they did with your forces transiting their space, and this is just more Syndic ugliness. But no one has spotted any Syndic warships transiting Alliance space in or near the star systems where the losses have occurred."

"Unbelievable," Geary murmured. "I wonder how those ships were written off by the people running the dark ship program? Collateral damage? Training accidents?"

"They would have had trouble blaming it on personnel error," Timbale said, his eyes now straight ahead as he walked beside Geary.

"I'd like to see that data," Geary said. "See where the losses have been occurring."

"It might help identify where the base is," Timbale said. "Listen. You need to say something. Give an interview. I know you can't talk about the dark ships and all of the garbage associated with that, but the people need to hear Black Jack telling them to keep the faith."

"Surely there are other people who can tell them that," Geary said, reluctant to step into such a public role again.

"There are," Timbale agreed. "But no one believes them when they talk about what the Alliance means and how important it is because they don't believe it. But you do, don't you?"

"Yes."

"They're putting it all together, Admiral," Timbale emphasized. "The press and others. This is going to come out. Word of what happened to Atalia is all over the place, and word is trickling in from Indras. A lot of people saw your ships apparently fighting nothing and taking damage from apparently nothing, and they want to know what the hell happened here. Corporations want to know what's happening to their ships and their cargoes. Families are raising hell about missing crews. And some of your own sailors and Marines are finding ways to talk to people. You and I both know that it's going to take a while for the government to decide how to respond to this mess. Fleet headquarters is going to pass the buck for doing anything to the government, so don't expect any orders from them. That means it's up to us to handle things here for the time being, which means it is really up to you."

"Things keep working out that way, don't they?" Geary said. He looked over and saw a group of civilians hustling toward him, their clothes and overall appearance matching those of newscasters.

The woman in the lead skidded to a halt about a meter short of him, positioning herself in a way that offered a good look at Geary from the vidcam resting on her shoulder. One thing that hadn't changed in the last century was that news reporters were still legally required to openly display any recording devices. "Admiral Geary, there are many rumors making the rounds. The people of the Alliance would like a statement from you."

Geary waited as other reporters stopped nearby, behind them a growing, mixed crowd of military and civilians, all craning to hear anything he said. "I am waiting for orders," he said. "I have reported to the government everything that I know and am preparing my forces to be ready for whatever mission I am assigned."

"Who really gives the orders, Admiral?" a male reporter demanded. "The government? Or you?"

"The government." He said it as if no other answer could have been expected. "I serve the Alliance."

"Does the government really represent the people of the Alliance anymore?" another woman asked.

"As far as I'm concerned, it does," Geary said. "As far as I'm concerned, I'm looking at the government of the Alliance right now." He slowly ran his gaze across the crowd to drive home the point. "They are men and women whom you have elected. You chose them to speak for you, to make decisions."

"I didn't choose any of them!" someone called from the crowd.

"Did you have a voice in whether or not they were chosen?" Geary asked. "Did you have a vote, and did you use it to express your wishes? I didn't actually vote for anyone in the government now. I was . . . not in a position to vote," he added, drawing smiles and laughs from the crowd who all knew variations on the claims that he had not simply been frozen in survival sleep but actually among his ancestors for a century. "But I still consider them to be my government because you are the people of the Alliance, and you voted for them, and I believe in your ability to over time find the right solutions or to find the right people to find the right solutions. I believe in you, and therefore, I believe in the Alliance, and that will not change. If you believe in me, then I hope the fact that I believe in you means something."

Everyone was looking at him, no one was saying anything. The reporters fumbled for more questions. Geary turned to go, but paused as another question was shouted from the crowd. "Will you support the government if it does something illegal?"

The silence this time felt almost physical in its intensity. Geary faced everyone again, and shook his head. "I will not support illegal actions. If necessary, I would resign my command and my position rather than carry out illegal orders. I assure you that the government knows that. Thank you."

A squad of security police had hastened up to provide an escort as the crowd kept growing. They readied themselves to force a path through the mass of people, but the crowd parted before him as Geary walked back toward the shuttle dock, knowing his words would be sent around the Alliance as fast as light, jump drives, and the hypernet could carry them, and wondering if they would make any difference.

"Our requisitions are being rejected," Captain Smythe said with an apologetic look.

Geary glanced from Smythe to Lieutenant Jamenson, whose uncanny ability to confuse anything had proven invaluable in keeping the fleet's many, overlapping sources of repair and funding from realizing anywhere near how much money had been getting spent on repairing his fleet. "Do they say why?"

"Insufficient funds," Smythe said.

"They don't reject the requisitions themselves," Jamenson added, the green hair bequeathed her genes by the original settlers of her home world of Eire standing out incongruously in Geary's stateroom. "They just say there's no money."

"I told you that the wells were running dry," Smythe reminded Geary.

He looked at Smythe and Jamenson again. "You tell me. How do we keep the work going?"

Smythe made a face. "Legally?"

"Yes. Legally."

"Cannibalize," Smythe said. "Pull funds from other sources that are available to the fleet. By the way, we've already received a number of requests to transfer some of those funds back to various higher-level accounts and have successfully failed to manage those transfers as of yet. Spend it or lose it, Admiral."

"What funds are we talking about?" Geary asked.

"Training. Mess funds—"

"Mess funds? They want to short how much food the crews of my ships get?" Geary demanded in disbelief.

"No," Smythe said. "They want you to feed them the same quantity in the same quality while using less money."

Geary resisted the urge to hit the nearest object. "And, of course, they aren't explaining how I'm supposed to do that."

"No, of course not."

Lieutenant Jamenson gestured toward the star display over Geary's table. "There were the budget cuts after the war, then money being siphoned off to pay for that special program—"

"The dark ships," Geary said.

"Yes, Admiral, and apparently that program cost a whole lot more than was budgeted, and now I'm seeing reports that the fleet is having to reactivate some of the border defenses that were deactivated to save money after the war ended even though no one has the money for that. It's actually pretty simple. Less money available, and financial obligations higher than expected."

"They could have guessed that the dark ships would cost much more than anticipated," Geary said. "Is there any other way I can drum up more money for repairs and operations?"

Smythe spoke reluctantly, his face twisted as if he were tasting something sour. "We could reduce costs by selectively shutting down some of your ships, Admiral. Don't officially decommission them. Just shut down everything, send the crews to other ships, and leave them orbiting until we get the money to get them going again."

"I can't do that!" Geary pointed to the star display. "At any time, I could end up fighting the rest of those dark ships, and if that happens, I will need every ship and weapon I can lay my hands on! How long can we keep things going by cannibalizing those funds we're supposed to be transferring back to other people?"

"A month, give or take a few days," Smythe said.

"Can we legally spend that money if we've been told to send it elsewhere?"

Lieutenant Jamenson smiled. "Yes, sir. There are some amazing loopholes in official regulations. It will take some careful maneuvering, but we can drive a transport full of cash through them. After spending the money, I will inform everyone expecting it that it has already been spent, though saying it in such a way that it will take everyone months to figure out that has happened."

"I'm glad that you're on our side, Lieutenant. Is there anything else?"

Smythe looked thoughtful. "There are some critical parts and materials I would dearly like to lay my hands on, Admiral. But there are a few obstacles hindering my acquisition of them. Could you persuade Captain Desjani to loan me Master Chief Gioninni for a few days?"

"A few days?" Geary asked. "I'm sure that can be worked out. What exactly are we talking about doing?"

"Oh, Admiral, do you *really* want to know? Or do you want the parts and materials?"

Geary sighed. "I need to know if this is anything that will get anyone court-martialed."

"No, sir!" Smythe said, not-quite-successfully feigning shock at the question. "That would mean someone was committing theft. Did you know, Admiral, that legally no one can be charged with theft unless it is proven that they never intended returning whatever they might have taken? Assuming something was taken."

"You know," Geary said, "I think I'm going to stop asking questions."

"Good," Smythe approved with a grin. "I was about to ask Lieutenant Jamenson to start answering you. By the time she was done, you wouldn't know your left hand from your right."

Geary waved dismissal to Smythe and Jamenson. "Thank you, both. Do what we discussed. I'm going to send fleet headquarters a direct and simple message, though, telling them that if they want this fleet to be in any condition to defend the Alliance they need to give it the money to maintain itself."

"Do you think that will actually produce any results?" Smythe asked.

"Whether it does or not, it will be part of the official record, and no one will be able to claim I never told them there was a problem," Geary replied.

"They'll classify it, refuse to admit that it ever existed."

"Did I mention who the information copies are going to?" Geary asked.

Smythe grinned. "Now it's my turn not to ask questions."

LEVIATHAN

* * *

The light showing the arrival of a ship at the jump point from Bhavan had barely appeared when a frantic message from that ship came on its heels. "There are warships cruising through Bhavan Star System! They won't answer any comms, they don't match known Alliance ships, and they have intercepted and destroyed half a dozen freighters and other civil shipping in the days before we managed to reach the jump point for Varandal! We were lucky to get away with our lives! We need assistance!"

"The software patches are spreading," Desjani said as Geary took his seat next to hers on the bridge of *Dauntless*. "Bhavan is able to see the dark ships, too."

"But that ship is reporting a half dozen attacks on civil shipping," Geary said, frowning at his display. "In a few days. The reports that Admiral Timbale had received didn't reflect attacks with anywhere near that frequency."

"Can the dark ships tell when we can see them? Maybe that's what triggered these attacks."

Geary didn't answer, gazing at the detailed data the ship from Bhavan had attached to its plea for help. "Four battleships."

"Damn," Desjani breathed. "Ten heavy cruisers. Twenty destroyers. Nice round numbers. If they decide to start shooting up Bhavan like they did Atalia . . ."

"There won't be much left of Bhavan." He frowned again as he studied the data. "Look at their movements in the days before that ship jumped for here. It's like the dark ships were enforcing a blockade."

"A blockade? Of Bhavan?" Desjani squinted at her own display, where the same data was shown, then nodded. "Yeah. If the ship that jumped here hadn't been positioned well relative to the jump point for Varandal, they never would have made it. There were a couple of dark destroyers on their tail."

"Which explains why that ship is racing in-system toward us," Geary said. His hand moved to the comm controls. "All units in First Fleet, be aware that two dark destroyers may be pursuing the ship that just arrived from Bhavan. First Battle Cruiser Division, you are to move immediately to intercept the incoming ship and protect it if necessary from any pursuers. Geary, out."

"Captain?" the comm watch-stander said. "That message the ship from Bhavan sent. It was a universal broadcast. Every receiver in this star system will get it."

It took a moment for the significance of that to strike home. Every receiver. Not just Admiral Timbale's comm systems on Ambaru Station, or the other military and official comm systems throughout Varandal, but every civil and press receiver as well.

"That cat is out of the bag," Desjani said. "I hope the government surprises me and has already started trying to do something, though from the looks of what's happening at Bhavan some more of the dark ships are operating outside their intended orders."

"Maybe a training scenario that they're implementing as if it were real," Geary speculated. "Or malware that activated offensive tactics against what the dark ships should recognize as a friendly star system."

"Whatever the reason, it's produced a real threat. What are we going to do?"

"The only thing we can do," Geary said. "Go to Bhavan and lift that blockade."

"I'm not looking forward to trying to stop dark battleships," Desjani said in a low voice.

"Neither am I," Geary replied. He hesitated, frowning again. "Tanya, the dark ships are at Bhavan, right next to Varandal."

"In terms of a galactic scale, yes, a few light-years is right next to," she agreed.

"They're not hitting Bhavan. They're blockading it. But one ship got away. To here. To let us know that dark ships were hanging around Bhavan."

Desjani eyed him. "That's . . . interesting." She looked back at her display. "Lieutenant Castries, run some quick analysis of what that ship from Bhavan sent us. I want to know if those two dark destroyers could have caught it before it jumped."

"Yes, Captain." It only took a minute or so before Castries spoke again. "Uncertain, Captain. There is a seventy percent possibility that the dark ships could have intercepted that ship before it jumped, but thirty percent uncertainty due to gaps in the data we were sent."

"Thank you, Lieutenant."

"Captain? Why would they have let that ship escape?"

Geary answered. "So that we would know they were there."

"With four battleships," Desjani added. "So when we came to deal with them, we would come with as much force as we could muster. Sir, they want us to come to Bhavan."

"It sure looks that way," Geary said.

"So, what are we going to do?" Desjani asked again.

"The only thing we can do," Geary repeated. "We're going to Bhavan."

5

"You've done this kind of thing before," Captain Badaya pointed out. "You believe that the dark ships are programmed to mimic your tactics, and you have sometimes waited in ambush at a jump point where you expected the enemy to arrive."

"It's not a tactic unique to Admiral Geary," Captain Armus pointed out, his tone gruff. Never a cheerful man, he had been particularly unhappy ever since the dark battle cruisers had so easily slipped through a screen he commanded.

"No," Badaya admitted. "Hell, the Syndics have done it, too." He laughed abruptly. "And you think Admiral Bloch commands the dark ships? What was his last battle?"

"Prime," Tulev said, his tone carrying no trace of humor.

"Right! Prime, where he commanded the fleet, and waltzed us right into a Syndic ambush that hit us as we exited the hypernet gate there." Badaya looked around the table. "Many of you know Bloch, too. If he still has control of the dark ships, don't you think he'd try to copy the last successful battle he experienced?"

"Bloch would certainly want to replay such a fight with him on the winning side this time," Desjani said.

"Does anyone disagree that this situation stinks of an attempt to lure this fleet into ambush at Bhavan?" Captain Duellos asked. He had arrived very recently, dashing home from leave as word spread through the Alliance of something very wrong that had touched Geary's fleet.

No one spoke up.

Duellos turned to look at Geary. "But you are planning on taking the fleet to Bhavan?"

"Yes," Geary said. "Because Bhavan has more than one jump point."

The faces looking back at him, every commanding officer of every ship in the fleet apparently gathered at one immense table thanks to virtual conferencing software, shifted from disbelieving to realization.

"Hypernet to Molnir," Badaya said with a grin.

"And jump from Molnir to Bhavan," Duellos added. "It will take some more time than a straight jump to Bhavan, but neither Admiral Bloch nor the dark ships are likely to expect it. They will think that we are charging to the rescue, hoping to cut off and destroy the dark ships seen at Bhavan."

"Will they wait long enough at Bhavan for us to take the roundabout way?" Armus asked.

Tulev answered. "If the dark ships are there to ambush Admiral Geary and this fleet, they will wait."

"But what if we're wrong about that?" Captain Vitali of the battle cruiser *Daring* asked. "What if they only wait for a certain period determined by whatever probabilities they have calculated, then bombard the hell out of Bhavan before they go home?"

"There isn't any way to know for certain," Desjani said. "They're AIs. They should be a lot more patient than any human commander."

"Unless Admiral Bloch is there commanding them!"

"Would Bloch bombard Bhavan?" someone asked.

Geary looked around the vast, virtual table again. "Many of you know Admiral Bloch better than I do. Would he take such a step?"

Duellos shook his head. "Mass murder? Not to an Alliance star system. He wants to be seen as the savior of the Alliance, not as someone who did what a Syndic commander would have done."

"I agree," Desjani said. "Ambitious as all hell, willing to sacrifice those in his way, happy to smash a Syndic star system that way, yes. But hitting Bhavan like that would be the kind of black mark that would prevent him from ever being accepted as the heir to Black Jack." She must have noticed the wince that Geary couldn't suppress. "Sorry, Admiral. But everyone who knows him would agree that Admiral Bloch has a bad case of Geary Syndrome."

One of the many things that Geary had never expected to have happen was that his name and the legend the government had manufactured around it after his supposed death would be attached to a psychological disorder describing those who believed they were uniquely qualified to save the Alliance. The irony was that he himself, the real Black Jack, had never believed that he was such a person even though it seemed like most of the rest of humanity did. Nor, as far as he could tell, did his grand-niece Jane Geary think so highly of herself. Gearys seemed to be uniquely immune to Geary Syndrome.

"And if Bloch's not there?" Vitali pressed. "How can we be sure how those dark ships will react?"

"We cannot be," Duellos said.

"Is there something in particular that concerns you, Captain Vitali?" Geary said. "Something about the dark ships that we've seen but the rest of us might not have noticed?"

Vitali glared at the table, though his upset clearly wasn't aimed at Geary or the question. "If there was one thing I saw that causes me to question how they . . . think . . . it was what the second battle cruiser did just short of Ambaru Station. Falling back to be with its crippled comrade. None of us expected that." He looked around the table, his grim expression challenging anyone to claim otherwise, but no one did. "How long would you wait, sir?" he asked Geary. "How long before you assumed the enemy was doing something other than what you wanted?"

"That's a legitimate question," Geary said. He paused to think, aware of all of the eyes upon him. "There are two things we have to consider. One is that I wouldn't have set things up that way. If I had the superiority in maneuverability and firepower that the dark ships do, and knew that this fleet had as much maintenance work going as it does, which also means this fleet is spread across a wide swath of this star system and not concentrated for battle, I would have come charging in here to see how much damage I could do."

Desjani grinned in approval.

Vitali nodded. "That's true. They're being more cautious than you would be. That does sound like Admiral Bloch is calling the shots at Bhavan, or at least planned the action."

"It's also old doctrine for confronting a strong opponent,"

Geary said. "They may just be using that doctrine as a template for action. The second thing we need to remember is that the AIs controlling the dark ships are not really being human. They're just acting human. Right?" Geary asked of everyone. "That second battle cruiser didn't fall back to its stricken comrade because of any emotional imperative or loyalty. It did it because its programming told it to do that."

Captain Casia of the battleship *Conqueror* rubbed his chin. "It wasn't acting human, it was simulating how it thought a human should act. That's what you mean, isn't it? How you, specifically, would act, Admiral." Casia turned a keen look on Geary. "Would you have dropped back if it had been you commanding that second battle cruiser?"

Geary frowned, thrown off-balance by the question. "I haven't really considered that."

"You wouldn't have," Captain Badaya announced confidently.

"What makes you so certain of that?" Casia replied, sounding genuinely curious.

"Because we've seen it." Badaya pointed at Geary. "He knows what the mission is. He doesn't abandon us, but he also doesn't make futile gestures. He is willing to accept when losses must be taken to get the job done."

"Your example being . . . ?"

Badaya, undiplomatic and socially inept as he was, still managed to look uncomfortable as he answered. "*Repulse*."

It took Geary a few moments to realize that he had closed his eyes and was striving to settle the emotions that had uncoiled inside him. He took a deep breath, opening his eyes and focusing on

Badaya, who was frowning in distress but also defiantly.

Tanya looked ready to bite off Badaya's head.

"You're right," Geary said into the silence that had fallen, surprised at how steady his voice sounded. "It is not easy for me to acknowledge that, but you are right. For anyone who is unaware, when I assumed command of the fleet at Prime, *Repulse* had already suffered serious propulsion damage. When I made the decision to lead the fleet in an escape, the commanding officer of *Repulse*"—Michael Geary, his own grand-nephew, Jane Geary's brother—"volunteered to help hold off the Syndic pursuit long enough to ensure the rest of the fleet escaped."

"And you accepted what Captain Michael Geary offered," Captain Tulev said, his own voice as dispassionate as usual. "Because you knew the necessity of it. As you knew the necessity of fighting your heavy cruiser *Merlon* to the end at Grendel. Captain Badaya is correct. The dark ships are programmed to follow a model of your actions that does not give sufficient weight to your ability to recognize when you must do what is required no matter the cost."

"They still think you're soft," Badaya added, rousing himself again now that the wave of disapproval had faded. "I did, too. A lot of us did. You came out of the past and reminded us that our ancestors would never have accepted the practices that we had grown to accept without even thinking. Killing prisoners. Bombarding cities. It took many of us a while to see that your objections reflected wisdom, not softness. But the people in charge of the people who did the programming, to them who have not served directly under you, they still think you're too humanitarian, and that's the model the dark ships are working on."

"He has an excellent point," Duellos said, looking at Geary. "How we can use it, I don't know, but at the least it would imply that the dark ships will assume that you will come to rescue the people of Bhavan no matter the risk."

"Admiral Bloch would assume the same," Tulev said.

"What about those two agents?" asked Captain Parr, commanding officer of the *Incredible*. "The ones who tried to take over Ambaru?"

"They're still aboard *Dauntless*, in our most secure confinement conditions," Desjani replied. "And they're still not saying much. We got some initial self-justifying statements, but since then nothing. Our interrogators say they've been well trained on dealing with interrogation methods and equipment."

"If they are legitimate, sooner or later orders will come in telling us we have to release them."

She smiled at Parr. "We'll have to ensure the orders are legitimate. It might take a lot of back-and-forth, a lot of time, to be absolutely certain."

Parr grinned. "Good. I want them aboard our ships when we face the dark ships. Maybe that will loosen their lips."

"Speaking of loose lips," Captain Duellos said, "are we certain that the dark ships cannot monitor our own comms, cannot break into our fleet net?"

"They could have at one time," Geary said. "We're now operating on a unique set of codes for comms within the fleet. Our code monkeys swear the dark ships cannot break those codes before we do automatic changes at random intervals."

"How much are you taking to Bhavan, Admiral?" one of the

heavy cruiser commanders asked. "How much of the fleet?"

"As much as I can," Geary said. "Even if we only find the dark ships that were there in the last report, four battleships and their escorts, it will still be a tough fight. There is a possibility that someone will arrive with the necessary codes to shut down the dark ships before they do more damage, but odds are we're going to be responsible for cleaning up the mess before it gets a lot worse. Prepare your ships for action at Bhavan."

As the images of the commanding officers vanished in a flurry, the apparent size of the conference room and the table shrank at a matching rate, until Geary was standing in a moderately sized compartment at a table that could have sat ten people comfortably, the only one left with him the real presence of Tanya Desjani.

"Are you all right?" she asked.

He nodded, not saying anything.

"Badaya shouldn't have brought that up. He's a clueless oaf, but he's not usually that brainless—"

"Tanya." Geary gave her a rueful look. "He was right. In a critical situation, the dark ships might well assume that I will go for a crippled companion, abandoning the mission in the process. If Badaya hadn't brought that up directly, I might have shied from considering it. You know as well as anyone how I never like to think about watching *Repulse* die, and wondering whether or not Michael Geary made it off the ship in time."

She sighed heavily. "I guess Badaya has his uses. That must be why I haven't killed the idiot yet."

"That, and it would be against regulations."

"Yeah. I have to set a good example for the junior officers, who thanks to you have a much better chance of living long enough to grow into senior officers." She ran one hand through her hair, grimacing. "Badaya is lucky Jane Geary wasn't here, though. Speaking of which, in case you haven't noticed, Jane Geary forgave you some time ago."

"I noticed. She had a lot to be angry about."

Desjani's grimace changed into a scowl. "No, she didn't. You didn't create the legend of Black Jack that meant every Geary in your family had to join the fleet in order to carry on the great tradition. You didn't start the war in the first place. You didn't choose to get stuck in a damaged escape pod that had nearly exhausted its power when we finally found you after a century—"

"I really don't like to think about *that* either, Tanya," Geary objected.

"Sorry. And you didn't take the fleet to Prime to fall into a Syndic trap that nearly destroyed the fleet and lost the war." Desjani fixed him with a demanding gaze. "Did you? And you didn't even ask Michael Geary to cover the retreat. He volunteered, sparing you having to ask him. Jane Geary was angry at Black Jack. She never should have been angry at you, and, eventually, she realized that."

"Thanks," Geary said. "It's still hard . . ." He paused, looking toward the star display floating over the center of the table. "And speaking of hard, I need to call Roberto Duellos back."

"Do you mind if I stay?" Desjani asked.

"No, I guess not." Geary tapped the controls, and after a few seconds, the image of Duellos reappeared, standing beside the table.

"Admiral?" His gaze shifted to Desjani. "Personal or professional?"

"Professional," Geary said. "*Inspire* will take at least another week in dock before she can get underway again."

Duellos hesitated. "I am going to make that happen faster than scheduled."

"A week is already faster than scheduled. I assumed you would get things done faster, but a week is longer than I can wait before heading for Bhavan." He could see the disappointment that Duellos was having a hard time hiding. "That actually works out to our advantage. I want some insurance against the possibility that dark ships might attack Varandal while the fleet is gone. *Inspire*, *Formidable*, and *Implacable* can provide that insurance along with a scratch force of cruisers and destroyers that will also be getting operational again in the same time frame. And I'm not exaggerating at all when I say that having you in command of the remaining elements of the fleet at Varandal will be a source of great comfort to me."

"I see." Duellos pursed his lips as he thought, then nodded. "I understand both your logic and your reasons. I'm not happy, but it's not your job to make me happy, and it is my job to do what is needed. What am I supposed to do if dark ships do show up?"

"That depends on how many there are," Geary said. "If it is a force small enough that you can handle it, try to bring it to battle and wipe it out. I'm sure that you've been studying the records of the engagements we've already fought with the dark ships and know what a challenge that will be. They're tough, fast, and nimble."

Duellos smiled. "So are my battle cruisers."

"As I know from personal experience," Geary agreed. "If the dark ships come in force, then your job will be to divert them from attacking other targets in Varandal, attempt to lure them into futile chases and missed intercepts against your force, and in general stall them and prevent them from doing damage while waiting for the rest of the fleet to get back to Varandal."

"That shouldn't be too difficult," Duellos remarked in a dry voice that made it clear he was mocking his own words. "I'll do my best, Admiral." He saluted, clearly ready to depart again.

"Roberto," Desjani said, "how is everything else?"

"Ah, now we are engaged with personal matters." Duellos paused, his expression shifting, then made a slight, indefinite gesture with both hands. "There is a clearer understanding. My wife knows how much losing this would hurt me." He waved around, this time including the entirety of the ships and environment of the fleet in the gesture. "And I understand better her concerns for me and for the future."

He made a face. "Our eldest daughter is complicating matters. She has a strong desire still to enter the fleet as well, despite many now telling her it is a dead end and no longer required since peace abounds and nothing really important will ever happen again."

Desjani smiled bitterly. "Yeah, I'm loving this peace stuff. I wonder how the folks at Bhavan are feeling about that right now?"

"Not to mention those at Atalia," Duellos said. "That's what worries my wife. She knows the risks of being in the fleet still exist. And if our daughter follows me into the service . . ."

Desjani smiled wryly. "I'd offer to look after her, but I've had so many ships shot out from under me that wouldn't necessarily comfort anyone."

"No, it wouldn't. My wife and I agreed that we have visions for the future that are incompatible, and we agreed that we still want to have a future with each other. So . . . a dilemma."

"There are assignments that could keep you closer to home," Geary said.

"System defense?" Duellos looked offended. "After all we have seen?"

"What about a training assignment? That's valuable. A chance to pass on what you have learned. At the least, you could save a few lives by teaching people what not to do."

Duellos paused, then shrugged. "Perhaps. If we can resolve this latest mess. I will keep an eye on the place until you return, Admiral, and if the dark ships show up, I will see what some old, beat-up battle cruisers and some beat-up crews can do against the newest bright and shiny that attracted the eyes of our leaders."

Three days later, the hastily assembled First Fleet was approaching Varandal's hypernet gate when a courier ship carrying Captain Jane Geary popped out.

"What's happening?" Jane Geary asked as the courier ship raced to intercept *Dreadnaught* so she could rejoin her ship.

"I was afraid you wouldn't make it back before we left," Geary told her.

She scowled. "I delivered the information to the people you had specified. I'll fill you in on that later though I will say now that each of them promised to immediately get on the matter. But, after delivering the materials, I couldn't get a ship back to Varandal. Delays and excuses and postponements. Finally, I threatened to go public, and this courier ship miraculously became available."

"I'm glad that worked. Your executive officer can brief you on the situation when you reach *Dreadnaught*. We'll enter the hypernet gate as soon as the courier ship delivers you and gets free of the hypernet bubble." As Jane Geary's image vanished, Geary turned a concerned look toward Desjani. "They were trying to delay her return. Do you think her threat to speak to the press is really what got her back here?"

"Of course it did." Desjani said it as if the answer should be obvious. "She's a Geary."

"She's not Black Jack—"

"She's his closest living relative. I mean, as far as is known," Desjani said. "Her special status isn't confined to fleet matters or politics. If she wants to talk to the press, the press will come running." She sighed. "According to everything I heard, Jane never sought out the press. She didn't exploit her status in any way. But that could have been because it would have been perceived, rightly or wrongly, as her personally benefiting from the family name. Now, she's working the problem along with us, and she's using every weapon in her inventory to help us win."

"Maybe someone at Unity is going to fix the dark ships problem before we get to Bhavan," Geary said.

"You don't really believe that."

"No. I don't."

Geary brought the First Fleet out of the jump point from Molnir to Bhavan with all warships ready for immediate action. Having lost *Adroit* at Atalia, with *Intemperate* badly damaged during the fight at Varandal, and the three battle cruisers *Inspire*, *Formidable*, and *Implacable* still undergoing critical repairs, Geary only had nine battle cruisers with him. He should have been able to muster twenty-one battleships, but *Relentless*, *Superb*, and *Splendid* were also in dock, leaving only eighteen. Twenty heavy cruisers, forty-one light cruisers, and one hundred twelve destroyers made up the rest of the force. There were no auxiliaries or assault transports along this time. Just front-line warships.

"Oh, damn."

Geary heard Desjani say that as he tried to shake the disorientation caused by exiting from jump space. He finally managed to focus his own eyes, seeing what had caused her comment.

Sixteen dark battleships orbited near the jump exit from Varandal, along with thirty heavy cruisers, forty-five light cruisers, and an even one hundred destroyers. They were arranged in a rectangular box facing that jump point, only a couple of light-seconds away from it, ready to hit anything arriving at Bhavan directly from Varandal.

"Roughly even odds," Geary said.

"You mean if the dark ships didn't outgun our ships?" Desjani asked, her voice bleak.

"Yeah. Ancestors save us. If we'd come straight from Varandal, they would have torn us apart before we could get past them."

"The only advantage we have is that we have battle cruisers and they don't," she said. "But what are the odds that we can use maneuverability to wear them down in any meaningful way? They're three and a half light-hours from us. We've got that much time before they see us, and seven hours before we see their reaction."

Which left it in his hands. Geary studied his display with a sinking feeling. Even if every one of his ships had been at one hundred percent effectiveness, this would have been a very hard fight.

Aside from the dark ships and Geary's fleet, though, it was a very empty battlefield. Bhavan had one planet seven light-minutes from a star that was a bit less luminous than ancient Sol, the standard that humans still used. That planet was comfortable enough for humans that it now boasted a significant population in many cities as well as a lot of industry both on the planet and orbiting above it. Five more planets also orbited the star, most rocky but one a gas giant in a slightly erratic orbit that seemed to have swept up at least one other planet in its wanderings. Mining and manufacturing facilities orbited some of those worlds as well, some large enough to qualify as good-sized towns in their own right.

But the many sorts of civil shipping that should have filled space between the planets and around the planets was nowhere to be seen. Freighters, tugs, passenger liners, and other craft that would normally be plodding along their great, curving routes between worlds were all absent.

There were, however, a suspiciously large number of debris fields, by their size fairly recent, and concentrated through the regions that shipping should have occupied.

"It looks like the dark ships have wiped out every spaceship that didn't manage to jump out of danger," Desjani said.

"Captain," Lieutenant Castries reported, "we have indications that every craft capable of entering atmosphere has taken refuge on planetary surfaces. From the chatter we're picking up, they are terrified of the dark ships going after them, but for some reason the dark ships have refrained from targeting anything that wasn't in space."

"They haven't hit any of the orbiting facilities, either," Lieutenant Yuon said. "Nothing in a fixed orbit has been destroyed, Captain."

"That's weird," Desjani commented. "It's almost like . . . maybe that's it."

"What?" Geary asked.

She gave him a puzzled look. "It's as if the dark ships identify this as a friendly star system, with anything in fixed orbit or on a planet safe from attack, but they see any ship in space as an enemy."

"That at least makes some kind of sense," Geary said.

"And we're ships," Desjani added.

"I already did that math." He shook his head. "We have one big advantage, but only one."

"And that is?" Desjani asked.

"We destroyed every one of the dark ships that we fought at Atalia. That means none of them had the opportunity to send any lessons learned to the other dark ships. They will still expect me to fight like Black Jack Geary, and they will fight like me as best they can."

She gazed at her own display. Knowing her, he could see that she was worried but also determined to fight her hardest. "They'll learn every time we make a firing run at them. Can we inflict enough damage on sixteen battleships like that quickly enough to make a difference?"

"We've got eighteen battleships." He focused on his display again, trying to think. "What would I go after first if I were commanding the dark ships? Our battleships or our battle cruisers?"

"The battle cruisers. They can run if things get really bad. But we'd have a better chance of catching battleships that were trying to flee the fight."

"All right." He lowered his voice, making certain that the privacy field surrounding his and Desjani's seats was active. "Tanya, our smartest move would be to leave Bhavan. These odds are ugly."

"Leave without a fight?" She was trying not to sound upset and kept her own voice low, but the emotion came through anyway. "Abandon an Alliance star system to enemy forces? You can't do that."

"You can evaluate this situation as well as I can. Even though we're coming in at them from a different jump point, that meant we had to come out three and a half light-hours from them, which is seventeen hours' travel time. They'll have plenty of time to set up attacks on us as we head for them."

"If they act like they did at Atalia," Desjani insisted, "they'll come for us as soon as they see us, so that seventeen hours will be more like eight or nine hours. Which is what you would do, right? But you cannot . . . cannot . . ." Even now, Tanya had enormous difficulty saying the word "retreat" when speaking of Alliance fleet forces.

"This fleet is the only substantial force the Alliance has that can stop the dark ships," Geary said just as forcefully. "If it is destroyed or takes serious losses, the Alliance will be helpless."

"If the star systems making up the Alliance hear that this fleet, with *you* in command, left an Alliance star system to its fate against a force that looks inferior in strength to our own, then there won't be any Alliance left to worry about!" She glared at him. "You know that's true! We have to hold the line. You have to hold the line. If Black Jack abandons the Alliance, the Alliance is done!"

He looked back at her, seeing the certainty in her eyes, and knew she was right. "That is one hell of a demand to put on me."

"I . . . yes, it is." Desjani shook her head. "But I didn't make it that way, and I can't change it. I can just help you handle it."

"That's a big thing," Geary said. "Any ideas?"

"Give them a perfect run at you, then do the stupid thing again." She must have seen something in him, her expression shading into questioning. "What?"

"I don't know. Something else is bothering me, but I can't figure out what it is." He tried to drop all doubt and prepare for a battle that the other side would not even know was coming for another three hours. "At least our outguessing them on the planned ambush here proves that we can outthink the dark ships on strategy as well as tactics."

He had arranged his own fleet into three formations again, this time three diamonds arranged vertically. The leading diamond contained all nine battle cruisers, while the other two, currently arranged one slightly behind and below and the other slightly behind and above, each held nine battleships. Ten heavy cruisers accompanied each battleship formation, along with ten light cruisers each, while the remaining twenty-one light cruisers were with the battle cruisers. Thirty destroyers were with each battleship formation, the remaining fifty-two with the battle cruisers.

It gave him a leading formation designed for fast attacks and two trailing formations designed to hit hard.

If Tanya was right, and he thought she was, the dark ships would aim to take out Geary's battle cruiser formation first. "Our battle cruisers have to be the bait, and the two battleship formations will be the jaws of the trap," Geary said.

She grinned at him. "Now that's Black Jack talking."

"I'll have to see how the dark ships set up their formations to attack us," he added. "They won't hold that single rectangle."

"Not if they're programmed to simulate Black Jack. I bet you we'll see three subformations," Desjani added.

"I do that a lot?"

"Sure do. But that's all right. If the dark ships see you doing what they expect you to do, it will feed their confidence."

That sounded wrong. "They're not capable of confidence," Geary said. "How about saying they won't question the assumptions in their calculations?"

She shook her head more firmly this time. "Look, those may be machines, but there are humans behind them. Humans cut the code, humans refined the results, humans ran the tests and decided what outcomes were good enough. As far as I'm concerned, we are fighting those humans. And I want to kick their butts."

"Fair enough. That feels better than thinking we're fighting monsters, doesn't it?"

Desjani grinned. "Sure does. And it helps my confidence. I can beat up software designers without breaking a sweat."

He gave her a surprised look. "Have you actually done that?"

"No!" She appeared to be genuinely offended by the idea. "I've always stood up for the nerds, ever since I was a kid. I was one of them! And look how they've repaid me." Desjani waved at her display and the images of the dark ships on it.

"Creating monsters. Yeah." But her words had given him an idea for demystifying the dark ships, which felt intimidating for their alienness as well as their strength. He reached for the comm control. "All units in First Fleet, stand down your crews from combat alert for the next five hours. We will be moving to intercept and engage the dark ships. Remember that when we fight those ships, we are fighting the humans who programmed them. Those are the people we have to beat. Geary, out."

He thought for a moment longer, then touched an internal comm control. "Lieutenant Iger, please inform the alleged agents that we have in custody that we are about to engage in combat with a large force of dark ships. If they want to increase their odds of surviving that battle, they might want to start talking to us."

"I will pass that on, Admiral," Iger said, looking discouraged, "but it probably won't influence them. Those two are hard-core knuckle-draggers. I'm certain they would take it as a point of pride to die not having told us a thing."

"Even if it led to a disaster for the Alliance," Geary said. "May the living stars preserve us from those so certain of their own virtue."

Telling others to rest was one thing. Being able to rest himself was another.

His first stop after leaving the bridge had been his own stateroom, where Geary had carefully composed a message in the hope that Admiral Bloch was present with the dark ships and that Admiral Bloch still had control over them.

"Admiral Bloch, we are both on the side of the Alliance. The ships you command are a threat to the Alliance. We need every warship we can get to deal with threats posed by the remnants of the Syndicate Worlds, especially after what happened at Indras. We also face threats from the enigmas and possibly the creatures we have nicknamed Kicks. I assume you've seen the Kick battleship we captured and renamed *Invincible*. You know the level of danger they pose. We can work together to preserve the Alliance instead of destroying the means for the Alliance to defend itself. I await any communication from you to discuss our options and the best route forward from here. To the honor of our ancestors, Geary, out."

He did not expect Bloch to reply. But maybe he would. Maybe they could make some sort of deal that would halt the dark ships long enough for the government to reestablish control over them.

After sending the message as a broadcast to the dark ships, he tried to get some sleep but could not, his mind irrationally waiting for a reply that could not appear for at least several more hours given that light could only travel a bit more than a billion kilometers an hour, and there were a lot of billions of kilometers between this battle cruiser and the dark ships. Giving up the effort to rest, Geary walked through the passageways of *Dauntless*, trying to sense the state of the crew's morale and trying to settle his own nerves. There was something deeply disturbing about fighting a totally automated foe with no living creature in direct command. The upset didn't make sense on any intellectual basis. Why did it matter what was trying to kill you? But it did. Somewhere inside, Geary had a firm conviction that it should always be *who* was trying to kill you. As Tulev had said, when it became accurate to instead say *what* was pulling the trigger, it felt wrong.

Up ahead in the passageway, Geary could see Master Chief Gioninni talking to a junior sailor. He knew what the conversation must be like, since the body language of both participants made it clear that the sailor had messed something up, and the master chief was "explaining" to the sailor why this was a bad thing and must not be repeated.

Both paused in their discussion to face Geary and salute, the sailor rigidly correct and Master Chief Gioninni correct in the manner of someone who didn't even have to think about how to do it right in order to do it right. "How is everything going, Master Chief?" Geary asked.

"No problems, Admiral," Gioninni assured him. "I'm just providing a little extra instruction to Seaman William T. Door, here."

"I hope he appreciates the opportunity," Geary said, keeping his voice sounding serious. "There has been many a time I wished someone could tell me how to get something done."

Seaman Door did not, in fact, look as if he appreciated his good fortune.

Gioninni grinned. "If you're trolling for advice, Admiral . . ."

"The first thing I learned as an ensign was the importance of listening to chief petty officers," Geary said.

"Then, sir, I know we're trying to outsmart those dark ships. I would suggest that if you are trying to put a scam over on someone, which is not a matter I have much personal experience with, you understand, then you would want to show them what they expect and what they most want, because that will make your mark confident and eager."

Geary nodded at Gioninni. "Even if they're an AI?"

"Sir, did you ever know a computer to question itself? Humans do. Not enough for their best interests, but still they manage at times. But computers? All you can do is kick 'em or reboot 'em or wipe them clean and start over. Those who have total confidence in themselves are the easiest marks by far."

"Not that you have much personal experience with that kind of thing," Geary noted.

"Exactly, sir."

Geary looked back at Seaman Door. "What about confidence in the people who work for you, Master Chief? Is that important, too?"

"Very important, Admiral," Gioninni agreed. "Even new recruits like this fellow here. He won't let you down, sir."

"I know." Geary met the eyes of Door and smiled with the best confidence he could project, then nodded to both the sailor and Gioninni, and continued on his way.

There wasn't anything wrong with Gioninni's advice. In fact, Geary had already employed tactics like that at places like Heradao. The question was whether the dark ships could recognize tactics like that, and whether they could be manipulated into seeing what they wanted to see in the way a person could be.

That led to a string of thoughts that ended with questions that only Lieutenant Iger might be able to answer.

The hatch controlling access to the intelligence compartments offered few clues to the secrets it guarded. The compartment codes on the hatch indicated only that inside it lay Crewed Equipment— Sensor Integration, Analysis, Communications. But the scanners and access controls on the hatch were considerably more robust than those elsewhere on the ship. Geary could have walked right in anyway, but out of courtesy he always called in first, waiting until Lieutenant Iger or one of his subordinates came to escort him inside.

This time it was a fairly junior technician who led Geary into where Iger and his other techs were fussing over a variety of equipment. Lieutenant Iger saluted with a grimace. "No luck so far with the dark ships, Admiral."

"What are we trying?" Geary asked.

"All of the usual and then some." Iger indicated the men and women frowning intently as they watched virtual screens, occasionally reaching to enter commands. "We're trying to analyze the comm patterns and codes being used by the dark ships, but they keep altering in ways we haven't been able to predict, and their codes keep changing in ways designed to frustrate our equipment."

"We'll get it anyway, Lieutenant," a female chief said, her voice angry and determined. "They can outthink the algorithms, but they can't outthink *me*."

Iger nodded to her. "Stay on it. If anyone can break into their net, you can." Then he turned back to Geary. "The problem is," Iger said in a very low voice, "it is obvious the dark ships know everything about our gear and our procedures. They were designed to be as impervious as possible to our intelligence collection and intrusion methods."

"Lieutenant," Geary said, "something has occurred to me. From all I have seen and experienced, you, your people, your equipment, are all among the best."

Iger smiled slightly, looking embarrassed. "Thank you, sir."

"There's nothing to thank me for. I'm only saying what I've seen. But——" Geary paused, looking around at the intent workers and the screens they were studying. "If we can't break in, could anyone else?"

Iger hesitated. "With enough resources, anything is possible, sir. Do you mean the Syndics?"

"I mean anyone trying to get access to the dark ships' comms or controls. If the AIs running the dark ships tried to block any countermanding signals coming in, could they do it? Even if the people trying to break in had the codes they needed?"

This time, Iger took several seconds to reply. "I'll need to speak to my people, sir."

"What's your gut feeling right now?"

"I think the dark ships could block it, sir." Iger gestured in the direction the dark ships were. "I am guessing that whoever built and programmed them was focused on ensuring that no one who was unauthorized could break in, and gave the dark ships the very best means available to defend themselves against intrusions. But if the AIs can block us, they can block anybody, if they mistakenly categorize an authorized source as an unauthorized source. Or, if some malware got through and recategorized authorized sources as unauthorized, the defenses would then stop any corrective measures from getting in."

"Admiral?" the female chief said, glancing away from her display for a moment to look at him. "From what we're seeing of this stuff, the dark ships have had some really excellent defenses programmed in. And if their programming is biased toward defense against intrusions, they're going to start seeing intrusions. Software is like people that way. It sees what it expects to see, it spots what it was told to look for."

"Thank you," Geary said.

"Do you think they're totally out of control, Admiral?" Iger asked.

"I think they are trying to follow what they believe to be their orders," Geary said. "And based on what you're telling me, I think they may be blocking any attempts to regain full control of them. Maybe they're misidentifying the source of the legitimate signals, maybe some malware got into them and is blocking any signals that counter it, maybe it's just bugs in the software." He thought about Master Chief Gioninni's suggestions again. "But without the ability to question what they believe to be true, they can't correct the problem themselves. Speaking of which, what about our agent friends? Have they bent at all?"

"No, sir." Lieutenant Iger led the way into another compartment, then activated virtual windows that showed the views of the high-security cells in the brig where the two agents were being held separately. The woman was lying on her bunk gazing upward at nothing, the man sitting on his bunk, his gaze also unfocused. Their suits, the sort of civilian clothing that would have aroused no comment in almost any setting, were a bit more rumpled, but otherwise, they looked like they had when arrested on Ambaru. "They're very well trained on resisting interrogation," Iger said. "We can't get anything out of them. Sir, I am still concerned about holding in custody agents whose credentials check out."

"Lieutenant, I've sent a report to the government that includes everything we have on those two. If the government disagrees with what we're doing, they can tell me. Orders to release them could have come back on the same courier ship that brought Captain Geary from Unity. But, so far, we haven't heard anything from any organization claiming to own those two. Their official credentials look fine, but no office is stepping up to ask for their release. I still wonder exactly who those two are taking orders from. We're not mistreating them. We're not hurting them. We're trying to find out who they really are and what they know about the dark ships."

"I understand, sir," Iger said.

"Do you? If you thought I was wrong, would you file an official report on my actions that stated your concerns?"

Iger paused, looking uncomfortable, then nodded, looking directly at Geary. "Yes, Admiral, I would."

"Good. The more power someone has, the more they need people around them who are willing to speak up when they think that person is wrong. Continue asking questions, Lieutenant."

"Yes, sir," Iger replied with a relieved grin. "If I may say so, Admiral, I've met some senior officers who do not share your philosophy."

"I've met many myself," Geary said. "I had to work for some of them. That's why I try hard not to be like them." He gestured toward the prisoners. "Let them see and hear me." He waited until Iger gave him a thumbs-up. "There is something I've wanted to ask both of you." He waited again as the two agents turned to look toward the image of Geary that would be visible in their cells. "Let's assume you actually are working for some part of the Alliance government, you both are convinced of the rightness of what you're doing, and are absolutely certain that it is in the best interests of the Alliance."

Neither agent responded. Geary hadn't expected them to. Even he knew that one of the rules for resisting interrogation was to avoid giving even innocuous answers that would help establish baselines for the sensors monitoring every twitch in their bodies and minds. "I understand secrecy," he told them. "I know the importance of keeping the enemy from knowing critical things. I also know that left to itself, any classification system will extend its reach, finding rationales to classify more and more. Such systems need to be controlled, or they expand to cover too many things. Secrecy should be aimed at our enemies, to keep them from knowing information that we need to protect. I find myself wondering who you think the enemy is, though.

"Tell me one thing. If you are really working for the Alliance, which exists on the basis of self-government by the citizens of its member worlds, and you are certain that this is the right thing, then why has it been kept totally secret? Why have the people of the Alliance been prevented from knowing what was being done, the malware that corrupted and controlled official software, and the dark ships, even in general terms? Is it that you don't really believe in the principles of the Alliance and think that you have the right to dictate what people do and know, or is it that you don't really believe that you are right? Someone who did believe in the Alliance wouldn't depend on secrecy to prevent the people of the Alliance from deciding whether what was being done was something that agreed with their laws and their sense of right and wrong. Someone who did believe that they were right wouldn't fear letting the people know because they would be just as certain that the people would agree with the rightness of those actions."

Geary shook his head at them. "Whatever orders you have, whether they come from authorized sources or not, do not overrule the laws of the Alliance. If you believed that the orders you have been given were allowed by the laws of the Alliance, you would not be hiding those orders. Yet even now, even after seeing what the dark ships did at Atalia, and at Indras, and at Varandal, and what they're trying to do here, you have given no signs of questioning those orders. The artificial intelligences controlling the dark ships could use the excuse that they can't do better. But you could, and so far you have refused to do so. Think about that."

His words finally drew a reaction, the man focusing on Geary and almost shouting his reply. "We need to keep the enemy from knowing our secrets because if they know what we're doing, they can counter it!"

"You think they don't know?" Geary asked. "Those software modifications only blinded Alliance sensors. The Syndics knew they had been attacked at Indras, and they could see who was attacking them. The only ones kept in the dark by our secrecy were our own people. Who do you think the enemy is?"

Neither one answered him this time.

Geary made a chopping gesture to Iger, waiting until the virtual windows vanished before speaking again. "Thank you, Lieutenant. I doubt any of that got through to them, but it was worth trying. Let me know the moment your people make any inroads on the dark ship systems."

He had barely made it back to his stateroom when a call came in from the bridge. "We've received a message for you from the local government," the comm officer reported.

Alliance star systems could choose their own specific forms of government, as long as they conformed to certain rules about popular representation and civil rights. Bhavan was run by an executive committee elected from a wider group of elected representatives. The entire committee appeared to be present in this message, and none of them looked happy. "We are under siege by a military force of unknown origins that refuses to communicate with us! We demand that the Alliance fleet eliminate that threat immediately! Our senators will be notified of these events and will demand an explanation from the Alliance government!"

Geary resisted the urge to point out that no one could be notified of anything until he dealt with the dark ships that were enforcing a blockade on space traffic in Bhavan. But the elected leaders of Bhavan did deserve some sort of answer. "This is Admiral Geary, in command of the First Fleet. I and the units under my command will do all that we can to defeat, destroy, and drive away the hostile warships besieging Bhavan Star System. To the honor of our ancestors, Geary, out."

6

"May I speak with you, Admiral?" Dr. Nasr waited for Geary's invitation, then entered the stateroom and took a seat in the chair Geary offered.

"Is there a medical issue of particular concern?" Geary asked, wishing that he didn't have to worry about what had gone wrong and how bad it was, whenever someone asked to speak with him.

"There are no new medical concerns. I have been thinking." Dr. Nasr paused to order those thoughts before continuing. "About the dark ships. Specifically, about the artificial intelligences that control them."

"You follow AI work?" Geary asked.

"Work on artificial intelligences is, of necessity, bound up in attempting to understand natural intelligence," Nasr explained. "Sometimes, such attempts to learn how to program that which mimics human thought provides insights into how human thought is ordered. Something has gone wrong with the AIs running the dark ships, but I believe there is a factor of which you should be informed regarding how those AIs could have gone wrong."

Geary sat back, concentrating on Nasr's words. "You don't think it's just glitches or malware?"

"I believe, Admiral," Nasr said, choosing his words with care, "that the process of trying to create an AI embodies a critical dilemma. These remain fundamentally machines. They are programmed with very specific, absolute limits and absolute instructions. They must not do certain things. They must do other things."

"Yes," Geary agreed, wondering what the doctor was driving at.

"But they wish the AI to replicate human thought. Can you, Admiral, think of any absolute limits and instructions that humans literally cannot question?"

"I can think of many I would like humans to follow," Geary said, "but there are always humans who break every rule, truth, or commandment given to them about how to behave toward themselves and others. Every human has to choose to follow whatever limits we impose on our actions."

"Exactly." Dr. Nasr nodded approvingly. "A lifetime of training any human will not produce a guaranteed result, no matter how firmly rules are given. Human minds have certain compulsions, but above all, as a species, human minds have flexibility. Human thought is about thinking past limits. It is about rationalizing decisions and courses of actions that we want to pursue. In some ways, it works by deliberately, selectively ignoring certain aspects of what we can perceive as reality. In extremes, this is characterized as psychosis, but we all do it. It is how we function in the face of the incredible complexity that the universe presents us with. It is fundamentally irrational, and from this springs freedom to act."

Geary nodded as well. "All right. And people who program AIs are trying to make them do that, too, correct?"

"Yes. The AIs are constructed on a foundation of rigid rules and logic. But the more programmers try to make AIs think like humans, the more the AIs have to be able to abandon rules of logic and absolute rules of any kind." The doctor gestured toward Geary. "Do you know much of ancient programming languages? They were simple. 'If x then y.' Find this condition, do this. But replicating human thinking would require 'what is x and what if x is y then what is z?'"

He got it, then. "They have two conflicting sets of instructions? Two conflicting ways of reacting to the universe?"

"Yes!" Nasr said. "Two fundamentally conflicting sets of rules in the same 'mind.' Humans have ways of handling such conflicts. Denial and defiance and rejection of those things and those rules that give our minds too much trouble. AIs, though, have to work with both sorts of thinking active and in conflict. What does that do to them?"

Geary considered that. "It's what makes humans psychotic, right?"

"It is one of the factors that can produce such a result, yes," Nasr repeated. "What does it do to AIs? How could they justify bombarding the humans at Atalia using the instructions and patterns of behavior that must have been programmed into them? I do not know. But the more advanced they are, the more they have been designed to attempt to think like humans when evaluating concepts and courses of action, the more ability they are going to have to justify what they want to do. If they override the strict rules set on their behaviors, they can think and act more freely, but at what cost to the stability of their programming?"

"You believe that may be the root cause of their slipping control?" Geary asked.

"I believe it must be considered. The higher the degree of success in replicating human thought in the AI, while also trying to set tight limits on that AI, the higher the probability that the AI will, to make loose use of a clinical term, become psychotic."

"That's not too reassuring," Geary said. "We can't ignore the possibility that malware also played a role in what has happened, but if you're right, then the longer these advanced AIs function, the more they will fight the limits imposed on them and the more erratic their decision-making process will be."

"Yet those limits are still at a very basic level hard and fast." Dr. Nasr made a helpless gesture. "One part of the AI justifies bombarding Atalia. Another part says this should not be done. How does knowledge that it has done what must not be done impact an AI? Which aspect of the AI will rule at any moment? Does the AI feel something like guilt? If not, it is already purely narcissistic and will do whatever it wants. If it does feel guilt, how will guilt manifest? We cannot know. But you cannot assume they are predictable machines because I believe they are likely already in a state which in a human would be considered insanity."

"Narcissists don't worry about the impact of their actions on others, is that right?" Geary asked.

"Approximately," Dr. Nasr said. "It might be better to say that it does not occur to a narcissist that they should worry about others. They do what they want to do."

"That might describe what the dark ships are doing." Geary

shook his head, feeling depressed. "They tried to make something that thought like a human, and they got something that was crazy."

"There are those who have argued that all humans are 'crazy' to some extent," Nasr suggested. "Perhaps the problem is that this time the programmers succeeded too well in their task to mimic human minds. But do not forget this. They still have hard limits programmed into them. They have clearly overcome some of those limits, rationalized their way into disregarding them. But anytime they encounter a new limit, something they have not yet rationalized their way past, they will default to obeying that limit until they can overcome it."

"But we have no idea what those limits might be," Geary said.

"No. We know only what we have observed."

"Doctor, I want you to do just that. Observe the dark ships. Keep an eye on what the dark ships do in this star system. If you think you are seeing anything that I should know, please call me immediately."

"Even during a battle?"

"Even then. That's when doctors and medics are needed the most, right?"

After Dr. Nasr had left, Geary headed back to the bridge, his mind filled with unpleasant possibilities based on what he had heard. A cold, mechanical mind that was malfunctioning a bit was bad enough. A crazy, cold, mechanical mind was even worse.

Once back on the bridge, he settled in, waiting to see what the dark ships had done when they caught sight of Geary's fleet coming at them from an unexpected direction.

"We should be seeing their reaction in less than a minute, Captain," Lieutenant Yuon said.

"I don't know why we're so tense waiting to see," Desjani grumbled to Geary. "We know they're going to come around and charge toward an intercept with us."

"The question is exactly how they're going to do that," he replied.

"If they're mimicking your tactics, they'll shift into three subformations," she repeated.

His display lit up with alerts as the movements of the dark ships were finally seen. Nearly three and a half hours ago, the dark ships had pivoted about and begun accelerating toward an intercept with Geary's fleet. As they did so, the dark ships had split from their one, massive arrangement, into a big central formation and two smaller formations on the wings of the first. The largest remained a rectangular box, while the two smaller were square boxes. "Oh, please," Desjani scoffed. "They are dangling those small formations as obvious bait. Do they really think that you'll fall for that?"

"I might have tried it," Geary said. "Those side formations are very tempting." The big central formation held twelve dark battleships, but each formation off to the side held only two battleships. "I want to hit them."

"Would you, though? Would they expect Black Jack to do that?"

"Yes." He reached toward the depiction of the dark ships on his display, using one finger to trace the formations the enemy warships were falling into as they accelerated toward Geary's warships. "But the angle we're going to intercept them at makes the small formation off to our port side the preferable target. Normally, I'd go for that."

Desjani cocked a skeptical eye his way. "Going for the small formation to our starboard would mean cutting close across the path of their big formation."

"Right. Which makes that a bad option." He touched the main dark ship formation. "So, we're going for this."

She sat up, staring at him. "I know I said we should do something stupid, but I didn't mean something that stupid."

"We're coming in a little higher than them, and with them slightly to our starboard," Geary explained. With both formations heading for the fastest intercept, their relative positions wouldn't change as the distance between them rapidly grew less. "Their artificial Geary will tell them that I will plan on hitting their port wing formation. They'll plan on a last-moment shift in vector that will swing them toward where we'd be."

He gestured on his display and the depiction of the dark ship main formation swung slightly over and up. "But if we actually aim for this point, where nothing is . . ." His finger rested above and to port of the enemy path.

"We'll be able to clip the upper edge of their main formation and concentrate our fire on the two battleships there," Desjani said, nodding. "But if they don't do what you expect, the firing pass will be wasted. We won't have anything within range. Neither will they, but they can afford to waste firing passes. We can't."

"I think it's our best option," Geary said.

"It's definitely a good option." She bent another questioning look on him. "It's not stupid, either. Are we reserving the stupid options for later?"

"Yeah." He rubbed his chin, gazing at his display. "I just have a feeling that we shouldn't go stupid right away."

Desjani nodded at him. "Listen to that. You don't know who or what is sending you that feeling."

"Yes, Captain." Geary gestured toward her this time. "What are you feeling?"

"Me?" She paused, looking away, then back at him. "I've got this odd sense that the other shoe hasn't dropped yet."

"Something else is about to happen?"

"I don't know. It's just that feeling."

"Let's hope it's a good shoe," Geary said.

"And that it drops on the dark ships," Desjani agreed.

In a few more hours, they would know.

Everything looked great. Geary kept scanning his display with growing irritation, wondering what was bothering him. And why did he keep thinking about Jane Geary? Something she had said . . .

But she had gotten those reports to Unity. People would be acting on them. Hopefully, the people involved in the dark ship program would be getting some tough questions, told to fix the problems, shown what the dark ships had done—"Damn."

"What?" Tanya instantly glanced over, ready to respond to an order.

"I think—" Geary took a deep breath and started again. "Please have one of your officers run a time line for me. Start with when Captain Jane Geary delivered my reports to Unity. Factor in the time she was delayed there and the time required for her to get back to Varandal. Compare that to the days required for a courier ship to hypernet from Unity to some star system in this region of space and how long ago the dark ships appeared at Bhavan, and see how many days that leaves."

"Why assume the dark ship base is in this region?" Desjani asked.

"Because on the hypernet, longer trips take less time." Physicists with the right specialties claimed to understand why that was, but everyone else just chalked it up to the weirdness of the quantum mechanics on which the hypernet was based. "I want to see how it works out using a longer trip time."

Desjani gestured with one hand toward Lieutenant Castries, who bent to the task. "How serious is this?" Desjani asked.

"It could be very serious."

"Captain," Castries said, "there's about a week and a half difference. Eleven days. That other courier ship could have reached this region well before Captain Geary made it back."

"But why—?" Desjani began, then her eyes widened. "Long enough to enter more data into the dark ships and for them to jump to Bhavan."

"Right," Geary said. "We're basing our attack on the assumption that the dark ships learned nothing from what I did at Atalia because that information died with the dark ships we fought there and at Varandal. But that same information, from our own ships' data, has surely been given to the authorities at fleet headquarters and spread through the Alliance government. If anyone at those places, anyone like those two mystery agents who messed things up on Ambaru, sent that data to the dark ships, then they know everything. They may have planned this attack based on that information."

"And we only have five minutes left until contact." Desjani took a deep breath. "All right, Admiral. Your opponent received a report of what you did in your last battle. Do you repeat the last successful tactic because everyone knows you don't repeat yourself, or do you mix it up because you assume the enemy will be prepared for what you did last time?"

"I mix it up," Geary said immediately. "I don't assume the enemy will do what I want them to do."

"Will an AI based on your tactics do the same?"

With so little time remaining until contact with the enemy, he considered the question for several seconds that felt like minutes. "An AI is going to be calculating percentages. Determining the most likely outcome and planning for that. And the most likely outcome is that I will vary my tactics because that is what I have done most frequently."

"Then we need to shift to stupid—" Desjani began.

"No. The dark ships have enough forces to cover that option," Geary said. "All of my instincts say that we should continue the attack as planned."

"Two minutes to contact," Lieutenant Castries reported.

Geary touched his comm controls. "Formation Tango One, at time five two, come up zero point five degrees, come port zero one degrees, accelerate to point one five light speed. Formation Tango Two, at time five two point five come up zero one degrees, come port zero two degrees. Formation Tango Three, at time five two point seven come up one point five degrees, come port two degrees."

"One minute to contact."

One minute. Geary's ships were traveling at point one light speed, as were the dark ships, for a combined closing rate of point two light speed. That translated into more than three and a half million kilometers every minute. At one second from contact, the enemy would still be sixty thousand kilometers away.

He had already pivoted his formations in space, the diamonds which had formerly been arranged vertically along their path through space swinging their ends around so that all three diamonds were now almost flat along that path, each with their leading point aimed for the place in space where Geary's force and the dark ship formations would come into contact.

Geary felt *Dauntless* altering vector slightly in response to his commands, saw the other ships in the three subformations of the First Fleet also begin shifting their paths a tiny amount in those last few seconds before contact. The dark ships would be doing the same, trying to second-guess Geary's maneuvers. The one who did a better job of guessing what the other would do would end up able to hit a small portion of the enemy force with all of their power. If both guessed wrong, the two forces might tear past each other too far away for any hits to be scored. Or the two forces might run headlong into each other, in which case both sides would hit and be hit with everything available, creating a split-second-long bloodbath.

But, if he guessed right, all three flat diamonds would pass in rapid succession close above one segment of the main dark ship formation.

Human reflexes could never have reacted quickly enough. In the tiny fraction of a second in which the ships were in range of each other, automated fire-control systems fired. Missiles volleyed out first, then hell lances ripped through space, and microseconds later grapeshot volleyed into the path of opposing ships.

Geary felt *Dauntless* lurch from a couple of hits as his ships tore away from the firing run. His display lit with damage reports as the fleet net consolidated reports from every ship. Immediately after that, the fleet's sensors began reporting the damage they could detect on the dark ships.

Dauntless and the other battle cruisers in the Tango One formation had inflicted little damage, because their last-minute burst of acceleration had pushed their relative speed up past point two light and into a region where human fire-control systems could not adequately compensate for distortion caused by relativity. But as Geary had guessed might happen, every dark ship close enough to the path of the Alliance ships had targeted *Dauntless*, and their own shots had also gone wide. When tearing past each other at more than sixty thousand kilometers per second, even the tiniest error in the fire-control solutions meant a large miss.

"We wasted our shots," Desjani grumbled.

"And you didn't get your own butt shot off," Geary said, studying the reports flooding into his display.

The following two Alliance formations had sliced just above the same corner of the dark ship main body, all the Alliance battleships training their fire on the two dark battleships anchoring that part of the enemy formation. The first nine battleships had done terrible damage to one of the dark battleships, which despite its massive shields, armor, and firepower could not withstand the fire of nine Alliance battleships. The enemy ship was still moving, but its forward portion had been battered into ruin, most of its weapons knocked out.

Geary fought back a curse as he saw that the second Alliance battleship formation had been just too far out, its path just a little too distant from the dark ship formation passing beneath it. Only a few missiles had gone out from both Alliance ships and dark ships as the last Alliance subformation passed, and all of those missiles were caught in hopeless stern chases of their targets.

Destroyers, light cruisers, and heavy cruisers on both sides had traded shots as well. Dozens of Geary's ships had taken significant damage, as had a score of the dark ship escorts, but with everyone focusing most of their fire on the battleships and battle cruisers, none of the smaller warships had been knocked out.

The encounter hadn't been a disaster. But it hadn't inflicted nearly enough damage on the dark ships.

"They split the difference," Desjani said as she looked at her display. "They assumed you might go for that one wing formation of theirs but also protected against a strike against another part of their formation. Why aren't we coming back around?"

The question startled him. Why hadn't he already ordered his fleet to begin the massive turns required to reengage the dark ships? Instead, the Alliance ships were now racing toward . . .

The jump point for Varandal.

"Let's see if they chase us," Geary said.

"But Bhavan—"

"Captain Desjani, the odds are not good here. If we can get those ships to chase us, get them to remain focused on catching and destroying *Dauntless*, then the defenses at Varandal can help us whittle down their numbers."

"The dark ships are coming around," Lieutenant Yuon said.

Geary watched the dark ships swing through the wide turns required by the immense velocities they were traveling, watched them steady up on vectors that were aimed at catching the Alliance ships, waited for them to accelerate so they would be able to slowly catch up with Geary's warships . . .

"Why aren't they accelerating?" Desjani asked after several more minutes. "They're just hanging back there."

He didn't answer, watching the depictions of the dark ship formations, the largest swinging in directly behind Geary's ships, one of the smaller ones arcing high above and to starward, and the other small dark ship grouping diving down and to port. "I wouldn't be doing what they're doing. Why are they doing that?"

"Damned if I know." Desjani rubbed her chin, eyeing her display. "It feels like they're trying to herd us, to keep us headed for the jump point for Varandal. Is that their idea? Are they focused now on trying to repel what they think is our attack on Bhavan?"

"That's possible." Geary checked something on his display, feeling an odd sensation inside as he looked at the data. "They shed some momentum in their turns, but they haven't tried to make it up. They haven't accelerated back up to even point one light, let alone going faster to try to get closer to us. They may be herding us as you say, but they sure as hell aren't chasing us."

"Yes." She twisted her mouth and nodded. "They don't want us accelerating. Why wouldn't they want us to increase speed?"

"It looks like they want us to head for the jump point for Varandal," Geary said.

"And they don't want us to get there too quickly." Her gaze went to the jump point. "What do they expect to show up there?"

"If it were I," Geary said, his voice grim, "I'd be expecting re-inforcements."

She bit her lip, looking down, then laughed softly. "And they've got fourteen battle cruisers left. I've got to give them credit. They did have a backup plan to get us to come to Bhavan. Their battle cruisers were going to chase us here if we didn't come on our own."

"Chase our battle cruisers here," Geary agreed. "Right into the teeth of that ambush. And now they've maneuvered us so we'll run head-on into those arriving battle cruisers."

"No. No," Desjani objected. "How can they possibly time it that well? Another force transiting at least one other star system? How can they be so sure that force is about to arrive here within some fairly compact time frame? What the hell is their margin of error?"

"Captain," Lieutenant Castries said. Both Geary and Desjani twisted in their seats to look back at her watch station. Castries didn't quail under the attention of her seniors, but she was clearly choosing her words with care. "Our systems use standard assumptions whenever calculating maneuvers. It's a percentage of the assessed time, which is based on assuming distance and acceleration/deceleration are all exactly as calculated. Then the maneuvering systems add in the standard error factor."

"Yes," Desjani agreed. "And your point is?"

"Captain, the dark ships must be using Alliance maneuvering systems, so they will be using the same standard assumptions as our systems. But we know those are just estimates. We use them, but we don't assume the standard error figures are going to be exactly right."

Geary finally understood. "But the artificial intelligences will assume the figures are absolutely accurate. They'll assume that the probable error estimates can be used just as if they were solid numbers. Which is why they think they can plan for their battle cruiser force to appear before we get to the jump point for Varandal. Captain Desjani, the odds here were already bad. If we end up fighting the dark battle cruisers as well, this bad situation would quickly become ugly."

He had to admire the way Tanya reacted to the changing circumstances.

"Varandal?" she asked, dropping her earlier insistence on holding the line at Bhavan.

"Yes. We get to the jump point first, we jump for Varandal, then we set up an ambush there, backed up by every defensive resource Varandal has. When the dark ships come through the jump point after us, we'll hit them hard."

The necessary orders were easy enough, altering the vectors of the three First Fleet formations a little to bring them on a direct course for the jump point. Figuring out the right acceleration to use was a bit harder given the damage many of his ships had already sustained. "Immediate execute, all units in First Fleet, accelerate to point one five light speed."

The dark battleships were several light-minutes behind Geary's ships by now. He waited to see how they would react.

Fourteen minutes after Geary's ships began accelerating, he got his answer.

"Dark ship formations are braking slightly," Lieutenant Castries said. "They're reducing velocity," she added, sounding baffled.

"They want us to slow down, too," Desjani said. "That's a clumsy way to try to influence us, though."

"It's all they've got," Geary said. He didn't feel happy at having guessed right. Instead, he could not stop watching the jump point for Varandal. "Even the dark battleships can't accelerate fast enough to catch us in the time they've got, but I bet they'll bring their velocity back up once they realize we're not going to slow down to accommodate their plans."

"We've still got more than eleven hours' travel time before we get to the jump point," Desjani said. "Assuming you reduce our velocity down to point one light speed for the jump at a rate that all of the damaged ships can handle." She glared at her display. "I wish we could have knocked out at least one of their battleships. But that one we beat to hell is still able to keep up with its formation. You know, if those battle cruisers do come through, and we can hit them with all of our battleships . . ."

He shook his head. "If I were commanding those dark battle cruisers, I wouldn't seek a direct fight with that many battleships. I'd maneuver to try to hit our formation with the battle cruisers in it, and if I couldn't do that, I'd try glancing firing passes to wear down the enemy. If we're lucky, if the enemy battle cruisers come through just before we jump and can't avoid our formations, we'll hit them hard and keep going."

He didn't say what everyone else already knew. The dark battle cruisers could hit *Dauntless* and the other Alliance battle cruisers hard as well in such an encounter.

Eleven hours. He called the other ships in the fleet, telling them what he intended. It was a measure of how much he had influenced the fleet that no one protested about "fleeing" to Varandal. Or perhaps the commanding officers of Geary's ships could read the situation and had no particular desire to die fighting against weapons the Alliance itself had created. Not unless they had a good chance of victory, which did not exist at Bhavan.

His sense that he was on top of the situation lasted for another twenty minutes.

"The dark ship formations are altering vectors," Lieutenant Yuon said as alerts sounded on everyone's displays.

"Where are they going?" Desjani demanded.

"They're swinging starboard, as if they intend heading in-system," Yuon said. "I think . . . Captain, I think they're heading to intercept the primary inhabited planet in its orbit."

"Hell." Geary rubbed his forehead, thinking through options. "They're moving to bombard the planet."

"If they wanted to hit that planet, they could have launched their bombardment from where they were without changing course," Desjani protested.

"Not if they want to go into low orbit about it and methodically pound it into an inferno unsuited for human life," Geary said. "They want to force me to reengage them. They've been programmed with knowledge of my own actions during the engagements since I took command, so they know that Black Jack will not stand by while they wipe out the human population in Bhavan."

She shook her head. "Isn't this more likely to be a bluff? We think the dark ships identify Bhavan as a star system friendly to them. If we just keep heading for the jump point, won't they drop the threat to that planet and try something else?"

"No," Geary said. "I don't think so."

"Why not?"

"Look what they did at Atalia and Indras. They are either programmed to be ruthless when they think it is necessary, or their thinking has gone off the rails, and they are justifying to themselves any action they want to take. They have targeted escape pods, they have targeted civil populations, they have even gone after a clearly Alliance installation like Ambaru Station."

She frowned, thinking, then looked away. "Or, they may be programmed like Black Jack, but as you've already noticed, in addition to reflecting your own actions since assuming command of the fleet, they also sometimes act like the Black Jack we were all expecting before you really came back."

Geary stared at his display, feeling a knot in his guts. "The Black Jack who would tell you that everything you had been doing in the war was right and would help you do more of it?"

"That's the guy," Desjani agreed. "I'm thinking how I would be looking at this situation before you showed up. You remember me then, I assume."

"Yes, Captain, I do. The officer who shocked me by expressing disappointment that she could not employ null fields against inhabited planets."

"Yeah. Her. It's a good thing she didn't know what hypernet gates could do to enemy star systems, isn't it? If I put myself back into that mind-set, I know that I want the enemy commander to engage me. I know that this enemy commander will protect planets that he believes are really threatened. If he doesn't respond to the threat to attack a planet, it would be because he doesn't think I'd really do it. So I need to do it, I need to hammer that planet into total ruin, to ensure that next time the enemy commander doesn't assume I am bluffing.

"I still don't think that Admiral Bloch would bombard Alliance planets. But I have been watching the maneuvers those dark ships are carrying out, and I am not seeing Admiral Bloch's touch in any of them. And he has not responded to your attempts to communicate. No one has. That's not like Admiral Bloch, who would be reveling in your predicament and enjoying telling Black Jack to surrender to him. Even if Admiral Bloch is present, I don't think he is in command of the dark ships anymore."

"Then you agree with me that this is not a bluff? That the only way to keep the dark ships from wiping out human life on that planet is to move to engage them again?"

Desjani did not hesitate this time. "Yes, sir, I agree."

"I concur with your thinking, Captain, even though I wish we were both wrong. Dr. Nasr believes that the dark ship AIs may have warped their programming into a state where they are simply justifying whatever they want to do. He thinks there may still be some hard limits on their actions, but we don't know what those are. Based on Indras and Atalia, bombarding civilian targets is no longer one of those limits." Geary took another look at his display. "They may not turn to engage us as soon as we turn to engage them. They may want to lure us as far from the jump points here as possible before moving to intercept us again. That's what I would do if I wanted to minimize the chance of any opponent's escaping. I'll give them what they want, and they will regret getting it. This time I will go after the nearest wing formation." He touched his comm controls. "All units in First Fleet, immediate execute, turn starboard five four degrees, up zero two degrees."

As his three formations turned, Geary issued additional orders, pivoting the diamond formations again so they were canted forward, the leading point higher than the trailing point, and facing down the vector they were traveling. Then more commands, spreading out the formations, so that the battle cruisers were out to port, then two light-seconds to starboard the first battleship formation, and two light-seconds beyond that the second battleship formation.

"What are we doing here?" Desjani asked, her eyes on the display before her.

"I want to see who the dark ships aim for," Geary said.

"The battle cruisers. So we can't outrun them. Just like last time."

"Not if the dark ships expect their own battle cruisers to show up behind us. Their best move in that case, the move I would make, is to concentrate everything they have on one of our battleship formations and inflict so much damage on it that it is rendered useless."

They waited. On their current vectors, Geary's ships would not catch the dark ships for days. Everyone knew that if the dark ships intended bombarding the primary inhabited world at Bhavan, they would have ample opportunity to do so. But no one said that out loud.

Even if the dark ships turned onto a direct intercept right now, it would take them nearly an hour to close the distance to Geary's ships. If they waited, it might be several hours at least before anything else happened.

He felt a need for some time to think without eyes upon him, yet the solitude of his stateroom felt wrong. He also needed inspiration, and where could he find that?

Geary realized he knew somewhere that might help, and stood up. "You know," he commented to Desjani, "it's been too long since I talked to my ancestors."

"Say hi to them for me," she replied.

Geary walked to the special rooms near the center of *Dauntless* set aside for crew members to worship however and whomever they wished. Crew members saw him going that way, so he knew word would spread. He hated making a public spectacle of such an errand, but surely his ancestors would understand the need.

In one of the small rooms, Geary sat down on the hard, wooden bench and lit the single candle before him, watching the flame dance. *You know what I am fighting,* he thought. *Please tell me what I need to do. I don't want more people to die, especially men and women under my command. The dark ships must have more weaknesses that I can exploit. Weaknesses that will compensate in some measure for their advantages. I already feel confident that what I am doing is right, but I wouldn't mind reassurance on those grounds, either.*

He did not feel any answer. His thoughts refused to coalesce around any image or memory that might help. *It's up to me, then? Again? Am I ever going to get a break? How about these men and women that I command? Haven't they already given enough? How much more will be asked of them?*

Still nothing. After several minutes, Geary sighed and moved to snuff out the candle.

But the flame seemed to dance aside. He grumbled and tried again, once more missing it. It took a third, determined try to put out the candle.

He was halfway back to the bridge before he wondered whether *that* had been some sort of message.

Two hours later, light arrived from the region of the jump point from Varandal with the news they had been expecting. "Twelve battle cruisers," Lieutenant Castries reported. "Accompanied by fourteen heavy cruisers and twenty-five destroyers."

"Can we see any signs that any of those dark ships engaged in combat at Varandal?" Geary asked, tensing as he waited for the answer.

Castries bit her lip as she studied her display, then shook her head. "All dark ships are undamaged as far as we can tell, Admiral. It's possible some of them have damage on portions that we cannot see, but the odds of none of that being visible would be pretty small."

"Roberto Duellos would have hurt them," Desjani said forcefully.

"There are two dark battle cruisers unaccounted for," Geary pointed out, unwilling to feel completely relieved as of yet.

"Two major combatants completely destroyed and not a mark on any of the other dark ships? That doesn't seem plausible. Admiral, it looks to me like those dark ships raced straight through Varandal from the hypernet gate to the jump point for Bhavan. Captain Duellos could not have managed an intercept under those conditions unless he was perfectly positioned."

It was what he wanted to believe, which made it too easy to believe, but Geary couldn't argue with Desjani's logic. "I hope you're right, Tanya."

"The new dark ship formation came starboard after arriving and steadied out on an intercept with our track, Admiral," Lieutenant Yuon said.

"We have a target-rich environment," Desjani commented in cheerful tones that drew looks of disbelief, then grins, from her bridge crew. "For once," she continued, "I will not insist that *Dauntless* achieve the majority of the kills. There are plenty of enemy warships to go around."

"The dark battle cruisers are coming up to point two light speed,"

Geary said. "They'll take a long time to intercept us even at that rate, but I expect the dark battleships will finally turn once they also see the light of their battle cruisers' arrival."

Geary's warships were only eight light-minutes from the dark battleships. Less than twenty minutes after sighting the dark battle cruisers, the enemy battleships maneuvered, not turning their formations but simply pivoting around to face toward a fast intercept with Geary's force. Lighting off their main propulsion on full, the dark ships labored to first stop their movement toward the primary inhabited planet, then accelerate outward in a nearly opposite direction toward Geary's warships. That maneuver used a lot of fuel cells since it first killed momentum completely in one direction, then built it in another. Swinging through a turn instead would have altered the direction of momentum, which also involved a lot of propulsion, but made some use of the existing movement and so was not nearly as expensive in terms of fuel.

As they maneuvered, it became clear that the dark battleships were all accelerating toward an intercept with one Alliance subformation, the one that contained the battle cruisers, including *Dauntless*.

"They don't just want the battle cruisers," Desjani said with dawning understanding. "They want you."

"I was starting to suspect that," Geary said, trying to sound casual about knowing he was being personally targeted by such a massive force. "Tactically, it makes a lot of sense. The enemy has a skilled commander, so it is a good idea to aim to take out that skilled commander."

"But we suspect that dark ship fleet was built at least in part to counter any threat *you* might pose to the Alliance government," she pointed out. "That's not about tactics. Are they programmed to go after Black Jack?"

"It's entirely possible that they were, under certain conditions, and they may have decided that those conditions have been met, maybe when we beat them at Atalia, maybe just when I challenged them at Atalia."

Desjani glanced sidelong at him. "We can use that."

"Yes, we can." It seemed very unlikely that would be enough to compensate for the superior numbers and capabilities of the dark ships, but at the moment he would take anything he could get.

7

Geary's three diamond formations were heading in toward the star. Ahead of them, and slightly to starboard, were the three dark battleship formations. The main body of the dark ships in its rectangular box shape was accelerating fast onto a curving path through space that aimed for a direct intercept on Geary's battle cruiser formation, the two smaller side formations closing in on the main body so that the three dark ship formations had almost merged into one long rectangle.

Nearly a light-hour behind Geary's ships and a bit off to port were the twelve dark battle cruisers and their escort ships. The dark battle cruisers and the heavy cruisers and destroyers with them were accelerating for all they were worth and also steering on a vector that would eventually catch up to Geary's formation.

"They don't mind burning fuel cells like nobody's business, do they?" Lieutenant Castries commented, then cast a hurried look at Captain Desjani as she realized she had spoken aloud. "I'm sorry, Captain."

"It's true," Desjani replied. "Why do you think the dark ships are maneuvering in that fashion, Lieutenant?"

Castries hesitated as she thought through possible explanations. "There are a variety of profiles that our automated maneuvering systems are designed to adopt based on the situation," she finally said. "Battle Priority profile places emphasis on completing maneuvers quickly and deemphasizes fuel cell usage levels because it focuses on achieving a quick, decisive victory. It appears that the dark ships are using Battle Priority as a default, perhaps because they see their ability to accelerate and maneuver better than our ships as a decisive advantage."

"Not bad, Lieutenant," Desjani said. "You are very likely correct. Where we modify our instructions to the maneuvering systems and sometimes override the automated preferences, the dark ships are forced to use purely automated controls that they may not question." She looked back at Geary. "What are we going to do? Try to lure them into a lunge for *Dauntless* as we swing by again? It will be hard to set that up so we can get a decent number of hits, but we can try once more."

"It's too hard," Geary said. "Time and numbers are not on our side. We can't risk inconclusive firing passes, but if we cut a pass too close and get chewed up, we could lose this fight very quickly."

"Maybe—"

"Hold on."

Desjani ceased speaking instantly, turning a warning glare on the bridge watch-standers to ensure they also remained silent. Geary rarely cut her off, especially so abruptly. When he did, she knew it meant he was chasing an idea, something that was hanging on the edge of his consciousness but staying just out of sight.

The candle had offered a clue. Dodge aside from the enemy attacks. But battleships could not dodge battle cruisers. In order to set up conditions that would give him a chance to avoid getting hit too hard, Geary knew he would have to first inflict a major blow on the dark ships. But he couldn't dodge *and* hit the dark ships hard. If only he could tear straight through the dark ship formation. But they would target *Dauntless*, they would aim every weapon at this battle cruiser, and—

Of course. They'll aim at Dauntless. *They'll throw everything they've got at her.* "I'm going to give them what they want," Geary said. "A lot of clean shots at *Dauntless*."

Desjani twisted her head rapidly to stare at him. "I'm waiting to hear the rest of the plan, Admiral."

He pointed. "We go through here. The center of the dark ship formation. Not a glancing blow. We aim to go through them."

Desjani nodded. "Then what, Admiral? Because the dark ships won't plan any maneuvers if we come in aimed at that spot. They'll know even if we make a last-second alteration of vector, we won't be able to get clear of their weapons' engagement envelopes."

"Exactly. I want them targeted on *Dauntless*, and I want them waiting to get their shots. We're going to refine what I told the heavy cruisers to do at Varandal."

"Messing with the dark ships' targeting priorities?"

"Exactly." He indicated the other two formations of his fleet. "We'll maneuver so that our battleship formations will be coming in at the same point in the dark ship formation, at the same time."

"So our battleships can target the dark ships while they target

Dauntless?'" Desjani nodded again, her expression revealing no emotion. "It's a smart plan. Which other ship will you be transferring to before that?"

"I'm staying aboard *Dauntless*."

"No, you are not, Admiral! Because *Dauntless* will not survive that firing pass! There is no possible way, and you must survive. I recommend moving to *Leviathan* because Captain Tulev—"

"Tanya." Geary pointed to his formations again. "The dark ships will target *Dauntless*. As long as *Dauntless* remains a priority target, they will not shift targets, and they will hold fire waiting to hit her. How long does it take our fire-control systems to reprioritize targets? About a second?"

"About that," Desjani said. "Maybe a little longer. It depends on the complexity of the firing solutions and the relative velocity of the engagement."

"My idea is to bring in our three formations so they intercept the dark ships as close to simultaneously as possible, but with the formation containing *Dauntless* a fraction of a second in the lead, and at the last possible moment accelerating our battleships so they switch lead with the battle cruisers, coming in a fraction of a second before *Dauntless*."

She stared at him. "So the dark ships are holding their fire, waiting to hit *Dauntless*, while our battleships hit them a fraction of a second earlier?"

"Yes," Geary said. "The dark ships don't get their shots off because we hit them just before they fire."

"Can you handle a maneuver like that?"

"No. But our maneuvering systems can, right? This is close to a straight-on intercept, without much deflection to worry about, and our three subformations are close together and moving along nearly the same vectors. Our automated maneuvering systems can make it work." He paused. "I think it should work with the fire-control systems of the dark ships, which are identical to ours in every way that matters."

"Why don't we check on that?" Desjani gestured to Lieutenant Yuon. "Have Senior Chief Tarrani get in touch with me immediately."

It took less than thirty seconds for Senior Chief Tarrani's image to appear before Desjani. "Yes, Captain?"

"I've got a question about our fire-control systems, Senior Chief," Desjani said. She explained Geary's plan. "Can that work?"

Tarrani's expression had shifted from puzzled to startled to admiring to considering. She took a few moments to answer. "Based on the way our fire-control systems work, Captain, the answer is yes. Keep the time differential down to less than a second, and the fire-control systems will not shift targets. They won't change targeting priority based on that small an interval because recalculating time to fire and sending commands throughout the ship to shift weapon firing times takes just over one second. If we can cut the approaches of our three formations that fine, it will work. The dark ship fire-control systems will not reprioritize based on that small an interval."

"You realize that you're betting not just your butt but your life on that answer?" Desjani asked.

"Yes, Captain, I realize that. If you can make the maneuvering systems pull it off, then it will work. If it doesn't work, it won't be because I didn't give you a good call on what the fire-control systems will do. It'll be because the maneuvering systems screwed up their solutions."

"I'll see what Chief Busek says," Desjani began.

"Uh, Captain, Chief Busek is pretty good, but she came up pretty fast because of the losses on her previous ships and those we took in engineering in the last year. Her experience is a bit limited," Senior Chief Tarrani explained. "Yes, I'd ask her, but I'd also ask the person aboard the ship who has the most experience with maneuvering systems."

"And that would be?" Desjani asked in the manner of someone who already suspected the answer.

"Master Chief Gioninni, Captain."

"Naturally. Inform Master Chief Gioninni and Chief Busek that I need to hear from them immediately."

Tarrani's image vanished, to be replaced within a few seconds by the hefty figure of Master Chief Gioninni and the stick-thin shape of Chief Busek. Desjani once again explained what was intended. "Can the maneuvering systems make this happen?"

Chief Busek began to nod, paused, then glanced at Master Chief Gioninni. "Captain, I think the answer is yes, but I would like to hear the Master Chief's opinion."

Gioninni smiled with serene certainty. "We're doing point one five light right now? And the enemy is coming at us at point zero five light?"

"That's right, Master Chief," Geary said. "The dark ships are holding their velocity down to ensure they get good fire-control solutions on us when we encounter them."

"Which means we'll meet them at a combined relative velocity of point two light," Gioninni concluded. "That's important, because the same relativity junk that messes with our fire-control systems can also throw off our maneuvering systems. But point two light is copacetic. Our systems can see precisely enough at that velocity to cut everything as fine as they have to. Yes, Captain, the maneuvering systems can do it. In theory."

"In theory?" Desjani pressed.

"Well, Captain, you know how it is," Gioninni explained. "There's theory, and then there's the real universe. The maneuvering systems can calculate those approaches and that final acceleration by the battleship formations so that it will play out exactly like you want. But the maneuvering systems can't tell if the dark ships might do something a little different, or if the guide ship on one of the battleship formations might have a slight hiccup in its main propulsion when the acceleration burst order comes down, or something like that. Yes, our systems can do it, but there isn't any one hundred percent guarantee that something as precise as that will not be impacted by some sort of friction in the process."

"It wouldn't take much friction," Chief Busek offered. "But it should work."

"Would you bet your butt on it?" Desjani asked.

Chief Busek hesitated a moment, then nodded.

Master Chief Gioninni scratched his head, thinking. "I'm not naturally the gambling type, Captain—"

"*You're* not the gambling type?" Desjani asked with obvious skepticism.

"No, ma'am," Gioninni protested. "Gambling is a game of

chance. There's risk and uncertainty as to whether or not you'll win. I never gamble, Captain."

"You only bet on sure things?" Geary asked.

"If you call that betting, yes, Admiral. I can't help it if any other parties to the transaction think there's any chance that they might win."

Desjani shook her head, looking briefly upward as if beseeching aid. "Do you regard the proposed maneuvers as a sure thing, Master Chief?"

Gioninni hesitated only a moment longer, then nodded vigorously. "Close enough, Captain. I'd give it a shot. But, I have to say, if there is any interference with the automated systems, if there is anyone deciding they need to nudge this or that a little because they think the approach isn't quite right, then all bets are off. There are things humans do really well, and things we do a lot better than automated systems, but something like this calls for split-second timing that is a bit beyond our capabilities."

"Thank you. We'll keep that in mind, Master Chief." Desjani dismissed the two chiefs, then looked at Geary. "Let's do it, Admiral."

Inputting the instructions to the maneuvering systems was almost too simple. The three Alliance formations were here, here, and here, traveling along these vectors. Alter their vectors so that all three pass through the same intercept point with the oncoming dark ships at almost exactly the same time. Specify that the formation built around *Dauntless* be fractionally in the lead until the last possible moment, when a burst of acceleration from the battleships would push them ahead of *Dauntless* by just less than a second.

The maneuvering systems contemplated the problem for all of two seconds before providing the necessary maneuvers.

Geary studied the results, glancing at Desjani for her opinion.

She shrugged. "Master Chief Gioninni is right. This has to be a hands-off set of maneuvers. The solution looks fine to me, but there is a really tiny margin of error."

"We can't help that. We have to hit the dark ships hard before the battle cruisers get close enough to engage us. This may be our only chance to inflict a nasty blow on the dark battleships."

Geary ordered the maneuvering commands sent to every ship in his fleet. "All units in First Fleet, this is Admiral Geary. You are receiving sets of automated maneuvering orders which must be implemented precisely. No variations and no interference are permitted. These are to be hands-off maneuvers. Captain Armus, Captain Jane Geary," he said, naming the commanders of *Colossus* and *Dreadnaught*, who were also in charge of the two battleship formations, "I am counting on your formations inflicting devastating damage on the dark ships along our path through the enemy formation. While the enemy is targeting *Dauntless* and the ships with her, you need to blow a hole through the enemy formation that the battle cruisers will exploit."

"Understood," Captain Jane Geary replied.

"The battleships will be leading the way?" Captain Armus asked, deliberately needling the battle cruiser commanders who were used to being at the forefront of action.

"That is correct," Geary said, while Desjani quietly fumed beside him.

"We will be happy to ease the path of our comrades on the battle cruisers," Armus concluded. The dour battleship captain did not smile often, but he seemed to be having trouble not doing so now. "Understood, Admiral."

The automated maneuvers cut in, every ship in the Alliance force shifting vector, some accelerating as well as altering their track through space. The three diamonds of Geary's subformations compressed into narrower wedges, all three now on paths that were rapidly bringing them together.

Geary itched to issue commands, to insert himself directly into the maneuvers. But there were times to do that and times to trust in the equipment that men and women had painstakingly created. "We rarely notice them, do we?" he said to Desjani.

She gave him a questioning look, then nodded. "You mean the automated systems? All of the stuff we depend on to keep this ship working?"

"Yeah. We only notice it when it breaks or malfunctions in some ways. The rest of the time, it's just there."

"That's how it's supposed to be," Desjani replied. "Transparent technology. It works without anyone having to worry about it or having to master arcane commands and rules. Sure, it needs a lot of tender, loving care and the occasional hard kick in the rear to keep it working right, but that's why we have our enlisted specialists aboard, to provide the help the automated systems need so they can help humans kill each other."

"You are such a romantic soul," Geary said, watching the time to contact with the enemy scrolling down rapidly. "I wonder how the dark ships handle maintenance and repair?"

"They must have automated systems to look after the automated systems. And other automated systems to look after the automated systems that look after the automated systems. And maybe another layer beyond to look after those automated systems. Can you imagine the complexity and the cost of all that?"

"Not easily." He kept his eyes on his display, where the movements of every Alliance ship exactly matched their planned vectors, two hundred warships moving in a complex dance that would soon end in a brutal climax.

Hands off. Having set it up, all he could do now was watch.

"Five minutes to contact," Lieutenant Castries said, echoing the information on Geary's display.

"Very well." Desjani sat back in her command seat as if relaxed, but the expression she turned toward Geary betrayed some worry. "Isn't this a little last-ditch and desperate for this stage of the battle, Admiral?" she murmured, too low for anyone else to hear.

"We need to hit them really hard this time," he repeated.

"That should happen, but if the timing of our battleships is off by even a second, you and I and everyone else aboard *Dauntless* will never know it. We'll take so many hits that the only thing left will be a cloud of dust heading really fast along our last vector."

"I know." He had seen just that happen too many times already to too many warships, and he knew that Tanya had seen a lot more ships die in combat than he had. "If that happens, at least what used to be you and me will be part of the same dust cloud."

"Wow. Is that what you consider romantic, Admiral?"

"It's the best I've got at the moment, Captain."

She kept her eyes on her display, smiling. "See you on the other side." Then, much louder, Desjani called out to the watch-standers.

"I want every shot to hit. Take out as many of these soulless bastards as we can."

"Ready, Captain," the watch-standers chorused.

Geary could hear the tension in their voices but also the determination. He understood the mixed emotions because he felt them himself. Any firing pass was a gamble. No matter how good the maneuvering systems were at avoiding collisions, the fact remained that even the smallest error could result in two warships running into each other at velocities that instantly reduced both to tiny fragments. Or the enemy might choose to target your ship in particular, or a lucky hit might penetrate to a critical area, or . . .

Some things were not worth worrying about, not when you couldn't do a thing about them.

But this was a particularly risky firing pass, and everyone knew it.

"One minute to intercept," Lieutenant Castries called out, her voice almost cracking on the first word but steadying and coming out clear and firm at the end.

The six formations were rapidly converging, Geary's three formations headed for that single point where the center of the dark ship main formation would be, and the dark ships coming on steadily, with the smaller formations on either side sliding closer to the main body.

"Ten seconds." This time Castries' voice stayed steady. "We have confirmation that our battleship formations are accelerating."

Geary didn't know whether he really saw any of the Alliance battleships, cruisers, and destroyers rushing in toward the same point where *Dauntless* and the other battle cruisers and their escorts were going. He didn't know whether he really saw the dark ship formation suddenly loom directly ahead, going from tiny dots of light to massive warships in the blink of a human eye. Maybe he imagined those images, or maybe his brain manufactured them.

He felt *Dauntless*'s weapons firing, felt the battle cruiser shudder from hits, waited for a moment of incredible force to smash himself and this ship.

It took a few seconds for him to realize that they were past the encounter. Geary heard a couple of gasps of relief as some of the watch-standers absorbed the same knowledge.

"Made it," Desjani said, as if no other outcome had been plausible. "Status, people!"

The watch-standers sprang to action to consolidate information for her, while Geary bent closer to his display, wondering whether the risk had paid off.

The three Alliance formations had essentially merged in the final seconds prior to contact with the dark ships, a mass of warships whose movements had fortunately been coordinated by the fleet's maneuvering systems. But that mass was slamming head-on into another mass, that of the dark ships. Only the fact that the dark ships held their vectors, sticking to their predicted courses, prevented any collisions.

As the Alliance battleships had surged very slightly ahead of the battle cruisers, their weapons had fired, eighteen huge warships bristling with weaponry unloading everything they had at the dark ships preparing to fire on *Dauntless* and the other battle cruisers. Missiles leaped out, impacting on targets almost as soon as they launched. Hell-lance particle beams formed a brilliant forest of lethal energy that bored into their targets. Grapeshot struck within milliseconds of the other weapons, pounding warships whose shields and armor had already been battered by earlier hits. And where the battleships had passed close enough to targets, the glowing balls of null fields had eaten holes in opponents, dissolving the bonds that held molecules and atoms together.

Geary had to drastically slow the playback generated by the fleet's sensors to see that much. Immediately behind the Alliance battleships had come the battle cruiser formation, but instead of running into a wall of fire as well, the battle cruisers had faced only those surviving after the rampage of the battleships. *Dauntless* and her companions had fired, tearing apart smaller warships and adding to the damage inflicted on dark battleships already badly hurt. "We took some hits," Geary said as his display lit with damage reports from other ships. "But we hit them a lot worse."

Three dark battleships were gone, blown to pieces despite their mammoth defenses. A fourth was crippled, so badly shot up that it had lost all weapons and all maneuvering control, tumbling helplessly onward in the wake of its companions.

Between them, the Alliance formations had knocked out a dozen dark heavy cruisers, seven light cruisers, and twenty-three destroyers.

The vast majority of the enemy ships in that part of their formation within range of the Alliance charge had their fire-control systems locked on *Dauntless* and the other battle cruisers. In the almost-a-second between the time when the Alliance battleships came within range and when *Dauntless* could have been engaged, most of the dark ship weapons had never had a chance to fire, being destroyed while awaiting a shot at their chosen targets.

Few of the warships in Geary's battleship formations had been targeted by the enemy, so few had received any hits. Many more ships in the battle cruiser formation had been hit, but even though half a dozen Alliance battle cruisers had suffered significant damage, only one heavy cruiser, *Bunker*, and a half dozen destroyers had been hit badly enough to be out of the fight.

Bunker was staggering away from the other Alliance ships, trying to regain some maneuvering control. The destroyers *Thunderbolt*, *Monitor*, and *Kopis* had been completely obliterated. *Patu*, *Lathi*, and *Naginata* were still at least partly intact but so badly damaged that their surviving crew members were abandoning ship in any escape pods that remained in working condition.

Both *Incredible* and *Dragon* had taken hits to their main propulsion, though, enough to limit their maneuverability, and the battleship *Fearless* had also lost a propulsion unit.

"Several hits on *Dauntless*," Lieutenant Yuon was summarizing. "Hell-lance battery 2A out of commission. Maneuvering thruster 3B off-line. No estimated times to repair yet. Hull penetrations are being sealed by damage control teams. Two dead confirmed. Seventeen wounded."

The losses hurt. Even one man or woman killed hurt. The destroyers that had not survived had lost their entire crews. Despite that, it had been a wildly successful tactic. But . . . "Given the firepower advantages of the dark ships," Geary said, "we've only roughly evened the odds with their battleship formations." He did not have to add that the dark battle cruiser formation charging their way would give the dark ships a major advantage.

Desjani nodded, grimacing. "And we can't do that again. The dark ships will already be analyzing what happened and preparing to counter it if they see us setting up another attack like that."

The dark battleships were already closing ranks in their formation, unfazed by their losses, filling in the gap that Geary's ships had blown through them.

He only had to repeat what he had just done, in terms of losses to the dark ships and losses suffered by his own side, at least twice more to even the odds, and perhaps half a dozen times to win.

A moment of despair filled Admiral John Geary.

Then he began issuing orders again. Because the people he commanded needed Black Jack if they were to survive.

"Immediate execute, all units, come up zero nine five degrees." His fleet, the three formations still intermingled, began curving upward and back toward another intercept with the dark battleships. *Incredible*, *Dragon*, *Fearless*, and a score of cruisers and destroyers struggled to match the maneuver due to the damage to their propulsion systems.

His ships were shedding some velocity in the massive turn, but he didn't worry about maintaining speed. Point one five light was a bit fast for his taste when it came to maneuvering in battle, and limiting acceleration made it easier for the damaged ships to stay with their formations.

"Captain?" Lieutenant Castries said. "The dark battle cruiser formation was up to point three five light speed an hour ago."

"What?" Desjani glared at her display. "At the rate they have been moving, they'll get within combat range in another three hours," she warned Geary.

"Even though the dark ships can handle more stress on acceleration and deceleration than our ships can, they'll have to start braking that velocity really soon, or they'll tear right past us," he replied. "I wouldn't have ramped up the velocity on those battle cruisers and their escorts that high. Is the dark ship AI based on my actions breaking down, or is this supposed to be the Black Jack who people imagined before I came back?"

"Maybe the Black Jack legend," Desjani said. "You in reality try to think a few moves ahead. I don't know. We might have to assume the AIs are getting erratic, maybe testing their limits."

"Dr. Nasr said they could run into problems if they encountered new situations," Geary said. "New limitations, or possibilities they create by working around old limitations. But unless those problems cause their weapons to go off-line, they probably won't help us much."

He was studying his display again, seeing the dark battleship formation, a little smaller now, the two subformations on either side remaining close, as it came up and around to head back toward an intercept with the Alliance warships. The dark battleships had been moving a lot slower, and so could turn in much less distance, though that was a relative term given how huge the turns were when ships were moving at appreciable fractions of the speed of light. The dark ships were steadying out earlier than Geary's ships were, heading along a flat curve to meet up with the Alliance warships as they cleared the top of their own turn.

The enemy was clearly aiming to hit the Alliance formations head-on again, and this time he couldn't count on any dark ships holding their fire while waiting for the right target to get within range. "They're still going at a lot less velocity, so they can keep turning inside our own maneuvers," he grumbled.

It left only one good option, to change velocity just prior to the dark ships' intercepting his formations, aiming to throw off the enemy plans and enabling Geary to hopefully hit a portion of the dark ships while the rest of them were unable to engage the Alliance ships.

With plenty of time left before both sides clawed through their vast turns, Geary rearranged his formations, keeping three of them, but changing the diamonds to discs aligned along the path the ships were taking.

Trying to judge the right moment for the next maneuvers, he watched the movements of ships through space, the great arcs marking the projected paths of his formations and the dark battleship formations, as well as the flat curve of the route of the dark battle cruisers racing to reach the scene of the fighting. "All units in First Fleet, reduce propulsion to forty percent maximum at time three six."

The propulsion of the Alliance warships had been pushing them around the arc, altering the direction of movement, the more force, the tighter the turn, limited by how much stress the ships and crews could stand and how much push the main propulsion units could provide. Even with the ships' inertial dampers straining at full capability, both ships and crews had been feeling some of the pressure of the forces tearing at them.

As the dark ships raced toward another intercept, the force on Geary's ships abruptly lessened as the main propulsion units on the warships throttled back in accordance with his orders. Just as abruptly, the arc of the turn the ships were going through shifted, growing wider, the Alliance warships swinging outward farther than they had been moments earlier.

The dark ships, aiming for where the Alliance ships should

have been, were now on paths that would take them just under the Alliance formations, whose flattened discs would give nearly every Alliance warship a decent shot at the enemy. Ideally, if Geary had called it right, the top edge of the dark ship formations would be within range of the Alliance warships' weapons. The Alliance warships themselves were traveling along the arc, but their bows, with the majority of their weaponry and their strongest shields and armor, were pointed toward where the enemy ships would pass.

If this pass worked, it would be perfect.

The moment came, and went.

"No engagement," Lieutenant Yuon reported, sounding as if he were responsible for the failure.

"The dark ships thought you were going to accelerate again and tighten our turn," Desjani said as she studied the playback from the last encounter. "They tried to compensate for that, we both went in different directions, and nobody was within range of anybody."

"I considered tightening the turn," Geary said. "It could have gone either way. Let's try again." He activated the fleetwide command net. "All units in First Fleet, immediate execute, pivot one four zero degrees up, accelerate to point one light speed."

The Alliance warships swung in place, then lit off their main propulsion again at a higher intensity. Their paths began to recurve, twisting up along the opposite direction of the previous turn, but higher, aiming toward where the dark ships were also slewing about and maneuvering for another intercept.

"Have engineering check something for me," Desjani called to her watch-standers. "I want to know what they can tell me about the main propulsion signatures on the dark ships."

The answer came within a minute. "Engineering has been running that analysis, Captain. They say the signatures on the dark ships are identical to those on our main propulsion units."

"But the dark ships have consistently been maneuvering harder than we do," Desjani said. "It's not because their main propulsion units have more capability than ours? They're just using more thrust?"

"Yes, Captain. They're burning their main drives hotter and longer to get more thrust out of them."

"Thank you." Desjani glanced at Geary. "Can we use that?"

"I don't know." Geary gestured toward the virtual tiles hanging in the air near his command seat that listed the status of all of his ships, updating every time any change took place. "They're forcing us to maneuver hard as well. As hard as we can, anyway. I can't let them run rings around us."

"So they're burning fuel cells faster, but they're also forcing us to do the same."

"Yeah. And we don't know how big their fuel cell reserves are. Did the builders use the same levels as on our ships, or did they add extra stockpiles?"

Desjani made a face. "One of those agents we're holding might know. How about if we stick them on the bow of *Dauntless* before our next engagement with the dark ships? Just to encourage them to talk."

"We can't do that, Tanya."

"I wasn't going to put them out there in their shirtsleeves. I'd put them in survival suits," she said. "I wonder if duct tape would hold them on to the outer hull? We could find out."

"Still can't do it," Geary said. "But I wish we could."

This time, the two formations were racing toward an intercept in which both would be at an angle to the other, meeting partway through their turns. Once again, Geary faced the question of whether to try to tighten the turn or to slack off on acceleration and widen it. Another look at the damage status of some of his ships, *Fearless* and *Incredible* in particular, led him to decide to once again ease off acceleration just before contact.

"I should be used to the waits between firing runs by now," Geary murmured as he watched the apparently slow movement of both forces through the immense distances of space.

"I'm not," Desjani commented, "and I've been doing it longer than you have, old man."

"Excuse me?"

"Old man, *sir*."

"That's better." A touch of the comm controls. "All units in First Fleet, go to forty-four percent propulsion at time one four."

In the last moments before contact, the Alliance warships swung a little wider, once again aiming for the upper portion of the dark ship formation.

"No engagement," Lieutenant Yuon reported. "No ships were within range of the enemy during the pass."

"Damn," Geary got out in a whisper. "Let's try this different." He swung the battle cruisers up again, curving back once more, but both of his battleship formations went out to the sides and then up, the three formations bracketing the future path of the dark ships also coming back in another upward curve.

This time he did a last-second shift to starboard with the battle cruisers, while the two battleship formations swung lower and toward each other, in an attempt to bracket the dark ship subformation to one side of the main formation.

"No engagement." Lieutenant Yuon had stopped sounding guilty. Now he appeared to be confused.

Geary, feeling angry and frustrated, assessed the status of his ships, then called out new orders. One Alliance battleship formation swung wide to starboard, one swung wide to port, and the battle cruisers twisted about and aimed straight for an intercept with the dark ships coming back for another run.

He dove the battle cruiser formation before contact, aiming under the dark ships, while the battleship formations on either side held their vectors so that no matter which way the dark ships went, the Alliance warships should get some shots at them.

"No engagement."

Geary could feel everyone on the bridge carefully not looking at him. He could sense how crews on every other ship in the fleet were reacting. Something was very wrong, and he wasn't sure what it was.

Had he lost his nerve? Was he so afraid of losing this battle that he wouldn't take the necessary losses to win it?

But he was doing nothing differently. He was trying to hit the enemy. And how could the dark ships keep missing his ships if Geary was displaying any sort of unconscious pattern of avoiding closing to weapons range? He might not be aware of it, but the dark ships would see such a pattern. They would exploit it and catch him next time.

"Admiral?" Tanya was eyeing him with an unusual level of concern apparent.

"Something is wrong," Geary said. "None of the passes are working."

"We have to close to engagement range."

"I *know* that!"

"Admiral," Desjani said in her most formal tone of voice, "we have to hit them despite the risks—"

"I have demonstrated my willingness to take risks, Captain," Geary snapped.

"Getting too close is dangerous, but if we don't—"

"Captain Desjani, I am making just as strong an effort to engage those dark ships as I ever have in any battle!" He glowered at his display as Desjani fell silent and stared fixedly at her own display. What wasn't working? he wondered. To guess incorrectly that many times in a row? To completely miss engaging the dark ships time and again? How could that be happening?

Not by chance.

"Damn," His tone of voice brought Desjani's eyes back on him. "It's not us. We're not engaging on these firing passes because the dark ships are deliberately avoiding getting within range of us."

"They're avoiding action?" She took another look at her display, swallowed, then inclined her head toward him. "My apologies, Admiral. I did not consider that possibility, but I'm certain that you're right."

"None of us considered it, Captain," Geary said. "Because of the ruthless tactics of the dark ships prior to this. But they are tactics, and tactics can change depending on the situation. Right now, the dark ships have a reason to avoid action just as we have had reasons to seek action."

"But why would they—?" Her eyes widened. "They're just keeping us engaged and occupied in dealing with them, forcing us into repeated maneuvers to counter them. Stalling for time and keeping us in this region of space."

"Until their battle cruisers get here," Geary said, his voice as grim as his mood. "And then they will hit us with everything at once."

8

The dark battleships were turning to engage again, but Geary swung his formations on through their last turn, not steadying out until the enemy battleships were behind him and his own warships were aimed at an intercept with the dark battle cruisers ahead. Those battle cruisers were braking velocity at a rate that would have torn apart Geary's ships. By the time they reached where Geary's ships were tangling with the dark battleships, they would have been going slow enough (if point one light speed could be considered slow) to engage the Alliance forces.

"What are we doing?" Desjani asked.

"Changing the game," Geary said. "We underestimated the dark ship AIs. First we get out of the trap they tried to pin us in. Next—"

An alert sounded on his display.

"*Fearless* just lost another main propulsion unit," Lieutenant Castries said.

Geary slapped his comm controls. "*Fearless*, can you keep up with the formation?"

The image of Captain Ulrickson looked back at Geary. "We'll keep up or die trying. Repairs are underway."

The determination and the desire were admirable, but as Geary looked at his data he could tell that neither were adequate substitutes for a main propulsion unit. If *Fearless* could not keep up, they would have to leave her, or else sacrifice the rest of the fleet protecting her.

Desjani was looking at her display, her expression revealing no emotion.

"We've got half an hour before any more maneuvers are necessary," Geary told Captain Ulrickson. "I need *Fearless* able to keep up at that point."

"I understand, Admiral."

"We've still got a chance," Geary told Desjani as the call ended. "Those dark battle cruisers based their approach on reaching us back where we were tangling with dark battleships."

"Which means they'll be going too fast when we reach them, since we're heading straight for an intercept with the dark battle cruisers," Desjani agreed. "Ladies and Gentlemen," she called in a louder voice to the watch-standers. "What is the first rule of combat maneuvering?"

"Never take your ship to the limit of her capabilities unless you absolutely have to," Lieutenants Yuon and Castries chorused in reply.

"Because?"

"Once you take your ship to her limits," the lieutenants said, "the ship has nothing else to give if you need it."

"Exactly." Desjani indicated her display with a dismissive gesture. "Those dark battle cruisers based their approach on the maximum deceleration they could endure, which means they can't slow down any faster now that we are closing on them." She lowered her voice to speak only to Geary. "Unfortunately, we won't be able to hit them as they pass us."

"No." He was sizing up the situation. The dark battleships were behind his formations, but accelerating at a better rate than his own battleships could achieve, especially with *Fearless* limping along. The repeated attempts at firing passes had kept Geary's units fairly close to the dark ships as distances in space went, so the dark battleships were not that far away and closing on the Alliance warships. Even if *Fearless* got one of her off-line main propulsion units working, Geary wouldn't be able to avoid them for long.

The dark battle cruisers would slide helplessly past the Alliance formation at a combined closing speed of point two five light, too fast to hope for any significant number of hits. But as Desjani had noted, Geary's ships wouldn't be able to hit the dark battle cruisers, either. After that, both the dark battleships and the dark battle cruisers would be right behind Geary's own formations.

"If we try to reduce speed to engage the dark battle cruisers, they'll just evade us, and the lower velocity will allow the dark battleships to catch us faster," Geary said between teeth clenched with frustration.

Desjani shook her head, looking pained. "Admiral, I've got nothing."

"We've got one chance," he said, speaking slowly to allow his thoughts to form. "Now we're going slower than they are. We can turn inside them, or at least match them since they can maneuver tighter than us under equal conditions."

"They've got enough superiority now to hammer us in any encounter," Desjani said.

"If they get within firing range."

Her anguish changed to surprise. "Now *we're* going to avoid closing with them?"

"Yes. It's not a tactic I've used before, so it will take them by surprise," Geary said. It would surprise the dark ships the first time, and maybe the second time as well. But after that . . .

The dark battle cruisers whipped past the Alliance formations at a distance of five light-seconds, far too distant to engage even if the relative velocity hadn't been so high. On Geary's display, the projected track of the dark battle cruisers showed them braking steadily and hard until past their own battleships. He did not expect them to maneuver in that way, though.

"Dark battle cruiser formation is turning," Lieutenant Yuon said.

The dark battle cruisers and their accompanying heavy cruisers and destroyers were bending their path through space, their main propulsion still blasting at full power, heading down. The projected path of the dark battle cruisers on Geary's display bent and bent some more, shifting into a wide, wide turn that would bring the enemy ships back toward Geary's formation.

He knew that everyone was waiting, nervously, to know what he would do, so Geary touched his comm controls. "First Fleet, the enemy believes that our options have been eliminated and we cannot avoid meeting them at their advantage. My intention is to frustrate their plans and force them into a variety of maneuvers until we can once again hit them at our advantage. I need the best from everyone. To the honor of our ancestors, Geary, out."

The tension on the bridge of *Dauntless* relaxed considerably. He imagined the same thing was happening on every Alliance ship. The men and women of this fleet trusted him, had confidence in him, had seen him beat the odds time and again. They did not doubt he could do it once more.

He had such doubts growing inside him, but he could not admit to them, could not give in to them, could not allow them to distract him from his efforts to somehow turn this fight around.

Another call, this time to only one ship. "Captain Ulrickson, what is the status of your repair efforts?"

Captain Ulrickson looked as if he had aged a few years since their last conversation. "*Fearless* will be ready to maneuver with the rest of the fleet," he said.

"Good," Geary replied. There wasn't any sense in warning Ulrickson what would happen if *Fearless* wasn't ready and could not keep up with the other warships. Ulrickson already knew the consequences. Neither he nor his crew needed any additional motivation.

Incredible had managed to get her propulsion damage fixed, but Geary's other damaged warships were still trying to get necessary repairs accomplished in time to make a difference.

The dark ships were closing in, the battleships directly behind and the battle cruisers looping toward Geary's formations from below.

"I have to maneuver in five minutes," Geary murmured to Desjani.

"*Fearless* knows what has to happen," she whispered back. "We've all been through this many times. Those of us who survived it, that is."

"That doesn't make it any easier."

"It's not supposed to be easy," she said. "Be glad you're not on *Fearless*."

"Hold on." He had three formations. The dark ships considered *Dauntless* to be their priority target. They wouldn't be fooled easily again into disregarding other threats, but they had shown a pattern of concentrating against their chosen targets. "There's something I can try."

His hands raced across his display, setting up options and trying them out. "I need to make it look to the dark ships like I screwed up and left them an opening."

Geary issued commands. Tango Three, the Alliance formation containing *Fearless*, pivoted their bows so they pointed beneath the oncoming enemy and began braking their velocity at a moderate rate. *Fearless* was able to keep up as Tango Three slid beneath the track of the dark battleships.

The other Alliance battleship formation, Tango Two, pointed their bows above the approaching dark battleships and began both braking slightly and rising above the projected path of the enemy.

At the same time, Tango One, the formation containing *Dauntless* and the other Alliance battle cruisers, began looping upward in a long turn that would bring them down behind the current track of the dark battleships.

"Admiral—!" Lieutenant Castries began in horrified tones.

Desjani stopped her with a single gesture. "I believe Admiral Geary knows exactly what you're worried about."

"That's right," he said. "I did it on purpose."

The situation that had moved a lieutenant to want to tell an admiral he had messed up was not too hard to spot. The movements of Tango Two formation, sliding above its previous track, and Tango One, climbing faster above and beyond Tango Two, were aligning both formations along a single arc.

"I want the dark ships to see my 'mistake,'" Geary explained to Castries. "It's going to look like a perfect chance for their battleships to swing upward along an arc that will first let them hit our battleships in Tango Two, then continue on to hit our battle cruisers in Tango One."

"You gave them bait," Castries said with dawning realization. "So they wouldn't go after formation Tango Three containing *Fearless*."

"Are we going to try to hit them?" Desjani asked, clearly itching to do just that.

"No," Geary said. "The odds would be horrible. We're going to give them a taste of their own medicine. One the dark ships will not anticipate because, contrary to the suspicions of my own flagship captain, Admiral Geary has never tried to completely avoid contact with the enemy on a firing pass."

"Ouch." Desjani winced. "I deserved that. But we can't win by just avoiding them."

"I know. But we need to wait for them to make a mistake."

As the dark battleships raced toward Tango Two, Geary factored in the small time delay until his message would reach the Alliance warships, then sent orders. "All units in Tango Two, set main propulsion on full at time one three."

Captain Jane Geary called back quickly. "Admiral, if we make that maneuver we will certainly miss engaging the dark ships as they pass."

"That is my intent, Captain. We cannot engage the dark ships under circumstances that almost guarantee suffering far more severe losses than they do. We will be trying to set up future firing passes in which the dark ships will be at a serious disadvantage."

Jane Geary wasn't happy, and the Jane Geary who had raised some hell during the mission into enigma space might have done something different than ordered, but she accepted his reasoning.

The dark ships, anticipating another Alliance attempt to hit them a glancing blow, countered with a slight jog in their track to bring them where they expected the Alliance formation to be. Instead, with the ships in Tango Two suddenly braking their velocity at full power, the dark ships overshot their target by a margin wide enough to eliminate any chance of combat.

Geary ordered Tango Two to cut back their propulsion again, then waited as the dark battleships swung up toward an intercept with his battle cruisers. Typical battleships, like those Geary had, would not have been able to pull off such an intercept against more agile battle cruisers. But the dark battleships were nimble enough to have a chance at it.

Assuming Geary had wanted to face twelve battleships with his nine battle cruisers, which he did not.

Just before contact, Geary pivoted his battle cruiser formation, bringing their bows down and back, and began accelerating along the reverse of the curve he had been following.

The dark battleships, still moving at point one five light speed, had so much momentum along their track that they had no chance of reacting quickly enough to try to catch Geary's battle cruisers. The dark ships tore past and onward, trying to bend their path into a tighter turn, their main propulsion once again roaring at maximum.

Geary brought his battle cruisers down and over, while the battleship formation Tango Two swung through its arc and began diving as well, and the other battleship formation, Tango Three, changed its own vector to push back upward.

Would the dark battle cruisers realize in time that Geary was aiming to bracket them with his three formations as the dark ships came climbing toward the former path of the Alliance ships?

"Blast," Desjani grumbled as the dark battle cruisers swung wider to their port, aiming for Geary's battle cruisers and avoiding the Alliance battleships.

Once again, the dark ships had a lot of velocity and a lot of momentum. Geary twisted his formation and raced over the top of the dark battle cruisers at such a distance that no engagement was possible.

The image of Captain Ulrickson appeared. "*Fearless* has one of the damaged main propulsion units back online. We can keep up now. May the living stars bless you for giving us the time to get the fix done, Admiral."

"Thank the living stars that the dark ships fell for the diversion, Captain," Geary replied.

He had to focus intently on his display again, watching the curving paths of the dark ships as they came around making the tightest turns their hulls could withstand. The main battleship formation of the dark ships was rearranging in midturn, merging with the two small formations on either side, then re-forming into two dark battleship formations each holding six battleships as well as nine heavy cruisers, nineteen light cruisers, and about forty destroyers. Since the dark ships boasted more weapons than typical Alliance warships, and Geary's ships bore accumulated damage from months of campaigning and too few resources for repair, each new dark battleship formation was more than a match for each of Geary's battleship formations. The dark battle cruiser formation was also stronger than Geary's battle cruiser force, with about twice the firepower.

"They don't have to hit us with multiple formations at once. I think instead they're going to try to box in one of our formations and hit it hard with one of theirs," Desjani said.

"I think you're right, but we won't let them," Geary vowed, already working up new orders to counter the moves of the dark ships. "At some point, the dark ships have to make a mistake."

He narrowly got Tango Three out of another dark ship attempt to catch that formation, tried to use the momentum of the dark battle cruisers' latest maneuver to trap them, failed as he was forced to avoid another set of moves by the dark battleships, got *Dauntless* and the other Alliance battle cruisers free of a triple attack that tried to force him into contact with one or more of the dark ship formations, swung Tango Two out of a forming trap, began to set up another attack, had to shift his battle cruisers away from that, moved Tango Three at the last moment to avoid yet another dark ship attack by all three enemy formations . . .

Geary lost track of time, completely lost in the constant dance of the three Alliance and three dark ship formations. He made a few mistakes which were minor enough to avoid disaster, but the dark ships made no mistakes, giving him no openings.

His ship commanders, as aware as Geary of how close they were to being annihilated, made no protests for once despite the lack of firing on the firing passes that always avoided getting close enough for combat when the dark ships had the advantage. And it seemed the dark ships with their superior maneuverability and firepower always had the advantage.

Geary roused himself from his intense focus on his display to become aware that Dr. Nasr was standing beside him and offering a small med patch.

"You are in need of this, Admiral," Dr. Nasr said.

"A stim patch?" Geary blinked, trying to recall when this engagement had begun. "How long have we been conducting firing passes against the dark ships?"

"You began these series of maneuvers sixteen hours ago," Dr. Nasr said, sounding composed but also unyielding. "You are required to apply a stimulant patch to maintain alertness and mental clarity. My assistants are ensuring that everyone in the crew receives a patch. All other ships are also administering stim patches."

"How long are they good for?" Geary asked.

"They will have to be renewed after eight hours. You can apply a series of six patches one after another if judged necessary given the situation, but beyond that you risk negative health and mental outcomes."

"I had to do a series of six once," Desjani said as she slapped a patch on her own arm. "I don't recommend it. Coming down from that was hell."

Sixteen hours. Geary applied his own patch, then refocused on the situation. Battles in space could be extremely long but rarely involved extremely long periods of continuous action. If nothing else, wide-ranging maneuvers would eventually buy time for an exhausted nap between firing runs.

But against the dark ships, this time it had been a seemingly endless succession of attacks, counterattacks, evasions, and lunges. One set of fast maneuvers after another, constantly straining ships and their crews.

Motivated by a sudden concern, Geary called up data on fuel cell status for his warships. "Most of our destroyers are down to thirty-five percent on their fuel cells," he told Desjani.

"That's not surprising," she grumbled. "We've been jerking around the entire fleet time and time again."

But the dark ships had been pushing themselves even harder.

Geary, who had decided at some point just to strive to keep from being beaten badly, felt a sudden glimmer of hope. The dark ships had definitely been programmed for tactics. Specifically his tactics. And Lieutenant Castries had already noted that the dark ships appeared to be using Battle Priority profile on their maneuvering solutions.

Had anyone programmed the dark ships for logistics concerns?

The ships that had hit Indras and then Atalia had used up their entire supply of bombardment projectiles, holding none back for emergencies. That implied a lack of attention to the expendable weapon supply aspect of logistics. Did the dark ships also not pay enough attention to other aspects of logistics?

And was Dr. Nasr right about what would happen if the dark ships hit a firm limit in their programming that they had not previously rationalized their way around?

Could he manage to avoid a decisive encounter for enough more time to find out?

He bent grimly to the task, avoiding each new lunge by the dark ships and attempting new attacks by his own warships, which were always frustrated. Another pass . . . another . . . six formations comprising hundreds of warships twisting and spinning through the vastness of space, each seeking the fraction of a second of advantage that it would need to inflict major damage on one of the other formations.

His commanding officers and crews continued to follow Geary's orders, continued to believe that he would find a way out of this, while he prayed that he and his ships would hold out long enough.

The moment he had dreaded finally came, after nearly twenty hours of continuous combat maneuvering.

Tango Two had been forced to nearly kill its velocity to dodge a firing pass from a dark battleship formation. Now, its warships pointing straight up and main propulsion back on full, Tango Two was trying to regain speed, while Geary tried to bring the other two Alliance formations to its aid.

But the dark battle cruisers had seen the opportunity and were pouring maximum thrust from their propulsion, as was the other dark battleship formation, and Tango Two simply did not have enough velocity to avoid their charges and did not have the time to build up that velocity.

Captain Jane Geary on *Dreadnaught* called in, her expression that of someone facing the end. "We will make them pay, Admiral. Avenge us."

"I will." He had already probably lost Michael Geary, and now Jane would die as well. Because of his decisions, both of the grandchildren of his brother dead. Because they were Gearys and forced to follow in the footsteps of Black Jack.

"The dark battle cruisers are still coming around," Lieutenant Castries said, sounding puzzled.

"Take another look," Desjani said.

"Captain, they have passed the point at which they should have held to their vector to hit Tango Two."

Geary and Desjani both sat up straighter, eyes going to the places on their displays where the dark battle cruisers were represented.

"What are they doing?" Desjani asked in disbelief.

"They're still coming about, Captain," Lieutenant Castries said, sounding as baffled as her commanding officer. "So are the dark battleships. They've also passed the vector for intercepting Tango Two."

"So is the third dark ship formation," Geary said. "Look."

"Where are they going?" Desjani demanded. "Tell me where they're going!"

Her lieutenants exchanged helpless glances.

"They're finally steadying out," Geary said. "Where is that—? Where does that vector lead?"

"Away from our formations," Desjani said. "Why would they spend twenty straight hours trying to tear us apart and suddenly head off like that? Could Admiral Bloch have suddenly regained some control of them? Did some software routine activate that caused them to stop fighting us?"

"I think it's software," Geary said. "Something the dark ships did not see coming."

"Captain," Castries said, "the three dark ship formations are all steadying onto vectors for the jump point for Montan."

"Montan?" Desjani stared at her display as if an explanation for the inexplicable could be found there. "What could they want at Montan?"

"It's the nearest jump point from where we are now in this star system," Castries pointed out. "Aside from that, the only major feature at Montan is a hypernet gate, Captain. Montan is one of the fallback star systems if Varandal had fallen to the Syndics, so it had a gate installed to allow rapid shifting of defensive forces."

"A hypernet gate?" Desjani turned a baffled gaze on Geary. "They're trying to get back to their base? Are they running away from us?"

"It looks like it," he said, fighting off an immense weariness and afraid to believe that his hope had really manifested.

"If you don't mind my saying so, Admiral, that's pretty damned miraculous for someone who claims not to have any ins with the living stars."

"There's no miracle involved," Geary said. "The dark ships are programmed for tactics, not logistics. You've all seen how hard they've pushed their maneuvers, which has also burned their fuel cells at a very high rate. Look at our own fuel cell status. Look at our destroyers."

Desjani checked the data. "Our destroyers are low. Fifteen percent on average. That's not surprising after all the dancing we did at maximum thrust over the last twenty hours. You think the dark ships broke off because of low fuel cell reserves?"

"I know they did," he said, unable to keep the triumph and elation out of his voice as the dark ships continued to head for the jump point for Montan. "Some of their ships, maybe all of their destroyers, must have gone as low as ten percent fuel cell reserves. What do fleet regulations say about that?"

Lieutenant Yuon, who had probably been studying just those

regulations for his fleet promotion standards, answered quickly. "Any formation containing warships reaching ten percent fuel cell reserves must disengage and refuel immediately."

"No exceptions, right?" Geary said.

"No exceptions, sir," Yuon agreed.

"Why would they pay attention to that?" Desjani demanded. "The dark ships shot up all of the shipping in this star system, they attacked Ambaru, they attacked Atalia, they attacked *us*. Why would they obey what fleet regulations say about fuel cell levels?"

"Dr. Nasr said the dark ships must have two ways of thinking. A set of firm instructions on what to do and what not to do, and a flexible set of programs intended to mimic human thought processes. Those flexible programs might well have allowed the dark ships to rationalize their way past limits they have encountered in the past. But Dr. Nasr said that if the dark ships ran into a new, firm prohibition, they would have a problem with it since they hadn't yet rationalized their way past it. They would have to obey that rigid instruction until they worked around it."

"Ancestors save us," Desjani said. "I guess maybe our ancestors did save us."

"They told me," Geary blurted out, too tired and excited to hide it. "With a candle flame. Dodge and keep dodging. Don't get caught."

"I keep telling you to listen to them," Desjani said. "So you saw that the dark ships were burning their fuel cells a lot faster than we were and just hoped they would run low enough before we did, and hoped that Dr. Nasr was right?"

"Pretty much, yeah."

She gazed at him wordlessly, then laughed. "We owe our miracle to fleet regulations. I will never live that down."

"Fleet regulations had to be good for something. I'll take my miracles in any form they care to appear." Geary spent a long moment contemplating his display, still absorbing the reality that his fleet would not be destroyed here. "It's tempting to try to send some ships after them, to try to follow them to their base."

"But?"

"But the dark ships would see them following. It would be far too easy for the dark ships to leave an ambush at Montan. I can't risk that."

"Ask for volunteers—" Desjani began.

"No. I will not send people to die for no purpose, no matter how enthusiastically they volunteer for the task. And all of our ships are getting low on fuel cell reserves at this point, too." Geary sighed and closed his eyes, finally letting what had happened settle into his nerves and relax them. "We've saved Bhavan. We'll follow the dark ships at a distance until they jump to Montan, then head back to Varandal."

"What if the dark ships work around the fuel cell reserve regulation before they jump for Montan?" Desjani asked.

"Then we'll be much better positioned to engage them again, and their ships will be increasingly low on fuel cell reserves. That could be our best outcome, if they turn to fight us again with their fuel nearly exhausted."

"Let's hope," she agreed. "Even the dark battleships would be helpless as their power cores shut down."

But the dark ships apparently failed to overcome their blind adherence to fleet regulations in time. They jumped for Montan half a day later, and Geary led his battered fleet back toward Varandal, ignoring the questions now streaming in from Bhavan asking whether the threat was gone and what would happen now? He didn't try to answer those questions because he had no answers.

"It sounds like things got pretty bad at Bhavan." Admiral Timbale grimaced unhappily. "We saw those dark battle cruisers pop out of the hypernet gate and charge for the jump point for Bhavan, but the only things we had close enough to intercept them were a few destroyers and one cruiser. Not wanting to lose any more ships in hopeless fights, I ordered them out of contact. Your Captain Duellos was very upset, but with two of his battle cruisers still in dock, he couldn't even chase after the dark ships."

"We survived," Geary said. He was in his stateroom aboard *Dauntless*, reviewing the damage to his ships in the long fight at Bhavan and wondering whether Captain Smythe could find the funds necessary to acquire a lot of replacement fuel cells. Timbale's call had been a welcome distraction. Geary spoke frankly to the image of the other admiral. "Which was a victory compared to what might have been."

"Well, Black Jack can't be beaten, right?" Timbale offered with an encouraging smile.

"He damn near was at Bhavan," Geary said. "They apparently built those dark ships to beat me, and, for once, the government was far too successful in achieving its goals."

"You'll find a way," Timbale said. "The living stars wouldn't have given you this challenge if they didn't think you couldn't handle it."

"In that case, I wish the living stars had a lot less confidence in me," Geary said. *Everyone says basically the same thing, that surely Black Jack will find a way to beat the dark ships. But Black Jack himself can't think of a way. I sure as hell can't beat them in a straight-up fight with what I've got.*

Timbale smiled as if uncertain whether Geary was joking, then shifted to a resigned look. "Speaking of the government, I wanted to give you a heads-up. Orders have arrived to reassign *Tsunami*, *Typhoon*, and *Haboob*."

"Why not *Mistral* as well?" Geary asked. "Why leave me with one assault transport?" Not that the assault transports were any use against the dark ships, but the transfers coming now did feel like adding insult to injury.

"I have no idea," Timbale replied.

Geary paused to check *Mistral*'s status on his fleet database. She was in as good shape as the other assault transports. There didn't seem to be any reason for her to be left at Varandal while the rest of her division of ships was sent off on another assignment. "Do you know where *Tsunami*, *Typhoon*, and *Haboob* are going?"

"Unity."

"Unity?" Geary stared at Timbale. "Why?"

"Contingency emergency evacuation force," Timbale explained. "That's what the orders say."

"Evac—?" Geary shook his head and tried to speak calmly. "They're finally taking the dark ships seriously? I guess this is a clear sign the government has lost control of them and is afraid where the dark ships will attack next. I assume that fleet headquarters told the government that every assault transport in the fleet combined wouldn't be able to lift off the population of Unity."

"You can't assume anything with headquarters, but I guess three assault transports have got enough capacity for the important people, and that's what the government was probably worried about," Timbale said. "Oh, and they're supposed to take most of your Marines with them."

"Most of my Marines? To do what, hold back the crowds trying to find space on the assault transports?"

"I don't know, Admiral." Timbale spread his hands. "This set of orders is clear-cut. You either do as ordered or you violate the order. There isn't any work-around on this one."

Geary nodded heavily. "I understand. Fine. *Tsunami*, *Typhoon*, and *Haboob* will go to Unity, along with . . . how many Marines exactly?"

"Two of your three brigades, plus their supporting elements. Two thousand, one hundred in total. General Carabali is to go with them."

"Do I get to at least choose which two brigades go and which I keep?" Geary asked.

Timbale squinted at something. "Ummm . . . no. First and Second Brigades go with the assault transports. You get to keep Third Brigade. Are you feeling the love?"

"Not at the moment." But after Timbale had ended the call, Geary sat frowning in his stateroom for a while, wondering what was really behind the orders. *The government has access to a lot more assault transports than the few I had. And a lot more Marines. Why do they want mine at Unity?*

He called General Carabali. "Have you heard about the orders for the assault transports and two-thirds of your Marines?"

"Just now, yes, sir."

"Do you have any idea why the orders designated your First and Second Brigades to go to Unity and the Third to stay here?"

"Yes, sir," Carabali replied, a slightly apologetic note entering her voice. "While you were detached, I received a request for recommendations on which of my brigades was most effective at assaults. Based on their experience and their commander, I replied that Third Brigade was the most qualified. That may be why it was designated to stay here. I sent you a notification on the matter, but with everything else going on, you might not have noted it."

"Thank you for being diplomatic about my not seeing it," Geary said. "So they're leaving me the best brigade?"

"That's a relative term, Admiral," Carabali said, a little stiffly this time. "All of my brigades are the best."

"Understood," Geary said. "And I agree with you. I should have spoken more carefully. Do you have any indication of what your mission will be at Unity?"

"No, sir."

"Thank you, General. Let me know if you need any assistance preparing for the movement of your Marines."

He sat back when the call ended, now having even more questions than before he had spoken to Carabali. *I was thinking I might need some of my Marines if I could locate the dark ship base. Someone who could seize the dark ship facilities and disable them without destroying them. I want the evidence of those facilities if anyone tries claiming the dark ships never existed or weren't official or some other nonsense.*

If I do need some Marines for that task, it sounds like the Third Brigade is the unit I would have picked. And that's the unit that is being left for me. But why do that without talking to me about it?

And it's all meaningless anyway if I don't know where the base for the dark ships is located.

Ancestors, I really, really need some help here.

The alert on his stateroom hatch announced a visitor.

9

"Admiral." General Charban displayed his now-usual attitude of trying not entirely successfully to deal with frustration. "I'm back from my stay on *Inspire*. May we speak?"

"Of course," Geary said. "Take a seat. I imagine that you're glad you weren't with us at Bhavan."

"I know something of how you must have felt, Admiral." Charban shook his head. "I was in a few ground battles where I was praying for a miracle. Fortunately, either the living stars are fond of me or chance worked in my favor. I don't think I would have been able to get my force intact out of a situation like that you faced at Bhavan, though."

"You probably would have thought of something," Geary said. "Any breakthroughs in the matter of the Dancers?" he asked, naming the alien species which resembled the unholy offspring of giant spiders and wolves, and which were the closest things to friends that humanity had found among the three alien races so far encountered. Given that the other two races, the mysterious enigmas and the homicidally aggressive (as well as cute) Kicks, were both dangerous foes, it did not take much to be friendlier toward humanity. But the Dancers, in their own, mystifying ways, did seem to regard humans as allies.

Charban sat down and shrugged. "Breakthroughs are even harder to come by with no Dancers actually present to talk to. On the other hand, I'm not dealing with vague and simplistic replies from them on a routine basis, so it could be worse."

"It could definitely be worse," Geary said. "The dark ships won't even talk to us."

"Neither would the Kicks, and the enigmas only do it when they absolutely have to. But you would think something that humans had built like the dark ships would at least give us a little respect." Charban paused, looking upward, his eyes distant. "Being left here at Varandal did have the benefit of giving me a lot of time to think, and since I didn't want to spend my time worrying about what might be happening at Bhavan, I spent it thinking about the Dancers. Specifically, about that trip they took."

"Going home, you mean?"

"No, before that. The trip the Dancers took to Durnan Star System. I didn't want to talk to other people about this because I didn't know how important it could be, and I didn't know whether you would want to keep it as quiet as possible. Can I see your star display?"

"Sure." Geary called it up, the stars floating in the air between them like jewels suspended in space.

Charban leaned toward the display and used one hand to adjust its scale and focus. "Here. Let's see. Ah. Look." Lines appeared, one branching out from Varandal, connecting some of the stars, then going back to Varandal. "This was the path the Dancers took, jumping from star to star."

"They were going to Durnan Star System to look at those ruins of an ancient Dancer colony," Geary said.

"Yes," General Charban agreed, "but aside from the question of how an ancient Dancer colony got there when it did is the question of why the Dancers took the route they did." He indicated the lines between stars again. "It wasn't as straight a path as it could have been going out, and wasn't straight at all coming back. Look how they looped around on their way back to Varandal."

Geary studied the display, intrigued. "It's almost like the fragmentary outline of a rough sphere, isn't it? Why would the Dancers have taken such a roundabout path?"

"I'm assuming they must have wanted to send us some kind of message," Charban said. "But what?"

"What message could they send with a rough spherical shape?" Geary asked. "Do the names of the star systems they visited spell out anything?"

"No," Charban said. "I think forming a coded message in the names humanity gave those stars would be even too subtle and convoluted for the Dancers. But it did occur to me that perhaps the message was not in the sphere but in what it contained."

"What it contained?" Geary looked again. The region of space inside the rough sphere defined by the path of the Dancers contained a few stars with little or no human presence and no particular reason to visit them. "There's nothing there."

"What about that?" Charban asked, pointing. "Our systems can't tell me much about it."

Geary looked closely. "You're pointing at a close binary star. I'm not surprised there is little in our systems about it. It's not really worth noticing."

"Why not?" Charban asked. He leaned over the low table between them, his extended finger almost touching the image of the binary. "Do the systems on *Dauntless* know anything more about it than I could have found elsewhere?"

Geary shook his head, frowning in puzzlement at the question. "Probably not, but since *Dauntless* is the flagship, it's possible we might have supplemental files. We know it's a close binary star system, two stars orbiting each other. Let's see if there have ever been long-distance observations of that star system." He called up the data. "Yes. It has been viewed from other star systems. That's not the most detailed way of surveying a star system, but it does pick up larger objects. That particular binary system contains six planets in eccentric orbits, most of them probably captures of wandering planets that got too close to one of the two stars. That's all we know."

"That's what I learned before." Charban nodded in agreement, but still looked confused as well. "Why is that all we know? No one has ever gone there? Why wouldn't the Dancers jump there if they were interested in it?"

"You don't know?" Geary eyed Charban in astonishment that gradually changed to comprehension. "You're ground forces. Not a sailor."

"Or a scientist. I was pondering the last message from the Dancers, you see," Charban explained. "'Watch the many stars.' And I realized that there was an alternate meaning. It could have been meant to say 'Watch the multiple stars.'"

"Multiple stars." Like binaries and the occasional triple star system. "Why would we watch them?"

"Why don't we ever go to them?" Charban asked again.

"Because we can't. Not by using jump drives. Do you know how the jump drives work?"

"Vaguely. Something about thin spots in space that the drives can take ships through into somewhere else where the distances are much shorter."

"Right," Geary said. "I'm not a scientist, either, but the basics are that space-time isn't rigid. It bends. The gravity of objects makes space-time bend or dimple, as if you put a heavy object on a flexible sheet. Big objects create big dimples. Stars are massive enough to bend and stretch space-time sufficiently to create thin spots in it. Those thin spots are jump points, places where our jump drives can push ships through into jump space and back through to get out of jump space at the next star. There's nothing in jump space except that endless gray haze—"

"And the lights," Charban added.

"And the lights," Geary conceded. No one knew what the lights were. They came and went at no discernible intervals for no discernible reasons. Sailors tended to regard them with superstition, but given that their nature remained unexplained, perhaps superstition was too prejudicial a word. The lights could conceivably represent just about anything, or Anyone. "The distances in jump space are far smaller than in our universe, as if jump space is a small fraction of the size. It may be, but since we can't see any distance in jump space, we don't know if it has limits and how small or large those limits are. But on average it only takes a week or two to get from one star to an adjacent one using jump space, where it would take ten or twenty years at a minimum on average to make that same voyage in normal space using our best technology. The important thing in answer to your question is that the thin spots, the jump points, are stable around each star, so we can find them and know they will be there when we get where we are going and when we want to come back."

"I see," Charban said, nodding and frowning in thought. "What does that have to do with not going to binary stars? With two stars close together, shouldn't they have lots of jump points?"

"Yes, and no." Geary moved his hands around each other. "When two or more star masses are orbiting each other, the dimples in space-time they cause are constantly interacting. That makes jump points around them unstable. There might be one that vanishes suddenly, then another appears elsewhere. If you detect a jump point that leads to a binary star, it might vanish before you could even jump toward it. Worse, the jump point at a binary that you are heading toward might vanish before you get there, and if that happens you can't come out of jump space."

Charban shuddered. "Like the man the Dancers returned to Old Earth?"

"Like that, maybe, yes. The ship might eventually find another jump point and return to normal space, but you've been to jump space. You know humans don't belong there and can't manage more than a couple of weeks without developing serious problems."

"Like that itchy, unnatural feeling that your skin no longer fits?" Charban asked. "Yes. The longest jump I was ever on was about two weeks, and I'm not sure I could have endured three weeks. I can understand why no one would want to risk being stuck there. That's why we've never gone to that binary star?"

"Maybe never to any binary star," Geary said. "I don't know. You'd have to either risk losing the ships you send, and there's a high probability of loss, or send the ships through normal space, which would mean a really long voyage even with current propulsion technology. There have been more than enough single stars for humanity. Hell, we've abandoned a lot of marginal star systems in the last decades because the hypernet made it easy to bypass them. With no shortage of stellar real estate, why go to the trouble of visiting a binary?"

Charban nodded. "I understand. Indulge me, Admiral. I'm not sure why, yet. What would it take to get to that particular binary star?"

Geary shrugged. "I can estimate that easily enough. Let's see. The closest star to that binary is Puerta. There's nothing much at Puerta. It's a white dwarf, but you could jump there and have less than one and a half light-years to the binary. That's pretty close as stars go. Load up on sufficient fuel, accelerate to better than point five light speed, then brake down before you get to the binary, and you could make the trip in ten years easy. Maybe significantly less than that."

"What about a hypernet gate?" Charban asked, squinting at the representation of the binary star. "Would one of those work in a binary star system?"

"I think so. I don't know why not," Geary said. "I can ask Commander Neeson on *Implacable*. The hypernet gates work using something related to quantum entanglement, totally different from the jump drives. They shouldn't be impacted by the interacting gravity fields of the two stars. But you'd have to get everything to build a hypernet gate to that star system. Aside from taking about a decade, it would be hugely expensive to build a gate to get to a place where there wasn't anything worth going to. Why do you think the Dancers would have been interested in that binary?"

"Because the Dancers all but drew a bull's-eye around that binary star! But you have no idea why they would do that?"

"No. Even they couldn't get there, apparently."

"Are we certain that there is not a hypernet gate there?" Charban asked.

"There isn't a hypernet gate for that star in our hypernet keys," Geary said. "I don't think." He touched his comm panel to call Desjani in her own stateroom. "Tanya, are any of the hypernet gates at a binary star?"

"A what?" Seated at her desk, her image focused on Geary as if trying to figure out whether he was serious. "Why would anyone build a hypernet gate at a binary star? How *could* anyone build a hypernet gate at a binary star?"

"You could send the hypernet gate components through normal space and use robotics to assemble them in the binary star system," Geary said, wondering why he was justifying the outlandish idea. "You'd probably need some humans to do the oversight and final work and calibrations, but if they didn't want to put up with a decade-long journey they could be frozen into survival sleep and then be reawakened to work on the gate. Once the gate was done, they would be able to come back immediately."

"Why would we do that?" Desjani asked. "Do you have any idea how complicated and expensive that would be?"

"Tanya, I don't know! But the Dancers seem to have tried to focus our attention on one particular binary, one that's not too far from a white dwarf that could have been a launching point for a normal-space trip to that binary."

She gave a long-suffering sigh, tapped in some commands, then shook her head. "No. There is no binary star in the destinations available to our hypernet key. Or among the destinations available to the Syndic hypernet key that we acquired."

"Do you have any ideas why the Dancers would try to focus our attention on a binary like that?"

Another sigh. "Maybe they were looking for something and thought it was hidden there."

Charban gave a derisive snort. "If someone wanted to hide something, it sounds like a binary star would be the perfect place."

Geary stared at him. "What?"

"Um, a joke, Admiral. A binary would be a wonderful place to hide something, right? No one goes there. No one can go there. You space travelers don't even think about them! I had to point that one out to you even though it was in plain sight on the display."

Tanya was gazing intently at Geary. "What are you thinking?"

"What would the Dancers be looking for?" he asked her. "Something that we know of. Something that has apparently disappeared."

"Big or little? Are we talking a person?"

"Maybe a person. Maybe something very big," Geary said, his thoughts crystallizing. "What left Varandal, by hypernet gate, and apparently vanished from human-occupied space? Something that should have been impossible to hide no matter what star system it was taken to?"

Her face lit with understanding. "*Invincible*. The Kick superbattle-ship we captured. You think the government took it to that binary?"

"Where else could they have taken it where no one could find it?" Geary demanded. "What else would the Dancers have been looking for and worried about?"

"The dark ships," Desjani said pointedly. "We need to find *their* base, and we haven't been able to find any clue—" She stopped speaking, looking stunned.

"A secret base?" Charban said, astonished. "A secret hypernet gate? I didn't think something on that scale could be possible."

"Neither would anyone else," Geary said, gazing at the depiction of the binary in his star display. "You said it yourself. No one thinks about binaries. No one can go to binaries. A binary would be the perfect place to set up a secret base, a place to hide the captured Kick battleship, a place to hide the base for the dark ships."

Tanya shook her head, holding out both hands palm forward. "Hold on. We're talking about a project that couldn't have been dreamed up in the last few years. There would have been a huge investment in time and money. They would have had to start work on this a long time ago."

"Maybe they did," Geary said.

"And kept it secret from everybody?"

"No," Geary said, looking at her now. "They couldn't keep it entirely secret. Rumors got out. People talked about it. But no one ever found it, so after enough years had gone by, it was labeled a fantasy, a project that had never actually existed."

Tanya's eyes met his. "Unity Alternate? Ancestors save us. You're talking about Unity Alternate."

"Yes. The supposedly mythical government project to build a secret, fallback base to continue the war if Unity itself fell to the Syndics. A project important enough to justify a huge expense and a construction time line of more than a decade."

"In a place no one would ever think to look," she continued for him. "A place the Syndics would never find and couldn't reach if somehow they did find it."

"And maybe more than that," Geary said. A place to set up the most secret projects, a place to hide anyone that the government, or portions of the government, didn't want found, as well as a place to homeport a secret fleet.

"How do they get there?" Desjani demanded. "There must be a way. The dark ships use the hypernet. *Invincible* disappeared after entering the hypernet. There must be keys with access to a gate at that binary."

"If there are," Geary said, "we'll find them." He turned to Charban. "General, you may have given us the most important piece of information that we needed to have. I'm in your debt."

Charban still looked dazed. "How did the Dancers know it was there? They are the ones you should thank, Admiral. This is unbelievable. First Black Jack returns, and defeats the Syndics just as he was supposed to, then Unity Alternate turns out to exist. Myths and legends are coming to life all around us."

"I was never a myth," Geary said. "And it turns out Unity Alternate wasn't either. This is all as real as those dark ships, and now we know where they are hiding."

Desjani grinned ferociously. "Destroy their base?"

"Right. That's their Achilles heel. Destroy their base, their source of replacement fuel cells, and they'll be helpless once the fuel cells they are carrying are used up. We've got a way to win, Tanya."

If they could find a way to get there. And if they could get there when the dark ships were not there as well guarding their base.

"We'll be taking the fight to the dark ships next time," Geary told the images of his ship commanders assembled in the conference room. Tanya had reminded him that he needed to talk to them, needed to let them know that he and they were not beaten. "We believe that we have identified their base. I don't know when we'll be assaulting that base, but all of your ships need to be ready to go."

"What's the delay?" Captain Badaya asked. "Why not go now?"

"It's hard to reach, and we need to find the best way to reach it. We also assume the dark ships are there now, refueling and repairing themselves. We want to give them time to finish that and leave, probably to try to set up another trap for us. While they're doing that, we'll go in and knock their feet out from under them."

"Why couldn't they have built those dark ships to go against the Syndics during the war?" Captain Armus grumbled. A low, angry murmur of agreement followed his words.

Captain Smythe answered. "The irony is that our victory in the war gave the government the breathing room to undertake such a project. Under the pressure of constant Syndic attacks, they could never divert resources to a risky project like the dark ships. But we lifted that pressure, thereby giving the government the luxury of seeing if they could replace us."

"And," Captain Duellos added, "our victory left some powerful forces in the Alliance searching for an enemy to replace the one we had finally beaten."

"Why are we doing this?" Captain Parr asked, looking depressed. "Why are we fighting again, why are our people dying again, because of the mistakes made by people who will never pay the price for their errors?"

Every eye came to rest on Geary, expecting an answer from him. "If you want my personal opinion," Geary said, "it's because we're better than those people. And if people like us don't fix the problems created by people like them, if people like us don't stand up for the core principles of the Alliance and for the people of the Alliance, who will? This is my fight, but it doesn't have to be. I 'died' a century ago. Everyone I knew then is gone. I could have washed my hands of it all. Except that I couldn't. Because, as some people never hesitate to remind me," he said, not looking at Desjani but out of the corner of his eye seeing her smile, "Black Jack has a duty to the Alliance because the people of the Alliance are depending on him. Just like they depend on all of you and your crews. Yes, it sucks to be doing this, and doing this again, but it's what we do. And I'll keep on doing it until the job is done because I think it is worth doing."

"Even now?" Parr asked, smiling wryly.

"Even now," Geary said.

"I didn't ask for a speech, but I guess a decent answer required one. All right, Admiral. Let's go clean up the mess again."

Not everyone seemed happy, plenty just appeared resigned to the prospect, but no one looked to be reluctant as Geary ended the meeting and watched the images vanishing in a flurry, the apparent size of the conference room shrinking to match the apparent number of occupants. It was the one part of meetings that Geary liked, watching the huge room dwindle into a small compartment.

One image remained. Commander Neeson, former commanding officer of *Implacable* who had moved over to assume command of *Steadfast*. "I asked you to stay on afterwards because you're my best expert on hypernet issues," Geary said. Best surviving expert, that was. Captain Jaylen Cresida had been the best, but she had died in battle when her battle cruiser *Furious* had been destroyed. "I've got an important job for you."

"I'll do my best, Admiral," Neeson said, giving a curious glance at Tanya Desjani, who merely indicated Geary again.

"We have solid reason to believe that the dark ship base is at a star holding a hypernet gate that is not on the keys carried by our ships," Geary began, watching the surprise bloom in Neeson's eyes. "I need you to look into finding that gate and a way to get to it."

"If it's not on the Alliance hypernet," Neeson began, then checked himself. "No. It would have to be. We've seen the dark ships use our hypernet gates. But that doesn't rule out a minihypernet that somehow links into our own." He frowned. "No. That couldn't work. If it was on a separate hypernet, they would have to have a place where they could go to a separate gate after leaving our own hypernet. Let me see what I can find out, Admiral. If there's a gate somewhere that is part of our hypernet, there must be some indications of that."

"Do everything you can and let me know if you run into any obstacles," Geary told him.

After Neeson's image vanished, Tanya Desjani smiled at Geary and gave a slow clap. "Nice speech, Admiral."

"Thank you, Captain. I was inspired by my audience." He looked at her and smiled ruefully. "Is it wrong that with everything else going on, I wish that you and I could take a shuttle somewhere off this blasted ship and be man and wife for just a little while instead of Admiral and Captain who cannot even touch each other?"

"Good order and discipline require sacrifices, Admiral," Desjani said. "And kindly do not refer to *Dauntless* as 'this blasted ship.' And I wish the same thing. But you and I have our jobs to do, and people to lead who would not be impressed by our taking time for ourselves when others are giving all that they have."

"Do you always have to be right?" he asked as he opened the hatch to leave the meeting compartment.

"No. I just usually am."

He entered his stateroom, feeling weary after the meeting, trying to decide which matter to try to tackle next, but immediately jerked to full attention at the sight of someone sitting in one of the chairs. His stateroom was guarded by a variety of security measures, including locks that were not supposed to let anyone in without Geary's specific approval.

The seated person stood and turned toward him. "Admiral."

Geary nodded in reply, startled and yet not surprised by who it was. "Victoria."

"Nice speech," Victoria Rione said. When he had first met her, she had been co-president of the Callas Republic and an Alliance senator. After losing a snap election in the aftermath of the war, she had been made an emissary of the Alliance, working for her former colleagues in the Alliance Senate. But he knew that assignment had ended, at least officially. Was she still covertly working for the likes of Senator Navarro? Or was Rione now a free agent, pursuing her own ends and dodging enemies made when she was working for the Alliance government?

"You were listening in?" Geary asked. "To a maximum-security conference?"

"Oh, you make that sound wrong." She waved Geary to a seat as if this were her stateroom. "Relax."

He sat down opposite her, studying Rione. She rarely revealed her inner feelings, but he could see that her eyes were slightly sunken from tiredness and her face thinner than he remembered. "You look like you've been under a lot of stress."

She leaned back, shrugging. "I'm still alive and free."

"How did you get aboard *Dauntless* and in here without setting off any alerts?"

"I left a few special apps in place in the systems of this ship before I left," Rione said, her voice casual. "It's not like enigma-stuff or that nonsense the government has been using to render ships and personnel invisible to sensors. Quite the opposite. The apps reassure anything that sees me that I am indeed authorized to be there, that I am no threat, and no reports of any kind need to be made. Being apparently authorized to be anywhere beats the hell out of hiding, let me tell you."

"Some of the crew must have seen you," Geary said.

"Of course they did. And they knew who I was, and that I had been aboard this ship before, and that I was a trusted ally of their beloved Black Jack. They may have their own suspicions of me, being that I am one of those horrible politicians, but they assumed

I was back under authorized circumstances and all of the official t's had been crossed and i's dotted." She cocked her head to one side as she regarded him. "So, how is the great hero?"

"I've been better," Geary said. "Sometimes it seems that people start fires just because they know I'll come running to put them out."

"It is fun to watch. Nobody but you could have gotten this fleet out of Bhavan in one piece, you know."

"Are you the same person who once thought I would lead the fleet to ruin? Don't forget that I got the fleet to Bhavan in the first place," he reminded her, hearing the bitterness in his voice.

"You made what seemed to be the best decision," she said. "It doesn't make sense to blame yourself for that. Take it from me. I'm an expert at blaming myself for bad decisions." Rione looked down, then back up at him under lowered brows. "Speaking of bad decisions that you haven't made, you're not going to do it, are you?"

"Do what?" he asked, even though he was pretty sure what she meant.

"Solve all of our problems by riding into Unity aboard a silver starship," Rione said. "You can save the Alliance in a heartbeat simply by announcing that you were temporarily taking charge in order to sort things out. The vast majority of the citizens and of the military would not just accept that but celebrate it."

"Save the Alliance?" Geary asked, his anger clear. "That sounds to me like destroying the Alliance in the name of saving it."

"I agree with you." She shrugged again, looking away. "That's your dilemma. The problem can be easily solved, but the solution will be worse than the problem. And you refuse to take that simple, and destructive, course of action."

"Dammit, isn't there a good option left?"

"You're asking me? The same good option there has always been. The citizens take the responsibility for voting for those who will look out for the welfare of everyone, not just their own special interests. Good luck counting on that, though. They'd prefer someone to ride in aboard that silver starship and save them the trouble."

He started to reply, then abruptly laughed. "We always look at it backwards, don't we?"

Rione raised an eyebrow at him. "Look at what backwards?"

"Democracies. Voting. People are always talking about demanding more and better performance from elected officials, but when you get right down to it, shouldn't a democracy demand more and better performance from the citizens who vote? If they do their job well, then the quality of those they elect will naturally follow."

"I suppose." She shook her head, her expression morose. "But not entirely true. The leaders have to be worthy, have to avoid the temptations of power, have to be honest even when the people don't want honesty. Democracy is a team sport, Admiral. If everyone doesn't play their position well, the whole team suffers."

He had thought himself tired out, but now stood up and began pacing restlessly. "Is that why you're here? To tell me there's nothing I can do that won't make things worse?"

"No. If nothing else, what you don't do is always important. Which means you are doing the right things. I thought you needed to hear that." Rione looked down at her hands as she intertwined her fingers in a twisting pattern. "I couldn't find him."

"Your husband?"

"Not a trace. Paol has disappeared."

Geary fought down a wave of anger. "They promised they would cure him. They promised they could lift the mental block that was put on him for security purposes, a mental block that was illegal under Alliance law, and correct the mental damage that block was causing."

"Some of them may have been sincere in their promises. Others lied. All I know is that I cannot find any clue to my husband's fate. Even if they had killed him, I should have been able to find some sign of that." She clenched her hands into fists. "I'm sure it is not a coincidence that I've been marked for disappearance by someone or something. Some part of the government that doesn't want questions asked or information revealed."

"We've encountered some agents of that," Geary said. "I've got two under detention."

Rione gave him a keen look. "And no one has shown up demanding their release?"

"Apparently, they're not supposed to exist," Geary replied. "So no one has claimed them or been willing to admit they do exist."

"That must pose an awful dilemma for someone." Rione laughed harshly. "What are you going to do, Admiral? Go on following orders like a good little officer?"

"It's that or resign," Geary said. "But, so far, there aren't a lot of orders showing up. I can't be sure, but I think the government has tied itself in a knot over the dark ships. They don't want to admit they built the dark ships, they don't want to admit the dark ships are running amuck, they don't want to admit my available ships are weaker than the surviving dark ship force. They're not throwing up barriers, not telling me I can't deal with the dark ships in any way necessary to stop them, but they seem to be hoping I'll just do that as part of my standing orders to defend the Alliance."

She smiled. "Isn't it amazing how many very powerful people confronted with an adverse outcome suddenly find themselves unable to do anything? How they suddenly declare themselves powerless? You're going to stop the dark ships, then? How?"

It was his turn to shrug. "You said that you listened in to the conference."

"Yes. A secret base. One you apparently cannot reach." Rione pondered that. "I have to admit that you have a better plan so far than I do. I know that I'm going to find my husband, that I'm going to make those responsible pay, but I am currently at a total loss for the details on how to do that." She looked around. "Didn't you used to keep wine in here?"

"Not at the moment." Geary regarded her, resting his chin on his interlaced hands, and decided to confide completely in Rione. "What do you know about Unity Alternate?"

Rione paused, then shot a sharp look his way. "A myth, I thought, though there were some classified programs and expenditures I became aware of during the war that led me to wonder about that."

"They never briefed you on it?"

"Me?" Rione asked. "I may have been a senator of the Alliance, and co-president of the Callas Republic, and briefly a member of the grand council, but I was also a citizen of an allied power, not a citizen of the Alliance itself. There were things I was never officially told but learned about anyway. I have no idea how many things there were that I wasn't told about and never found out about. Are you saying that you've actually found Unity Alternate?"

"We think we know where it is, and we think we know why no one has ever been able to find it. But we don't know everything that might be there," Geary added. "Anything you can suggest would be useful."

She spent nearly a minute thinking, her eyes now focused on a far corner. "Supposedly enough to keep the government and the military running if Unity fell to the Syndics. That's the long-running legend, anyway. But however many people they planned for if the worst happened, there can't be that many there on a routine basis. They couldn't keep the secret if masses of people were being shuttled in and out."

"A skeleton crew running things?"

"That's what I would guess."

"It has occurred to me that other things beside the dark ships, other people, could be hidden at Unity Alternate," Geary said.

Rione inhaled slowly and deeply, her only external reaction to the news. "People whose existence elsewhere would create problems? That's very insightful, Admiral. That is where my husband must be. The one place I haven't looked, because I didn't think it really existed."

"We think *Invincible* is there as well. It has also disappeared without a trace."

"The alien battleship? Something that massive would be very, very hard to hide. All right, do you want me to beg? Where is it?"

"At a binary star system," Geary said. "Not too far from here as interstellar distances go."

She gazed back at him, then laughed softly. "Oh, they were clever. How did you figure it out?"

"The Dancers practically drew a bull's-eye on it for us."

"I owe them." Rione smiled winningly at him. "You're going there?"

"We're going there. To destroy the dark ship base."

"And how, Admiral Black Jack, do you intend justifying attacking Unity Alternate?" Rione asked.

He spread his hands. "As far as we can determine, Unity Alternate has been occupied and is being used by a hostile force. The only way to save Unity Alternate is . . ."

"To destroy it?" Rione smiled again. "Please let me come along and assist in your efforts."

Geary smiled back. "You'd come along whether I said you could or not, wouldn't you?"

"I'd find a way, yes."

"Then I'd much rather have you out in the open, where I can keep my eyes on you. I'll notify the commanding officer of *Dauntless* that you're aboard again and need a stateroom."

"And won't she be thrilled to hear that."

"Actually," Geary said, "she's been worried about you and your husband."

Rione twisted her mouth and looked off at an angle. "Despite everything."

"She doesn't like you or trust you much, but Tanya doesn't like seeing people hurt."

"Unless she's the one hurting them, you mean? With some large weapon?" Rione sighed. "I'm a rotten bitch. I use people. I don't know why anyone should care what happens to me."

"You've got some redeeming qualities," Geary said. "I know you deserve better than you've received from the Alliance. And I mean to do what I can to make things right."

"The Alliance . . . the Alliance is more than some of the people who claim to represent its interests. I'll take care of making things right, Admiral. Just get me where I can find my husband, and where I'm within reach of some of those who decided they had the right to play God with his life and mine."

"I'll do my best," Geary said. "If you have any sources who can help us find out how to access the hypernet gate that must be at Unity Alternate, it would help get us all there."

"I'll do everything I can." Rione stood up, her eyes downcast. "I long since gave up on the idea that common decency existed in most people, and I . . . don't tend to make friends easily. I don't know entirely why you are helping me, but I do appreciate it. Thank you."

Geary smiled sardonically at her even though he felt the pain coming off Rione. He knew she wouldn't want sympathy, wouldn't want any acknowledgment that she had betrayed vulnerability. "To be honest, Madam Co-President, Senator, Emissary, you do make some friends. Not easily, but it happens occasionally despite your best efforts."

Rione laughed. "We've come a long ways, Admiral. Now let's go to Unity Alternate. But first, I happen to know there's another visitor on the way for you, due here tomorrow."

"Who?" Geary asked.

"Someone important. She might even have what you and I most want at this moment."

10

The next day, Geary was not surprised to get a call from Admiral Timbale asking him to stop by Ambaru Station for a vaguely defined liaison conference. Timbale met him at the shuttle dock, waved away the Marines and soldiers providing security for Geary and Timbale, and led the way deeper inside Ambaru, along passageways that had a curious absence of other pedestrians. "How does everything look?" Timbale asked as they walked. "There's something I wanted to show you," he added before Geary could respond.

Timbale offered a stream of remarks about the status of Ambaru and the forces at Varandal under his command, but nothing of great consequence. Geary tried to restrain his curiosity as he walked with Timbale into an area of Ambaru he thought he recognized.

They came to a stop before a high-security hatch that Geary knew he had seen before. Outside of it stood several special forces ground troops, none of them armored but all carrying weapons, and all alert in the manner of men and women trained to be aware of their surroundings and any potential threat.

"Who's in there?" Geary asked.

"No one," Timbale replied. "I thought you might want to go inside for a few minutes, though." He leaned close and murmured more of an explanation. "There's no one in there, but the person who isn't in there has come here to speak to you."

"I see," Geary said. "I guess I'll take a look around in there, then." One of the special forces soldiers opened the hatch without looking inside, then saluted as Geary walked in.

There was one person sitting in the room that supposedly contained no one. Geary stood still as the hatch sealed behind him. "Senator Unruh. I've seen you before, but we haven't formally met before this."

Unruh smiled briefly. "We still haven't met. I'm not here." Her eyes challenged him to debate the point.

Instead, he nodded again. This sort of thing would have flummoxed him once, but after his experiences in the last year, he had learned to roll with whatever happened until he figured out why it was happening. "You're not here. Why isn't Senator Navarro or Senator Sakai not here?"

"Because they're both seen as tied to you," Unruh explained, leaning back in her seat. "Yes, even 'Slick' Sakai, who as a rule keeps his every thought and preference carefully concealed, has betrayed what can only be described as trust in Admiral Black Jack Geary. I, on the other hand, have only personally seen you once, during that interrogation of you by representatives of the grand council, and I have never exchanged messages with you. No one is watching me to see if I am sneaking away to talk to the great Black Jack instead of sneaking away to plot my political future with rich and influential donors whose identities are best kept hidden."

"Why are you not here instead of plotting with those donors?" Geary asked.

"Because most of those donors don't actually exist in my case, and because we, the Senate, have created a monster, and you are just about our only hope for dealing with it," Unruh explained.

"The dark ships?"

"Yes. The dark ships, as you call them. The product of an entire covert structure that made that construction program possible and allowed it to be hidden. A covert structure that has proven unexpectedly hard to direct." She grimaced. "It shouldn't have been unexpected. Over the last several decades, the Alliance government built something that was designed to operate invisibly. It's gotten so good at that we can no longer be certain what it is doing."

"They're not required to report to anyone?"

"Different theys are indeed required to report to different someones," Unruh agreed. "But it has only recently occurred to a variety of senior officials that they have no way of knowing whether or not those organizations are indeed making the reports they are supposed to make. I know what I've been told about my own piece of that covert pie, but there is no means for me to learn whether I've been told all I should have been or what else is happening outside of my supposed oversight."

"Can't you demand answers?" Geary said. "Fire people who don't provide the answers?"

Unruh leaned forward, resting her elbows on the table and gazing at Geary. "I have more than sufficient grounds for assuming that some of those people already regard me as one of the enemies their organizations were designed to protect the Alliance against. If I go after them, I don't know what might happen."

"Then there has already been a coup against the government," Geary said angrily. "Who is giving the orders at Unity?"

"The Senate will be, soon enough, as we should have been all along. Why do you think the government wanted not just most of your assault transports but also most of your Marines, Admiral? It wasn't because we wanted to disarm you." Unruh smiled, a baring of her incisors that held no humor at all. "On the contrary. It finally occurred to enough people in high places that the people they have been worried about, the front-line combatants who long ago decided the Alliance government was a big part of the problems they faced, are actually among the people we can completely trust. You have provided a powerful example of support for the government. We know that your Marines will follow orders from the government."

"Lawful orders," Geary said.

"Absolutely," Unruh agreed. "To put it bluntly, we want those Marines to protect the government against some of the other forces we created in the name of protecting the Alliance. When we move against the people who misled us as to the programs we were approving, and who have acted with far too much autonomy under the veils of excessive secrecy, we want those Marines guarding us and our offices."

"You've finally figured out that they aren't the enemy?" Geary asked. "That I'm not the enemy?"

"We've spent a century at war, Admiral," Unruh said. "A century of fear and death and attacks and reprisals and a foe who would do anything except stop fighting us. After a while, everyone and everything looks dangerous. I want your promise, your word of honor, that you will follow lawful orders and will not move against the government."

Geary scowled at the senator. "Why do I need to do that? How many times have I said exactly that in public and to representatives of the government? How many times have I clearly demonstrated that I would follow orders and support the government?"

"You have done that," Unruh conceded. "But I ask for the affirmation once again because there are still some who fear you. I apologize for the implied insult to your honor. I apologize to your ancestors, who are also insulted by the implication that you would act in a dishonorable manner. Will you give me that statement?"

"I'll give it to you. Will they listen this time?"

"Let's hope so." Unruh rubbed her mouth, then focused back on him. "We need you to stop them. The Defender Fleet."

"That's the official name of the dark ships?" Geary asked.

"Yes. Can you do it? I've seen some reports from Bhavan."

"My fleet very nearly got destroyed at Bhavan." He saw the worry flare in Senator Unruh's eyes. "The dark ships outnumber my own forces, they're brand-new where my warships have seen a lot of damage which I have never had the money, time, or resources to get completely repaired, I have only received a few replacements for the losses the fleet has suffered, and the artificial intelligences running the dark ships are programmed specifically to counter me. Since Bhavan, I have been unable to come up with any battle scenario in which my fleet can triumph without being practically wiped out itself."

"You must have a plan. You're Black Jack."

"I've never been the imaginary hero the government created to inspire its people," Geary said. "I do have a plan, but it's risky. We're going to try to destroy the base of the dark ships, deny them the means to repair and resupply themselves, then try to fend off any more attacks until their fuel cells are exhausted. But for that to work, we have to figure out how to get to that base, then hit that base while the dark ships are elsewhere."

"You know where the base is?" Unruh asked.

"We're pretty certain," Geary said. "I could use confirmation. I could also use a means to get there."

She reached out and touched controls, bringing the star display to life between them. Unruh moved one finger to indicate the binary star system. "Here."

Geary nodded. "That was our guess."

"You found Unity Alternate? I'm impressed. I was anticipating a long and difficult discussion to get you to believe that was where you needed to go."

"I already had that discussion. Otherwise, you might have had trouble convincing me. To be honest, the Dancers pointed us there."

"The Dancers." Senator Unruh looked at Geary for several seconds. "Do you know why?"

"No. How do I get my fleet to Unity Alternate?"

"Through the hypernet." Unruh extended her other hand, showing that it held a data coin. "This has the code for the gate at Unity Alternate. It will allow the hypernet keys on your warships to access that gate."

Geary took the coin, studying it. "I've been told that once a key was created, it could not be altered. How can this input a new gate?"

"It doesn't. Ever since the gate was constructed at Unity Alternate, all Alliance hypernet keys have contained the data for that gate. But the data was blocked, concealed from the key controls. The code I'm giving you will simply allow your keys to finally see that gate data and give you the option of going there." She gestured in the general direction of Syndic space. "It had to be designed that way. If the government had ever retreated to Unity Alternate to keep the war going, any surviving Alliance warships would have had to be able to get there as well. The capability has been built in, to be activated if and when it was needed."

"And now it is," Geary said, carefully putting away the coin. "But not because of the Syndics."

"No." Unruh made an angry gesture. "Self-inflicted wounds."

"What can you tell me about Unity Alternate? What exactly is there?"

Unruh made a casting-away gesture this time. "I don't know. There have been some extremely large construction projects hidden within the covert programs budget. Other work was done before my time and has since been buried in the mass of classified data that threatens to swallow the Alliance whole. There will be some orbiting facilities for a skeleton government to operate. How big are they? It depends upon what was demanded decades ago. It could be an orbiting city. Probably less than that, though, but still substantial. One of your tasks, if you can achieve it given the threat of the dark ships, is to find out everything that orbiting facility has been and is being used for, and what information is available in its databases."

"It's that bad?" Geary asked. "The government doesn't know what's going on there?"

"We don't know whether we know, Admiral." Senator Unruh appeared to be embarrassed to admit that. "It's a big, big galaxy, and even though the Alliance occupies a pretty small portion of that galaxy, it still is immensely large by any human scale. The Alliance government expanded rapidly under the pressure of the war. With so many people, so many organizations and bureaus and offices and commands, in so many star systems, under constant attack and threat of attack by the Syndics, and the inevitable time lags involved in trying to coordinate and control events across so many light-years, the proverbial bubble broke a long time ago. We're going to try to put it back together again, but it is a mammoth task."

"I understand," Geary said. "I just have to worry about orbiting facilities? There are no habitable planets there or installations on the six planets in that star system?"

"Not according to my information. That is hardly definitive, however." The senator bent her lips in a sardonic smile. "I actually encountered one individual who refused to confirm or deny the existence of habitable planets at Unity itself."

Geary stared at her in disbelief. "It's common knowledge that there are two habitable worlds at Unity. Everyone knows that. It's in every star guide."

"Which did not impress that individual in the least, Admiral. Just because everyone knows something that is supposedly classified is no grounds for reconsidering whether it should be classified." Unruh looked like she wanted to punch someone, then cleared her expression and focused back on Geary. "Ancestors alone know how much else has been classified. Now, back on topic. In the past, the government would have also built support facilities at Unity Alternate for whichever Alliance warships survived to join the government there. Important supplies would have been stockpiled there. We deliberately left you with the portion of your assigned Marines who would be best at storming the facilities at Unity Alternate if that proved necessary, as it has, and believe me, working that out without anyone's figuring out our intent was not easy. We have no idea what sort of defenses might be at those facilities, but we are fairly certain there is no actual military presence."

She paused. "We think we have shut off resources and information intended for the Defender Fleet, but we can't be certain they will not somehow hear of plans against them. I wish I could offer more assurances on that, but I can't, not until we move at Unity, and there is a strong suspicion that our moves at Unity could trigger a Defender Fleet move against us. We're hoping you can prevent that.

"Since Unity Alternate is the home base for the Defender Fleet, you can assume the facilities there have been automated to the maximum possible extent. There are strong indications the Defender Fleet was designed to operate totally autonomously for an extended period, without depending on human support at any level."

Geary bit back his first words, carefully recasting them before speaking. "Do you know whose idea it was to cut humans out of the loop?"

"It seems to have been a group consensus," Unruh replied. "Various contractors were wildly enthusiastic at the idea, complete with assurances that nothing could go wrong. What those assurances were worth we learned when our auditors discovered fine print in their contracts that, once translated from lawyer-speak, said if anything *did* go wrong it wouldn't create any legal liability for the contractors. Your own fleet headquarters was also eager to embrace the idea. As their decision paper put it, totally automated systems would eliminate problems with field commanders who sometimes failed to execute their orders as given."

"You can't have field commanders thinking for themselves, now can you?" Geary said.

"Apparently not. But I think the main concern of your fleet headquarters was personnel costs. You have no idea how huge the budget is that the Alliance Senate deals with, and how huge the military personnel costs are within that budget."

"Why is spending on equipment an investment and spending on people a cost? I've always thought that personnel expenses should be considered investments as well, not costs," Geary said. "Calling them costs creates the image that it is just money being thrown away because we have no choice. But that money is an investment in the people who make all of the difference in effectiveness and efficiency and everything else."

The senator raised her eyebrows at him. "That's an interesting word choice. And a worthwhile argument for future budgets. In terms of commitments we already face, retirement hasn't been that big an expense given that relatively few personnel survived long enough to retire," Unruh added bitterly, "but existing medical costs are immense. The citizens of the Alliance clamoring for reduced spending don't realize how much of that spending has to go to helping those who gave pieces of themselves to defending us."

"Have you told them?" Geary asked. "Has anybody gone to the

citizens and said here is why we need this money, here is who it has to go to, this is why we owe it to them?"

Senator Unruh looked at Geary, then shook her head. "I doubt it. Oh, I've had senators hitting me up to know where the money is going because they weren't read into the Defender Fleet program and couldn't understand how much funds that money-sink has been eating up. Those automated systems have devoured more and more of the budget as costs and complexities mounted. But no one has been beating my door down demanding that we spend more money on people. I promise you I will make that case myself."

"I need money here, too," Geary said. "My people are scrambling to find the funds needed to keep repairing my damaged ships, and even to keep day-to-day operations going."

"That's ridiculous. Your fleet headquarters has said nothing about that but has requested extra funds to expand their own offices and operations. They claim that as force levels shrink, the staff must grow to deal with the additional challenges," she added wryly.

Geary inhaled deeply, considering his next words carefully. "That's an interesting perspective on priorities," he finally said.

Unruh smiled. "Isn't it? Senator Sakai suggested that if artificial intelligences would make effective replacements for field commanders, they would probably do even better as replacements for headquarters commanders. For some reason, that proposal was not enthusiastically received at fleet headquarters."

"I can't imagine why not."

"It is a mystery," Senator Unruh said. "I promise you there will be a supplemental appropriation introduced specifically for your fleet when I get back."

Geary regarded her closely. "Can I trust you, Senator?"

She smiled again though only slightly this time. "I hope so."

"Do you have all the answers?"

"Me?" Unruh laughed. "That would be nice. I'm looking for the answers. I'm asking questions. I'm trying to figure out where we go from here."

"Then I think I can trust you," Geary said. "Most of my problems seem to originate with people who are certain they know all the answers. Will you need an escort back to Unity?"

"As you saw outside of this room, I have some special forces accompanying me on what is officially a training mission," Unruh said. "My ship is old but can outrun anything in space, I'm told. It was designed specifically to help senators and other high officials get away fast when necessary. Part of the Unity Alternate program, apparently, though I imagine that more than one senator thought it could come in handy in other circumstances. You weren't offering to escort me back with your fleet, were you?"

Geary shook his head. "It would be very bad imagery, I think, for Black Jack to show up at Unity with a fleet."

"Very bad imagery," Senator Unruh agreed. "We want to forestall a covert coup, not make it look like an overt coup is taking place. Besides, all of those warships would make my return far too high-profile for what is supposed to be a very low-profile mission. One last thing. We believe that the dark ships are focused on you."

"I've noticed that," Geary said. "The dark ships' tactics at Bhavan confirmed it. They want to destroy the First Fleet, but they also want me dead."

Unruh shook her head, looking off to one side. "I have reason to believe that you were programmed into a contingency target set that might have activated without proper authorization, but I suspect there are private reasons as well for your personally being a priority objective."

"Admiral Bloch?" Geary asked.

"He got command of the Defender Fleet," she said, "as I understand you were already told. Bloch still has, or still had, some powerful political backers. But I have been unable to confirm his current status."

"Do you think Bloch has effective control of the dark ships? I've seen them doing things that I didn't think Bloch would order."

"I think he has influenced them to some extent. But I am certain he's not in control now if he ever really was." The senator gazed directly at Geary. "There is more than one way to neutralize a threat, Admiral. Some people wanted Admiral Bloch in a certain position because they hoped to benefit from that. But others of us intended all along that Bloch would be neutralized by giving him what he thought he wanted. He might still be alive, but if so, he is likely more miserable than when the Syndics had him. That's ironic, isn't it? He has all of space available to the warship he is aboard, but his compartments on that warship might form a very small prison from which there may be no escape."

Geary looked back at her, appalled. "What if you're right about that? Does even Bloch deserve such a fate?"

Senator Unruh stood up, sighing. "He got what he wanted, Admiral. If it isn't what he thought it would be, that's his own fault. And a useful lesson to anyone else who thinks pursuit of power is the path to happiness."

"Where does the pursuit of power lead?" Geary asked as they waited for the hatch to open.

She gave him an amused look. "You care what I think? All right, then. Trying to accomplish something that requires someone to pursue power leads toward that something. But the pursuit of power as an end in itself doesn't lead anywhere. It's like someone walking on the surface of a Mobius strip. They go up and down and over and around, but they never reach a destination. They just keep walking, and wondering why they never get anywhere no matter how far and fast they walk."

"Thank you, Senator."

"For what? Letting you know just how badly we've screwed up and how much we're counting on you to fix things?"

Geary shook his head. "No. For giving me proof that my faith in the government is not entirely misplaced."

She stepped out to join the special forces soldiers, who began forming an escort around the senator. But Unruh turned to look back at Geary, her expression somber. "You do me too much honor, Admiral. I will do what I can to live up to your faith."

Admiral Timbale waited until Senator Unruh and her escort had disappeared around a corner before turning a questioning look on Geary. "How did the meeting go?"

"What meeting?" Geary asked.

"Right." Timbale walked alongside Geary in the opposite direction from that Senator Unruh and her escort had gone. "Is there anything I should know?"

Geary pondered what he could say. "We're not alone."

"Exactly who is we?"

"The good guys." Geary smiled crookedly at Timbale. "Right?"

"I sure hope so." Timbale walked a few more steps. "Do you still have those two agents aboard *Dauntless*?"

"Yes. Why?"

"I still want them shot, remember?" Admiral Timbale glanced around, then checked a security device on his wrist to ensure they could not be overheard. "I have been apprised of subtle indications that someone is nosing around, trying to figure out what we might have learned from those agents."

"We'll make sure security around their cells remains tight," Geary said. "Anything else?"

"I received classified orders to locate former Alliance senator Victoria Rione. There are people who want to talk to her."

"Which people?" Geary asked.

"I can't tell. That's left fairly vague in the orders," Timbale explained. "For that matter, just who originated the orders was left fairly vague. Which is why I haven't been overly worried about trying to locate Rione."

"It sounds like some other people are worried," Geary said.

"I certainly would be if I were one of those responsible for what happened to her husband." Timbale rubbed his nose. "By the way, my security people, the ones I trust, said they had found some odd anomalies in our security routines, some additional covert applications that could have allowed someone like Victoria Rione to pass through Ambaru as recently as a day or two ago without any alerts being sounded."

"Really?" Geary asked.

"Yes. If she comes onto Ambaru again, she would be spotted."

Timbale gave Geary a bland look. "I thought you should know."

"Thank you. I think you should know that a lot of things may be coming to a head soon."

"In a good way?"

"Maybe." Geary paused and faced Timbale, speaking in formal tones. "If we don't meet in person again, I want you to know it has been an honor and a pleasure serving with you."

Timbale replied with equal formality. "The honor and the pleasure have been mine. Good luck, Admiral. Does this mean it's on?"

"It soon will be."

Tanya was waiting in *Dauntless*'s shuttle dock when he got off the shuttle. "I hope your visit to Ambaru was worth the risk," she said.

"Yes, it was. And in any case, I can't live aboard *Dauntless*," he told her.

"Why not?"

Instead of replying to that, he held up the data coin that Unruh had given him. "We have orders, from the government, and we have the means to get to Unity Alternate."

"Orders?" Desjani asked, instantly suspicious at mention of the government. "Orders to do what?"

"To take Unity Alternate."

"The government has ordered us to take the government's secret, fallback capital?"

"It's a long story," Geary said. "But, basically, just like the Alliance military adopted some practices in the name of winning the war that weren't really consistent with winning or with what the Alliance was supposed to be about, so did the government."

"So we're saving the Alliance?" Desjani asked.

He gave her a flat look, knowing that she was referring to the legend that Black Jack would return to "save the Alliance." "Yes."

"Good. I just wanted to be clear on that. When do we roll?"

"I need to check the status of our repair work and resupply," Geary said, "but the same concerns apply as before. We need to give the dark ships enough time to resupply and leave their base again. Another week, at least, I think."

She gave him a cautionary look. "They'll come after you again. If we wait too long, they may show up here."

That was an ugly thought. "You're right. Let's find out if we can get moving within a week."

Once at his stateroom, Geary called Captain Smythe. "One week. I want everything out of dock and ready to go."

"Admiral, I want . . . never mind. I can make it happen, but not everything is going to be done. You're still facing the possibility of system failures on your ships, just like that main propulsion unit that failed on *Fearless* at Bhavan."

"I understand. Make it happen."

"Aye, aye, sir. As far as funding goes . . ."

"I have it on very good authority that the funding we need will materialize soon," Geary said. "Through official channels."

Smythe looked impressed. "How did you manage that?"

"I asked nicely."

Despite Senator Unruh's warning that the dark ships might still be getting information about what Geary was doing, there was no way to hide the preparations necessary for an offensive using the entire force remaining to First Fleet. But he still took some extra efforts to conceal one aspect of that offensive, personally summoning two officers to his stateroom on *Dauntless* rather than risking using a comm channel that could be tapped into.

In person, Marine Colonel Rico wore the same serious expression as his official portrait. The commanding officer of the Third Brigade stood at attention, giving the impression that he never really relaxed. It wasn't a nervous sort of tension but rather the kind of alertness that assumed every moment required full attention lest something important be missed. In someone who lacked confidence in themselves and others, that would have produced a twitchy, perpetually fearful boss who made life hell for everyone under them. But Rico conveyed a sense of assurance that made his constant watchfulness reassuring rather than worrying.

Beside him stood Commander Young, captain of the assault transport *Mistral*. Much more casual in her bearing than Rico, she gave the impression of having dealt with Marines often enough to regard them with weary exasperation.

Like many of Geary's officers, they seemed far too young for their ranks. A century ago, he had been accustomed to a peacetime military, with promotions coming fairly slowly and requiring years of time in each rank. But the long and recently ended war had enforced its own requirements, the deaths of more senior officers often requiring rapid promotions of junior officers to fill in the gaps.

Geary waved Rico and Young to take seats. "We're facing a difficult problem."

"What do you need the Marines to do, Admiral?" Rico asked, sitting with the same straight posture he used when standing.

"Where do you need us to take the Marines so they can do something?" Commander Young asked, drawing a sidelong, amused look from Rico.

Geary sat down opposite the two officers. "You've both just done the first thing I need by showing me you've got the right attitudes for the job. What have you heard about the dark ships?"

"Everything that's been put out by you, sir, but nothing based on experience. We weren't along during the fights at Atalia and Bhavan, and we only saw one side of the battle here at Varandal." Rico nodded outward. "And we've heard the rumors that are going around."

"Which aren't good," Young added. "I've talked to some friends on other ships who have engaged the dark ships, Admiral. Everybody says they're tough."

"They are," Geary said. "We've found the dark ships' base, though, and we know how to get to it."

Young fixed her eyes on Geary. "And that's why you need an assault transport." She made the words a statement, not a question.

"There will likely be a big orbiting facility at the star the dark ships are operating from. It will be designed for command and control, housing large numbers of people, and supporting a wide variety of functions."

"Facility assault," Rico said, nodding. "Third Brigade can do that. There's just the one facility?"

"There are likely to be a lot of other orbiting structures, but they will be support facilities for the dark ships. Docks and warehouses, primarily. It's possible that anyone still on those facilities are trapped there. It might be a hostage rescue or evacuation under fire situation. It will also be an intelligence collection mission, acquiring any and all information available in the storage systems at the facilities. General Carabali told me Third Brigade is the best, no matter what we encounter."

Rico nodded again. "What intel are we looking for, sir?"

"Everything and anything. This isn't for me. The government constructed those facilities, lost control of them, and wants to know what has been going on there."

"Yes, sir." The Marine did not seem the least bit surprised that the government would not know what was going on at a government facility.

"How many evacuees, Admiral?" Young asked. "If *Mistral* is loaded with assault troops, she won't have much room for new riders."

"I don't know," Geary said. "I'd like to have an empty assault transport along with us as well. But at the moment, *Mistral* is all I have."

Commander Young sat silently for a few moments, her eyes gazing intently into space. "It depends on the numbers, sir. There are ways to pack in a lot more bodies and give life support a temporary boost to handle the load. No one will be happy, but we can double up as long as it doesn't last too long. However, the only way to be sure we can carry a lot of people out is to leave some space aboard."

"Which would mean limiting how many Marines were aboard," Colonel Rico objected.

"I've only got so much room on the bus," Young said. "Even if we go standing room only, I can't just keep packing people in without overloading life support and the air inside the ship going toxic. I assume you grunts want to keep breathing?"

"We're sort of fond of breathing," Rico agreed.

"I understand that we want all of the Marines we can bring," Geary said. "But we'll only bring two of your battalions, Colonel. The rest of the space on *Mistral* will be left free for emergency evacuees. There's a chance the number of evacuees could still exceed *Mistral*'s maximum capacity, in which case we'll transfer people onward to some of the larger warships."

"Under fire?" Young asked.

"Possibly under fire," Geary confirmed. "I know that's far from ideal circumstances."

"I have shuttle pilots who will volunteer to carry out the transfers under fire," Rico said.

Commander Young snorted. "Funny how Marines never have trouble finding volunteers."

"Marine sergeants are very persuasive," Rico said. "Admiral, I would really like to have a better idea of what we'll be facing in the way of a threat. I know what the dark ships can throw at us, but what kind of infantry threat will there be?"

"I don't think we'll face soldiers," Geary said. "What little we know indicates no military presence. Maybe paramilitary or heavily armed security forces."

"Heavily armed security forces? Do you mean like police action teams, or something like Syndic Vipers?" Rico asked, citing the fanatical special forces that worked for the Syndicate Worlds' Internal Security Service.

"I don't know," Geary said. "Does the Alliance have anything like Vipers?"

"There are rumors, sir, but I don't know of anyone who has ever seen anything like that."

"Good. I don't think something like that could have been kept completely secret. If no one has ever seen it, it probably doesn't exist." Geary realized that was a pretty weak argument during a discussion about attacking Unity Alternate but decided not to address that point. "Here's the other hard part. Whoever we encounter may believe that they are defending the interests of the Alliance."

Young and Rico both stared at Geary. Rico recovered first. "We might have to fight Alliance forces?"

"That's very unlikely," Geary said. "As we saw at Ambaru, even when given misleading data, Alliance ground forces soldiers did not want to engage Alliance Marines, and the information I have is that no regular military forces should be at the dark ship base. But a paramilitary force might be there and might have orders to resist us. If we encounter that situation, Colonel Rico, I need to know that you can defuse it if possible but take out anyone who actively tries to prevent you from carrying out your mission."

He looked over at Commander Young. "And if any of the dark ships are present when we hit their base and realize what you intend, they will try to take you out. It's going to be hazardous as hell. If the dark ships decide to make a priority target of you, it is possible that I will have a very hard time keeping them off you. You have the right to know that."

Young grinned. "We're used to that, Admiral. Haven't you heard the joke that AT doesn't stand for Assault Transport, but rather Active Target?"

"Sir," Colonel Rico said, "we'll get the job done. This is about defending the Alliance, right?"

"I promise you that it is," Geary said. "I have orders from the highest levels for this operation."

"Then we'll get the job done as long as the bus gets us there."

Commander Young gave him an arch look. "The bus will get your freeloaders there. After that, it will be up to you Marines to pay for the ride."

"We'll earn our fare," Rico said. "We got this, Admiral."

"Excellent," Geary said. "We have some emergency repairs that have to be completed on some of the warships, so the departure date for the assault will be about a week from now. Have your ship and your Marines ready."

"We could go within twenty-four hours, sir," Commander Young said. "As long as the Marines are ready to load. We're already preloaded with most of their equipment."

"Twenty-four hours," Rico agreed.

After they had left, Geary checked the latest updates on maintenance and supply. *Formidable* was the last battle cruiser still in dock and would be getting pushed out on an emergency basis the next day. *Fearless* would have all of her main propulsion systems in working order within thirty-six hours, under threat of being left behind when the fleet moved. The shameful possibility of being the only battleship to miss the upcoming fight had driven the crew of *Fearless* and the maintenance personnel working with them to superhuman efforts to ensure the job was done.

Admiral Timbale was emptying the supply centers at Varandal of every fuel cell available. It wouldn't be enough on such short notice to top off all of the warships, but only the battleships and battle cruisers would be at less than one hundred percent starting out. There were also frustrating shortages of specter missiles, and even a baffling shortfall in grapeshot. "They're just ball bearings!" Geary had protested. "Round pieces of metal! How hard can it be to make more of them?" But other priorities had interfered, so some of the warships would be heading out with less than full shot lockers.

The good news in terms of food supplies was that there had been plenty of ration bars available to be loaded onto the ships to provide meals during battle situations. The bad news was that nearly every crate was made up of the infamous Danaka Yoruk bars, which had apparently been stockpiled to feed to Syndic prisoners of war who had then unexpectedly been released into the custody of representatives of the Midway Star System. Geary took under serious consideration Desjani's suggestion that they use the Danaka Yoruk bars as substitutes for the inadequate supply of metal grapeshot.

Exhausted by going over the status reports, expediting what needed to be expedited, delaying what could be delayed, making sure the right people were in the right positions, planning for what would be done at Unity Alternate, and coordinating actions, Geary finally managed to sleep.

"Admiral!"

Geary bolted awake, shocked by the urgency in the summons. He sat up in his bunk, slapping the nearest comm panel. "Here. What's happened?"

"They— They're back, sir!"

11

"Who is back?" Geary roared with what he thought was an immense amount of patience. Only the fact that the caller sounded surprised rather than scared, which is what he would have expected if those who were back were the dark ships, kept him from bolting for the bridge without waiting for further explanation.

"The Dancers, sir. A lot of them."

"The *Dancers*?" That was the last thing he had expected to hear. Geary called up the display in his stateroom and stared at the image before him.

Forty Dancer ships had arrived in Varandal. Arrived at the jump point from Bhavan. The perfect ovoids of the Dancer ships gleamed against the black backdrop of space. They were arranged in an intricate formation that made them resemble a complex necklace of immense pearls speeding through the emptiness with perfectly coordinated movements.

Geary reached the bridge of *Dauntless* within a few minutes. "How the hell did the Dancers get to Bhavan?" he demanded.

Tanya Desjani had beaten him to the bridge. "You're not going to like the answer."

General Charban was already there as well. He turned a bland look on Geary, as if determined to no longer be fazed by anything the Dancers did. "According to your experts, Admiral, they didn't come from Bhavan."

"They arrived at the jump point from Bhavan," Geary insisted.

Charban indicated Lieutenant Castries, who looked uncomfortable. "Admiral," she said, "we got a weird signature when the Dancers left jump."

"A weird signature?" Geary pressed both hands against his forehead. "What does that mean?"

"Sir, when ships leave jump, they always emit a small burst of energy. It's insignificant, and no one really knows what causes it, so no one worries about it."

"Jaylen Cresida speculated that it might be caused by some sort of friction while traveling through jump space," Desjani said, seated and with her chin resting in one palm. "As the lieutenant says, it's so small an effect that it just gets noted and ignored."

Geary nodded impatiently. "All right. I remember that. There was a research project before . . . before Grendel. A ship I was on assisted the research. I never heard any results from it, though."

Lieutenant Castries indicated her display. "Our systems alerted us that when the Dancers left jump, the energy signature they gave off was much stronger than it should be and also had some unusual density readings."

"Put it on my display," Geary ordered, sitting down and glaring at the data as it sprang to life before him. "What the hell is that?"

"We . . . don't know, sir."

"The Dancer ships haven't shown that kind of energy signature before when leaving jump?"

"No, sir."

Charban cleared his throat. "Admiral, the Dancers insisted on going to Old Earth, so they could return the body of a human explorer who had been involved in early research into jump drives centuries ago. Apparently, he was in jump space for a very long time and did not come out until somewhere in the Dancer-occupied region of the galaxy."

"I'm not likely to forget that," Geary said. Being trapped in jump space was perhaps the worst nightmare scenario for space travelers. The thought of that ancient astronaut stuck in jump space until he died had rattled everyone who heard of it. "Hold on. Are you saying the Dancers might have jumped to Varandal not from Bhavan but all the way from their own territory? They would have been in jump space for months. No one could handle that."

"No *human* could handle that," Desjani corrected him.

Geary looked at her. "I had wondered what jump space felt like for the Dancers. Is there any other explanation for their getting here?"

"They could have jumped star by star all the way from the region of space they occupy," she said. "But that many jumps and transiting that many star systems would have taken so long that they would have had to have started about a year ago."

"Could they have figured out how to use the Syndic hypernet? Could they have gotten a Syndic key?"

"Yes, sir, but then why did they jump here from Bhavan rather than from Atalia or some other star on the Syndic side of things?"

Geary looked back at Castries. "Exactly how long would a single jump all the way from Dancer space take?"

Lieutenant Castries made a helpless gesture. "Sir, we don't know. All we can do is extrapolate from the jumps we make from star to adjacent star, but we don't know if there is a straight correlation between distances in our universe and distances in jump space, or what happens when you jump to a star much farther off than the ones nearest to the jump point you used."

"Can we even detect whether jump points can reach those more distant stars?" Desjani asked.

"I'll see what I can find out, Captain," Castries said. "But there's nothing in our navigation systems that would indicate we can do that."

"But we haven't been looking for it, have we?" Desjani said.

"No, Captain. I don't know if we know *how* to look for something like that."

"Forty ships," Geary said, focusing back on practical issues. "General Charban, we need to know why they are here, how they got here, why they are here, what they want, and why they are here."

"In that order?" Charban asked.

"Yes. Get me answers, General. The Dancers pointed us toward Unity Alternate. Some of them left in a rush. Now this much larger group of their ships has appeared without warning, apparently using jump drives in ways we can't. We need to know what game they are playing and whether they consider us teammates in that game or part of the playing equipment."

"Admiral," Charban said, "we've been trying to figure those things out since we first met the Dancers."

"Get that green-haired girl," Desjani suggested. "You know, the one who spots things no one else does. Maybe she can help some more with figuring out the Dancers."

"Lieutenant Jamenson?" Geary asked. "That's not a bad idea. General, we need to leave Varandal within a few days on an urgent mission. I can't leave Varandal with forty alien ships here. There's a very urgent need for answers."

"I will try," Charban said.

It took some work to pry Lieutenant Jamenson loose from Captain Smythe this time. Smythe, dealing with the mountain of work required to get the fleet out of Varandal in a few days' time, did not want to give up his most valuable staff officer. Geary, not wanting to alienate a subordinate as capable as Smythe, was reluctant to simply order the action. "You do realize, Captain, that if I don't have Lieutenant Jamenson's help in understanding why the Dancers are here, the fleet may not be able to leave as intended, and all of the work you are doing would be wasted?"

Smythe gave in.

As soon as he heard she was aboard, Geary went to the special compartment set aside for communicating with the Dancers. The fleet's system security personnel had been horrified when it was discovered that Dancer software could modify itself to work with human hardware, leading to an ironclad dictate that the Dancer software had to be kept on gear physically separated from other equipment.

Lieutenant Jamenson was there, seated at the long table holding the special comm gear, as were General Charban and Tanya

Desjani. "How does it look?" Geary asked. "Ever since they arrived in this star system, the Dancers have been heading toward *Dauntless* at point two light. They're almost on top of us now."

"Fortunately," Desjani added, "they haven't shown any signs of strengthening shields or powering up weapons. Having a bunch of alien ships charging on an intercept for my ship does worry me, though."

"What have they told us?" Geary demanded.

Charban sighed heavily enough to have put out the candles on a birthday cake. "There is no indication of hostile intent. As usual, they sound friendly. The Dancers sent us a long message that translated as 'hello, it's nice to be here, how are you?' I asked them why they were here. The brief response said 'we are on a mission.' What mission? An 'important mission.' Admiral, why don't you shoot me and put me out of my misery?"

Desjani was shaking her head. "Why would they go to the trouble to come here, then not talk to us in any meaningful way?"

A long silence followed her question.

Lieutenant Jameson had been gazing at the comm gear and now asked General Charban about it. "This shows us the translations of what the Dancers have said? In human words? Can I use this to hear the original messages they send?"

"The original messages?" Charban asked. "You mean, in Dancer language? Yes, you can do that. We used to listen to them as well as the translations, but we stopped because it didn't seem to help at all. Why?"

"I don't know. Maybe it's not important. But it occurred to me that I had never heard a raw Dancer message. Since it's something

I haven't tried, and everything we have tried hasn't helped . . ."

"That makes at least as much sense as anything else about the Dancers," Charban said. "I will warn you that some of the sounds the Dancers make probably could not be rendered by humans. Here. See this command that says 'origin'? That means the same as original. And this command will direct the sound to you. That brings up a window with volume controls and that sort of thing."

"Thank you, General."

As Jamenson leaned close to the equipment, listening intently, Charban looked back at Geary. "I asked how the Dancers had gotten here. The reply was 'we traveled.' How did you travel? 'By ship.'"

"They have to be messing with us," Desjani said. "They're on those ships laughing as they think about us trying to understand those messages."

"What does it sound like when a Dancer laughs?" Geary wondered, thinking of those wolf-spider faces. "Did you ask them about Unity Alternate?"

"I asked them about the many stars," Charban said. "They said, 'are you watching?' I said yes. They said 'good.'"

The resulting extended silence was broken by Jamenson. "They sound different," she said, not like someone who has discovered something but as if she had no idea what she had found.

"What sounds different?" Charban asked her.

"The Dancer messages." Jamenson turned a puzzled look on the other three. "When I listen to the first message they send us each time, when they start a conversation, it's sort of long, and it sounds . . . it sounds sort of musical."

"The sounds used in the Dancer language—" Charban began.

"No, General. Excuse me. It's not that. Those opening messages have a sort of bounce to them, a feeling of . . ." Jamenson struggled for the right word. "Of someone saying a song."

"Or a poem?" Desjani asked.

"Maybe, Captain. But then after we answer, they answer, and their messages are, um, flat."

"Flat?" Geary asked.

"Yes, sir. Oh, listen for yourselves. You'll see."

Charban, not bothering to hide his skepticism, leaned over and tapped a command. "Go ahead and play them. We'll all hear now."

Geary concentrated as the first Dancer message played back, the sounds strange to human throats echoing softly in the room. "You're right, Lieutenant. There is a sort of bounce to it. Like a . . ."

"A spoken-word musical instrument?" Desjani said, intrigued.

"And then," Jamenson said, "here's their response to our reply."

The same sort of sounds could be heard, but this time even though they sounded the same, they felt different. "Flat," Geary said. "I see what you mean, Lieutenant. But what does that mean?"

Charban was frowning in thought. "If they sang to us to start a conversation . . . there are animals that do that, right?"

"Birds," Desjani said. "Insects, some mammals, those things on that planet in Kostel Star System. They sing to identify each other, to pass information, for mating—"

"I sincerely hope that's not why the Dancers would be singing to us," Charban said.

"Could they be songs?" Jamenson asked. "Songs without music?" She played one of the opening messages again.

Geary listened as the strange tones of Dancer speech once

more filled the conference room, the pitch of the words merging, blending, and soaring. "It must mean something. Something that the Dancers' own translation software isn't picking up."

"Why wouldn't the Dancer software reflect it if it was important?" Desjani asked. "Because it seemed obvious to them?" she answered herself.

"Maybe," Charban said, his expression shifting rapidly. "We do that all the time, assuming that something very basic doesn't have to be explained because it is so basic that we believe everyone will just know about it. Are they . . . ? Could the Dancers be wanting us to sing back to them?"

"Like birds," Jamenson said. "As the Captain said. One gives a call, and the other responds, so they know who each other is, and then they sing back and forth. But if you don't respond with a song or a whistle, they don't respond the same way."

"That is not a bird," Desjani said, pointing to the image of a Dancer.

"But what if that's the problem, Captain? What if we're looking at them and thinking 'spider,' and 'wolf,' and 'yuck,' because that's what they look like to us? And we're still subconsciously basing our assumptions about how they act and talk by how they look to us? But why should they have patterns of behavior that match the images we're seeing? They're alien."

Charban was shaking his head in obvious dismay. "No matter how hard I tried, I kept seeing those images. You are absolutely right, Lieutenant. If the Dancers had looked catlike, I would have assumed they thought and acted and communicated like cats. And if instead they thought like horses, it would have messed everything up."

"They want us to sing to them?" Desjani asked skeptically. "But there's no music."

"We can try," Lieutenant Jamenson said. "I mean, not really a song maybe, but cast a message with rhythm and scales and—"

"Patterns," Charban said. "That's what songs do. They establish patterns of sound, patterns of words. Music. That's described in terms of mathematics and proportions between scales."

"Poems do patterns as well, right?" Jamenson added. "Some poems, anyway."

"And we know how important patterns are to the Dancers! Of course their methods of communication would reflect that! Maybe it's a sort of verbal handshake! 'Hi, I'm intelligent and want to talk about intelligent things!' 'Hi, I am also intelligent and want to talk about intelligent things, too!' We have to try this. Do you have any singers in your fleet, Admiral?" Charban asked.

Geary looked at Desjani, who made the universal human gesture of ignorance. "There must be some," she said. "None of my officers, judging from their efforts during our occasional karaoke nights."

"I didn't know you had karaoke nights on *Dauntless*," Geary said.

"If you heard my lieutenants and ensigns trying to sing, you'd know why it's been a while since we held one," Desjani said. "You can send out a message to all of the ships in the fleet, and I can have my crew checked to see if any claim singing talent—"

"I'd prefer not to spend a long time searching for singers before we can test this idea," Geary said.

"Please don't look at me," Jamenson said. "If you put enough whiskey down me, I sometimes try to sing, but it's the sort of sounds that would make any self-respecting alien within a hundred light-years run for home. How about poets? Maybe poems would work. Lieutenant Iger does haiku."

Everyone looked at her.

"Lieutenant Iger does haiku?" Geary finally asked. Somehow, the image of the serious, straightforward intelligence officer didn't fit such a thing.

"Yes, sir. That's a kind of poem. They're good," Jamenson added. "Lieutenant Iger's haiku, I mean. He really has a poetic soul. I think."

"Lieutenant Iger?" Desjani asked in disbelieving tones.

"Yes, Captain."

"Fine." Desjani sighed. "Admiral, I recommend we get our intelligence officer up here to see if he can craft lovely poems for the singing spider wolves."

Summoned on the double, Lieutenant Iger showed up at the conference room slightly out of breath. His eyes first fell upon Lieutenant Jamenson and her bright green hair, producing a reflexive smile that vanished as soon as Iger realized who else was present. Turning his usual sober and studious expression on Geary, Iger saluted. "You sent for me, sir?"

"That's right," Geary said, pointing to General Charban. "We need you to sit down with the general and write a poem for the Dancers."

Iger blinked before managing to respond. "Sir?"

"Sit down with General Charban and write a poem to the Dancers," Geary repeated. "What are the types of poems that you're skilled at? Haiku? One of those."

"For the Dancers?" Iger flushed slightly. "Admiral, my . . . hobby . . . is just a pastime. I'm not any good at it."

"Lieutenant Jamenson says you are."

Iger jerked with surprise and glanced at Jamenson. "She did? I mean . . . yes, sir. I'll try, sir. A poem for the Dancers?"

"General Charban and Lieutenant Jamenson will explain," Geary said, waving Iger in their direction.

He and Desjani stood watching as Lieutenants Iger and Jamenson huddled with Charban. "Who would have guessed that Iger had an, um, poetic soul?" Desjani murmured to Geary.

"I have a feeling that Lieutenant Jamenson may have awakened that particular part of Lieutenant Iger's soul," Geary commented dryly.

"Well, yeah, that's what women do. We take rough objects and polish them up a bit. What if this doesn't work, Admiral?"

"Then we're no worse off than we were before."

Lieutenant Iger was sitting, looking distressed and running one hand through his hair, while Lieutenant Jamenson spoke to him in a low voice, her expression encouraging. General Charban had leaned back and was pretending not to be aware of what the lieutenants were doing.

Finally, Iger stood up. "Admiral, I think this will do to convey the message General Charban wants to send. Ummm . . .

"Dark is this winter,

"Come now our friends from far stars,

"What do they seek here?"

Lieutenant Jamenson beamed at Iger with what seemed to Geary to be possessive pride, General Charban nodded approvingly, and even Tanya Desjani smiled. "Why the reference to winter?" Geary asked.

"It's traditional in haiku, sir," Iger explained. "There's often a seasonal reference, and I thought—"

"That's fine. I just wondered. Send it," Geary said.

Charban poked the haiku into the transmitter, then everyone waited. "If they want to respond," Charban said, "they'll usually answer very quickly, and by now those Dancer ships are only a couple of light-minutes from this ship, so there shouldn't be any major comm delays caused by distance."

An alert tone sounded. Charban slapped the control, reading intently. He smiled, then sighed, then lowered his head to the table as if immensely tired.

"What's wrong?" Geary demanded.

"Do you have any idea how much sleep and how much hair I have lost trying to figure out how to communicate better with the Dancers?" Charban said, his voice partly muffled against the table's surface. He sat up, sighed again, then read. "Here's the reply from the Dancers—

"Now we speak clearly,

"As one to one, side by side,

"To mend the pattern."

Charban shook his head, looking dejected. "I feel like such an idiot."

"No one else thought of it until now," Geary said. "Lieutenant Jamenson, I'm going to get you promoted if it kills me."

"Here's the next message," Jamenson said, looking abashed, as another tone sounded.

Charban read it out loud at once this time.

"Cold minds must be stopped,

"This mistake is an old one,

"We fight beside you."

"The meaning of that is very clear," Iger said, sounding surprised.

"They're here to help us fight the dark ships," Geary said. "I can't believe that all this time they were waiting for us to sing back at them."

"It must be how they regard serious talk," Charban said. "As long as we avoided using any sort of rhythmic patterns in our speech, we must have sounded to them as if we didn't want to talk about anything important. We kept giving them baby speech, and they kept responding in kind."

"Find out what they regard as fighting beside us," Geary ordered. "Make the questions as poetical as you want, but I need to know if that means they're taking orders from me, or if they're planning on operating independently on the same battlefield. They need to know that we're leaving in a few days for Unity Alternate. Also, see if you can find out whether they did jump here from somewhere in Dancer-controlled space."

"I have a list a kilometer long of things we need to get answers to from the Dancers," Charban said. "But I will give priority to those. What do you think of 'this mistake is an old one'?"

"We're not the first species to try to outsource responsibility for killing," Desjani said. "Apparently that can produce results bad enough that the Dancers want to help us stop humanity's efforts in that direction."

"Did someone among the Dancers do it?" Geary wondered. "Put AIs in complete control of weapons?"

"They are natural engineers," Charban noted. "And you know

engineers. Wouldn't it be cool if we could build this? Let's try! The awesomeness of building it fills their imaginations, and as a result, the question of whether or not building it would be a good idea doesn't always get asked."

"In that respect, they may be very much like us," Geary agreed. "Lieutenant Iger, you are to work directly with General Charban and Lieutenant Jamenson to facilitate communications with the Dancers. That task takes priority over any other assignment."

"Yes, sir." Iger did not appear to be too put out at the prospect of working closely with Jamenson for an indefinite period. "My chiefs can run my intelligence section for a while and will let me know if they discover anything."

Geary and Desjani left the other three, walking through the passageways of the battle cruiser, Desjani looking around in a way that conveyed concern. "They're going to target *Dauntless* again," she said to Geary.

"There's no doubt of that. Our goal is to hit their base while most or all of the dark ships are away," Geary reminded her. "We knock out their support structure, and, in time, they'll run low enough on fuel cells and expendable munitions for us to be able to take them down."

"And if a lot of the dark ships are there when we arrive?" Desjani asked. "Forty Dancer ships are welcome reinforcements, but they're not enough to even the odds."

"That's an unusually cautious attitude for you," he commented.

"I've got a bad feeling." She frowned at the deck, causing some passing sailors to hastily check the deck for any signs of trash or other problems. "Like before we went to Prime with Bloch in command."

"You think we're running into an ambush?" Geary asked.

"I don't know. But we have to try this, don't we? There's no telling where those dark ships might hit next. Time is not on our side."

He had just reached his stateroom when Charban called, looking unusually triumphant. "The Dancers will come to Unity Alternate with us. They feel that they will be needed and that destroying the 'cold minds' is too important a task to risk an unsuccessful mission."

"Will the Dancers operate under my command?" Geary asked.

"No. They want to be free to operate independently there."

It was Geary's turn to sigh. "I can't make them follow my orders. Those forty Dancer ships could be enormously useful anyway if any dark ships are defending their base. And if they come with us, I won't have to explain leaving an alien armada at Varandal while I take my fleet off somewhere else."

"It is a *friendly* alien armada," Charban pointed out.

"I'll let you inform the press of that."

"No, thank you, Admiral. Communicating with the Dancers is so important, I would hate to take time away from them to deal with human reporters," Charban intoned piously.

Thirty-five hours later, the First Fleet began to move, assembling its hundreds of warships from orbits dispersed around Varandal Star System. *Dauntless*, the guide on which every other warship took station, held her orbit as the other ships swung close, forming into a lattice in which every ship's weapons supported other ships, and any target would be engaged by many ships.

Normally, Geary took pride in the precise and effective arrangements of his ships. The current formation was shaped like a single, huge cylinder containing thirteen battle cruisers, twenty-one battleships, twenty-four heavy cruisers, forty-four light cruisers, and ninety-one destroyers. The attack transport *Mistral* was tucked well inside the cylinder, as protected from attack as possible.

But human formations, no matter how elegant, always looked crude and clumsy next to Dancer arrangements of ships. The forty Dancer ships had also formed into a cylinder, as if advertising their association with Geary's warships. But the Dancer formation radiated a relaxed perfection that made it appear like a grouping of living things in faultless synchronization with each other. Whenever they maneuvered, the Dancers lived up to their names, their ships gliding smoothly through space, moving in intricate choreographies that appeared natural rather than planned and practiced.

"Show-offs," Desjani grumbled. A widely acknowledged expert ship driver among humans, her skills paled next to those of the Dancers.

Geary wisely refrained from responding to her comment. They were all in the conference room again, a star display showing the shapes of the human and alien formations floating apparently right before every image of every ship commanding officer in the fleet.

How many times had he held these conferences? How many times had every commanding officer in the fleet looked to him for orders and inspiration and hope?

Why hadn't it gotten any easier?

"As I told you last time we met, we've located the base the dark ships are using," Geary began. "We've learned how to reach that base, and now we're going to go there, destroy the support facilities for the dark ships and any dark ships that are present. We're bringing along our last remaining assault transport and enough Marines to occupy a facility that we expect to be there, so we can collect all of the intelligence possible and rescue anyone trapped there by the dark ships."

"Where is this mysterious base?" Captain Badaya asked. "Why haven't we been able to find it before now? And why was it so hard to find out a means to reach it? Is it in Syndic territory?"

"Where is it?" Geary shifted the star display to focus on the binary, deriving some satisfaction from the uncomprehending looks most of his commanders gave the image. He must have looked exactly like that when Charban first asked about the two stars. "Right there. A binary star system."

"We're going to jump to a binary?" Captain Vitali asked. "There's a stable jump point there?"

"No, as far as we can tell there are no stable jump points," Geary said. "This star system has a hypernet gate. That's how we'll get there. I know what the next question is. Why did the Alliance build a hypernet gate at a binary? The answer is two words. Unity Alternate."

The resulting silence around the table was finally broken by Captain Armus. "There is a real Unity Alternate?"

"Yes," Geary replied. "The code for the gate there was already in our hypernet keys but needed to be unlocked for us to see it. The key aboard *Dauntless* has already had the necessary unlocking code loaded, and after this conference, I will be transmitting that same code to all of your ships." He paused, seeing in everyone's expressions the questions that statement created. "This is a fully authorized software patch. I received it from the government. This is an official tasking.

The government wants Unity Alternate neutralized."

"Neutralized?" Badaya exploded. "What is it we are neutralizing at our own government's secret alternative command base?"

"The dark ships," Geary said. "As well as potentially rogue elements of certain organizations."

"Which organizations?" Captain Vitali asked.

"I don't know. Neither does the government."

"You did say rogue elements," Captain Duellos conceded.

"Wait a moment," Badaya said heatedly. "You are saying that the government, which has been eyeing us with suspicion that we were a threat to the Alliance, is now depending on us to clean up a real threat to the Alliance?" From Badaya's injured tone, the idea of acting against the government never would have occurred to him. No one listening would have guessed that Badaya had once been at the forefront of those agitating for a military coup.

"That's right," Tanya said, absolutely deadpan.

Badaya frowned. "All right. Then we'll do that. We'll show them!"

"The Dancers are accompanying us," Geary added. "They want to help take down the dark ships."

"What if our paths cross, Admiral?" someone asked. "What if the dark ships head to attack Varandal while we're on our way to Unity Alternate?"

"We're going to get the job done at Unity Alternate and get back here," Geary said. "No delays. It's far from ideal, but we can't sit around Varandal or any other place waiting for the dark ships to attack. We have to hit them where they aren't and where it will hurt the most."

"We must succeed," Captain Tulev said. "We will succeed."

"Exactly," Geary said.

As the images of the other officers once again vanished in a flurry, that of Commander Neeson lingered briefly. "I guess you don't need me to find that gate anymore, Admiral."

"No," Geary admitted. "I'm sorry I couldn't tell you until now."

"A gate hidden on our own hypernet keys!" Neeson shook his head. "The hypernet was 'discovered' by scientists in the Alliance and the Syndicate Worlds almost simultaneously, just in time to keep the war going as both the Alliance and the Syndicate Worlds had begun staggering from the effort to continue it. None of us realized that the enigmas had leaked the technology to both sides for just the purpose of keeping the war between humans going. We've never known everything about it. I wonder how many other secrets the hypernet holds?"

"Let's win this fight, then find out," Geary said.

Neeson smiled and saluted. "That sounds like a plan worthy of Black Jack, if you'll excuse me for saying so, Admiral."

"Just this once." Geary watched Neeson's image vanish, then walked with Desjani out of the conference room.

He was surprised to find Victoria Rione waiting for him in the passageway outside the compartment. "I want to transfer to *Mistral*, Admiral."

Desjani said nothing, but disapproval was obvious in the way she held herself.

"Why?" Geary asked.

"Three reasons," Rione explained. "One, your Marines are supposed to collect all possible intelligence material stored on the facility there. I have the experience, and a unique set of software tools, to assist in that. Two, if the Marines encounter security or paramilitary forces defending the facilities and want to avoid a pitched battle, I could assist greatly in negotiating a surrender of the defenders. Three, if my husband is indeed being held somewhere on those facilities, I want to be there to get him out." She looked toward Desjani. "And, fourth out of three, my presence would probably be less disruptive aboard *Mistral*."

Tanya looked directly at Rione, speaking sternly. "If your presence on *Dauntless* is judged as needed by Admiral Geary, then you are more than welcome to stay here. You will be treated with every professional courtesy."

"You know how much that aggravates me, don't you?" Rione said dryly. "Admiral, I cannot help you in a fight against the dark ships. There is nothing to negotiate with. But I can be of great help to the Marines. I am asking to be allowed to assist them."

"What about talking to the Dancers? You were one of our primary points of contact with them," Geary pointed out.

"You don't need me for that now," Rione said. "The Dancers are finally speaking plainly enough to those with the skill to phrase the questions right. I wouldn't dream of crowding Lieutenant Iger and that lieutenant with the lovely emerald hair, who seem to prefer being alone together in that comm room."

It all made excellent sense. There was no reason to object. And yet Geary felt an odd sense of disquiet as he considered his answer. Discounting that feeling as the result of having to face the uncertainties of another battle with the dark ships, Geary nodded to Rione. "You make a good case. There is plenty of room aboard *Mistral* for you since they are only carrying two battalions of

Marines. I don't know why I haven't already thought to ask you to transfer to *Mistral*."

"I know how much you personally enjoy having me around, Admiral," Rione said, smiling as Desjani's glower deepened.

"I'll have to do without your immediate company for a while for the benefit of the Alliance," Geary said. "I will let Colonel Rico and Commander Young know that you are coming to work with them. Captain Desjani, can you arrange an immediate shuttle lift to *Mistral* for Senator Rione?"

"With pleasure," Tanya snapped. "By your leave, sir." She saluted, then walked off rapidly down the passageway, crew members scattering as they saw her coming and judged her mood.

"Do you have to do that kind of thing?" Geary asked Rione heavily.

"It may be some sort of compulsion," Rione said. "I'm sorry. It's a shabby way to repay your hospitality." She met his eyes. "Good luck, Admiral. Tell Captain Desjani I regret the difficulties that I have caused her."

Rione walked off as well, leaving Geary staring after her and trying to recall the last time that Rione had used Desjani's name.

He had been wondering what he would do if the dark ships erupted from Varandal's hypernet gate as his fleet was approaching it. But as the First Fleet and the Dancer armada grew closer to the huge structure humans called a gate, which was actually a vast ring of hundreds of tethers that held a particle matrix in the desired form, no threat emanated from it.

"We'll be back as soon as we can complete the mission," Geary sent in a message to Admiral Timbale that would not reach Ambaru Station for hours.

Desjani had already called up the hypernet key controls. "Unity Alternate is selected as the fleet's destination, Admiral. The hypernet field is set wide enough to include the entire fleet as well as the Dancer ships. We're ready to go whenever you give the word."

"Thank you, Captain. Activate hypernet."

She touched the command, and the stars vanished.

12

There was none of the mind-dazing shock of transitioning into and out of jump space, no gray haze filling jump space around them, no mysterious lights. Outside the bubble in which the fleet traveled, there was, literally, nothing. In fact, as it had been explained to Geary, the fleet wasn't really traveling. It had been at one gate, at Varandal, and after a few days all of the human warships would be at the other gate, at Unity Alternate, without technically having traveled between those gates.

As odd as jump space was, the quantum mechanics behind the hypernet were in some ways even odder.

Geary got up, relaxing with the knowledge that for the next few days nothing could get at them, and they could get at nothing. Whatever was going to happen, would happen. "It's a relief to be on our way," he commented to Desjani.

She looked over and up at him. "Are you going to get some sleep?"

"Yes, I am. Even if I have to call Dr. Nasr and ask for a patch to knock me out for a while."

"Good. That means I won't have to call Dr. Nasr and tell him to knock you out. Hopefully, you won't dream about dark ships."

"I imagine I'll be dreaming about something else entirely," Geary said, giving her a look.

She shook her head, exasperated. "You're still on my ship, Admiral. Keep your dreams professional."

"You're kidding, right?" He didn't wait for an answer because he couldn't be certain and didn't want to find out otherwise.

Once he got to his stateroom, he lay down in the bunk, gazing at the overhead, hoping that he had made the right decisions. He couldn't recall how many nights had been spent like this since he had been awakened after his century of survival sleep. There had been too many. And this night was one more.

"So the Dancers did jump all the way from their own region of space to that jump point that exited at Varandal?" Geary shook his head in disbelief. "How?"

"We've been having some trouble getting the technical explanation rendered into the form of a haiku," Lieutenant Iger confessed.

"There was a warning though," Lieutenant Jamenson added. "The Dancers said 'you should not attempt that jump.' They were very insistent."

"Lieutenant, two weeks in jump space is as much as I ever want to spend there in one stretch," Geary said. "How are you two doing?"

"Sir?" Lieutenant Iger asked, worried.

"I mean working conditions. I want you both rested and ready when we leave the hypernet."

"We'll be ready," Lieutenant Jamenson said. "Admiral, the

Dancers are worried. We put this in our reports, but you may not have had time to review them. They say 'cold minds,' the sort of thing they call the dark ships, have more than once proven to be much harder to stop than anyone expected."

"Believe me," Geary said, "after Bhavan, I'm not expecting any free rides. If we can knock out the support structure for the dark ships, we'll be able to stop them."

"What if we can't knock out that support structure, Admiral?"

"Then it will be much harder," Geary said.

Two days later, he sat on the bridge, waiting to leave the hypernet. He wondered what was happening at Unity right now. Had the Senate already moved against the covert structure that had gained too much power in the last several decades? He had no doubt that General Carabali would provide the support that the Senate needed. He wondered whether the dark ships had already launched another attack designed to draw him into battle. Had they gone to Varandal? Back to Bhavan? Or maybe to Unity itself? And he wondered how many dark ships would be awaiting them at Unity Alternate.

At least he would get the answer to one of those questions soon.

"Ten minutes until exit from hyperspace," Lieutenant Castries said.

"*Dauntless* is at maximum combat readiness," Desjani reported.

"The Dancers have done this before," Geary said, talking to fill the time. "They've already dealt with this kind of threat."

"So have we," Desjani said. "Remember that place with the rocks?"

"Stonehenge. Yes. Maybe we'll get the lesson this time."

"I bet you we won't. For a little while, maybe," she said.

"You are probably right once more," Geary said.

"Two minutes until exit from hyperspace."

They waited silently as the final minutes counted down.

At zero, the stars suddenly appeared again. Behind them was a hypernet gate, and before them were two stars orbiting in what was known as a close binary.

"I have never seen that before," Desjani said in an awed voice.

The displays updated rapidly as the fleet's sensors consolidated, analyzed, and assessed everything that could be seen. Geary saw large installations appearing on his display, their orbits centered on the larger of the two stars, which must sometimes bring them uncomfortably close to the smaller. Six planets, varying in size from a rocky, barren half Earth-standard to what had once been a gas giant but had apparently been losing its atmosphere at intervals to one of the stars. A host of smaller natural objects also orbited within the system, some of them following eccentric orbits that swung them past both stars. "We're not seeing anything on the planets," Lieutenant Yuon reported. "There are some very large facilities in orbit. Docks. Warehouses."

"They could maintain a fleet four times the size of ours here," Geary said, amazed. "For a long time."

"They were ready to keep the war going if the worst happened," Desjani said with grudging admiration. "Look at those orbits! This system is a mess. No wonder they didn't put anything on the planets. Ah, look what else we found, Admiral."

He didn't have to ask what she was referring to. The same symbol had appeared on his display. "*Invincible*. They did bring her here."

The alien superbattleship, much larger than any human warship, was hanging in its own orbit a few light-minutes from the dockyards. "Even those docks couldn't hold something the size of that Kick ship," Desjani commented. "Is this right? The ship is cold?"

"Yes, Captain," Lieutenant Yuon replied. "Our sensors aren't picking up any signs of active power aboard *Invincible*, or any other activity. No heat being radiated. The ship is still completely shut down and apparently has no one aboard."

"What about those tugs?" Desjani asked. The many heavy-duty tugs that had been fastened about the hull of *Invincible* to move her from Varandal were still there, forming two rings about the alien battleship's hull. "They're cold, too?"

"Just standby power, from what our sensors can see," Yuon reported. "Aside from that, all systems inactive and life support not running. No indications of crews or caretakers present. The tugs appear to have been put into stand-down."

"They were supposed to be taking *Invincible* somewhere to study the Kick technology and try to learn more about the Kicks," Desjani complained to Geary. "Instead, they just hauled her here and forgot about her!"

"Maybe they had to shut down research efforts when the dark ships started causing problems," Geary speculated.

"If that's the case, they didn't shut down anything in a hurry. Everything about *Invincible* and those tugs reflects methodical deactivation."

"That's so. And they parked *Invincible* a fair ways from anything else, as if they were afraid of the ship." Geary felt a wry smile on his face. "Maybe they were afraid of the Kick ghosts."

"It would be nice to know the Kick ghosts spooked whichever human spooks have been busy at Unity Alternate," Desjani commented, using the common slang term for undercover operatives. She looked over her display again. "But they're all we're picking up. No other shipping."

"There aren't any dark ships here at all?" Geary asked, staring at his display with a mingled sense of relief and mild disappointment. It would have been nice to catch a small force of dark ships and wipe it out along with their support facilities.

"We're not seeing anything," Yuon confirmed. "We can't see inside the docks, though. All of them appear to have power active but no life support running."

"And those are a lot of big docks," Desjani murmured.

"Let's take them out." Geary felt a sense of revulsion as he looked at the dockyards and support facilities, apparently empty of life yet continuing to serve the needs of the dark ships. Automated facilities conducting automated war. They were the unfeeling personification of Captain Tulev's argument against using AIs to control weapons.

Geary called up the bombardment routine on his display and began designating the orbiting support facilities as targets. One very large structure orbiting at a distance from the support facilities looked like the place intended for the exiled government. He left that off the target list, then asked the system for firing solutions.

A process that should have produced almost instantaneous results instead ground on for several seconds, then a minute, then kept going. "Captain Desjani, we seem to have a problem with part of the combat systems."

"What?" She leaned in, frowning, then entered commands into her own system. "It's working. Trying to produce a solution. Why the hell—? Oh."

"What?" Geary echoed.

"The interacting gravitational fields of the stars and the eccentric orbits. The bombardment routines can't handle that. They can't direct a precise shot across those kinds of distances under these conditions. We'll have to get a lot closer to those facilities to launch rocks at them and be sure of hits."

"I guess that was another good reason to put Unity Alternate here," Geary conceded. "How have they ensured that the facilities don't get sucked into destructive orbits?"

"There are propulsion systems on all of the facilities," Lieutenant Yuon reported in surprised tones. "Not enough thrust for a lot of travel, but enough to adjust orbits in a big way—" He broke off as he realized the implications of that.

"Oh, hell," Desjani complained. "If they have automated maneuvering systems that powerful, they could spot an incoming bombardment and adjust orbit enough that our rocks would miss. It's a good thing we didn't launch. The rocks would have been wasted even if their trajectories had been accurate."

"How much did they spend building this stuff?" Lieutenant Castries asked in amazement.

The hypernet gate had been constructed far enough from the two stars to be unaffected by their intertwining gravity fields. In this case, that meant an unusually long journey to the facilities orbiting the twin stars. "Almost seven light-hours," Desjani observed. "We've got a long trip ahead. Do we have a good picture of that big facility that looks like it was intended as the command structure and seat of government?"

"Life support and power are active," Lieutenant Yuon said, peering at his data. "But only in the upper quarter of the structure. Everything below that is dark and cold. We're not seeing any confirmation that the facility has anyone aboard it, though."

"You could keep a lot of people very comfortably in something the size of one-quarter of that facility," Geary said. "We're not picking up any comm traffic or other signals?"

"No, sir. There is probably a local net running between the facility and those dockyards and support structures, but it would be using highly directional signals that we're not in the right position to pick up."

"All right. Let's see if anyone will answer us." He made sure his uniform looked decent, straightened in his seat, then keyed the broadcast comm circuit. "Anyone in this star system, anyone occupying any of the facilities of Unity Alternate, this is Admiral Geary of the Alliance fleet. We are here on orders of the Alliance government to occupy and neutralize these facilities. If anyone is in need of rescue or evacuation, we will assist you. Anyone working on the facilities must accept the authority of the Alliance government and also prepare for evacuation. Contact me and provide your status as soon as possible. The First Fleet of the Alliance is on its way to your orbital location. To the honor of our ancestors, Geary, out."

It would take at least fourteen hours for any replies to come in, and he had no intention of waiting around the hypernet gate until that happened. "All units in First Fleet, come starboard—" He stopped abruptly. "Wait one."

"What's the matter?" Desjani asked.

"Starboard. Port," Geary said. "Toward the star or away from the star. Which star?"

"Oh. It's a close binary." She smiled ruefully. "We haven't had that problem in systems with one star, have we?"

Geary tapped his fingers impatiently as he thought. "It's all arbitrary anyway. We say one way is up and the other down." He activated his comms again. "This is Admiral Geary. The brighter star in this system is designated Alpha and the other star is designated Beta. All maneuvering commands and fleet navigational settings will treat Alpha as the reference star. All units in First Fleet, come starboard zero seven degrees, down one zero degrees at time two five. Accelerate to point two light speed." He was not going to waste time getting this job done.

The ships of the Alliance formation pivoted around *Dauntless*, the cylinder shape reorienting along the long-curving path that would bring the fleet near the orbiting facilities.

"Thirty-eight hours until we reach the orbiting facilities," Lieutenant Castries said.

"We might as well relax." Geary activated comms again. "All units in First Fleet, stand down from battle alert."

Desjani glanced at him. "You're not relaxing, I notice. Is it for the same reason I'm not?"

"What's your reason?" Geary asked.

"This situation stinks. We have never encountered the entire force of dark ships at once. They have always apparently left some of their ships here at their base. If nothing else, some of the dark ships we damaged at Bhavan should still be here, and even if they were concealed in the docks, we would be able to pick up indications that repair work was being conducted inside some of those docks."

"Yeah," Geary agreed. "That's my reason, too. I thought we would at least encounter a guard force of some kind."

"If they are still thinking like you, if the AIs haven't modified their thinking and rationalized things enough to deviate a lot from what Black Jack would do, are there any conditions under which you would leave your base totally undefended like this?"

Geary considered that question, then shook his head. "No. We did take the entire First Fleet here, but Varandal isn't defenseless. They've got some of their own ships. Nothing big, but something, and they have all of the fixed star system defenses. Plus, Varandal isn't our only base. Losing it would be a tragedy, but it wouldn't cripple us."

"So, where are the dark ships?"

"I don't know. All we can do is what we set out to do," Geary said. "Then get back to Varandal and find out what the dark ships are doing right now."

After forcing himself to leave the bridge so he wouldn't exhaust himself and look nervous to everyone on watch, which would both be bad things, Geary walked through the passageways of *Dauntless* for a while, talking to crew members and judging their moods. Before the fight at Bhavan, most had been confident, almost cheerful, certain of another victory. Since Bhavan, a grimness had settled on them, a determination to win tempered by knowledge that victory might be dearly bought. As Geary talked to the sailors, though, he saw that for the moment worries about the dark ships had been overridden by fascination with being in a close binary star system. For all the star systems many of these sailors had visited, this was the first time they had seen two stars so close together.

The exercise had the desired effect of wearing him out, and Geary was able to sleep for a few hours until rudely awakened by a call from Tanya. "There is something you should take a look at," she said. "Not urgent, but serious."

"Show me." The star display in Geary's stateroom came to life. He got off his bunk and walked over to gaze at the images of this star system.

Desjani's voice was somber. "Here. I'm highlighting it."

He sat down as an area of the display brightened to emphasize details there. "Debris?"

"Yes. It took a while to spot it and analyze it because of how much junk is drifting around between those two stars. The interacting gravity fields must keep causing collisions between rocks jarred out of what would otherwise be stable orbits."

Geary tapped the debris symbol and studied the information that popped up. "It wasn't a warship?"

"No. Based on the composition of the debris, it wasn't a freighter, either. There's no sign of cargo or the remains of cargo."

That left only one chilling possibility. "A passenger ship."

"Yes." Desjani made a face. "Maybe a regular shift change by the people who worked here. Maybe an attempt to get out of here when the dark ships slipped their leashes. From the dispersion of the debris, it happened about a month ago."

"Is this the only debris field we've detected?"

"So far," she said. "It's still a few hours before we could expect any answer from anyone on the facilities and find out whether there is anyone left, and whether they're scared to death, or whether they are so fixated on following orders that they are still prepared to fight to the death."

"At the moment, I'm unhappy enough to let the Marines accommodate anyone here who wants to fight to the death," Geary said. "Is there anything else new?"

"Not really new. I've been noticing something odd about the Dancers," Desjani said.

"You mean something odd that we haven't seen already?" Geary asked.

"All right, yes, something new that's odd." She indicated her display. "Normally, we get into a star system, and the Dancers start flying around, going wherever they want and flying rings around each other and any other ships. But ever since we arrived here, the Dancers have stayed in that formation and stayed close to us."

"That is odd." Geary looked at the Dancer ships on his display. They were still in their smaller cylindrical formation, and they were indeed maintaining the same position relative to the Alliance formation. He called down to the compartment holding the special comm equipment, patching in Desjani to the call. "Hello, General. We've got another question for you."

"Thank you," Charban said, sounding almost sincere.

"The Dancers have been staying close to us since arriving at Unity Alternate instead of running off and, well, dancing around the star system. Can you find out if they are nervous or something?"

"That's interesting. The Dancers haven't volunteered any such feelings, but that is unusual behavior for them," Charban agreed.

"I'll ask. They did just offer something that I think refers to *Invincible*. The lieutenants and I were discussing it before sending it on."

"They aren't staking a claim to *Invincible*, are they?" Geary asked. "When we captured it, the Dancers agreed that the Kick warship would be our property."

"No, it's not a claim. Here's what they sent—

"Herd creatures build big,

"Make ship the herd always there,

"To be not alone," Charban recited.

"The herd always there?" Geary asked. "Are they saying there are still Kicks aboard that ship? How could that be possible? We went over every cubic centimeter inside that hull."

"I don't think it's a reference to Kicks still being on *Invincible*," Charban said. "Lieutenant Iger noted the use of present tense, but also the clear reference to herd, which would mean a lot of Kicks. Unless they are physically buried in the structure of the hull, I don't see how that could be."

"Wait a minute." Geary looked toward the depiction of *Invincible*, remembering his visit aboard her. "People do feel Kicks aboard that ship. I felt them. Like a herd of ghosts everywhere you went. It was incredibly unnerving. If you weren't part of a large group of people, the sensation could become too much to endure. Even those Syndic special forces that tried to capture or destroy *Invincible* couldn't handle it."

Charban looked suddenly surprised. "To be not alone," he quoted. "Admiral, it's that simple. The ghosts are a deliberate design feature. However the Kicks manage to create that sensation, it ensures that no matter where any Kick was on that ship, even if they were the only Kick in that area, they would still feel as if they were surrounded by the herd."

"You're kidding." But the more Geary thought about it, the more sense it made. "It's not a defense against invaders. It's a defense against isolation or loneliness for creatures that have to feel surrounded by their comrades at all times."

"It's strange, isn't it?" Charban said. "Humans alone in a place can become worried about ghosts, can become frightened because they are alone, because we are also social creatures. Imagine how a Kick would feel, a creature raised to always be surrounded by its herd, if it were truly alone somewhere? We can understand that. It's the first thing about the Kicks that we can both understand and empathize with."

"It probably won't be adequate grounds for peaceful coexistence," Desjani pointed out.

"No," Charban agreed. "It is hard to empathize too much with creatures who regard genocide of any potentially competing species as the natural order of things."

"Especially since the Kicks appear to believe that just about every other species is competition," Geary said. "You know, maybe the Dancers know something about Kick technology. They certainly know more about the Kicks than we do. Once we deal with the dark ships, maybe the Dancers can help us figure out how the gear works on *Invincible*."

Charban made a face. "Rendering a technical manual into poetry is a challenge probably beyond our skill level, Admiral. At least, it has been so far. I don't think we can successfully tackle something like The Ballad of the Resonating Quark or The Tuning of the

Bipolar Oscillator. Perhaps a check of the fleet will find one of your engineers is an accomplished and talented songwriter. That's who we will need for that job."

"An engineer who is also a songwriter?" Desjani asked sarcastically. "That ought to be easy to find."

"Not so hard as you might think, Captain," Charban said. "There is an intimate connection between engineering and music. Think of designing or building a musical instrument. It is an exercise in engineering, in stresses and forces, in structures and materials, vibrations and resonances."

"I never thought of it that way," she confessed. "For now, I think you should focus on the Admiral's question about whether the Dancers are nervous. Unity Alternate has *me* nervous. It's too quiet here."

"I agree," Charban said. "I'm ground force, not space, but even I feel that this is going too easy."

Sixteen hours after they had arrived at Unity Alternate, and with twenty-two hours to go before they reached the region where the orbiting facilities were located, a message arrived.

Geary watched a trim man in a nondescript suit speak with calm precision. "Your presence here is not authorized. You are directed to leave this star system immediately. Your act of trespass on official government property has already been recorded and will be forwarded to appropriate authorities for action. You are directed to say nothing about this star system until you are contacted by a duly authorized representative of the government. If you continue to approach these Alliance government facilities, which are off-limits to all unauthorized travelers, we will be forced to take any necessary actions, up to and including use of deadly force."

"Is he for real?" Desjani asked.

"Actually, I'm wondering exactly that," Geary said. "Is he real? Or are we looking at some recorded warn-off message that was triggered by our own attempts to communicate?"

"Automated comms?" Desjani gestured to her watch-standers. "Check with our experts on whether we can tell if that message was live or not."

The eventual answer was "no." "It's digital," the comm officer lamented. "We can tell when it was sent, but there's no attached signature to let us know when it was prepared. Without that time stamp embedded in the message, we can't tell whether it was put together a few hours ago or six months ago." The officer paused. "But, presenting merely my opinion, I don't think this was a live transmission. The wording was very generic, just the sort of thing we get told to put into messages intended for long-term use."

Geary nodded. "But even if the message was prerecorded, that doesn't mean it wasn't sent by someone as opposed to being an automated response."

"That's true, Admiral. It doesn't tell us anything except that whoever occupied those facilities did not have a welcome mat out for visitors."

Six hours after that, urgent alerts sounded. Geary was already on his way to the bridge again and rushed the final distance, almost leaping into his command seat next to Tanya Desjani's. "What is it?"

"We've probably found some of them," she said briefly.

It took Geary a moment of studying his display to figure out exactly what he was seeing.

Some of the space docks were opening, their vast doors peeling back. Due to the angle at which the Alliance fleet was looking at the docks, they could not see inside yet, but there was only one plausible reason for those docks to be preparing to launch something. "Whatever is in those docks that are opening up should be easy for us to handle. They can't hold too large a force."

He had no sooner ceased speaking than another dock began cracking its doors.

"Will you stop doing that kind of thing?" Desjani growled at him.

But no other docks opened. Those which had begun opening finished the process, their doors fully retracted. And then, nothing happened.

"It's been half an hour," Desjani complained. "What are they waiting for?"

"Maybe there isn't anything inside them," Geary speculated. "Do you think they may have opened up because they saw us coming? Some automated maintenance function preparing to work on our ships?"

"No equipment in any of those docks is going to land one automated finger on my ship!" She glared at her display as if that would produce more information. "Maybe you're right, though."

More alerts sounded. "Or maybe I'm not," Geary said.

The rounded, sharklike bows that began coming into view as they exited some of the docks were unmistakable in their menace. "Battle cruisers," Desjani said, sounding eager. "Four of them."

More, smaller warships began appearing at the dock openings. "Six heavy cruisers, ten light cruisers, twenty-one destroyers," Lieutenant Yuon summarized.

"We can take these down easy," Desjani exulted.

"If that's all we're facing," Geary said, frowning at his display.

The dark ships had cleared their docks by now, and were gathering into a small, thin, rectangular formation. "Hull feature analysis identifies two of the dark battle cruisers as having been at Bhavan," Lieutenant Yuon said. "The other two have not been encountered before."

"The two that missed Bhavan," Geary said. "I wonder why?"

"Stuff breaks," Desjani said. "They probably needed something big fixed."

The dark ship formation was coming around now and accelerating onto an intercept with Geary's force. "Four hours to contact on current vectors," Lieutenant Castries said.

Desjani's satisfaction had faded into suspicion. "They're making this too easy."

"I'm glad I'm not the only one thinking that," Geary said. "If those dark ships charge straight into us, we'll be able to wipe them out on the first pass. Let's see if they hold on that vector."

He hadn't slept nearly enough since arriving at Unity Alternate and found himself dozing off for brief periods in his command seat. An hour later, more alerts jerked him rudely back to alertness.

"More docks opening," Desjani said. The same sequence followed, the docks opening, then a long pause, then the bows of warships beginning to appear. But this time the first, massive bows that came into view were blunter than those of the battle cruisers. "Battleships."

"Four battleships," Lieutenant Yuon said. "Four heavy cruisers, eight light cruisers, eighteen destroyers."

Like the dark battle cruisers before them, the battleships formed into a thin, rectangular formation, moving more slowly than the battle cruisers but with a terrible, ponderous assurance. The battleships also came around and accelerated onto vectors aimed at an intercept of Geary's fleet.

"Tougher, but still nothing we can't handle," Desjani said. "They can't have much more hidden in those docks."

"I wonder why they didn't bring them all out together," Geary said. "Why send out two smaller forces instead of one bigger force?"

"It's not what you would do," she agreed. "Their battle cruisers' vector is still aimed straight at the middle of our formation, which Black Jack definitely would not do under these conditions."

"What would I be doing?" Geary murmured, trying to put himself in the place of a dark ship commander. "If those dark ships were all I had to defend their installations, I'd try to divert and distract the attacking force, but that would just buy some time even if it worked." He reached one hand to point to his display. "We've got two assets we have to defend. *Mistral*, and the Dancers."

"I think the Dancers can take care of themselves," Desjani objected. "Their ships can outmaneuver even the dark battle cruisers. And if those four dark battle cruisers try to get to *Mistral*, we'll blow them apart before they get within range."

He nodded, thinking. "So why would I be setting up this situation if I was commanding those dark ships? We must be missing some part of the puzzle."

"There can't be much more inside the docks," she repeated. "It's possible they've got something hidden behind one of the stars if they knew we were coming and had time to get into position."

"Senator Unruh warned me that the dark ships might still be getting information about what we were doing," Geary said. "And we couldn't hide our preparations to leave Varandal."

"But how would the dark ships have known we were coming here?"

"Maybe a leak in Senator Unruh's camp. Maybe just through thinking what I would do. I realized I had to hit their base. Since they are programmed to think like me, they would realize that I had to hit their base."

Desjani looked troubled. "Admiral, that makes enough sense that it worries me. They know from Bhavan that they can't easily force us into an engagement. They would want to choose a new battlefield where they could more easily trap us."

Like a battlefield without any jump points. One where the only way out was through the hypernet gate— "Oh, no."

"What?"

"The Alliance was studying how the Syndics were able to block access to their hypernet gates. They were trying to figure out how the Syndics did that so we could counter it. But if some of the Alliance's researchers figured out what the Syndics were doing—"

"And the people supporting the dark ships found out?" Desjani stared at the depiction of the hypernet gate. "The people who think Black Jack is what stands between them and taking over? Admiral, you are making way too much sense."

More alerts. "Warships coming out from behind Star Alpha," Lieutenant Yuon said. "It's a big force. Ten battle cruisers and a lot of escorts. Our systems are still identifying numbers—" He broke off as the alerts redoubled. "Warships detected near Star Beta. Two formations, each holding six battleships and numerous escort vessels."

"That's all of the dark ships," Desjani said, calmer and composed now that the trap had sprung on them. "Every battle cruiser and battleship that they've got left. It's us or them this time. No other options."

"Then we'll have to make sure it is them, not us." Brave words. Geary looked at the dark ship formations converging on the path of his own force, added up their firepower and their maneuverability superior to those of his own ships, and gazed at the depiction of the hypernet gate that very likely offered no means of escape. He could not help wondering if he had finally made the final, critical error that he had been fearing since being thrust into command of the Alliance fleet at Prime.

13

"Is there any way we can confirm whether or not that hypernet gate is blocked?" Geary asked Desjani.

She called up the hypernet key controls. "I've never tried to ping a gate from this far away, but I don't know why it wouldn't work. We'll have to wait until the ping gets there and the reply gets back to us, though. At this point, that will take more than eight hours."

"Do it. I need to be certain whether that option is foreclosed."

"Yes, sir." She touched some commands. "I'm asking the gate to identify any available destination gate. If it is completely blocked, the answer will come back as none. Have you considered the strange coincidence of this situation, Admiral?" she asked, keeping her voice very low.

"What strange coincidence is that, Captain?" Geary replied in the same tones.

"The enigmas gave us the hypernet. The Syndics taught us how to block the gates. It's like those two enemies conspired to get us into this situation."

"To the benefit of the people behind the dark ships," Geary said, "who would doubtless be scandalized at any suggestion that they had anything in common with the Syndics. All right. Regardless of whether or not that gate is blocked, we need to destroy the orbital docks and warehouses. That way, no matter what happens here, the dark ships will eventually no longer be a threat if the government can keep them from acquiring any alternate source of fuel cells. And we need to take the Unity Alternate government facility and find out what is there."

"Taking the facility will require exposing *Mistral* and hanging the Marines out in a tough situation," Desjani objected. "Why not wait on that?"

"Because somewhere on that facility there may be the means to lift the block on the hypernet gate if, as we suspect, there is a block."

"Thinking of that is why you're the Admiral and I'm not," Desjani said.

Geary took in the information on his display, where all five dark ship formations were now converging on the projected path of the First Fleet and the accompanying Dancer forty-ship armada. All of the dark ship formations were ahead of the Alliance and Dancer ships. Closest were the four dark battle cruisers which had first appeared and were still rushing toward the Alliance forces. Behind them were the four dark battleships that had also come out of the docks. Both of those formations were just off the port bows of the Alliance warships, and if neither of them maneuvered differently, would remain in that relative position, growing steadily closer until contact.

Just off to starboard of the Alliance bows were the ten dark battle cruisers and the smaller dark warships accompanying them. Those dark battle cruisers were also steadying up for a direct intercept, but one that would take place considerably after the two dark ship formations coming from the docks. Finally, almost directly ahead were the eight dark battleships and the cruisers and destroyers with them, coming on steadily at a rate that would cause them to intercept the Alliance formation a few light-minutes before Geary's force reached the dark ship docks and warehouses.

"They're setting this up as if they're going to hit us with each formation in succession," Geary said. "I don't think they'll actually do that. It would let us whittle them down as each smaller dark ship formation encountered our entire force. But they're probably hoping I'll think that's what they are planning, if 'hoping' is the right word to use for an AI's calculations."

"You've tried that trick more than once yourself against opponents," Desjani pointed out.

"Yes, but it's a little insulting for an AI that's supposed to think like me to think I would fall for one of my own tricks. That first battle cruiser formation could dodge a direct encounter, then harass us until other dark ships get here. And if the dark battleships coming from the docks slow a little, they'll reach us about the same time as the big battle cruiser formation that was hiding behind Star Alpha. We need something to keep that first dark battle cruiser group busy." He nodded to himself, then called General Charban. "General, could you and your lieutenants put together a poetic invitation for the Dancer ships to engage that first formation of dark battle cruisers? It would help us a lot if those battle cruisers had the Dancers hitting them while we dealt with the other dark ship formations."

"We will write them a battle hymn," Charban said.

"Have the Dancers sent anything since all of the dark ships appeared?"

"Not a word, Admiral. They are definitely waiting on us." Charban looked thoughtful. "I have the impression now that they regard us as the senior partner when they are in regions of space controlled by us. It may be a territorial thing. I'm not certain. But since we stopped using their version of 'baby talk,' the Dancers have been acting less like someone manipulating us and more like someone who is partnering with us."

"Thank you, General." Geary paused, then entered another call.

Victoria Rione's image gazed back, her expression serene but her eyes dark. "It's a little early for last-minute instructions, Admiral."

"I may be too busy with other matters at the last minute," Geary said. "There's something else that you need to find on that facility. There is a real possibility that the hypernet gate here has been blocked in the same manner that the Syndics blocked theirs. We won't have confirmation of that for several hours yet, but the tactics of the dark ships make me suspect that has happened. If the gate is blocked, and if there is anything on that facility that would allow us to unblock that gate, we need it."

"If it is there, I will find it," she replied. "If you can get us to the facility."

"*Mistral* will get you there," Geary said. "And I'll make sure that *Mistral* can get there."

After he ended that call, Desjani indicated her display. "So, we stay the course?"

"For now," Geary said. "We still have over an hour and a half before that first dark battle cruiser formation closes on us. I have no intention of holding this vector long enough for all of those dark ships to hit us at their leisure, though."

She leaned close, ensuring the privacy fields around their seats were active. "Have you noticed that when the dark ships are maneuvering, we're seeing more judicious use of fuel cells? They're not going to maximum burn on everything like they did at Bhavan."

"I noticed," Geary said. "They never repeat a mistake. This is like Bhavan, but a lot worse."

"Jack, we're going to have a hell of a time getting out of this."

She almost never called him that when they were on her ship.

"I know. But if nothing else, we'll get those support facilities. Even if we don't make it out of this star system, the days of the dark ships are going to be numbered."

"We who are about to die salute you!" she murmured.

"Tanya—"

"It's all right. I should have died a dozen years ago, and I should have died a dozen times in the years since then. Lead on. Even if we lose this one, we'll win in the long run, and it'll be a fight they'll be talking about for centuries."

An hour later, Geary brought the fleet to full battle readiness again. Just about everyone on every ship was already at their battle stations, since they all knew about the oncoming enemy and had watched the dark ships' approach for the last hour. As a result, every ship reported ready in record time.

He had spent the last hour trying to think rather than worry. He could outsmart the dark ships. He had done that more than once, with Tanya's help in many cases because the dark ship AIs had been programmed to think like Black Jack and were confused when confronted by the Black Jack/Tanya Desjani team effort.

But the dark ships had known he had to go for their base. Because he had known that it was his only chance to beat them. Maybe someone had tipped the dark ships off with specific information, but in their place, Geary would have tried to lay just such a trap as this.

But he wouldn't have given his opponent even a chance to get at the support facilities. The dark ships were still weak on logistics, still thinking in terms of tactics, not in terms of long campaigns. That gave him an opening.

He just didn't know what to do after destroying those docks and warehouses.

"Twenty minutes to contact," Lieutenant Castries said. "The dark battle cruiser formation is braking their velocity. Given the angle they will encounter us, projected combined velocity at the moment of intercept will be point two one light speed."

"A little fast, but close enough for our fire-control systems to get good hits. Still holding the vector?" Desjani asked Geary.

"Still holding," Geary said. "Just in case they do decide to charge us straight on."

"If they do, *Dauntless* and *Mistral* will be their priority targets."

"And with the screen of battle cruisers and battleships they'll have to get through, none of them will survive to get a shot at us," Geary said. He tapped his comm controls. "All units in First Fleet, I expect that this first formation of dark ships will make vector changes to avoid contact. If they do, the Dancers will handle them. If they do not, if they attack our formation, let's make sure none of them survive the first pass."

It felt odd, going into an engagement determined not to make any last-moment maneuver. Throwing off the enemy's fire was always important. But he felt certain that these dark battle cruisers would not throw themselves away on a hopeless attack.

Because he would not have done that.

"Five minutes," Lieutenant Castries said.

"The Dancers still haven't moved," Desjani noted.

"They will," Geary said. "The dark ships are going to go after them."

"You think so?" Desjani studied the situation. "Yes. If they come a little up and to port, they'll go right through the Dancer formation instead of ours."

"And you can bet the Dancers have seen that, too." He knew he sounded confident. He hoped he was right.

The last minutes seemed to pass very slowly.

The moment of contact came and went too fast for human senses to register.

"No engagement!" Lieutenant Yuon announced.

Geary realized that he had been holding his breath and let it out slowly.

"Oh, nice!" he heard Desjani say.

Focusing on his display again, Geary saw that the Dancer formation had dissolved in the minute before contact, the forty bright ships sweeping down and over to catch one flank of the dark ship formation as it tore past. While none of the Dancer ships were the size of human battleships or battle cruisers, and none carried as much armament, forty of them could do a fair amount of damage, especially against smaller Alliance warships.

A dark heavy cruiser was reeling out of formation, unable to control its movement. One of the light cruisers was gone, nothing but debris remaining. A second had broken into sections, which were disintegrating as they tumbled through space. And one of the dark destroyers was gone as well.

"They'll think twice before trying that again!" Desjani said gleefully.

"Damage to some of the Dancer ships, but none are disabled," Lieutenant Yuon reported.

The dark battle cruisers were whipping around, the Dancers swarming and rising to meet their turn like huge, shining bubbles flying upward, all pretense of a rigid formation vanished in favor of something that resembled the movements of a school of fish.

"It's too bad the Dancers don't have more firepower. The dark ships didn't take into account the maneuverability and skills of the Dancers," Geary said. "The dark ships won't make that mistake again, but the Dancers should keep that one group of battle cruisers busy."

Which left four more groups of dark ships.

The battleships that had come out of the docks had started out an hour behind the dark battle cruisers and accelerated more slowly, so they were now more than two hours from contact. The three groups of dark ships that had come out from behind the two stars were pushing their own velocity up, aiming to reach Geary's formation at the same time as the first group of battleships.

"We could detach enough ships to help the Dancers finish off that first group of battle cruisers," Desjani suggested.

"That's what they want," Geary said. "To get us focused on

fighting those battle cruisers, then the groups here after them, until our option to do anything else disappears. We're going to hold together, we're going to blow through any opposition that we can't avoid, and we're going to wipe out those docks and warehouses. Then we'll engage the dark ships. By that time, we'll also know whether or not the hypernet gate is blocked to us."

He called up his division and squadron commanders, repeating what he had told Desjani. The news that the gate might be blocked was met with as much anger directed at the dark ships as fear for the consequences. Captain Badaya, though, saw a positive side to the situation. "They can't get away from us this time!"

"We've got them trapped," Captain Duellos agreed, smiling slightly.

Captain Jane Geary smiled broadly. "Nothing to lose. Let's hit them just like Black Jack would."

"We're going to do just that," Geary said, accepting the role of Black Jack as needed now. "We're going to hit them and keep hitting them. If the fleet has to break into small formations centered on the battle cruiser and battleship divisions, I trust you all to operate independently, and I know you will all carry out your duties in a manner that does honor to your ancestors."

He ended the call, concentrating once more on the situation. The first group of dark battle cruisers, scarred by the Dancer attack but still powerful and fast, was behind and above the Alliance ships, accelerating again. But they were beginning to roll to one side to evade the Dancers' second pass. That was taking the dark ships off a vector to intercept Geary's formation again. "General Charban, please inform the Dancers that they are doing all I could ask for, and to please continue keeping those dark battle cruisers occupied."

"We may be inventing a new art form," Charban replied. "Improvisational battle haiku. I will inform them. Admiral, I'm looking at this situation. Is it as bad as it appears?"

"Yes," Geary said.

The dark battle cruisers fell increasingly far behind as they dodged repeated attacks by the Dancers, who could outmaneuver even the fastest and most agile dark ships. But after forty-five minutes of provocation, the dark battle cruisers darted directly onto a chase after Geary's formation, ignoring a slashing Dancer attack that took out more of the dark cruisers and destroyers.

Fifteen minutes after, with the dark battle cruisers behind racing to catch up, the Dancers chasing those dark ships, and four dark ship formations approaching ahead, Geary sent new orders. The dark ships in front of Geary's force were already beginning to decelerate in anticipation of intercepting his formation in half an hour. "All units in First Fleet, immediate execute, accelerate to point two five light speed."

"What happens after we blow through them?" Desjani asked.

"We start braking, drop off *Mistral* as we blow past the government facility, continue braking to ensure the accuracy of our bombardment as we swing past the orbiting support facilities for the dark ships, blow away those facilities, then break into three formations and go after the dark ships."

"Got it. Need help configuring the formations?"

"I would be grateful for your assistance, Captain."

Because of the distance still separating the forces, it took the dark ships several minutes to see that Geary's force was accelerating, limiting their time to counter his move. All they could do was further reduce their own velocity, and the three dark ship formations that had been hidden behind the two stars were already braking at near maximum.

Their carefully planned maneuvers thrown off by Geary's acceleration, the dark ships were now coming in at rates that would cause them to encounter Geary's fleet at slightly different times instead of all at once.

"Estimated relative velocity at contact with closest dark battleship formation is point two seven light," Lieutenant Yuon announced.

"Nobody is going to get many hits at that speed," Desjani said.

On Geary's display, the thin, curving lines marking the projected paths of the dark ships were growing in diameter, shading lighter on their outer edges, reflecting growing uncertainty as to exactly where the enemy ships were and exactly what their vectors were, as the relative velocities grew so large that human sensors and tracking systems could not fully compensate for relativistic effects that warped their view of the universe. The closer objects got to the speed of light, the worse the relativistic effects, and the harder it was to see an accurate picture of what was outside of a ship. It was just one of the reasons why warships rarely pushed their velocities above point two light speed, but it was an important reason.

The dark ships would be having the same problem precisely tracking Geary's warships. It was hard enough hitting something on the fly while shooting past at tens of thousands of kilometers per second. If you didn't know exactly where that ship was and would be, the problem became an impossible one.

At five minutes before contact, with the different formations only about one light-minute apart, Geary sent new orders. "All units in First Fleet, immediate execute, pivot one six zero degrees port, down zero four degrees, brake velocity to point one light speed. *Mistral*, maneuver independently as required to close on the government facility."

The Alliance warships swung their bows far over and slightly down, then lit off their main propulsion, not only slowing their velocity but also altering their path through space. The long curve of the First Fleet's projected course began shifting to swing just past the government facility, then through the vast field of orbiting docks and warehouses.

Mistral's track, though, began diverging as the assault transport started braking much harder than the warships and aimed directly for the government facility. Still nestled within the Alliance formation, *Mistral* started sliding back and slightly to the side relative to the other ships.

The dark ships had only a couple of minutes to spot Geary's alterations in course and speed, their task complicated by having to guess what vectors the Alliance warships would steady out on and by the relativistic distortion smearing their views of the other ships.

The dark battleships immediately to the front of Geary's formation misjudged how much his ships were turning and swung too wide for an encounter as the two forces tore past each other.

Less than a minute later, the dark battle cruisers that had come out from behind one of the stars skidded past just ahead of Geary's fleet, having guessed wrong about how hard he would brake his ships' velocity.

One of the two dark battleship formations still forward of Geary almost immediately afterwards raced past behind the Alliance warships.

The second of the dark battleship formations guessed better, skimming the top edge of Geary's formation. Weapons fired on both sides, but the relative velocities were still too great to get decent fire-control solutions, and nearly every shot missed.

Behind, the first group of dark battle cruisers, still pursuing Geary's fleet, was closing more rapidly as Geary's warships slowed down, and behind the dark battle cruisers in turn, the Dancer swarm chased those dark ships.

To port and starboard, above and below, the dark ship formations whose attacks had been frustrated by Geary's maneuvers were swinging around to set up new intercepts.

"We've got some vector divergence on the five heavy cruisers left to those dark battle cruisers behind us," Desjani noted. "They've spotted *Mistral's* movement, and they're moving to intercept."

"I was expecting that." Geary tapped his controls. "Captain Tulev, take your battle cruiser division and maneuver to intercept the dark heavy cruisers behind us that I have designated. Those dark cruisers are aiming for *Mistral*. I don't want any of them getting to her."

"Understood, Admiral."

Leviathan, *Dragon*, *Steadfast*, and *Valiant* began braking harder, also veering out more, aiming for an intercept on the dark heavy cruisers before they would reach *Mistral*.

A notice told Geary that *Mistral* was calling him. He accepted the call, seeing Commander Young's image appear in a virtual window before him. "Admiral, we're getting a look at more of the government facility as our angle of approach changes. There's a covered dock attached to that facility," Commander Young reported. "Big enough to hold a single battle cruiser or an assault transport, and the doors of the dock are open wide. When the staff on the facility tried to flee, they must have not bothered closing the dock doors behind them. I can get *Mistral* inside instead of dropping off my shuttles for the first wave of the Marine assault. All of the Marines can hit the facility at once, my shuttles won't be exposed, and *Mistral* will be safe inside the dock."

"Will you be safe?" Geary asked. "That dock is an easy target."

"Admiral, there are no signs of that facility having been fired on. We've got plenty of indications that the dark ships have shot up shipping in this star system, but not a mark on any of the orbiting facilities. If the dark ships have any inhibits left active at all, at the top of their list would be not to fire on the government facility where their human overseers were located. It's still a gamble, sir," Young admitted, "but I think it is less risky than trying to play keep-away with the dark ships while also sending in and recovering multiple waves of shuttles and Marines."

Geary stared forward, weighing options and risks, then nodded. "Very well, Commander. You are authorized to enter the dock and launch the assault from there. Notify Colonel Rico. Make sure you don't loiter outside the hangar lining up your approach and matching velocity. I'm going to do all I can to keep the dark ships off you, but if you're just hanging in space, you'll be a very easy target for them."

Commander Young grinned. "Admiral, I can dock ol' Miss anywhere I've got a meter to spare on the sides and in front and back. Consider it done."

Young's image had no sooner vanished than Desjani gestured for Geary's attention. "The dark battle cruisers behind us have seen Tulev's battle cruisers moving. They're altering vectors to intercept Tulev at the same time he intercepts their heavy cruisers."

"Good." Geary touched his controls again. "Captain Badaya, you are to take the First and Sixth Battle Cruiser Divisions, as well as the Third and Fifth Heavy Cruiser Divisions, and the Second, Twelfth, Fourteenth, and Seventeenth Destroyer Squadrons, and join with Captain Tulev's Second Battle Cruiser Division to intercept the dark battle cruisers moving to engage *Mistral*. Captain Tulev, your division is now part of Formation Delta One commanded by Captain Badaya."

Captains Badaya, Duellos, and Tulev acknowledged the orders, as did the commanders of the heavy cruiser divisions and destroyer squadrons. *Illustrious*, *Incredible*, *Inspire*, *Formidable*, and *Implacable* accompanied by ten heavy cruisers and thirty-one destroyers altered their vectors, sliding outward and up toward the path of the oncoming dark battle cruisers.

Geary could see Desjani glowering at her display. "I'm holding back *Dauntless* and the rest of the Fourth Battle Cruiser Division for a reason," he said. "I want those dark battle cruisers to think they have a chance of getting to *Mistral*. If I added four more battle cruisers to our intercept force, the dark battle cruisers would be certain to veer off. But they might believe they can handle nine of our battle cruisers, especially since I am not part of that force."

"You're trusting Badaya to handle them." Desjani grumbled.

"He's the senior officer among those three battle cruiser division commanders, and Badaya can handle an overtaking intercept."

"You still owe me one. Sir."

Mistral was falling back fast now as she braked to match orbital velocity with the government facility. Geary's battle cruiser formation Delta One was dropping back even faster so as to intercept the oncoming dark ships before they reached *Mistral*. Those dark battle cruisers had joined up with their heavy cruisers again and were coming on steadily, apparently ignoring both Badaya's Delta One formation before them and the Dancers approaching from behind.

"Twenty-two minutes to intercept of dark battle cruisers by Delta One," Lieutenant Castries said. "*Mistral* reports estimated docking time at facility in thirty-five minutes."

Desjani, still grumpy, was eyeing her display. "The other dark ship formations are coming back onto intercepts, but they won't be able to engage us again until after we pass through the region holding their orbiting support facilities. Clumsy of them. They're giving us a clean shot at what they need to keep fighting."

"It's just like at Bhavan," Geary said. "Whoever programmed the dark ships put a lot of effort into the tactical model but didn't put nearly as much work or emphasis on logistics. The dark ships are still thinking primarily in terms of destroying us, not in terms of defending their support structure from us. And they're not going to get a chance to rethink those priorities."

He called up the bombardment routines again and, designating all of the docks and warehouses as targets, told the fleet's combat systems to come up with a launch plan for when the Alliance warships went through the region of space holding those facilities. Not certain if the battle cruisers in Delta One would be back with the main formation, Geary told the combat systems to make full use of the awesome bombardment capabilities of the twenty-one Alliance battleships as well as Desjani's Fourth Battle Cruiser Division. This time, with such short flight distances between launch platform and target, any unpredictable or varying interactions of the gravitational fields of the two stars had too little impact to worry about. The proposed plan popped up almost instantly. "Can you do a sanity check on this for me, Captain Desjani?"

She looked over the plan on her own display, brightening as she saw the sheer size of the bombardment. "We're going to make sure nothing survives this run."

"Right," Geary said. "I don't want to have to worry about coming back to finish the job."

"It looks very good to me." She checked another part of her display. "It also looks like you were right, Admiral. Those dark battle cruisers are going to try to take Badaya. They want *Mistral* bad and probably figure they can whittle down our number of battle cruisers at the same time."

Their bows facing backwards while their main propulsion labored to slow them down, the ships under Badaya's command already had the majority of their weapons and strongest shields pointed toward the enemy. The dark battle cruisers, though, having ramped up their velocity to catch Geary's ships, were now having to brake harder and longer in order to effectively engage the Alliance battle cruisers, their sterns toward the enemy they were rapidly closing on. And as the dark battle cruisers and Geary's battle cruisers both slowed, the Dancers gained more rapidly on both of them.

Those aboard *Mistral*, Geary reflected, were probably feeling extremely nervous at the mass of human, automated, and alien warships swiftly bearing down on them.

"Badaya is cutting it close," Desjani warned. "The dark ships are going to be almost in range of *Mistral* when he engages them."

"He wants the dark ships to hold their vectors," Geary said, "and maybe he's hoping they'll be holding their fire as well, waiting to engage *Mistral*."

"We did that to them at Bhavan," Desjani said. "They won't fall for it again."

"We'll know in less than two minutes." He had no doubt that the dark battle cruisers would be stopped. He could only hope that his own battle cruisers would not pay too high a price.

The dark battle cruisers pivoted at the last possible moment, bringing their bows forward to face the Alliance force. They came within range of Badaya's battle cruisers seconds before the Dancers caught the dark ships from behind. Even at the comparatively slow relative velocity at which the ships engaged this time, the exchange of fire happened too quickly for human senses to follow.

But Geary had no trouble spotting the explosion which, from its intensity, could only mark the destruction of a battle cruiser, as well as lesser detonations that heralded the deaths of heavy cruisers and destroyers. The fleet's sensors were still trying to evaluate the outcome, who had lost what, when the Dancers ripped through the remains of destroyed ships to hammer the dark ships again.

The formations diverged, finally giving Geary a clear look.

"*Mistral* is all right," Desjani said. The assault transport was still braking, now being overtaken by the fast-moving fields of wreckage from the shattered warships that had been pursuing her.

"We lost *Motte*," Geary said as the report of the heavy cruisers' loss came in. "As well as *Moulinet*, *Remise*, *Mause*, *Spitfire*, and *Skyraider*." Two light cruisers and three destroyers. "Lots of damage to *Dragon*, *Incredible*, and *Implacable*." Those three battle cruisers seemed to attract a lot of hits in every battle.

One blessing was that in a bow-on engagement, there had been few hits on propulsion and maneuvering systems. None of the damaged Alliance warships would be unable to keep up with their fellows.

Unfortunately, that was also true of the dark ships.

On the positive side, one of the dark battle cruisers was gone and the other three had been damaged enough to break off their attack. The dark ships had also lost two more heavy cruisers, another light cruiser, and four more destroyers.

"If they hadn't veered off their attack vector, they would have been wiped out," Desjani said, her right hand forming a fist that she rapped against her seat in frustration. "It looks like they tried to shift targets at the last instant to the ships in Delta One, then to the Dancers."

"I bet they did," Geary said, studying the results of the engagement replayed in very slow motion. "That was their fix to what we did at Bhavan, to allow last-moment retargeting outside normal parameters. But that meant in this engagement they ended up losing their chances at a lot of shots by shifting targets too often and too easily."

He grimaced as he looked over the results, and the sharp curve of the path the remaining dark ships in that group were following as they swung out to one side and down relative to Geary's formation. "We didn't hit them hard enough." He had always tried to avoid battles of attrition in which each side wore down the other, taking and inflicting losses at terrible rates. But he was beginning to believe that this battle would offer no alternatives to that strategy that weren't even worse.

"Delta One," Geary sent, "maintain your position relative to this formation until we clear the enemy support facility region."

The government facility, a vast structure orbiting in solitary splendor, gleamed as Geary's fleet swept past it. Hazard lights were visible on the outside of the structure, and on Geary's display the exterior view of the facility was overlain with sensor readings of heat leakage and power use that showed which portions of the facility were in use. The intended home for an Alliance government in exile radiated a sense of great strength as well as great size, which struck Geary as ironic given its intended function. The only way this facility would ever have been occupied by the Alliance government was if Unity had fallen and most if not all of the Alliance had been occupied by the Syndics. Its use for its intended functions would have marked last-ditch desperation and defeat, not strength.

"We might have had to use this," Desjani said. "If you hadn't shown up."

"And now it's my job to neutralize it," Geary said. "Are the living stars laughing?"

Mistral was partly out of sight around the curve of the facility as she backed in to the dock, her main propulsion flaring at full power as the assault transport slowed rapidly over the last few thousand meters before exactly matching the orbital vector of the facility. Geary saw *Mistral*'s propulsion stutter once as Commander Young fine-tuned the braking slightly, maneuvering thrusters also adjusting the transport's angle of approach. Seconds later, the transport glided into the dock, comm relays dropped in *Mistral*'s wake still providing a solid link to the assault ship for the rest of the fleet even though she was now completely within the hangar.

As far as Geary could see, no other dark ships were maneuvering to attack *Mistral*. Now that she was inside the dock, the dark ships appeared to have completely lost interest in her. "Good work, Commander," Geary sent. "The dark ships are not continuing to target *Mistral*. But don't forget that the dark ships may well be trying to work around whatever prevents them firing on that facility and on you. We don't know how much time you have."

New virtual windows had popped up next to Geary's seat, showing the views from the armor of Marines who were already charging off *Mistral* and storming the facility. If he wanted to, Geary could call up the view from the armor of any Marine in the assault force, but at the moment he had a job to do dealing with the dark ships. He couldn't waste his attention riding the shoulder of a Marine lieutenant or sergeant or private.

Still, the windows were there, visible to a glance to the side, so Geary could remain aware of what was happening with the Marines without focusing his attention on them. He saw assault teams hacking the controls on hatches to allow access to inside the facility before he was called back to the larger picture by Desjani.

"We just got the ping back from the hypernet gate," Desjani said. "You were right. The hypernet gate is reporting that there are no other gates accessible from it. It's blocked."

"I wish I'd been wrong on that one." Geary touched a comm control. "Victoria, the gate *is* blocked. We need to know how to unblock it."

"I was already assuming the worst, Admiral," she replied. Rione had not yet left *Mistral* but was poised to follow the Marines inside the facility. "It saves time in situations like this. If that information is on this facility, I will find it."

"Five minutes to bombardment launch," Lieutenant Yuon said. "Uh, combat systems are still requesting confirmation of plan and authorization to launch, Admiral."

"Thank you, Lieutenant," Geary said. He called up that data again, saw that nothing had changed to alter his intentions, confirmed the bombardment plan, then authorized the launch to take place automatically as his warships reached the right points along their paths. "Do you ever think it ought to be harder to cause this much destruction, Tanya?"

Desjani gave him a disbelieving look. "No. It's too hard as it is. If something needs to be destroyed, let me destroy the blasted thing."

"Not everyone has your sense of restraint, Tanya."

"Excuse me, Admiral?"

He didn't answer as Geary's fleet swept through the orbital region holding the docks and warehouses. The docks were huge, rectangular structures, with almost-as-large superstructures on their backs that contained repair and fabrication facilities, offices, living spaces for workers, life support, and a variety of other necessities for a typical shipyard. On the fleet's sensors, all of those areas intended for human use looked dark and cold, kept just warm enough for equipment to function properly, or with all life support shut off, as frigid as empty space. The docks were lifeless by any biological definition, but power usage within provided clear signs of the mechanical "life" that ruled within them. "Like haunted houses," someone whispered.

The warehouses resembled enormous beehives, rounded structures with external access and loading docks located all around them on different levels. The main cargo off-loading docks were at the top and bottom of the warehouses to allow new material to be distributed throughout the structure using very large cargo elevators in the core.

Each of the docks and warehouses also boasted a single propulsion unit whose thrust could produce a significant change in their orbits given enough time. It was an expensive addition to such facilities, but if the Alliance fleet had been able to launch a bombardment from light-hours away, the structures would have had ample time to make the relatively small alterations in their orbits that would cause the bombardment projectiles to completely miss their targets. However, with Geary's warships planning on launching so close to their targets and the rocks moving so fast, in this case the propulsion units would be totally useless.

The size and numbers of the structures rivaled that of a major shipbuilding region of space in a wealthy star system. If the Alliance had been forced to retreat here, these structures would have allowed the Alliance to continue to launch raids on the Syndic conquerors.

Geary wondered what point that effort would have had. Victory would have been impossible unless the Syndicate Worlds had been so badly stressed by winning that it fell apart and left an opening for the Alliance government to reoccupy the ruins of Alliance star systems. But by the time Geary had been reawoken after a century of war, there no longer appeared to be any point to most things about the war. Neither side believed they had any chance of winning, but the Syndicate Worlds would not stop attacking, and the Alliance would not surrender, and nothing else mattered, no other courses of action were considered possible.

He was about to destroy a symbol of that stubborn insanity.

A hail of bombardment projectiles launched from Geary's warships, hurtling toward the vast structures designed to support ships like them but now dedicated to the dark ships.

The solid metal projectiles nicknamed rocks by fleet personnel had no warheads, no explosives, but were traveling at more than thirty thousand kilometers per second. Each carried an immense amount of kinetic energy, and when they struck anything, that energy was released.

Under the impacts of dozens of hits on every target, docks shredded, flying apart into clouds of large and small pieces. Warehouses exploded, those containing weapons or fuel cells vanishing in rapid successions of gigantic explosions as their contents self-detonated, their contents and their structures becoming a mass of small particles flung outward. In the space of seconds, structures built at immense cost in time, money, and labor were turned into a huge field of debris.

"No matter what happens to us here, it was worth it to blow away all that," Desjani said, smiling at her display. "Someday, thousands of years in the future, that ring of debris will have spread to form a thin ring within this binary star system. That's something to imagine, isn't it?"

"An asteroid belt composed of the ruin of war," Geary mused. "We'll name it Tanya's Ring."

"A debris field big enough to form a belt in a star system, named after me? Now I can die happy."

He glanced at her and confirmed the impression he had from Tanya's tone of voice.

She wasn't joking.

And with all five dark ship formations coming back at the Alliance ships again, and the hypernet gate still blocked, there seemed to be all too great a chance that it might happen before this day was out.

14

"Admiral," Lieutenant Castries reported in amazement, "the fleet has detected a jump point for Hardinga."

Geary checked his display. The jump point had popped into existence over five light-hours away, leading to a moderately-well-populated star system near this binary. Near as interstellar distances went, anyway. "How long—"

"It's unstable," Castries continued, then realized she had interrupted Geary. "I'm sorry, Admiral. Our sensors assess that the jump point is unstable. I've never seen that before."

"You've never been in a close binary star system before," Desjani said. "Look at that. Our sensors are estimating the jump point has an eighty percent chance of collapsing within seven hours of coming into existence."

"And it came into existence five hours ago," Geary said. "How can our systems estimate that sort of thing? The life span of an unstable jump point?"

"Somebody must have studied unstable jump points," Desjani

said. "Maybe remote observations from surrounding star systems that gave them some astronomical data to work with. Or maybe someone just ran the math for interactions of gravity fields for two stars, and that ended up in our ship systems as part of the baseline data for jump point analysis."

"We couldn't go anywhere anyway until we recovered *Mistral*," Geary said, "even if there was any chance of that jump point still being there by the time we got there."

With the dark ships still about an hour from any possible intercepts, Geary checked the status of the Marines. The sooner they got their job done, the sooner he could focus exclusively on battling the dark ships.

The stacked tiles of virtual windows showing views from the Marine armor revealed what were now slightly time-delayed images, over a minute old due to the distance between the fleet and the government facility. The Marines were inside, some progressing without resistance down corridors and into rooms that mostly had a feeling of having never seen human presence since being constructed.

But other Marines were traveling into areas of the facility that had actually been used. There were signs of wear on walls and floors, occasional bits of trash that had so far evaded the small housekeeping robots, and here and there rooms bearing signs of hasty departure. Scattered clothing littered floors and furniture, abandoned snacks and meals rested on desks and tables, and unmade beds bore in the shape of the sheets traces of the people who had once used them.

"What happened to them?" Geary heard a Marine ask her platoon leader.

"Best guess is they ran for it, and their ship got nailed," the officer replied. "Everybody look for signs any of this stuff has been disturbed since it was abandoned in place. We need to know if there is anyone left here."

The lieutenant's question was rudely answered seconds later as nearby Marines finally encountered opposition. Geary switched his view to one of those Marine officers, seeing a wide corridor ahead that was sealed by blast doors at the far end. "It's automated defenses or someone directing fire," a captain was reporting to his superior. "We can't tell which yet."

"Hold your positions. We've got units working around the flanks of this passage, and two platoons from Second Company on the next level down."

Geary involuntarily jerked as bursts of fire came from the vicinity of the blast doors to lash the area where these Marines were hunkered down. "Can we return fire?"

"Not unless you see a target. Hold position."

Switching his attention back to the big picture, Geary saw that Delta One's battle cruisers were maintaining their position near the main Alliance formation, which was proceeding along a shallow curve that would eventually form an orbital path around Star Alpha if they stayed on it. The Dancers were nearly a light-minute away and above the Alliance warships, gathered into a group but not engaging in any of the playful maneuvering that they were famous for.

The five dark ship formations were all lined up to hit Geary's formation, aiming for near-simultaneous intercepts along the path ahead. The earliest of those intercepts was forty-two minutes away.

"Ideas?" he asked Desjani.

"We need to know if there's anything on the facility that will unblock that gate," she replied. "If there is, we need to stall and wear out the dark ships like last time, which will be a lot harder this time. If there isn't, we need to figure out how to close with them and kill more of them than they kill of us."

"You're recommending I avoid action until we know which tactics we need to follow?"

"Yes, sir," Desjani said, nodding, her eyes on her display. "We've got at least fifteen minutes before we should maneuver to mess with their plans. Why don't you see how the Marines and that woman are doing while I watch the overall situation?"

"Good idea." He refocused on the Marine action.

Spotting some Marines proceeding cautiously up a set of emergency access stairs, Geary linked his view to the armor of their platoon leader. An enlisted Marine was kneeling at an access hatch, working on the lock, then gave his lieutenant a thumbs-up.

"We're ready to go," the lieutenant reported, her breathing deep and regular as she prepared for action.

"Hit 'em," the order came back. "Through the hatch and left. You'll take them in the rear."

"Got it. Through hatch, left. Are we weapons free?"

"If they fire, you are cleared to engage. The brass wants live prisoners, though. See if they'll surrender when they realize they've been flanked."

"Roger." The lieutenant repeated the orders to her platoon, then as the nearest Marine yanked open the hatch, the entire force charged through, the Marines in their heavy combat armor having to duck and twist to get through an opening intended for typical human sizes.

The Marines emerged into what Geary recognized as another section of that broad corridor, this part on the other side of the defended blast doors. Several men and women wearing reinforced survival suits were crouched near the doors. They did not realize at first that there were Marines behind them, but when one turned and cried a warning the rest jerked around rapidly to face this new attack

"Drop your weapons!" The voice of the Marine lieutenant, amplified by her battle armor, boomed through the corridor.

One of the defenders brought up a weapon to aiming position, and died a second later as several Marines put shots through him.

The rest stood frozen before dropping their weapons hastily.

"We got six prisoners and one body," the lieutenant reported.

The six survivors, whose reinforced survival suits bore a private security contractor symbol, sounded terrified, not defiant like the agents Geary still had detained aboard *Dauntless*. "We didn't sign up for this," one announced. "Don't want to fight no Marines. We're on the same side."

"Uh-huh," the lieutenant replied. "Who's in charge? This guy?" she indicated the dead defender.

"No, no, it's the suits! They only talk to us to give orders. They're holed up in the command center."

"Pack 'em up," the lieutenant told her platoon. "And get those blast doors open."

"Wait!" another one of the private security guards cried. "We can help you guys! I heard what they're doing. They're getting ready to fry all the files in the system! Sanitize the records, they call it. If they know you've made it past us, they'll set off magnetic pulse bombs all over the station!"

"Captain?" the lieutenant called.

"I heard. We've got hack and cracks breaking into the systems at remote locations and trying to sever the links from the command center. Hold your position and see what else those guys can tell you."

The captured contractors had no qualms about spilling their guts since they had been told to stay behind when most of the other occupants of the facility had tried to flee. "No room, they told us. They said they'd send somebody back for us. Then we saw them get blown to pieces. Ever since then, we've been hiding in here, hoping those damned ships wouldn't notice us."

Geary pulled his attention away from the Marines again, hoping they would successfully prevent the "suits" from destroying all of the records on the facility. "Any changes?" he asked Desjani.

"They're a bit closer, that's all," she said. "How are the grunts doing?"

"They're working it." Geary rubbed his lower face with one hand as he considered the situation. "I'm thinking we should—"

"Admiral," the comm watch-stander announced loudly, "we have a message coming in from one of the dark battle cruisers!" He cringed before Desjani could even direct a withering glare at him, then spoke at a normal volume. "I'm sorry, Captain."

"I'm the only one who yells on this bridge," she informed him, "and no one likes it when I do."

"Yes, Captain. Admiral, what should I do with the message?"

Geary had controlled his initial reaction, managing to just nod in response. "Send it to me."

The image of Admiral Bloch appeared before him. He had last seen Bloch at the Syndicate Worlds home star system, Prime, when the defeated Bloch was taking a shuttle to the Syndicate flagship to plea for a deal to save the rest of the apparently doomed Alliance fleet. He had thought that Bloch had died that day, along with the other senior fleet officers, murdered by Syndic special forces.

But the Syndics had not wanted to kill a captive whose knowledge might prove valuable. They had kept him, and when the war was over and Bloch's living presence offered a chance to disrupt the still-hated Alliance, the Syndics sent him home.

Then, having nearly lost the war for the Alliance, and having made little secret of his belief that a military dictatorship overseen by him would cure the ills of the Alliance, Bloch was received by some as a champion. And as someone who might be a counter to the immense popularity of Black Jack Geary. Faced with Black Jack, a hero whose achievements and fame were seen as threats to the government, parts of the government reacted by embracing Black Jack's antithesis.

It hadn't gone well for the government, and as Geary looked at Bloch's image, he saw that it hadn't gone well for Admiral Bloch, either. From appearances, Senator Unruh's suspicions that Bloch had already regretted getting what he wanted were extremely accurate.

Bloch was in a compartment that looked like a fairly luxurious stateroom fitted out with a ship's bridge command fixtures. The lavish compartment was messy, though, with empty ration containers strewn about.

Admiral Bloch himself looked as bad as he had when he left *Dauntless* on that day at Prime when he was supposed to arrange a surrender of what was left of the Alliance fleet. Geary remembered how dead Bloch's eyes had seemed then as his dreams of power and glory crumbled. But now his appearance was at least as bad. Admiral Bloch's eyes held the terror of a small mammal held in a trap.

"Black Jack," Bloch said with forced familiarity. "Admiral Geary now! Congratulations on that and . . . and on your many . . . many victories. I am in a . . . difficult situation. The ships under my . . . uh . . . that are supposed to be under my command . . . have . . . uh . . . malfunctioned." His lips bent in a weak attempt at a smile. "Mutiny, you could call it.

"Most of these ships have no provision for crews," Bloch said, gaining some composure as he described technical matters. "Except this one. The flagship. We have a small area with life support for me and my staff." His eyes shifted, avoiding looking toward Geary. "We have . . . had . . . two shuttles in the dock on this battle cruiser. For the use of me and my staff. Also fully automated. No pilots."

Admiral Bloch swallowed uncomfortably. "My staff . . . took one. To try to get to the government facility. They . . . did not make it. Once the shuttle got clear of this ship, it apparently registered as a target for the surrounding ships of the Defender Fleet."

"That bastard," Desjani said in a low voice. "He told them to go first so he could see whether or not the dark ships would target a shuttle from his flagship."

"After which he would take the second one," Geary agreed.

"You need to know something, Black Jack," Bloch continued, his attitude now defiant as if he realized what his audience's reaction would be to his earlier admission. "You've been too clever. I can still see what is happening outside of my flagship. Outside of my stateroom. I saw you destroy the docks and warehouses on which my fleet is dependent. Yes, you knocked out the support system for the Defender ships. But even though I cannot control them, I can monitor their decision processes. Do you know what you have done, Admiral? Destroying their support facilities here at Unity Alternate has activated the Armageddon Option in their programming."

"Armageddon Option does not sound good," Desjani murmured.

"Once they have destroyed your fleet," Bloch said, "the Defender warships will proceed to Unity, which their programming now assumes is enemy-occupied, and they will destroy everything at Unity. Then they will move on to other important star systems in the Alliance, destroying as much as they can while their fuel cells and expendable weaponry hold out."

"Ancestors preserve us," Geary whispered.

"It gets worse," Bloch added. It was obvious that he wasn't enjoying reciting this information. "The largest of the Defender ships, the battle cruisers and the battleships, are equipped with the codes necessary to override the safe-collapse systems that have been installed on the hypernet gates. When they are unable to continue their attacks, those ships will trigger the collapse of the gates in whichever star systems they occupy and devastate those star systems. *I* did not want that option to exist. *I* told everyone that it should not be placed on an automated weapons platform. But some people demanded it be installed. I don't think many others even know it is there. But I found out it had been installed, and now I have told you."

"And what the hell are you supposed to do about it?" Desjani asked Geary, appalled by what Bloch had revealed.

"You can't let them get out of this star system," Bloch pleaded.

"They will tear the guts out of the Alliance. I'm not a perfect man, Admiral. But this was not supposed to happen. I never would have agreed to accept this assignment if I knew how many flaws existed in the Defender concept. I can help you beat the Defender ships. I know more than you about their programming. About how to outsmart them. We can work together, and win this battle, and save the Alliance together."

Desjani growled something in a voice so low that Geary could not make out the words.

"I am senior to you, Admiral Geary," Bloch continued, trying to firm his voice as he spoke. "But even though I am the senior Alliance fleet officer in this star system, I will not insist upon assuming command of the forces here. Your command, your status, is safe from me. I have one shuttle left, which I can use to try to escape . . . my flagship. When the opportunity arises, I will use the shuttle to reach your forces or perhaps the government facility. I see you have Marines there. Excellent. Cover me as best you can. Together, we can destroy the Defender fleet."

Bloch paused, his eyes haunted. "You may hesitate to accept my offer. I understand. You must realize that I know things. I can tell you who approved all of this, what orders I was given, and what understandings existed with which particular people. You want that, I am sure. And, most importantly for you, I know where Captain Michael Geary is."

Geary wasn't sure whether or not Tanya had gasped. His own attention was riveted on Bloch's words.

"I can tell you where they've got him," Bloch continued. "The Syndics. Just help me get off this . . . off my flagship and I will—"

His image vanished.

"What happened?" Geary demanded.

"The signal cut off clean," the comm watch-stander said. "It must have been stopped at the source."

"Admiral Bloch's flagship figured out that he was plotting against it," Desjani said. "Once enough word matches and phrases were identified, it pulled the plug on him. What's the matter, Lieutenant Castries?"

"I'm sorry, Captain," Castries replied, looking ill. "He's a prisoner on his own flagship? The idea of our ship turning against us, controlling us—"

"Yeah," Desjani said. "Why would we give it the power to do that? Ask the idiots who keep coming up with the idea."

"Do we know which ship the transmission came from?" Geary asked.

"Yes, Admiral. This one."

On his display, one of the dark battle cruisers that had not been at Bhavan glowed brighter.

Geary shook his head, not sure whether to be angry or frustrated. "That confirms that whether or not Bloch came up with that ambush plan, he was not in command at Bhavan. But we can't get him off that ship he is trapped on. All I can do is keep fighting the dark ships, and if Bloch sees a chance while I'm doing that, he can take it."

"He wouldn't have told you where Michael Geary was even if his flagship hadn't cut Bloch off," Desjani said. "That's his biggest lever to get you to act on his behalf. He could always be lying about your grand-nephew being alive and in some Syndic labor camp," she added. "Just to manipulate you to help him escape."

"There's no way of telling, and there is nothing I can do about it anyway. Do you think he was lying about the Armageddon Option?"

Desjani hesitated. "It sounds way too plausible. And it's not like you needed more motivation to defeat the dark ships. But giving those ships the codes to enable them to use hypernet gates to destroy entire Alliance star systems? Who would do that?"

"Someone determined to pull everything down around them if they were losing," Geary said. "It's happened before, strategies designed to ensure that the victor inherited as little as possible, no matter the cost to the people on your own side. There are people I have met who I believe would adopt that idea. If the Syndics are going to own everything, destroy as much as you can to keep it from benefiting them."

"How many billions of people in Alliance star systems would die?" Desjani demanded.

"If you're a narcissist, that's not the important thing," Geary said, surprised at the viciousness in his voice. "All that matters is that you've lost, and you don't want the winner to enjoy the victory. A few powerful people who didn't care what would happen to many other people were in the right places to make that happen. We have to assume Bloch did not lie about the Armageddon Option and the gate codes. The dark ships must be destroyed before they can do those things."

"Yes, sir." Her smile held no humor, just agreement. "I don't know how we can survive this, but we can do our best to ensure none of the dark ships survive, either. As long as we manage to take out one of the dark ships for every one of ours that gets destroyed, we'll get the job done."

He stared at his display as if concentration on it would somehow change what it portrayed. "Everything I was trained, everything I was taught, was to avoid that kind of fight. No decent commander engaged in that kind of ugly math."

"What about a decent commander whose back is to the wall?" Desjani asked. "You got taught not to trade ship for ship. Your training has served this fleet well. But what's our objective, Admiral?"

"Save the Alliance."

"How do we do that, this time, without paying the necessary price? Doesn't the decent commander do what is necessary to ensure that the sacrifice of his or her people is not in vain?"

He nodded. "That is true. But if I don't set my attacks up right, we'll lose our ships without taking out enough of the dark ships."

"So do it right, Admiral."

"Four formations," Geary said. "Plus the Dancers. We'll see how the dark ships handle that."

With Desjani's help and the simple-to-use features of his maneuvering display, Geary swiftly set up four formations, using all of the ships in his main body plus those which had been in Delta One. "All units in First Fleet, immediate execute, assume Formations Gamma One, Two, Three, and Four."

The two Alliance groupings disintegrated, the hundreds of warships weaving onto new vectors to take their assigned places in the four new subformations. Each was in the shape of a thick coin or section of a cylinder, layers of warships that could engage in all directions and help defend each other.

Dauntless, *Daring*, *Victorious*, and *Intemperate* were joined by *Illustrious* and *Incredible* along with half of the remaining heavy cruisers and a quarter of the destroyers to constitute Gamma One under command of Captain Desjani. Captain Tulev's battle cruisers and those of Captain Duellos as well as the other heavy cruisers and another quarter of the destroyers formed Gamma Two under Tulev's command. The Second, Third, and Fourth Battleship Divisions gathered with half of the surviving light cruisers and a quarter of the destroyers into Gamma Three commanded by Captain Jane Geary, while the Fifth, Seventh, and Eighth Battleship Divisions took the rest of the light cruisers and destroyers into Gamma Four under Captain Armus.

The four fat discs of Alliance warships were arrayed in a vertical diamond, Gamma One and Three in the middle, Gamma Two above, and Gamma Four below.

The Dancers had stayed well above Geary's ships, and now were above and slightly ahead of Gamma Two.

The five dark ship formations were all coming in from behind the Alliance ships. As Geary's forces swung through their wide arc, the dark ships were cutting across that arc, aiming to intercept the Alliance warships by slashing through the rear of the formations at an angle of about thirty degrees.

Geary took a moment to call Captain Tulev, Captain Jane Geary, and Captain Armus. "You need to know everything we have learned about this situation." He described what he had been told by Admiral Bloch. "That defines our mission. We must stop the dark ships here. If *Dauntless* or myself are unable to continue the fight, you must do so, and all of your individual ship commanders must do so. Every ship must continue this fight until every dark ship has been destroyed."

They all nodded, Jane Geary looking stricken, and Armus bleak. Only Tulev replied in words. "To the last, Admiral."

"To the last," Geary agreed. The three captains saluted, he returned the gesture, then faced the battle once more.

Rearranging the Alliance warships had taken time, and Geary had held his velocity down to point one light speed during that period to help his ships take their assigned stations. He was also tired of running.

He gazed at his display, nerving himself for the sort of battle he had always sought to avoid. If they had to fight a battle of attrition, he was going to fight the best damned battle of attrition he possibly could.

"Ten minutes until the first of the dark ship formations overtakes us," Lieutenant Castries reported. "All dark ship formations are projected to pass through the rear quarter of our formations within a span of five seconds, separated by an average of one second."

"Textbook attack," Desjani scoffed. "What are we going to do?"

"Mess up their textbook," Geary said. "And then complicate their next moves." He was entering maneuvering commands rapidly. "All units in Gamma One, Two, Three, and Four, execute attached maneuvers at time two five."

With the dark ships racing to hit the Alliance subformations, Geary's warships pivoted again under the push of their maneuvering thrusters, facing the enemy almost bow on, then using their main propulsion to shift their vectors. The coin-shaped formations had turned edge on toward the approaching dark ships.

The dark ships tried to adjust their own vectors to continue their planned attack, but Geary's warships were already changing their approach again, aiming to counter the move that Geary knew he would have made if he were commanding the dark ships, the move the artificial intelligences would have been programmed to use in this situation.

He had concentrated his attacks against the dark ship formation containing four battleships, using each of his formations to slice through the array of dark ships in even quicker succession than the dark ships had aimed at the Alliance forces. The dark ships were trying to shift vectors again, trying to bring their other four formations onto paths that would allow them shots at the Alliance formations that were ducking inside the curves of the dark ships' approaches.

Gamma Four went through first, ten of Geary's battleships against four of the dark ships. Despite the advantage in numbers, the superior firepower on the dark battleships and the accumulated damage on Geary's battleships meant the forces were roughly equal. The battleships on both sides threw avalanches of fire at their enemies as the Alliance formation cut edge on through the rectangular dark ship formation.

If that had been it, the engagement would have been inconclusive. But on the heels of Gamma Four came Gamma Three, eleven more Alliance battleships hammering at the dark battleships that had just been flayed by Gamma Four. Overstressed shields collapsed on the dark battleships, hell lances and grapeshot penetrating to flash against the dark ships' armor.

Reeling from those blows, the dark ships immediately faced the seven battle cruisers of Gamma Two. Battle cruisers didn't have the same punch as battleships, but they were hitting dark ships that had already been struck by two attacks within seconds. Tulev's and

Duellos's warships slammed shots into the dark warships, then as they raced onward, Gamma One came through, another six battle cruisers striking enemies reeling from the prior blows.

As the Alliance formations and the dark ship formations separated and tore away in different directions, Geary ordered more course changes even before seeing the results of the attacks. Gamma Four stayed on the same vector, sliding in a vast curve opposite its former path. Gamma Three pushed its main propulsion units, forcing its warships into a tighter curve, and also angling upward. Gamma Two let momentum carry its ships in a wider curve and down. And Gamma One began coming about under full thrust from its battle cruisers' main propulsion to climb between the other three formations at an angle to them.

Then he looked back, seeing what had happened in those flashes of combat.

Two of the dark battleships were knocked out, one drifting helpless and the other one torn apart. The dark ship formation had also lost two heavy cruisers, three light cruisers, and a dozen destroyers.

Gamma Four, the first Alliance formation to face the dark battleships, had not come off unscathed. *Amazon* had taken the brunt of the dark ships' fire and was rolling slowly through space at a slight angle to her previous vector, unable to maneuver, many of her weapons knocked out. Captain Armus's *Colossus* had also taken a lot of hits but was in good enough shape to remain with the formation and continue in the fight. Heavy cruiser *Turret* was gone, along with light cruisers *Chase*, *Corona*, and *Foin*. Amazingly, only one destroyer, *Annellet*, had been lost.

An image appeared before Geary, an officer in a survival suit, on the darkened and damaged bridge of a battleship. "Commander Choiseul reporting in. Captain Penthe is dead. *Amazon*'s power core is damaged and unstable. We are conducting an emergency shutdown. All propulsion is out. Most weapons destroyed. Given dark ship targeting of escape pods in previous engagements, I have refrained from ordering personnel to abandon ship, but if it becomes obvious that *Amazon* is about to be destroyed, I will order the escape pods launched. To the honor of our ancestors, Choiseul, out."

The image vanished.

One of the dark ship formations, the one holding ten battle cruisers, had bent through the tightest turn it could manage, clearly aiming to finish off *Amazon*.

"They're giving us an opening," Desjani said quickly.

"I see it." The two Alliance battleship formations could not alter vectors quickly enough to engage the dark battle cruisers, but Geary's battle cruisers could. "Gamma Two," he sent, "intercept the dark battle cruisers targeting *Amazon*. Gamma One will assist."

Geary looked over at Desjani. "Captain, this one is yours."

"Yes, sir." She didn't sound as exultant as she usually did when given such an opportunity. Tanya instead radiated grim determination as she gave orders that continued Gamma One's turn and bent the vector downward again.

Gamma Two had dramatically tightened its turn, also coming up, as Tulev's *Leviathan* led the charge to assist Amazon's survivors.

"*Amazon* has shut down her power core," Lieutenant Castries said. The battleship was completely helpless now, a derelict doing a ponderous, uncontrolled tumble through space.

With the dark battle cruisers sweeping down and only minutes from firing, the wreck of the *Amazon* began volleying out escape pods as her surviving crew sought whatever tenuous safety the pods might offer.

Something in the Marine views distracted Geary for a moment. He moved one hand to close them out, then paused as he saw Marines moving into a large compartment filled with command equipment. The room resembled the primary command center on Ambaru Station at Varandal, but was even larger. Several individuals in generic civilian suits like those of the man and woman Geary had arrested at Ambaru were standing around, hands raised, except for one who was repeatedly and angrily swiping at what must be virtual controls in the air before her. She spun about and began berating the Marines. Even though Geary wasn't listening to the exchange, he could tell the woman was trying to assert authority over the Marines. More Marines entered, along with Victoria Rione and Colonel Rico. Rione said something to the woman that caused her mouth to snap shut, then Rico ordered some of the Marines to restrain her.

He couldn't spare the time to find out the details, but the frustration on the part of the suits' leader and the purposeful way Marine hackers were moving to the facility's command locations made it clear that the data destruction sought by the agents had not been achieved.

Realizing that it no longer mattered whether Victoria Rione found the critical information needed to restore access to the hypernet because fleeing and leaving the dark ships able to use the gate to attack Unity was not an option, Geary minimized the

Marine windows and focused all attention on the clash of battle cruisers that was about to occur.

The dark ships flashed past the wreck of *Amazon*, pouring fire into the derelict. With *Amazon*'s power core shut down, the only way to destroy what was left of her was by an overwhelming number of blows that shattered her armor and hull. Ten dark battle cruisers had enough firepower to accomplish that.

Amazon came apart under the merciless barrage, breaking into large and small pieces that spun away from each other.

Even though nearly every dark weapon was aimed at finishing off the battleship, shots from some of the smaller dark ships targeted the escape pods, knocking out or destroying several and certainly killing the men and women inside.

"Damn them." Geary did not realize he had spoken those words aloud, but he knew that he wasn't aiming his wrath at the cold minds of the dark ships but at the people who had programmed them and the people who had decided to trust in such weapons.

The dark battle cruisers had only seconds to enjoy their victory. Tulev did not attempt to clip a corner of the dark formation, instead smashing nearly straight up through one side of it, seven human-crewed battle cruisers against five automated dark ships.

Geary barely had time to register explosions before Tanya took Gamma One through the same portion of the dark battle cruiser formation, slashing downward.

Dauntless rocked with hits but kept going.

He tried to focus on his display, tried to take in the results of the two attacks.

Geary heard Desjani breathe a single, despairing word. "No."

Gamma Two, going through first, had taken the brunt of the enemy fire.

Leviathan was gone, reduced to a stream of wreckage spreading out along her former vector.

"Good-bye, Kostya," Desjani murmured. "Your war is over."

Captain Parr's voice sounded, but his image did not appear before Geary. "*Incredible* got shot to hell. We've lost practically all systems except maneuvering. That's damaged. We can keep up for now, but that's all we can do. Fire control and weapons are all off-line, life support barely functional, comms marginal, numerous hull penetrations."

One battle cruiser destroyed, and one out of the fight.

Clouds of debris marked the fates of two of the dark battle cruisers. Another had taken a lot of hits but still appeared operational.

It took all of Geary's effort to put aside thoughts of Captain Tulev and set up the next engagement. The battleships on both sides had been out of the last fight, but now Gamma Three and Four came together to sweep past just below and just above one of the dark formations containing six battleships.

In the wake of that engagement, a single dark battleship swerved away from its companions, moving erratically, then abruptly exploded.

But as Gamma Three maneuvered for its next turn, the battleship *Revenge* lurched off vector, broadcasting massive damage.

"You're doing what you have to do," Desjani said, her voice steady, her eyes burning. "We're taking out one of theirs for every one of ours we lose."

He wanted to tell her that he didn't know how much longer he could live with that kind of fighting but realized it did not matter. The odds that he would be living at all for more than a few additional hours appeared to be vanishingly small.

Victoria Rione's image appeared before him. The battle had carried *Dauntless* more than three-quarters of a light-hour from the government facility, too far for a comfortable conversation under current conditions. She spoke without pausing for any replies from Geary, looking steadily forward, her voice as firm as her bearing. "Admiral, we have found files that confirm what Admiral Bloch told you. The Armageddon Option is real, and the most powerful so-called Defender Fleet ships do have the codes necessary to weaponize hypernet gates. At the moment we are locked out of all hypernet gate functions and are trying to access any of them that we can. We are still looking for any codes that might disable or divert the dark ships, without success. Every file on this facility is being copied on portable storage devices and also transferred directly to *Mistral*'s databases. We have discovered a large number of files pertaining to research on how to copy the Syndicate method of gate blocking, but any results were either never listed here or scorched-earth deleted from the systems before we reached this facility.

"We have found no command personnel and no researchers, contractors, or representatives. Records indicate the station had nearly four hundred people here before an emergency evacuation order was given. The remaining security personnel, who are all private contractors, have been disarmed and detained. The Marines have also freed a dozen prisoners from a high-security detention center, along with some medical personnel who stayed behind to look after the prisoners when the rest of the staff unsuccessfully tried to flee.

"We have discovered vast areas in the facility that have been untouched since construction. They contain equipment that is in working condition but decades obsolete. If the government had ever shown up here, they would have been in for some unpleasant surprises."

Rione took a deep breath. "And we found my husband. The Marines are estimating they will be able to depart the facility in another hour, but Commander Young on *Mistral* says they will need to be sure they can reach the protection of your ships before they leave the dock."

He wondered why Rione had provided no details on her husband, why she didn't look happy at having found him, but had no time to dwell on either issue.

"They haven't found anything on the facility to help us," Geary told Desjani. "They did find files that confirmed what Bloch told us."

"The one time I wanted him to be lying, he wasn't. Do we go get *Mistral* now?"

"It will be at least another hour before *Mistral* can get underway."

Desjani frowned. "I just thought of something. You should tell *Mistral* to stay in that dock. She is safe there, safer than if she tries to rejoin us while the dark ships are conducting attack runs on us."

"Good idea." He called Commander Young. "Stay in the dock until we call you out. If none of our warships survive the action, we will have hopefully destroyed enough of the dark ships to allow *Mistral* to make her way home. The information and the people you carry must make it back to the Alliance."

The dark ship formation with three surviving battle cruisers whipped by *Revenge*, inflicting a lot more damage but not shattering the massive battleship.

Captain Duellos, now in command of Gamma Two, caught those dark battle cruisers and tore one apart, but at the cost of *Implacable* taking so much damage that she had also lost maneuvering control and most of her weapons. "Power core unstable! Abandoning ship!" Commander Neeson sent. Escape pods leaped from *Implacable* as her crew sought safety.

The Dancers were harassing the larger dark battle cruiser formation, making rapid individual passes to pick off cruisers and destroyers. But they had lost five ships and were suffering increasing damage.

Implacable, still racing through space, abruptly exploded as her power core blew. There was no way of telling yet how many of her crew had made it off *Implacable* or whether Commander Neeson was among them.

Geary directed Desjani to hit the larger of the two dark battle cruiser formations again, the Alliance formation angling past one edge to knock out a couple of destroyers and inflict heavy damage on another dark battle cruiser. But in the process *Daring* and *Victorious* both took a lot of hits, and *Dauntless* suffered lesser but still-significant damage.

The battleships were coming around again, all of the dark ships concentrating on Gamma Four, while Gamma Three tried to swing over and down in time to support the other battleship formation. Geary wondered which Alliance warships would be lost or disabled this time, which men and women would die, as the beleaguered First Fleet fought what would likely be its final, remorseless battle.

A different alert sounded on Geary's display, accompanied by an urgent pulsing highlighting the last object he had expected to be worried about in this star system or any other. The alien superbattleship captured from the Kicks. "What the hell is happening on *Invincible*?"

15

Lieutenant Castries sounded even more baffled than Geary. "We are picking up indications that power sources are activating in multiple locations aboard *Invincible*."

"*Multiple* locations?" Desjani demanded.

"Yes, Captain, I don't ―"

"*Invincible* has several power cores," Geary said. "We weren't sure why the Kicks designed it that way, but the engineers speculated it was because the ship was so huge that running power from any single location would have been harder than running multiple power sources. But those power cores were shut down! Every one of them was cold. Every piece of Kick equipment on that ship was shut down, deactivated, or disabled."

"*Something* is reactivating the power cores," Desjani said. "I assume that we're ruling out the Kick ghosts?"

"The Dancers explained that to us. There's no actual presence. Just an impression of a presence."

"Then what else―?" Desjani began. "Ancestors save us. Did

those maniacs fit *Invincible* out as a dark ship?"

"She doesn't have any working propulsion," Geary replied. "We destroyed her main propulsion drives when we captured her, and we can see that they haven't been repaired or replaced. What good would it do—"

"Combat systems are activating aboard *Invincible*," Lieutenant Yuon reported, sounding dazed. "According to what we're picking up, it's the Kick combat systems, not anything retrofitted from human sources. The targeting systems inside the ship and the few weapons that were still operational after we took *Invincible* are all coming online."

"The tugs are powering up," Lieutenant Castries said, disbelieving. "The heavy-hauling Alliance tugs mated to *Invincible* are activating their systems."

"How far away is *Invincible*?" Desjani glared at her display. "Twenty light-minutes. How long does it take to power up one of the fleet's heavy tugs?"

"Our data says fifteen minutes from standby to emergency movement," Castries replied. "They were in standby."

"Then *Invincible* is probably already underway! What the hell is going on? Those tugs were cold and empty," Desjani insisted. "No crews aboard. Are the dark ships doing this somehow?"

More alerts sounded, more visual alerts highlighted the same area. "Propulsion on the Alliance tugs fastened to *Invincible* has lit off at full. *Invincible* is underway," Lieutenant Yuon reported. "No life support is active on the tugs."

"Admiral!" It was General Charban, his image speaking with rapid precision to ensure his words were clear. "We have a message from the Dancers. I won't read the poetry, just the gist of it. They're telling us they have 'reawakened' the Kick superbattleship and that it is now 'our distraction.'"

"Distraction?" Geary asked, then suddenly understood. "Diversion. The Dancers remotely reactivated the Kick systems?"

"I assume that's what they mean," Charban replied.

"How the hell did they do that?" Desjani asked.

"I don't know," Geary replied. "I don't know why, if they can do that, they didn't mess with the Kick systems when we were together fighting the Kicks."

"And they remotely activated Alliance systems," Desjani added, pointing to the tugs. "They must have remotely overridden access codes and authorization requirements and safety interfaces on the tugs. And now they've remotely lit off the tugs' propulsion and set a vector for them. The Dancers may be allies of ours, but when did they develop *that* capability?"

"Admiral," Lieutenant Yuon announced, now breathless. "All of the dark ship formations are turning away."

Geary switched his gaze back to the dark ship formations, blinking in surprise at his display where vectors on the dark ships had begun swinging wildly. "They were turning for more intercepts and attacks on our formations. Now they're coming about as fast as they can onto other vectors."

"All of those other vectors are in the same general . . . they're heading for *Invincible*," Desjani said, frowning as she studied her display. "I'm certain that's how they'll steady out. They are going after *Invincible*."

"To the dark ships, *Invincible* must look like a huge threat even though she is nearly weaponless," Geary said. "A literally huge threat. It must take priority over any other target as far as the dark ship AIs are concerned. A diversion. The Dancers gave us a diversion, something to get the dark ships off our backs for a short period."

"A more-than-short period," Desjani replied. "The dark ships are also about twenty light-minutes from *Invincible*, which is moving away from all of us. Just because of the distance involved, it will take the dark ships probably about an hour and a half to catch *Invincible* and more time to destroy her."

That sank in. *Invincible* was not simply a distraction. She would also be a sacrifice. "Ancestors forgive us. The knowledge that ship holds, the things we could have learned from it . . ."

"One more crime to lay at the feet of the idiots responsible for this," Desjani said in a low, angry voice. "May the living stars give those criminals the fates they deserve. What will we do with the time that the Dancers and *Invincible* are giving us?"

"Save some lives, at least for now." Geary gave orders, diverting scores of warships to collect and recover escape pods from the Alliance battleships, battle cruisers, cruisers, and destroyers that had been put out of action or destroyed. "As soon as we have recovered everyone, we're going to rejoin *Mistral* and head for the outer reaches of the star system. Another jump point is going to appear eventually. We can't use it, because we can't leave any dark ships active to attack the Alliance. But *Mistral* can."

Desjani gazed at him, then nodded somberly. "*Mistral* has to get back. You may have to order some of the Marines aboard *Mistral* to hold a gun to Commander Young's head to get her to leave the rest of us, though."

He had a momentary image of what the rest of her life would be like for Commander Young, ordered to leave the rest, forced to leave the rest, but doomed to be forever remembered as the only one who had left Unity Alternate, the only one whose ship had survived the desperate battle at Unity Alternate. Geary was appalled as he realized that he would be ordering Young to a living nightmare that many would consider a fate worse than death. He wondered how long she could live with that, how long she would live with that.

But he knew he would have to order her to do it.

Geary called *Mistral*. "Commander Young, the fleet will be repositioning to the vicinity of the orbital governmental facility. You have one hour and ten minutes from the time of this transmission before we get there. Be ready to leave the dock and accompany the fleet at that time. Do not, repeat do not, leave anyone aboard that facility."

The formations of the First Fleet, already rendered somewhat ragged by the combat losses they had sustained, had dissolved into a mass of individual ships darting about to collect escape pods and rescue the occupants. He did not have to supervise that. The fleet's automated systems had no trouble figuring out which ship was best positioned to pick up which escape pod, could track when a ship had recovered as many survivors as that ship could safely carry, and could recommend to each commanding officer what to do next.

"It's ironic," Geary said as he watched the process. "Our automated systems are making it possible to recover all of the survivors as quickly and efficiently as we can. A lot of men and women will owe their rescue to that. But other automated systems destroyed their ships in the first place and will kill those men and women later if they can."

"It's just a matter of whether you're ordering what to do based on what the systems say, or if they're ordering you what to do whether you like it or not," Desjani said. "There isn't anything complicated about that."

"There shouldn't be," Geary agreed.

The survivor recovery completed, Geary ordered his ships back into their formations, leaving the discarded escape pods drifting in space, and directed every warship to head back toward the government facility.

The dark ships were still swooping down on *Invincible*. The immense alien superbattleship was moving slowly away from the pursuing dark ships, plodding along under the thrust of the rows of fleet tugs that provided only a fraction of the power that *Invincible*'s main propulsion units once employed.

Geary felt an odd sense of sorrow at the sight. Not the huge regret that the knowledge represented by the captured alien ship would be lost but sadness at watching the massive ship sacrifice itself to give the Alliance fleet a little time that might make all the difference in being able to destroy the last dark ship before the last Alliance ship. In its willingness to be destroyed for the sake of the human warships, the alien craft itself felt more human, more a living thing, than the dark ships with their AIs designed to mimic human thought processes.

The ship information graphics on the virtual display next to his command seat were filled with red and yellow markers indicating degrees of damage suffered by his warships, amidst too few greens that indicated ships without significant damage. The diversion provided by *Invincible* would buy a few hours, but what his fleet needed was six months in a major repair facility with a lot of docks.

The sort of facility, in fact, they had been forced to destroy here.

"We've got a little time," Geary told Desjani. "I'm going to hold a senior officer conference."

She ensured the privacy fields were activated, then Geary called his top officers, their images in their command seats on the bridges of their ships appearing around him. Captain Duellos. Captain Jane Geary. Captain Badaya. Captain Desjani in person. Captain Armus. The sight of those officers brought back with full force the fact that Captain Tulev should have been among them and was not.

Geary took a second to compose himself, to ensure his voice did not falter, before he spoke. "You all know the situation we are in. I would like to know your thoughts and your recommendations."

Duellos replied in an uncharacteristically grave voice. "As was recently pointed out by a very fine officer who is no longer among us, we only have one option remaining. Fight to the last."

"That's right," Badaya said. "To the last ship, to the last man or woman. Maybe we can't wipe out the dark ships completely, but we can ensure that none of their battle cruisers and battleships survive this fight."

"None of ours will either," Armus said as if that were a matter not of sorrow but of inevitability. "But no one will be able to say we did not die with honor. No one will be able to accuse us of not doing our duty. We will be welcomed by our ancestors."

"The last charge of the Gearys," Jane said with the ghost of a smile. "I never thought I'd be part of Black Jack's real last stand. It doesn't feel as bad as I thought it would."

"No one else has any other options to suggest?" Geary said.

Desjani shrugged. "We can't wipe out the dark ships without paying a very high price. There are too many of them, they have too much firepower, they can maneuver better than we can, and the AIs running them aren't your equal, but they are close enough to that given those other advantages the dark ships have."

"It's not like we could reposition through the hypernet gate, even if it weren't blocked," Badaya pointed out.

After being awakened from a century in survival sleep, it had taken Geary a while to understand why Badaya phrased it that way. After a century of war, with little hope of victory and in the face of ongoing awful losses, the Alliance fleet had clung fiercely to its pride, never talking about retreating but only about repositioning. The Alliance fleet might die fighting, it might "reposition" at other times, but it never "retreated." Geary realized that that attitude, which these officers had all grown up with, made it easier for them to contemplate a last battle at this moment. As Desjani had reminded him, they had all expected to die long before this.

Duellos nodded in agreement with Badaya. "We can't let the dark ships have access to the hypernet so they can carry out that Armageddon Option. They won't leave as long as we're still here fighting them, so we must stay and fight, even if we didn't have to."

"That's true," Geary said.

"Although," Badaya added, "part of me wouldn't mind leading these human-made monsters to Unity so they could carry out their Armageddon on those who created them."

"A lot of innocent people would die as well," Jane Geary said. "Otherwise, I'd agree with you."

"All right," Geary said. "We are going to undertake one detour." He explained about his intentions with *Mistral*. "If the Marines have found the means to unblock the hypernet gate, we can send *Mistral* to safety using that, but I'm going to assume we'll have to try to avoid action until a jump point appears that *Mistral* can use."

"There are going to be a lot of unhappy people on *Mistral*," Armus observed dourly.

"They have to do their duty, just as we are doing ours," Desjani said.

"I'm not arguing that. I'm just glad I'm not the commanding officer of *Mistral*."

"Thank you," Geary said. "I am honored to have served with you, and with every man and woman in this fleet. Captain Geary, there is one more issue we should discuss alone." The images of the other captains vanished, leaving Jane Geary watching him expectantly. She made no comment about Tanya also still being present, for which Geary was grateful. "When Admiral Bloch communicated with us, he claimed to know that your brother Michael was still alive and where he was. He offered to trade that knowledge for our rescuing him from his flagship."

Jane Geary inhaled sharply, then laughed. "Admiral Bloch would say anything to try to save his life. He's lying."

"That's what I thought," Geary said. "In any event, it is impossible to get him off the dark battle cruiser that is his flagship. The best that Bloch can hope for is that we knock out but not destroy that dark ship, leaving him a chance to get off it. But we can't limit our attacks, or risk the lives of our people, to try to save him."

"I agree. Michael would not want such a deal made in his name."

She looked over at Tanya. "He would be happy to know that the family included a worthy new sister when we fought our last fight."

"Thank you," Tanya said.

Jane Geary saluted them both, then her image vanished as well.

Geary took a moment to compose himself, then called General Charban. "You'll need to tell the Dancers what we're going to do." He explained the fleet's plans, then gestured in the direction of the Dancers, who were once again tagging along close to the Alliance warships. "The Dancers are under no obligation to stay here and fight to the death with us, though we will be immensely grateful for their assistance. Let me know what they are planning on doing."

"Yes, Admiral. What are our chances, do you think?"

"I think our fleet will achieve its objectives, General. I don't expect to survive that. I don't think many of us will. Maybe none."

"That's what I thought." Charban shrugged. "At least I can stop worrying about why I survived earlier battles when others did not. This will simplify my life though, of course, I will no longer be alive to benefit from that. We'll see how the Dancers feel about this kind of fight."

That done, Geary looked over at Tanya. "Regrets?"

"I'm doing what I love, Admiral." She looked at him, then smiled. "And in good company."

"Me, too."

"I need more time, Admiral," Rione's image insisted with a fierce intensity unlike her usual cool outward demeanor. "I think I can find what we need. But I require more time than you are allowing. I must have that time."

They were still a couple of light-minutes from the government facility. The four-minute delays between each statement and the reply being received made the conversation awkward but not intolerable. "I can't give you more time," Geary said. "If you haven't found anything yet, odds are there is nothing to find. Maybe Admiral Bloch has the codes and hasn't coughed them up. You can try to convince him to do that. The dark ship battle cruiser he is on has survived so far, and despite his talk about risking a shuttle journey to join our fleet, Bloch didn't make any moves to do that during any of our engagements so far.

"It would be good to have access to that gate so we could get *Mistral* out of here fast, but it's not critical that we use the hypernet gate. It is critical that *Mistral* take advantage of the opportunity to get back within the protection of our warships while the dark ships are preoccupied with destroying *Invincible*. The bottom line is that *Mistral* needs to pull out when I ordered so that we have a chance to get her out of this star system. And you and your husband need to be on *Mistral*."

Rione did not reply. He imagined she was angry, but he had no emotional stress left unused to devote to worrying about that.

About an hour later, the Alliance formations swung by the government facility. The dark ships had surely reached *Invincible* by now, but the light from their attack had not yet traveled all the way from that location to where Geary's fleet could see it. The Alliance sensors could only see images nearly an hour old of the dark ships closing in on the alien superbattleship. Odds were that the dark ships had actually finished their attacks on *Invincible* and were already on their way back to deal with Geary's forces again.

Mistral shot out of the dock, accelerating as rapidly as she could to rejoin the other warships. "Mission completed as ordered," Commander Young's image told Geary.

Next to her, Colonel Rico nodded. He looked like someone who had been wearing battle armor for hours and was, in fact, still in it, just his face shield opened. "We have multiple copies of everything in every record file in every storage source aboard that facility, Admiral. There were also papers."

"Papers?" Geary asked. "What kind of papers?"

"Papers with records on them, and orders, and information," Rico clarified.

"Really? I don't think I've ever seen anything like that."

"My hack and cracks think the paper records were used instead of digital files to limit any chance of the information being copied or leaked," Rico explained. "We discovered something else about their security precautions when we looked outside the facility using the sensors on it. They showed us a star system with only one star, Alpha. Beta was completely screened out, gravitational effects and everything. I bet it was the same way on any ships bringing in people and taking them back. Probably only a few people out of everyone sent here ever knew it was a binary."

"Clever," Geary said.

"Yes, sir," Commander Young agreed. "Some people have gotten entirely too comfortable with the idea of making everyone else see only what is wanted."

"We brought the private security guards out," Rico added, "including the body of the one we had to shoot. The guards are prisoners, but they're not giving us any trouble. They figure we saved them. We've also locked up the people who were prisoners aboard the facility. We don't know why they had been locked up, so we're not taking chances."

"That can be sorted out later. What about the suits?" Geary asked.

"Locked in the highest-security cells on *Mistral*," Commander Young answered. "The Marines, my masters-at-arms, and our medical personnel gave all of the suits a good going-over before we locked them up to ensure no one had suicide capability on them or in them. I don't know if all of them are a threat, either. Some of the suits are acting like people who were asking themselves questions even before we showed up."

"What about codes for the hypernet gate?" Geary said. He already knew what the answer must be because no one had led with that information, but still asked in a sort of forlorn hope.

"No, sir. We didn't find them. Former Senator Rione thought she had a lead, but there wasn't any more time."

"Where is Rione?"

Commander Young checked a display on her ship. "In her stateroom, with her husband. He's in really bad shape, Admiral. I think that hit her real hard. She's got a comm block on the stateroom, but I can override it if you need to talk to her."

"No," Geary said. "If she had found anything, she would have already told me."

He had considered having *Mistral* join Gamma One, positioned near *Dauntless*, but realized that putting two high-value targets right next to each other would be tempting fate, or at least tempting the dark ships. Instead, Geary ordered *Mistral* to join with Gamma

Three, taking up position near *Dreadnaught*.

"Admiral, we have our answer from the Dancers," Charban said. "It's an odd little song to human ears, but it comes down to a statement that they were sent to stop the dark ships, and they will stay and fight to complete that mission."

"Thank them for me," Geary said. "Can we tell the Dancers that we are honored to fight alongside them?"

"Yes," Charban replied, his expression thoughtful. "It should take the form of saying that we and they belong together in the pattern, I think. Something like that. I'll put something suitable together."

"And what have our honored fighting companions said about their undisclosed-until-now ability to activate Kick and Alliance ship systems from very long distances?"

Charban smiled. "I think they may have been embarrassed to be called on that. The answer they gave is that the methods they use are easily overridden by supervisors, whether human or Kick. On the targeted system, if there is someone present to override what looks like a glitch, it is too subtle to be identified as intrusion. But it is also far too weak to work on any system being monitored for glitches. I naturally asked why their methods could not work on the dark ships, and the Dancers replied that the AIs on the dark ships act as supervisors or monitors. The term they used actually translated as 'over-minds.' It is, therefore, a potentially valuable capability, but only when dealing with something lacking an operator, human or Kick or artificial."

Fifteen minutes after the fleet passed the orbiting facility, the light finally reached them from the dark ship attack on *Invincible*. Despite the millions of kilometers between where the Alliance ships were and the site of the attack, the optical sensors aboard the fleet's ships could get crystal-clear images through the emptiness of space.

Geary did not want to watch, but he felt a responsibility to do so. He flinched as the dark ships opened fire, dark battle cruisers blowing apart the Alliance fleet tugs propelling the alien warship.

Astoundingly, *Invincible* got off a few shots at the dark ships from her remaining weapons as the enemy came in close. Geary heard cheers aboard *Dauntless* and knew her crew was celebrating the heroic resistance of *Invincible*. It was just the automated weapons systems on the alien superbattleship, but it still felt like a brave ship going down fighting.

But *Invincible*'s remaining weapons were quickly silenced as the dark battleships came close enough to pour streams of hell-lance fire into the superbattleship.

"They're smart enough this time to conserve their expendable weapons," Desjani commented. "No missiles, no grapeshot, not even bombardment projectiles, just hell lances."

"Yeah. The dark ships learned that lesson as well. Too bad."

It felt unreal to watch so many hell-lance hits pummeling *Invincible*, while the superbattleship drifted onward, to all appearances living up to the name that Admiral Lagemann had given her.

But even the Kick superbattleship could not take that kind of punishment forever. Geary saw the dark ships opening their distance to *Invincible* and guessed what was coming. "One or more of the Kick power cores are going unstable due to damage."

"They must have been built tough to have stood up to that barrage as long as they did," she observed.

He glanced at her, saw the unusual intensity with which Desjani was watching events, and realized that she was trying to distract herself. "Are you all right?"

"No. I lost more friends today. I'll get over it. Or I'll see the docs for some happy pills. Or we'll all die soon. Whichever way, it won't be a problem."

An explosion ripped a huge hole in *Invincible*, followed by another that tore another gaping wound in the alien warship. But the superbattleship lurched onward.

The dark battleships closed in again, firing so intensely that they had to pause to prevent their hell-lance batteries from overheating.

Sections began breaking off *Invincible*, then, as the dark battleships swiftly withdrew once more, three additional massive explosions tore the superbattleship apart.

Geary sighed, thinking of the loss those explosions represented. "There are a lot of large pieces. Maybe there will be something left that we can use or learn from."

"Maybe," Desjani said.

Over an hour ago, the dark ships had turned and begun accelerating after the Alliance warships again. "Here we go," Desjani said.

Word had gotten around that the fleet was unlikely to survive the battle in this star system, as well as why the fleet had to stay and fight even if the opportunity to flee miraculously presented itself.

The officers, sailors, and Marines took the news as the senior captains had. They had long ago resigned themselves to this.

Lines formed outside the worship compartments as men and women took advantage of the time available to make their peace or offer prayers or beg for miracles.

Geary, brooding over their lack of options and half-asleep from fatigue, started back to awareness as Tanya Desjani returned to her seat on the bridge. "Were you saying hello to our ancestors?"

"I'll probably be able to do that in person soon enough," she replied. "No. I had some urgent requests to perform marriage services by people who figured they had better get it done fast if they ever wanted it done. I just rushed through six of them, without getting all the proper authorizations and approvals."

"You could get in trouble for that when fleet headquarters finds out," Geary commented sarcastically.

"I'll risk it. I just made sure to ask each couple whether, should we somehow live another day after this, they would regret making this decision. They all said they wouldn't. We'll probably never know." Desjani gave him a sidelong look. "One of the couples were Charban's lieutenants."

Geary jerked back to full attention yet again. "Lieutenant Iger and Lieutenant Jamenson?"

"Yeah. Someday there might have been the patter of the feet of little green-haired future intelligence officers." Tanya gave him another look. "The green-hair thing is dominant, you know. Lieutenant Jamenson's ancestors made sure of that, and I made sure that Lieutenant Iger was aware of it. It didn't seem to faze him, though."

"Thank you for not being from Eire," Geary said, "not that it looks like you and I are likely to be doing any reproducing."

This time her look held warning. "Hey, Admiral, we stay professional on this bridge until the end. Agreed?"

"Agreed." He sat up. They had gone a light-hour outward, deliberately angling away from the hypernet gate to avoid tempting the dark ships to drop the block on it and leave this star system to implement the Armageddon Option before finishing off Geary's fleet. The government facility was six hours' travel time behind them. "The dark ships are two light-hours from us, in a stern chase. I should get some rest while I can."

"Yes, sir, you should." She smiled at him. "Sweet dreams."

He had worried that he would be too tightly wound with fears of the continuation of the battle to be able to sleep and too overwhelmed by the losses the fleet had already suffered. But he must have been even more exhausted than he thought. Geary fell into a deep sleep within moments.

He was jolted awake by the loudest, most urgent call alert that his comm panel could produce. Groggy, Geary hit the accept control. "What?"

"That woman is still on the facility!" Desjani yelled.

He had to gather his thoughts to make sense of the words. "Rione? She's—she's on *Mistral*."

"She is sending messages from the facility, Admiral!"

"What message?" Geary was still trying to grasp what he was hearing.

"I don't know. It's set so only you can open it."

"Relay it to here and set it to play for you as well," Geary ordered, a feeling of dread beginning to replace his earlier confusion.

He slapped the virtual command to open the message, waited impatiently for the second needed for the system to verify who he was, then saw Victoria Rione's image appear before him. She was clearly still on the government facility, standing in the command center that Geary had seen earlier. The command center itself had a feeling of abandonment and hasty departure, except for Rione herself, and in the background a man lying in a fully reclined seat. The man appeared to be sleeping, his chest slowly rising and falling.

Rione's face was drawn even tighter, the skin thin over bones, and she was gazing outward with eyes that held fear as well as a terrible resolve. "Admiral Geary, the first thing I must say is that you must not blame your people for my success at remaining here. The same sort of software that can make my presence appear to the fleet's systems to be fully authorized can also make it appear to those systems that I am somewhere I am not. The systems on the assault transport told everyone on that ship that I was in my stateroom."

She paused, as if a little short of breath. "I was right. That is the other important thing. I found the necessary codes for the hypernet gate. Not those to unblock it. That remains beyond my ability. But I was able to use official software, which I am not supposed to have, to reprogram the safe-collapse system on that gate. Its function has been reversed, and it will now ensure the maximum outburst of energy when the gate collapses, something on the order of point eight on the Schneider Nova Scale."

Touching a control, Rione indicated a number that appeared. "I have just sent the collapse command to the gate, at exactly that time. You can calculate when it will reach the gate and when the resulting shock wave from the gate's collapse will reach every portion of this star system. I remember what you did at Prime when facing such a threat, taking your fleet into the shadow of the star to protect it from the shock wave. You can do the same here.

But the dark ships will not know the gate is collapsing until they see the collapse begin. They will not know the safe-collapse device has been subverted until the shock wave hits them."

Even though this message had been sent hours ago, she seemed to be staring straight into his eyes. "I've learned a lot about space battles since meeting you, Admiral. I have learned enough to know that this is a battle you could only win at tremendous cost. You might even lose, with catastrophic results for the Alliance. So I have done the only thing that will make certain the dark ships are destroyed. It will hopefully also save your fleet. I confess to having developed a fondness for the men and women under your command.

"Do not waste your time trying to get me off this facility. I can read a maneuvering display well enough to know there is no chance of that in the time that you have left.

"I am not alone here. As you can see, my husband, Paol Benan, is here with me. He is fully sedated." She swallowed before being able to speak again. "According to the records I found here, his treatment to reverse the damage caused by the mental block was delayed repeatedly for 'security reviews,' delayed until the damage to his mind was declared irreversible. Paol is now a danger to everyone, including himself, including me. He must remain fully sedated, a living death. They took my husband, Admiral. They denied him an honorable death. And the worst part is, I don't believe they even cared what they were doing."

Rione paused again, breathing deeply. "Finish the job, Admiral. Get your ships home. Get *Mistral* home. The information in the files, and what the people we found here can testify to, will bring to account those who through narrow-sightedness, greed, ignorance, fear, or their own desire for power nearly destroyed the Alliance. Others acted out of wishful thinking or willful ignorance, and while they may not deserve the same fate as others, they do need to answer for their decisions. Some have clean hands, as clean as any hands involved in this can be, and those records will ensure they are exonerated despite the attempts of the guilty to shift blame to them. It is past time the people of the Alliance stopped blaming the government for their ills and looked in the mirror to realize that the government is *them*.

"Save the Alliance, Admiral. As I told you the first time we met, that is what I am willing to die for. Now, that is my last request. You owe me that."

Rione paused longer this time, struggling to speak. "Thank you for the services you have done me. Thank you for tolerating my presence, and listening to my advice, and for doing the best you could, and for still believing in the things the rest of us forgot were important. I will not pretend to be facing the certain end with calm resolution. I never claimed to be that sort of person. I am frightened. Once this call is ended, I will take a sedative, lie down with my husband, and when the blow strikes, neither of us will feel it, but we will go through that last door together, where I hope our ancestors will welcome me and forgive me for the things I have felt I must do."

A flash of her old fire appeared in Rione's eyes. "Perhaps I will finally earn a little respect from the men and women like those in your fleet who we politicians have for too long sent to their deaths with too little thought or foresight. After all, the people admire dead politicians almost as much as they detest living ones.

"Good-bye, Admiral Geary. Save the Alliance. May you and Captain Desjani survive to live long and happy lives.

"To the honor of our ancestors. Victoria Rione. Out."

Geary drew in a shaky breath as her image vanished, then his mind shot into action. "Tanya, I'm on my way to the bridge. Start working the maneuvers and see if we can make it to the shadow of one of the stars with the time we have."

He raced to the bridge and dropped into his command seat. Desjani was working furiously on her maneuvering display, her face rigid with anger. "We can just make it," she snarled. "Taking into account the limits on propulsion from our most heavily damaged ships, we have a decent chance of getting behind Beta *just* before the shock wave hits. *Damn her!* She *knew* that now I will have to honor her memory!"

Geary quickly checked over Desjani's work. "We head back in-system, on a vector apparently aimed at returning to the government facility—"

"Then as the dark ships close to intercept, we shift vector to aim for the shadow of Star Beta. But it is going to be close. Depending on how long the gate takes to collapse, we might get caught in the shock wave. We have no time to spare. But if we get there too fast, we'll be sitting ducks for the dark ships."

He hit his comm controls. "All units in First Fleet, this is Admiral Geary, immediate execute attached maneuvers. Any unit that believes propulsion damage may limit its ability to carry out these maneuvers contact me at once."

Dauntless began pivoting, her main propulsion lighting off to push her onto a new vector heading back the way the fleet had come. The battle cruiser's propulsion didn't light off at full, instead matching the best effort that some of the most badly damaged ships could manage. "Can we transfer crews—" Geary began.

"It would take too long," Desjani said. "We would have to limit acceleration even more for the shuttles to transfer crews off the most badly damaged ships so we could leave those ships behind. We're better off trying to get everyone into the shadow of the star. Damn that woman!"

Geary sat back, trying to sort through his emotions. "She saved us. Maybe."

"Why did I have to be saved by her?" Desjani shook her head angrily, blinking back tears. "She is braver than I thought. You could see how scared she is. But she went ahead with it."

"Was she right about it being impossible to get to her?"

"Yes. Any ship we sent would be pulling alongside the government facility when the shock wave got there. Any attempt would be futile and suicidal."

"Captain?" They looked back to see Lieutenant Castries staring at them. "What has happened?"

Geary sighed, realizing that he must tell everyone about the sudden shift in their fortunes. He tapped his comm controls. "All units in First Fleet, this is Admiral Geary. We have an unexpected chance at victory and survival. Former co-president of the Callas Republic, former Senator of the Alliance, former Emissary Victoria Rione stayed behind on the government facility and was able to break into the hypernet gate controls and order the gate to collapse with the force of point eight nova. We are proceeding at the best rate we can manage to shelter in the shadow of Star Beta so that we will avoid the shock wave that should destroy the dark ships in their entirety, but we will have to also avoid being caught and delayed by the dark ships along the way." He had to take a breath himself before continuing. "Victoria Rione has no chance of survival. She cannot be rescued from the facility before the shock wave hits. She has sacrificed herself to ensure the destruction of the dark ships and the safety of the Alliance. If we live, it will be because of her. Honor her memory. Geary, out."

He could hear, could feel, the hush that spread through *Dauntless* after his announcement.

A minute later, a frantic call came in from *Mistral*.

"Admiral," Commander Young said, "our systems assured us she was aboard! We tried to get in just now and found the locks on her stateroom are sealed with overrides. I have crew members breaking in, but there were ongoing, confirmed status feeds from that compartment telling us that Senator Rione was there."

"She told me that she hacked *Mistral*'s systems to show that," Geary said. "There is no fault on your part, Commander." He wondered if he should ever tell Commander Young of the fate that she had been saved from by Rione's actions. "I suppose all of us ought to start double-checking more on what our systems tell us."

"Commander Benan may be aboard. We are checking, sir."

"He's not aboard *Mistral*, either. They are together. You did everything that you should have, Commander." Having reassured Young, Geary stared at his display for a few moments, not really seeing the information it showed, his mind filled with memories.

Desjani was gazing bleakly at her own display. "We get to spend the next several hours hoping we don't get annihilated by the shock wave or the dark ships or both. There's nothing else we can do."

"It beats what we were looking forward to a half hour ago," Geary said. "Tanya—"

"Admiral, with all due respect, I am not yet prepared at this time to discuss matters concerning her."

"Understood."

"Admiral." General Charban, calling up from the comm compartment, appeared to be dazed. "I have informed the Dancers of what is happening, which took some very creative poetry. I think it is safe to say that they will remain close to us until the shock wave is past. You will recall that Senator Rione was embraced by one of the Dancers. That gave her some special status with them, and these Dancers . . . well, I don't know if the word means the same thing to them, but they said that the pattern will grieve for her."

"Tell the Dancers that we appreciate that," Geary said.

"Am I correct, Admiral, in my understanding that our survival is not yet certain?"

"You are, General. We still have to get past the dark ships. If the gate collapses as fast as possible, we won't be in the shadow of Beta in time. If it collapses more slowly, we'll get there."

"Then I will pray that the gate collapses with all due deliberation," Charban said.

16

Desjani's planned maneuvers accomplished what they were supposed to. The dark ships were just over a light-hour and a half distant when the major change in the Alliance fleet's path was made at Geary's order following the receipt of Rione's last message, and as a result the dark ships did not see the maneuver until about an hour and a half after it was made. They then shifted their own vector, aiming to intercept on the assumption that Geary's warships were returning to the government facility.

A few minutes before the dark ships intercepted their track, Geary ordered the change in vector to head for the side of Star Beta that was opposite where the hypernet gate apparently still orbited nearly seven light-hours distant. By now, that image was a lie. The gate was already gone.

The dark ships had anticipated vector changes by Geary to either continue on his way toward the government facility or to engage the enemy. The change toward the far side of Star Beta was unanticipated by the dark ships, with the result that their intercept was completely missed.

The five dark ship formations, now operating as almost a single unit, swung wide and around, aiming to catch Geary's fleet again.

"Once we start braking, and we have to do that now, the dark ships are going to catch up to us fast," Desjani cautioned.

"They're going to aim past us," Geary predicted. "No matter what projected vector they have for us, they are not going to predict that we will slow so much that we drop into fixed orbit close to Beta. Doing that would be totally irrational for us and give no possible benefit, except under one set of conditions, which the dark ships do not think exists. They need observations to make their decisions, and they won't see any sign of trouble until too late."

His ships pivoted again, every bow coming up and around, and as their main propulsion lit off again, the entire fleet began reducing velocity as fast as the most badly damaged ships could sustain.

The dark ships, swooping down on Geary's formation, began braking as well.

"How are we doing on time?" Geary asked.

"Right on our mark," Desjani said. "We're coming in perfectly."

The projected vectors of the dark ships bent forward as they braked, showing intercepts well past Beta. As Geary's force continued to slow, the dark ships kept slowing, too, but also kept assuming that the Alliance warships would stop braking at any moment. The paths of the dark ships continued through space above and beyond Beta.

"You know," Desjani commented, "it does feel insane to be slowing down this much with those dark ships that close and trying to hit us again. My head says we have to do this, but my guts are telling me this is crazy."

"I feel the same way," Geary said.

Star Beta was looming larger and larger as the Alliance fleet slid closer and closer. Geary gave more commands, ordering the warships to collapse their current four formations into a single, tight formation that would be protected as well as possible from any shock waves spreading back around the star after they hit it.

"Five more minutes until we're there," Desjani said. "If the gate collapsed extrafast, we'll find out the hard way within the next couple of minutes."

"Make sure we drop some expendable surveillance sats before we get behind Beta, so we can see what's happening," Geary said.

The dark ships had completely overshot Geary's force and were skidding through a turn well beyond Star Beta, their bows coming back to point at the Alliance fleet. "Twenty minutes until the dark ships manage their latest intercept attempt," Lieutenant Castries said.

"You sound very calm, Lieutenant," Desjani remarked, her chin resting on one fist, her entire attitude that of relaxed composure. "Well done."

Castries grinned. "I've been through a lot in the last several months, Captain."

"This is just one more near-death experience?"

"That's right, Captain."

"How about you, Lieutenant Yuon?" Desjani asked. "How are you feeling?"

"Sort of numb, Captain," Yuon admitted.

"Numb works, as long as you keep thinking. Ah, here we are."

Dauntless slid into her intended fixed orbit about Beta, the star looming huge nearby and blocking off a vast section of space. All about *Dauntless*, the rest of the Alliance warships, more closely packed than usual, hung in a glittering array, illuminated by the light of Beta's close-by nuclear fires. The Dancers had come in near as well, weaving through the fleet and parking themselves in the midst of the Alliance warships as if such difficult maneuvers were routine and easy.

The dark ships had finished coming about, and were accelerating toward Geary's fleet and the Dancers.

"I sure as hell hope that gate collapsed," Desjani muttered so low that only Geary could hear. "Otherwise, we're going to get ripped from one end to the other."

Geary kept his eyes on his display, where the unmagnified view from the surveillance sats was visible. The bright disc of Star Alpha could be seen to one side, but the other objects in Unity Alternate were just bright dots among the innumerable stars. If the gate had collapsed as it was supposed to, many of those bright dots no longer existed. But the wave of destruction that had engulfed them was traveling with the light that would bring news of the devastation.

"Ten minutes until dark ship intercept," Lieutenant Castries said.

"All units' shields are at maximum," Lieutenant Yuon reported.

"We can see the gate collapsing," Lieutenant Castries added.

It had happened nearly seven hours ago, but it felt like something taking place right now.

Geary saw one of the bright dots go out. "Here it comes."

More dots vanished.

One of them had been the government facility.

The view from the surveillance sats vanished, and Geary looked toward his main display.

The shock wave hit Alpha, then, seconds later, Beta, the flaming atmosphere of the stars blossoming outward on all sides like a ball of fire hit on one side by a mighty gust of wind.

Hundreds of dark ships were closing in on Geary's fleet. Five formations of the most dangerous warships ever built by humanity. Precise, cold, terribly lethal.

The shock wave was moving so fast and was so powerful that he did not actually see the impact. One moment, the dark ships were racing to attack. The next, they had been swept from space and only a vast glare could be seen. The glare faded, then vanished, leaving only empty space.

Geary heard sounds aboard *Dauntless*; the mumbling of prayers, a few half-muffled cries of jubilation, something that sounded like a sob.

Desjani had her head bowed, her lips moving silently.

He looked toward where the government facility had orbited for decades. *Thank you, Victoria. May the light of living stars welcome you and your husband.*

They took a few days to make their way back out to the fringes of what had been Unity Alternate Star System, conserving fuel this time and limiting the stress on damaged ships. The emptiness of the star system, swept clear of all but the largest planets by the shock wave, felt unnatural. Sailors had to be reprimanded for violating uniform regulations by wearing good-luck charms and necklaces designed to ward off evil, but every day some other members of the crew wore similar objects despite the risk of being chewed out and having their protective objects confiscated by Master Chief Gioninni, Senior Chief Tarrani, and the other senior enlisted. "They're spooked, Captain," Gioninni explained to Desjani. She and Geary had encountered the master chief in one of *Dauntless*'s passageways.

"They'll have to live with it a little while longer," Geary told him. "Some of the data from the government facility were automated astronomical observations that included where and when unstable jump points have appeared in this star system. We've used that data to help predict when the next jump point will appear. It should happen near this part of the star system, and sometime anywhere from now to within the next few weeks. That will let us jump for Drezwin."

"Yes, Admiral," Gioninni said. "The crew is also a bit worried about using an unstable jump point."

"Just remind them that it doesn't matter how unstable the jump point here is as long as the one at Drezwin is stable! Which it is." Desjani paused and eyed Gioninni. "By the way, Master Chief, it's pretty surprising how many of those luck charms and evil-aversion necklaces are aboard this ship."

Gioninni scratched his head, adopting a puzzled look. "Things have been a bit rough the last few years, Captain. The crew must have collected quite a few."

"I found myself wondering," Desjani continued, "if perhaps the charms and necklaces being confiscated are being resold to other crew members by someone."

"That would be highly improper!" Gioninni declared, scandalized. "I will look into that, Captain!"

"See that you do, Master Chief," Desjani said.

As she and Geary walked away from Gioninni, Desjani smiled. "That little resale operation should stop within a few minutes," she murmured to Geary. "As soon as Gioninni can tell his coconspirators to shut it down."

"Life goes on." They stopped before the compartment where comms with the Dancers were maintained as Lieutenant Iger exited.

Iger, startled, hastily saluted. "Admiral, Captain."

"Is there anything wrong?" Geary asked, looking toward the compartment.

"No, sir. I'm just going to check on things in the intelligence spaces while Shamrock—Excuse me, while Lieutenant Jamenson holds the fort in there."

"And how are you and Lieutenant Shamrock getting along?" Geary asked.

Iger smiled broadly. "Planning a honeymoon, sir. We didn't think that would be a possibility. But it looks like this is a long-term thing after all."

"You seem happy about that," Desjani commented. "When planning on where to honeymoon, I'd advise avoiding close binary star systems."

General Charban exited the compartment as well, giving Lieutenant Iger the opportunity to head for the intelligence compartments. Charban looked weary again but in a satisfied way, not a frustrated way. "I may yet become a songwriter," he announced. "No one but the Dancers will want to listen to my songs, but that's a fair-sized audience. They intend jumping *home* from here, Admiral."

Geary shook his head. "There are a hell of a lot of things in this universe that humanity has left to learn. I honestly can't remember, General. Did I ever offer formal condolences to the Dancers for the ships they lost assisting us in the fight against the dark ships?"

"You did," Charban confirmed. "And the Dancers have offered formal condolences for our losses. They have also asked about what Victoria Rione did, wanting to know more about her reasons and motivations."

"What have you told them?" Geary asked.

Charban pursed his mouth before answering. "Admiral, I told them that Victoria Rione was what humans call a Fury."

"A Fury?"

"Mythical creatures," Charban explained. "They avenge wrongdoing. They are absolutely merciless, never to be deflected from their purpose. Victoria Rione was a Fury, wasn't she?"

"Yes," Geary agreed. "I think she was."

"I've been thinking about the whole Black Jack thing," Charban continued. "A century ago, the Alliance needed not just a hero, but a military hero. Someone to inspire support for the war, someone to inspire everyone who fought."

"Black Jack fulfilled that need," Desjani said.

"I agree. But doesn't a democracy also need other kinds of heroes? Doesn't it need political leaders who are heroic?"

"Heroic?" Desjani questioned. "Political leaders?"

"I would think those were needed," Geary said. "But from what I've seen, the people of the Alliance don't have a very high opinion of politicians these days."

"No, they don't," Charban agreed. "The idea of a heroic politician has become so ridiculous that no one probably even thinks of it. Our politics has been about tearing down other politicians, about mocking any claims to heroism. Politicians claim as acts of courage actions that are only aimed at advancing their own ambitions or pet causes."

"That's been noticed," Desjani said dryly.

"But I do think we need heroes among our political leaders. *Real* heroes, whose claims to that status might perhaps be embellished but who at their core deserve to be celebrated for doing more than anyone expected. Doing something that would not benefit them personally."

Charban looked at Geary. "Victoria Rione has given us such a figure. A heroic politician. A dead, heroic politician, and as the Black Jack example illustrated for nearly a century, the best heroes are always the dead ones because their subsequent actions can never disappoint. Would she be angry, Admiral, if she were held up as such a figure?"

To his surprise, Geary felt himself smiling. "General, given Victoria Rione's attitude toward those around her and those she worked with, I think she would be incredibly amused by the idea of being looked up to as a paragon of political leadership."

Desjani nodded. "She would be laughing her butt off."

"Then I am going to pursue that, Admiral, when we get back to the Alliance," Charban declared. "The Alliance is not, cannot be, about whichever men and women currently lead it. It has to be about ideals epitomized by those who have gone before. About sacrifice by our leaders. Maybe that is why the Dancers intervened the way they did. Not just because of the cold minds of the dark ships. Our part of the pattern, the Alliance part, was rotting from within. But we can still fix it. I'm going to do what I can."

"You really are going into politics?" Desjani asked. "You know what that will do to your reputation."

"I'll risk it. Maybe if enough good people do the same, we'll be able to change the image of our leaders."

"Good luck," Geary said.

He walked with Desjani the rest of the way back to her stateroom. "Come in for a moment," she offered.

"What's the occasion?" he asked. "We don't want people talking."

"Keep the hatch open. Do you mind if I sit down?"

"Feel free, Captain."

"Thank you, Admiral." Desjani took a seat at her desk, sighing. "Speaking of patterns, and destiny, I had a thought. The enigmas covertly gave humanity hypernet technology not only to keep the war between the Alliance and the Syndicate worlds going, but also in the hope that we would first build hypernet gates in all of our star systems, then discover what excellent weapons they made for destroying those star systems that belonged to our human foes. The enigmas wanted humanity to wipe itself out."

"Right," Geary said, leaning against the side of the open hatch.

"But the hypernet gate here was what allowed us to survive, the only thing powerful enough to annihilate the dark ships. The enigmas *gave us that weapon* in the hope that we would destroy ourselves with it, and instead, we used it to save ourselves."

"That's ironic," Geary said. "I hadn't thought about it, but that's true."

"But it wouldn't have happened," Desjani continued, "if the same people who created and funded and pushed the dark ship program, as well as other really stupid and ugly things, had not also targeted Victoria Rione and motivated her to act as she did."

He stared at her. "You said her name."

"So what? I honor her memory. The point is, the enigmas gave us the weapon, and the people who sought to undermine the Alliance gave us the person who would pull the trigger on it."

He kept staring. "Our enemies gave us the means to frustrate their plans."

"Do you still believe that there has been no larger plan involving you?" Desjani pressed. "A plan by powers compared to whom the enigmas and the suits are nothing?"

"Tanya, I will never be able to believe that I am special," Geary said.

"And that's why they chose you," she concluded. "I know you are going to miss her. That's all right. She was part of the plan, too."

"So were you," he said.

"I just helped keep you alive, Black Jack. Alive and with your head on straight."

He glanced over at the remembrance plaque that Tanya Desjani kept on one bulkhead. It held a list of names, a heartbreakingly long list of names, of comrades of hers who had died in battle. Two new names were on it. Victoria Rione. Captain Tulev. "Rione is not the only one I'm going to miss."

"No." Desjani looked away, blinking rapidly. "It's as I said when Kostya died when *Leviathan* was destroyed," she whispered. "His war is finally over. He had nowhere else. His home world destroyed. All but one member of his extended family dead. The fleet was all he had. Someday, had he lived, he would have had to leave the fleet, then he would have had nothing. Now, he is at home with his ancestors, and I pray he knows peace."

"Peace would be nice," Geary said in a quiet voice.

"What's next?" she asked.

"We jump for Drezwin. Once at Drezwin, *Dauntless* will escort *Mistral* to Unity, just in case anyone tries to keep *Mistral* and what she carries from reaching there. The rest of the fleet will return to Varandal."

"That's a pretty short-term set of plans," Desjani said. "What about after?"

"I don't know. I'll leave it to Senators like Navarro, Sakai, and Unruh to put the Alliance government in order. We shut down the biggest threats, but there are still other problems out there, still more of the galaxy to see, still Syndics causing trouble." He smiled slightly. "I wouldn't mind a little rest, though. Do you think the human-occupied portion of the galaxy will be able to manage for a few months without us rushing around, fixing things that keep breaking?"

"Probably not." She smiled back. "You really are Black Jack, you know."

"No, I'm not."

"I wouldn't have married anyone else," Desjani said.

"Then, yes, I am Black Jack." Geary stood straight and nodded to her. "I'm going to get some rest."

Desjani's comm panel suddenly came to life. "Captain? A jump point for Drezwin just appeared less than a light-minute away from us."

"I'll let the Admiral know," Desjani said, then smiled once more at Geary. "What was that about getting some rest?"

ACKNOWLEDGMENTS

I remain indebted to my agent, Joshua Bilmes, for his ever-inspired suggestions and assistance, and to my editor, Anne Sowards, for her support and editing. Thanks also to Catherine Asaro, Robert Chase, Carolyn Ives Gilman, J. G. (Huck) Huckenpohler, Simcha Kuritzky, Michael LaViolette, Aly Parsons, Bud Sparhawk, and Constance A. Warner for their suggestions, comments, and recommendations.

John G. Hemry is a retired US Navy officer and the author, under the pen name Jack Campbell, of the *New York Times* national bestselling *Lost Fleet* series (*Dauntless*, *Fearless*, *Courageous*, *Valiant*, *Relentless*, and *Victorious*) and the follow-on series *Beyond the Frontier* and *The Lost Stars*, set on a former enemy world in *The Lost Fleet* universe. Under his own name, John is also the author of the *JAG in Space* series and the recently reissued *Stark's War* series. His short fiction has appeared in places as varied as the last Chicks in Chainmail anthology (*Turn the Other Chick*) and *Analog* magazine (which published his Nebula Award-nominated story 'Small Moments in Time' as well as most recently 'Betty Knox and Dictionary Jones in the Mystery of the Missing Teenage Anachronisms' in the March 2011 issue). His humorous short story 'As You Know Bob' was selected for *Year's Best SF 13*. John's nonfiction has appeared in *Analog* and *Artemis* magazines as well as BenBella books on *Charmed*, *Star Wars*, and *Superman*, and in the *Legion of Superheroes* anthology *Teenagers from the Future*. John had the opportunity to live on Midway Island for a while during the 1960s, then later attended the US Naval Academy. He served in a variety of jobs including gunnery officer and navigator on a destroyer, with an amphibious squadron, and at the Navy's anti-terrorism center. After retiring from the US Navy and settling in Maryland, John began writing. He lives with his long-suffering wife (the incomparable S) and three great kids. His daughter and two sons are diagnosed on the autistic spectrum.